A HOUSE WITHOUT WINDOWS

ALSO BY NADIA HASHIMI

The Pearl That Broke Its Shell
When the Moon Is Low

A

HOUSE
WITHOUT
WINDOWS

❧

Nadia Hashimi

wm

WILLIAM MORROW
An Imprint of HarperCollins*Publishers*

A HOUSE WITHOUT WINDOWS. Copyright © 2016 by Nadia Hashimi. All rights reserved. Printed in the United States of America. No part of this book may be used or reproduced in any manner whatsoever without written permission except in the case of brief quotations embodied in critical articles and reviews. For information address HarperCollins Publishers, 195 Broadway, New York, NY 10007.

HarperCollins books may be purchased for educational, business, or sales promotional use. For information please e-mail the Special Markets Department at SPsales@harpercollins.com.

FIRST EDITION

Designed by William Ruoto

Library of Congress Cataloging-in-Publication Data has been applied for.

ISBN 978-0-06-244968-9 (hardcover)
ISBN 978-0-06-247784-2 (international edition)

16 17 18 19 20   OV/RRD   10 9 8 7 6 5 4 3 2 1

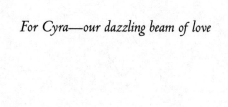

For Cyra—our dazzling beam of love

The message, the rain, and the divine light come through my window

Falling into my house from my origins

Hell is that house without a window

True religion, O servant of God, is creating a window

Do not raise your ax to every nook, come

Raise your ax to frame a window

Do you not know that sunlight

Is only the image of the sun that appears beyond her veil?

   — RUMI, MASNAVI III, 2403–2406

A HOUSE WITHOUT WINDOWS

I SUPPOSE THIS BLOODY MESS MIGHT PARTLY BE MY FAULT. HOW could it not be? I lived with the man. I salted the food to his taste. I scrubbed the dead skin off his back. I made him feel like a husband should.

He did a few things for me, too. He would sing to me, something between a song and an apology, whenever I was most upset. I could never stay mad then. Something about the way his eyebrows danced or the way his head bobbed . . . he was like ice to my hot moods. I would curl up against him just to feel his breath tickle the back of my neck.

To think that it all would come to an end just a few feet from where we'd lain together as husband and wife. And only steps away from where unholy blood had been spilled before. Our little yard with a rosebush in one corner and a clothesline running across it—it has been the theater of much gore in the last year. I question the sanity of the roses that still dare to bloom there.

Those roses are deep red and would look lovely on a grave. Is that an odd thought?

I think most wives imagine their husbands dying—either out of dread or out of anticipation. It's an inevitability. Why not guess at how or when it might happen?

I'd imagined my husband dying a million different ways: as an old man with his children at his bedside, shot in the head by insurgents, keeled over with his hands on his unticking chest, struck by lightning on his way to somewhere he shouldn't have been going. The lightning was always my favorite. Allah, forgive me for my colorful imagination. I blame my mother for that lovely bit of inheritance. Lightning would have been easier on everyone—a shocking and poetic little bolt from the heavens. It would have hurt, but only for an instant.

I hate to watch anything suffer.

No, I never imagined my husband dying the way he did, but what's a wife to do? Thunderstorms don't show up when you need them.

Since I was a young woman I've managed to hold myself together by stringing words into rhyme, creating order and rhythm in my head when there was none to be found in my world. Even now, in this miserable state, my mind turns a verse.

My full height, my beloved husband never did see
Because the fool dared turn his back on me.

CHAPTER 1

IF ZEBA HAD BEEN A WOMAN LESS ORDINARY, KAMAL MIGHT HAVE seen it coming—a gnawing feeling or at least a few hairs standing on end. But she gave him no warning, no reason to believe that she would be anything more than she had been for the last two decades. She was a loving wife, a patient mother, a peaceful villager. She did nothing to draw attention to herself.

On that day, the day that changed an unchangeable village, Zeba's afternoon was a bland repetition of the many afternoons before it. The clothes hung on the line outside their home. Stewed okra simmered in an aluminum pot. Rima, the puffy tops of her feet blackened from crawling around the house, slept a few feet away, a dark, wet circle where her innocent mouth met the bedsheet. Zeba watched her daughter's back rise and fall and smiled to see the soft pout of her lips. She traced her finger through a mound of freshly ground cardamom. The scent lingered on her fingertip, sweet and soothing.

Zeba sighed and flicked the end of her white head scarf over her shoulder. She tried not to wonder where Kamal was because that inevitably led to wondering what he was doing, and Zeba was in no mood to entertain such thoughts today. She wanted today to stay an ordinary day.

Basir and the girls were on their way home from school. Basir, Zeba's eldest son, was only sixteen years old but more hardened than other boys his age. Adolescence had gifted him with the unfortunate insight to see his parents for what they were. Home had not been a refuge. Home had been, for as long as Basir could remember, a broken place—broken dishes, broken ribs, broken spirits.

At the heart of the problem was Kamal, Zeba's husband, a man who had disintegrated over the years. Now he survived only by believing that the man he was for minutes at a time could make up for the man he was the rest of the hours.

Zeba watched the embers flicker beneath the pot. Maybe Kamal would bring home a cut of meat today. They hadn't had any in half a month. Last week, he'd brought a bag of onions, so fresh and sweet Zeba's eyes had watered just looking at them. She'd cried tears of gratitude into everything she cooked for days.

Rima shifted languidly, her pale leg twisted back under the knit blanket and her arm pulled back to her side. She would be waking soon. Zeba brushed the cardamom grinds into a small empty jar. She took one deep breath before sealing the lid, letting its scent tingle her lungs.

Some days were difficult. Food was often scarce and the children sometimes ill. Zeba had already lost two little ones and knew just how easily God could take away. Kamal had moods she didn't understand, but she'd learned to weather them, like an experienced pilot navigating through stormy skies. She numbed herself with housework. She focused on the good. The girls were attending school. Basir, her first and only son, was bright, and his help around the house was a relief to her aching back. Rima, the baby, had survived illnesses that had claimed others before her, and her pink cheeks buoyed Zeba's spirit.

Rima. Incredibly, it was the youngest of the household who changed the course of history. Most children had to start walking before they could do such a thing.

Had Rima not shifted her leg at that moment, had the scent of cardamom not breathed life into Zeba's weary lungs, had there been anyone else around to see or stop her, perhaps the life that transpired

in their humble courtyard and within the solitude of their mud walls
would have continued on for another year, another decade, or their
entire lives. As it were, a soft breeze drifted through the open window
and Zeba thought it best to bring the laundry in before Rima awakened, before Basir and the girls came home.

Out the back door, into the courtyard, and over to the clothesline where she stood for a few moments before hearing something she
couldn't deny.

It was the kind of sound no one wanted to hear. It was the kind of
sound people would much rather walk away from.

Zeba's chest tightened. A white heat flushed her face and made
her jaw clench tightly on a day that could have been so wonderfully
ordinary. Zeba debated for a moment before deciding she—a wife, a
woman, a *mother*—had to see.

BASIR AND HIS SISTERS ENTERED THROUGH THE GATE IN THE
clay wall that separated their home and courtyard from the street and
neighboring houses. At the sound of Rima's wailing, the cry of a child
with outstretched arms, Basir's stomach lurched. The girls hurried
into the house and, in a flash, Shabnam had Rima balanced on her
narrow hip, the baby's face runny and red. Kareema looked at her sisters wide-eyed, the smell of burnt okra thick and ominous in the air.
There was no sign of Madar-*jan*. Something was wrong.

Basir said nothing to the girls. He scanned the two bedrooms
and the kitchen quickly. He felt his hands tremble as he reached the
back door. Pantaloons, head scarves, and shirts flapped on the clothesline. A soft whimper pulled Basir's attention to the far corner of their
courtyard, where the outhouse backed against the neighbor's outer
wall.

Basir took another step. And another. How much he yearned to
go back to this morning, when everything was ordinary and normal.
How much he yearned to go back into the house and find his mother

stirring green beans in a heavy pot and worrying that her children hadn't enough to eat.

But nothing would be ordinary again. Basir knew this as he turned the corner and the life he knew melted into a bloody, brutal mess. Zeba, his mother, looked up at him, her face drained and empty. She sat with her back against the wall, the air toxic. Her hands were dark and bloody, her shoulders shaking.

"Madar-*jan*," Basir started. A crumpled shape lay a few feet away by the outhouse.

"*Bachem*," Zeba's voice faltered. Her staccato breaths quickened. Her head sank between her knees as she began to sob.

"Go back into the house, my son . . . go back into the house . . . your sisters, your sisters . . . go back into the house . . ."

Basir felt his chest tighten. Like his father, he hadn't seen this coming.

CHAPTER 2

YUSUF, AS A YOUNG BOY, NEVER DREAMED HE WOULD ONE DAY BE a lawyer, much less a lawyer in America. He was like any other child and gave little thought to the many days beyond tomorrow.

He remembered well afternoons spent rustling through the low-hanging boughs of the pomegranate tree in his grandfather's orchard. Plump red balls hung like ornaments on outstretched arms. Three proud trees grew enough fruit to keep Boba-*jan*'s children and grandchildren with red-stained fingers through the fall. Yusuf would pluck the heaviest and roundest pomegranate he could reach and slice through its leathery peel with a knife he'd snuck from his grandmother's kitchen. He would crack the globe in half, careful to catch any loose ruby-colored gems. A careful fingertip wiggled each seed free from its white membrane. He worked diligently, painstakingly. Sometimes he ate the pearls one by one, feeling the tart burst on his tongue. Other times, he popped a handful in his mouth and teased the juice out before mashing the fibrous pits between his teeth.

Yusuf would throw the peels over the adobe wall that separated his grandfather's yard from the street—not because he shouldn't be eating pomegranates but because he didn't want his siblings or cousins to know how many he'd devoured.

The youngest of four children, Yusuf adored his brother, who was six years older, handsome, and quite self-assured. He loved his two sisters, too, sitting by them while they crumbled stale bread between their palms and tossed it to the grateful pigeons and sparrows outside their home. Yusuf was a boy who loved stories, particularly ones that frightened and surprised. When he slept, he imagined himself a hero, chasing djinns into the jungle or finding treasures at the bottom of a well. Sometimes he was brave in his dreams, rescuing his family from the grips of evil villains. But more often than he cared to admit, Yusuf would wake to a mattress wet with a child's fear.

When Yusuf was eleven, his father decided it was time to leave Afghanistan. The rockets were nearing their town, a village that had escaped the past decade relatively unscathed. Yusuf's mother, who had worked as a teacher for just one year before the schools were closed, was glad to leave. She carried a few token items into their new life: a handful of photographs, a sweater her mother had knit, and an intricate peacock-blue shawl her husband had brought for her from his travels in India when they were first married. Her copper urns, their crimson hand-knotted carpets, and her silver wedding tray were all left behind, along with most of her clothing. Yusuf's father, a trained pilot, hadn't flown in years because the airlines had been grounded. He still made certain to pack his diplomas and certificates as well as the children's. He was a practical man and did not lament leaving the rest behind.

The journey from Afghanistan to Pakistan was treacherous. The family crossed mountains, sometimes in the darkness, and paid suspicious-looking men large sums of money to help them. All four siblings, close in age, huddled with their parents in the darkness, in the back of a truck, as they climbed over rocks. They trembled when gunshots echoed through the valleys. Yusuf's mother, stumbling beneath her *burqa*, urged them to press on and insisted the guns were too far away to reach them. Yusuf might have believed her had her voice trembled a bit less.

In Pakistan, Yusuf's family settled in a refugee camp. Though they were far from wealthy in Afghanistan, the camp was a harsh adjustment for them. Pakistani police officers shouted and waved off any questions. They stood in lines for food, for housing, for documents that never seemed to materialize. They lived in an open field, a dust bowl full of tents and listless souls. They slept side by side, trying to ignore the stench of poverty, loss, and destitution. "The devil finds work for idle hands," Yusuf's mother would warn her children. They kept to themselves and spoke to no one in the camps of anything more than the interminable waiting and the abominable heat. This refugee camp was temporary, Yusuf's parents promised, and soon enough they would join their relatives in America.

Weeks passed and no news came. Yusuf's father searched for work, but the airline office scoffed at his appeals. He couldn't find work as a mechanic or even as an assistant to one. Disheartened and with dwindling funds, he took a job as a brick maker.

"Dignity is not in what work you do," he insisted to his wife and children who were unaccustomed to seeing him covered in mud and dust. "It's in how you do that work."

But his shoulders hung low as he washed the clay from his hands. Yusuf's mother bit her lip and rested her hand on his arm in the thin privacy of their tent. Dignity was hard to find in the camp. They insulated themselves as much as possible and kept away from what went on: cockfights, opium clouds, the stench of unbathed masses, and the moans of mourning for a child who'd succumbed to disease.

Yusuf's older brother worked alongside his father. His two sisters stayed with their mother, and Yusuf was sent to the local school, twenty boys sitting under a log shelter, open on three sides. There was a weathered chalkboard and a teacher who distributed small, stapled notebooks with onionskin paper. Yusuf's relatives in America swore they were doing all they could to bring them to the United States— they had filled out forms, submitted bank statements, and even hired lawyers they could barely afford. The local consulate officials told Yusuf's father his application was still being considered.

"Padar-*jan*, I can go work with you and Fazil. I'm not a child anymore. I can earn money, too." They sat in their tent at dusk, drinking bowls of thin soup his mother had cooked over an open fire.

Yusuf's father had stared at the ground, as if he expected it to drop from under him.

"Padar?"

"Yusuf-*jan*," his mother interrupted softly. "Let your father eat his dinner."

"But Madar-*jan*, I want to help. That school is crowded and the kids are . . ."

"Yusuf." The unmistakable edge in her voice silenced him. Yusuf's father slept that night without saying another word.

Weeks stretched into months. They grew despondent as they watched the camp swell with new families. When they finally received the letter saying they had been granted visas to the United States, Yusuf's mother pressed her face into her husband's chest to muffle her sobs. Kaka Rahim's persistence had paid off. They were among the fortunate few who would turn their backs on this camp; but years into their lives in America, the mark was still on them, heaviest on Yusuf's father who never managed to walk as tall as he had when he was an out-of-work pilot in their village.

Yusuf's family settled in New York, in a Queens neighborhood that was home to the Afghan diaspora. They took it all in: the elevator buildings, the swarms of people walking to work, the reliable tap water, the grocery stores so bountiful that their fruits and vegetables practically spilled onto the sidewalks. The reunion with family was thick with embraces, tears, and meat-laden meals. They stayed with an uncle and his family in their three-bedroom apartment until they were able to secure assistance and enough work to rent an apartment of their own. Yusuf and his sisters were enrolled in school; his father and Fazil started working at Kaka Rahim's pizza shop.

YUSUF'S ELDEST SISTER, SITARA, FELL IN LOVE JUST AFTER FINISH-ing high school. She had met an Afghan boy who lived in the same apartment building. Flirtatious looks in the dank elevator turned into stolen moments in the humidity of the basement laundry room. Yusuf's parents warned their daughter to stay away from the boy, who worked part-time as a bank teller and whose parents were of a different ethnicity. Doors were slammed, phone calls were intercepted, and seething looks were exchanged. Predictably, the young lovers grew all the more desperate for each other and embraced on public buses, caring less and less that their parents would learn of their improprieties.

To stave off rumors, the families agreed to have the two married, and after a modest ceremony, Sitara moved in with him and his family to start her new life just two floors above her parents and siblings in the apartment the boy's family had occupied for years. Yusuf's second sister, Sadaf, opted to stay in school and pursue accounting at a city community college. His brother, removed from books for too long, sharpened his English by repeating lines of dialogue from television sitcoms. He rose quickly through the restaurant ranks and became a bartender. Yusuf's mother enrolled in ESL classes at the local library and began working as a clerk in a department store. Yusuf's father, grateful to Kaka Rahim for getting them on their feet, decided it would be safest not to mix work and family and driving a taxi, resigning himself to a flightless future. Almost overnight, Yusuf became an adolescent who had mastered the nuances of the English language and the crowded subways. He excelled in school and impressed teachers who urged him to apply for scholarships and pursue college.

He did well by day but woke in cold sweats at night at least once a week. He simply couldn't go seven nights without fumbling in the dark to change his panic-soaked shirts and pillowcase without waking his siblings.

The family lived modestly but comfortably. They had one, then two televisions. Their closets filled with new clothes. They replaced their lost possessions with new ones. Yusuf's mother burst into tearful laughter when his father came home with a silver tray, almost identical to the wedding tray they'd left behind. They watched television together, one person always with a ready finger on the remote should the actors and actresses fall into a love scene. Yusuf's father followed Afghanistan in the newspapers and on the news. They all braced themselves after September eleventh and were shocked that strangers on the street would shout angrily at them in the disaster's aftermath. Yusuf's father cheered the U.S. decision to invade Afghanistan though he had no intention or hope of returning there.

Only fools run into burning buildings, he would joke.

When Yusuf was a freshman at NYU, news about Afghanistan was everywhere. It was tedious. Afghanistan was suicide attacks, battered women, and corruption. In his second year, Yusuf had enrolled in a course on human rights on a whim, thinking it would be an easy way to bring up his grade point average. By the second lecture, a fire was lit. In a flood of memories, Yusuf was back in Afghanistan. Death tolls. Small boys working as blacksmiths. A promising journalist murdered along with his wife and children. Dehumanizing refugee camps. A young girl sold to pay off a poppy crop debt. Untouchable warlords.

How could he turn his back on all that?

Others did not. Others were brave. Others championed the cause of the voiceless.

Yusuf had lived and breathed the American belief that one person could make a difference. Flyers in the student union and the optimistic rhetoric of professors swelled in him. He attended his first protest and liked the way it felt to chant with the crowd. He raised his voice. He developed a taste for the fight, the fury it brought out of him. Feeling angry was better than feeling afraid.

Two semesters passed, and Yusuf realized it had been weeks since he last woke in a cold sweat.

Yusuf chose law because it was the difference between right and wrong—because the law was the only way to protect the weak and punish the aggressors. He studied for weeks and burned through books of practice LSAT exams until he sat for the test and scored surprisingly well. He filled out a dozen applications but kept his fingers crossed that he would get accepted into a program in New York. With nervous excitement, Yusuf tore open a thick packet from Columbia. It was good news, but his parents shook their heads in disappointment.

Are you sure you don't want to be a doctor? Doctors save lives every day, they reminded him.

I don't want to save one life at a time, Yusuf declared. *There are better ways.*

His parents shrugged their shoulders and hoped for the best. At least he would be a professional, more accomplished than his siblings who had little interest in graduate school. They would have done more to stop him had they known what he would go on to do.

Yusuf took courses on human rights law and immigration law. He volunteered as an interpreter and sharpened his native Dari. He had professors make phone calls on his behalf to land internships with human rights organizations. He was thankful his family had settled in New York where opportunities abounded. He kept his nose buried in books.

You'll be blind before you're thirty, his mother had lamented. She was proud of her son but worried about him, too. Some weeks it seemed he barely slept at all.

Yusuf graduated from law school and was hired by the advocacy organization where he'd interned for two years. They'd been impressed by his drive and created a position for him. He wasn't making as much as his classmates who had gone the corporate route, but it was more than he or anyone in his family had ever made and he was thrilled to have purpose. He worked hard and turned no project away.

Yusuf did carve out time to socialize, though he felt compelled to tell himself he was networking so he would not feel as though he was wasting time.

IT STARTED WITH HAPPY HOUR, A CHEERFUL EXCUSE TO DRINK upon exiting an air-conditioned office building. Over time, Yusuf acquired a taste for dark lagers. A cold beer in his hands made him feel like he was bonding with his colleagues. He kept this part of his life private from his parents and siblings. Though they'd shared tight living spaces all their lives, he still felt compelled to keep his sins to himself. It was not a matter of deceit, as he saw it, but a show of respect for his parents' ideals.

Happy hour was where Yusuf had started dating. It had taken him that many years to feel like the girls around him wouldn't see him as foreign or inferior. When an Asian girl named Lin leaned across a bar table and rested her hand on his forearm flirtatiously, Yusuf felt his confidence soar. He went out with a few girls but never let anything go further than five or six dates. If he sensed they were interested in more, he would slip away, letting a few phone calls go unanswered or confessing his reluctance to commit to any one person.

It was immature, he realized, but he had decided, after listening to his parents rant about his older brother's diverse parade of girl-friends, that he would find someone his parents would adore. He wanted someone who could speak Dari with them, who would raise bilingual children with him, who would understand both American and Afghan culture. It was the practical and respectable thing to do.

Then he'd met Elena—beautiful and irresistible Elena who had immigrated to the United States with her family at a very young age from Peru. She had chocolate brown hair and her cheeks dimpled when she smiled, which she did often. She was a friend of a colleague and stopped when she spotted them drinking beers at a sidewalk café. She was making her way home from her job at an accounting firm, wearing a white peplum top and smartly creased, navy blue pencil pants.

She was sweet and smart and, importantly, did not flinch when Yusuf told her his family had come from Afghanistan. On their first date, they went to see a free Peruvian music concert in Central Park. On their second date, they ate artisanal ice cream in the East Village. Yusuf couldn't resist slipping his arms around Elena's waist and pulling her close when he was with her. She was five inches shorter than him, and when they embraced, Yusuf breathed in the sweet, tropical scent of her shampoo. She clung to him just enough that he felt adored and not so much that he felt trapped. She could talk about the implications of a trade agreement and the latest One Direction song in the same breath. Yusuf's friends raised their eyebrows and beer mugs in approval. Elena was a catch.

When Yusuf met her, he'd already made plans to move to Washington, D.C., to work with a nonprofit that focused on crimes against humanity. He convinced himself they both understood things would come to an end once he left. Elena didn't fit into his plans. And yet, Yusuf found immense happiness in a hundred quiet things: the way her nose crinkled when she laughed, the way she slipped a playful finger into his collar, the urge he felt to call or text her a moment after they'd kissed good night.

The fact that they had so little in common seemed to draw them to each other. Language, religion, professional fields—they studied each other with almost academic interest.

Elena listened to Yusuf talk about the headlines that pulled his attention: the unearthing of thousands of Muslim corpses, men and boys who'd been executed in the Bosnian genocide, the flogging of a dissident journalist in Saudi Arabia, the disappearance of a Malaysian passenger plane. Elbows propped on the table and eyes focused, she filled in with details she'd read in online news reports. She made Yusuf question his plan. Maybe he shouldn't limit himself to women from his own background. Maybe a common culture and language wasn't everything.

Maybe Elena was everything.

They were on their way to the subway station after a dinner with friends when Elena and Yusuf paused at a crosswalk. He turned to her and adjusted the paisley scarf knotted around her neck. It was fall and the evenings were brisk.

My niece's baptism is this weekend. You'll come with me, right?

The red hand turned into a white stick figure, prompting them to move forward. Yusuf didn't immediately obey. Elena had to tug at his elbow.

Maybe, he had said. *Let me see how much I get done with work this week.*

They'd settled into two empty seats on the 7 train, New York's version of the Silk Road. Elena would get off soon after they entered Queens, before the neighborhoods turned distinctly Asian. Yusuf had another nine stops to go before he got to Flushing.

You know, I already miss you, baby, Elena had said to him as the torque of the subway car nudged them closer together. *I'm going to want to visit you every weekend in D.C.*

Yusuf had kissed her squarely on the lips, long enough that Elena interpreted it to mean he would miss her equally. But something in Yusuf was rattled by the expectation that he would go to something as alien as a baptism, and, as their lips parted, Yusuf withdrew. When the conductor announced her stop, Elena smiled at him and walked off the train. He was already sorry for what he would have to do, but it could be no other way. Yusuf no longer saw all that Elena was—he only saw what she was not.

A REMORSEFUL YUSUF TRAVELED TO WASHINGTON, D.C., AND spent a year with a team of lawyers putting together a case against militia officers accused of genocide in Africa. He did his best not to think about Elena. When he missed her, as he often did, he busied himself with research or called his mother, which reminded him how Elena would not fit in with his family. Conversations with his mother were, by this point, fairly predictable. She would fill him in on the latest happenings with his siblings and gossip from his cousins. Inevitably, her attention would circle back to Yusuf.

You've finished school, you have a job. It's time to get married. Are you waiting for all the good girls to be taken by boys that don't even have a quarter of your looks or smarts?

Yusuf ducked out of the conversations. He missed having *someone* at his side, but he could not imagine taking a wife now. He could not imagine someone waiting for him to come home each night, asking him why he worked so late. He could not be bothered with a second set of parents and cousins and uncles. He had no desire to become a father. He made false promises to his parents that he would be better prepared for commitment next year.

But Yusuf had other plans. He would sacrifice, he believed, so that he could follow the path he was meant to follow. And he'd had no choice but to walk away from Elena.

Turning away from Elena would have been harder had he not felt a strange twinge in his chest.

It came from the land of clay and mountains. It was as if a siren had appeared in his dreams, begging him to save her from herself. He heard her name on the talk radio stations; he saw her face on magazine covers. The Internet screamed her sorrows, telling the story of the unjust blood shed on her land, the imprisoned and the persecuted. Each injustice called to him as if he were the only hope.

Afghanistan.

Yusuf picked up the phone. He sent painstakingly constructed e-mails. If he did not answer her call, who would? His resolve hardened.

On a bustling sidewalk, Yusuf realized he could not remember the last time he'd woken in a cold sweat. He smiled to himself, growing stronger just by thinking about her. Hurt and beautiful, she was home.

CHAPTER 3

"HER HUSBAND'S BEEN MURDERED! THIS IS NO TIME TO ASK RIDIC-ulous questions! Where's your honor? This man needs to be washed and prepared for burial. His parents, his family—has anyone spoken to them?"

Zeba clenched her hands together. If only they would stop shaking, maybe then she could understand what had happened. Maybe then she could explain. Her head was in a vise. There was too much talking. Kamal's body was still by the outhouse. Certainly the flies must have noticed by now.

"This man was killed in his own home! We need to know what happened here!"

Basir and the girls were in the second bedroom. Kareema and Shabnam, eight and nine years old, were trying to be brave. They'd run to their mother when she finally came into the house, but the look in her eyes and the way her knotted hands trembled had unnerved them. They retreated, turning back to Basir who had tasked them with looking after Rima.

"Please, everyone, dear neighbors and friends, please understand that my mother, my family has suffered today. I have to get word to my uncles, the rest of the family."

"But the police, they have to be called."

"They've been sent for already."

"Who called?"

"It doesn't matter. The chief will be here shortly and he can decide what will be done."

The screaming had cracked the neighborhood doors open, one by one. Scandal was an irresistible temptress. It was unclear who had been shrieking, and now neither Basir nor Zeba was sharing any information. Basir stood in the front courtyard biting his cheek. He fought back tears and kept his gaze to the ground. The men and women had gathered, word spreading through the mud-walled neighborhood like a drop of ink in water. Basir stole glances at the faces he'd known all his life. Women pinched their head scarves primly under their chins and clucked their tongues softly. The men shook their heads and shrugged their shoulders.

"Someone should call the mullah."

"Yes, call the mullah!"

"And for God's sake, someone needs to send word to his family! Rafiqi-*sahib*, send your son."

Basir's eyes darted to his mother.

"But why isn't she talking? What happened here, Khanum? Did you kill your husband?"

"Of course she did! There's a hatchet in the back of his neck! Do you think he killed himself?"

Zeba and Basir both winced at the mention of the hatchet. Basir crouched down next to his mother who sat with her side against the clay wall of their home.

His voice cracked in a nervous whisper.

"Madar, I don't know what to . . . can you tell them what happened? Did someone come in here?"

Zeba's eyes pleaded with her son. She said nothing.

Basir pressed his palms against his closed eyes, the pressure making the world go black for only a split second. He still saw blood.

"What are we to do now?"

Basir cried silently. Zeba pulled her head scarf across her face. Eyes were watching her, sentencing her. Her three daughters cowered in the room behind this wall. Zeba inhaled sharply and forced a deep breath.

"Basir, *bachem*, please go inside and look after your sisters. They must be so frightened."

Eyes narrowed. Ears cocked to the side—the grieving widow was speaking. They waited for a confession. Basir didn't move. He stayed at his mother's side, angrily wiping tears away with the back of his hand.

What else will she say? he wondered.

"Dear God, what have you brought upon us? What did we do to deserve such a fate? What are we to do?" Zeba moaned, loud enough to elicit sympathetic head shaking. "How could this have happened here . . . in our own home?"

The women looked at the men around them. They looked at one another. Zeba was as close to death as any woman could be. And then they began to echo her laments.

"This poor woman—without a husband—may Allah protect her and her dear children!"

THE CHIEF OF POLICE, AGHA HAKIMI, WAS IN HIS EARLY FORTIES. He was the grandson of a warlord who'd been conquered by another warlord with more men, more guns, and more money. Hakimi was the living legacy of impotence and failure. The village treated him as such.

When Hakimi entered the courtyard, he was immediately led to the back of the house. At the sight of Kamal's body, he shook his head and narrowed his eyes, hoping to look more pensive than disgusted. The flesh of Kamal's neck had been torn apart. Chunks of bone, puddles of blood, and bits of brain—a spray of pink, red, and white scattered just behind the dead man.

The police chief was updated in a series of interrupted accounts, his eyes darting from the morbid debris to the widow slumped against the wall and then to the many faces staring at him expectantly.

Zeba was moaning softly, mournfully.

Hakimi stared hard at the woman before him. Her eyes were glazed, her hands still trembled. When he spoke to her, she looked at him blankly, as if he spoke a foreign tongue. Exasperated, Hakimi turned to the crowd.

"No one knows what happened back there? God have mercy. What happened to Kamal? You were his neighbors? Did no one hear anything?"

Then Hakimi raised a hand for silence. He turned to Rafiqi. Agha Rafiqi had the grayest beard present, and his home abutted Zeba's on one side.

"Agha Rafiqi, you share a wall with this family. You have known them for years. What did you hear?"

Over the years, Agha Rafiqi had heard plenty—not the same sound that had drawn Zeba into the yard, but other sounds that were easier to name. He looked at the woman slumped on the ground, trembling like a bird caught in a net.

"I . . . I have known them for years, indeed. Kamal-*jan*, may Allah forgive his sins, gave me no trouble. He looked after his family, he was . . . oh, what can I say? His widow now sits here. She has four children to look after. My wife knows her well. I cannot believe she would commit such a heinous crime."

There were groans and shouts and fists pumping in the air.

"Enough!" Hakimi cried, feeling a trickle of sweat trace his spine. He felt his breath catch to think how the gathering mob would react to any plan he might propose. They hated him, he knew. Why oh why had he agreed to take on this job?

"I want to hear what Agha Rafiqi has to say." He turned again to Agha Rafiqi, who looked more than a little uncomfortable with the power vested in him.

Agha Rafiqi cleared his throat and started cautiously.

"I am no judge but . . . I . . . I would say, as a matter of decency, that she should be allowed to stay here and tend to her children until these matters can be sorted out."

The women buzzed in agreement.

Hakimi nodded authoritatively. People respected Rafiqi and wouldn't question their neighborhood elder. The accusing shouts fell to a grumble. Hakimi cleared his throat, fidgeted with his police belt, and took a step away from Zeba.

"Very well, then I suppose there's the issue of the body . . ."

"We will wrap his body and move it closer to the back door of the house. His family can tend to his washing there," one of the men called out.

Basir felt his stomach settle a bit. Hakimi looked all around, peered into every corner of their home, and examined their courtyard one square foot at a time. He had two officers with him, young boys barely older than Basir, bushy haired and smooth faced.

Someone pulled a bedsheet off the clothesline. Hakimi, hands on his hips, thanked them for helping with a nod. He avoided Zeba's eyes.

Basir could see the neighbors were more than a little interested in the gory scene. The women filed out in respect but found reason to linger in the street, necks craning as they hoped for a glimpse. Was it really as bad as people had said?

It all might have ended there had Fareed not stormed in, breathless and enraged. Fareed, Kamal's young cousin. A man who could curse and exchange pleasantries in the same breath. Fareed's tunic hung from his body, and his face was flushed. Agha Hakimi was startled and nearly dropped his pocket pad.

"What happened here? Where's my cousin?"

Fareed's eyes fell upon the four men carrying the rolled bedsheet. The pale floral pattern was darkened with splotchy red stains.

"So it's true? Is that him? Let me see my cousin! What happened to him?"

He pushed his way closer, but three men held him back, muttering words of condolence.

"Somebody tell me what happened here!" Fareed roared.

All faces turned to Hakimi. The police chief straightened his shoulders and summarized what he'd learned thus far.

"Your cousin was found in the courtyard. We are not sure who killed him at this moment. No one heard anything until Khanum Zeba came out screaming. We believe she'd found her husband's body. So while we investigate this further, we'll leave Zeba to look after the children for tonight."

Fareed looked at his cousin's wife, whose shaking had worsened since he entered the gate. She was rocking with eyes half closed. Fareed turned to stare at the circle of onlookers, some shifting under his grief with a guilt they could not explain. His nostrils flared and his brow knotted with fury.

"Have you lost your minds—all of you?" The men looked at one another.

Fareed did not wait for an answer. In that second, he pounced on Zeba, and before anyone could stop him, his hands closed around her neck.

CHAPTER 4

ZEBA, LIKE A TODDLER WITH A FEVER, YEARNED FOR HER MOTHER in those bleak hours. But she did not cry out for her. After the venomous words they'd exchanged, Zeba was not yet desperate enough to reach out to Gulnaz. She would wait.

It was a shame, really. Once upon a time, Zeba and her mother, Gulnaz, had been as close as a flower to its stem. Zeba had been a radiant child, a manifestation of the name her father had bestowed upon her. She would slip from her father's lap to her mother's side, giggling as her parents took turns tickling her tummy, kissing the top of her head, or tossing her in the air.

Zeba's brother, Rafi, was five years older and more serious by nature. He was a simple and docile son who gave his parents neither reason to boast nor to complain.

While most of the women around Gulnaz grew round with their next child by the time the previous had taken its first steps, Gulnaz was not like any other woman. She thrived on having control—control of her emotions, her body, and her family. Her husband was content to let her exert her will. She drew much envy for that, which further fueled her need to be in command.

Gulnaz would have a child only when she wanted. Whether she did this by denying her husband's attentions or by some trickery of herbs was not known. She simply smirked when her sisters-in-law dared to ask.

It was 1979 and the Soviet troops had started to roll into the country, the end result of a flirtation between Afghanistan and the great power that had begun when Gulnaz was born twenty years earlier.

Rafi, her firstborn, was old enough to bathe, dress, and feed himself when Gulnaz decided she was ready for a second child. Nine months after she declared her desire, Zeba was born. Gulnaz loved Zeba all the more because her cherubic existence was proof that Gulnaz was the captain of her own ship.

Afghanistan changed hands that year, one president replacing another who had either died of natural causes or had been smothered by mutinous hands. The truth would remain elusive. Since chaos breeds chaos, the new president would be replaced before the year was over. It was an inauspicious time to bring new life. Gulnaz wondered if even Zeba had been a mistake.

Imagine a home led by three different patriarchs in one year, she thought to herself. No, this kind of home could not survive, nor could a country.

We will have no more children, Gulnaz had declared to her husband and their family. No one doubted her when she made the vow. They knew, by then, that she could circumvent nature to make it so.

GULNAZ WAS A SORCERESS, A SKILLFUL TEASER OF FATE JUST AS her grandmother had been. While Gulnaz maintained that her grandmother had never taught her any of the trickery she was known for, it was obviously not true. What Gulnaz practiced was an intricate and complex art honed over generations, not one that could be picked up casually.

She hummed as she concocted, which made it seem all the more innocent to her children and husband. They, after all, only benefited from her skills. When the children burned hot with fever, she dripped holy water into their mouths and placed amulets beneath their pillows. When Rafi writhed with pain as a boil the size of a tomato grew on his calf, Gulnaz set off for the lake. She found a frog, sliced it open with a paring knife, and butterflied it onto the mass, wrapping its bleeding corpse in place with strips of fabric. Within an hour, Rafi shouted loudly. The boil had erupted and pus flowed freely down his leg. Gulnaz tossed the frog's body outside, and Rafi's leg was completely healed two days later. Gulnaz was as loving and devoted as any wife or mother could be—she was just a bit more potent. Her children took comfort in their mother's magic even when it hurt.

When Rafi was six, he broke his leg. It happened the day after his aunt had commented on his remarkable height. Cursing under her breath, Gulnaz held a sewing needle over a flame and used it to pierce Rafi's earlobe, tears in her eyes as he writhed and screamed beneath her. And until he turned fourteen years old, she left one lock of hair uncut until it reached the middle of his back.

"To protect you from *nazar*," she'd said grimly. The evil eye was powerful. These things had to be done.

The rest of the family was discomfited by Gulnaz. The cousins, sisters-in-law, and aunts bit their tongues and clung to their prayers like they were antidotes. The green-eyed beauty made them quite anxious.

Zeba sat at her mother's side and watched as she plunged hot needles in chunks of animal fat or boiled eggs that she would leave at an unsuspecting doorstep. These habits became as routine to her as washing the bedsheets or peeling potatoes. This was life with Gulnaz. Zeba recited multiplication tables along with other children her age but understood the mathematical property even better when Gulnaz showed her how a knot threaded five times was five times as powerful in its ability to turn friction between two resentful women into a fire so angry it could burn a house down.

But Gulnaz used her powers only when necessary or when those closest to her called upon her for help. She was judicious about it because she knew it made her husband uneasy, though he never outright forbid it. Her trickery, like everything else in her life, was under her control and she could exercise it as much or as little as she saw fit.

All that changed when Zeba's father disappeared. Gulnaz recalled a shift in her mother, a tightening of the jaw that never eased.

Zeba's father had disappeared just as she'd learned to read. She remembered it only as a time when a string of letters made more sense than the happenings in her small home. Gulnaz told Rafi and Zeba only that their father had gone off to fight the godless communists. The children wished quietly for him to come home but quickly learned it was not a topic to discuss with their mother. When relatives did bring up his sudden departure, Gulnaz would spend the rest of the day beating the dust from the carpets or scrubbing the blackened pots with vengeance. It was best not to mention Padar, even if his absence was a window left open in the winter. The war was bloodier each day, and soon, it seemed, the martyred would outnumber the living.

Gulnaz withdrew from the rest of her husband's family within their shared compound and pulled her children in closer, taking on the appearance of the sullen, abandoned wife. When enough time passed that some began to refer to her as a widow, Gulnaz took advantage of their assumptions. She dressed in black, drew the curtains on the windows, and spoke in hushed tones. She stayed up when the children slept and watched over them by the wan light of a flickering candle. With her children, she was cheerful and loving but only when they were alone. The children had loved their father and missed him sorely. Rafi grew more subdued than he already was by nature, emasculated by his father's absence. Zeba, with a child's magical thinking, believed her father would return. She'd fallen asleep to the soothing rhythm of his heartbeat too many nights to think she would never lay her head on his chest again.

Gulnaz and the children drew looks—some sympathetic, some suspicious. Gulnaz despised them equally and added those people's names to her list of enemies. She doled out bits of retribution to them all. Sheltered by her mother, Zeba grew accustomed to being an outsider. Rafi, though quiet and reserved, became her best friend. He was the only other person in the world who could possibly understand what it meant to have Gulnaz as a mother.

WHEN A MAN'S HAD ENOUGH, HE'S HAD ENOUGH, ZEBA'S AUNT HAD once commented at a holiday dinner, as the conversation turned to a neighboring couple whose arguments could be heard from the street. The women, while clearing the dinner dishes, had been arguing that the husband was a stubborn brute deserving of his wife's near-public berating, but Ama Ferei, her father's sister, considered other possibilities. *No wife or husband is without fault. Only those two know the truth of their story.*

Zeba had not thought much of the conversation, and Gulnaz had only nodded and smiled. Her aunt had been the voice of reason, she'd believed. But once Gulnaz and her children were within the confines of their own home with the curtains drawn, everything changed.

"He's had enough, she thinks," Gulnaz snapped at no one in particular. "Of course he's had enough. What a terrible wife she must be!"

"What's wrong, Madar-*jan*?" Zeba had asked cautiously. She was around twelve at the time, hovering in the space between childhood and adolescence. She and the other cousins her age spent their time with the women, learning the nuances of gossip and etiquette.

"Your aunt always says what's on her mind with that look that she's being so noble and above gossiping. I don't know what's more insulting—the way she hints that I drove your father away or that she thinks I'm too stupid to know what she's really talking about!"

Rafi never knew what to do when their mother went into one of her fits. Hating to feel helpless, he would busy himself with work outside the house. On this particular occasion, he picked up the yellow plastic container and headed out the door to draw water from the well. Zeba watched him go. She had no such escape, especially in the evening hours.

"But Madar-*jan*, I didn't hear her say anything about our father," Zeba protested cautiously. If she had, she would have been duly offended. She missed him still, even as the memory of his face was starting to blur.

"You didn't? Oh, Zeba." Gulnaz sighed. "My daughter, a one-inch scorpion can be just as deadly as a hulking tiger. You've got to learn to pay attention and respect every threat for what it is. And the way she watched you! I'm sure she's jealous because you're much taller than her daughter and your skin is so much fairer. Your cousin is sweet, but she doesn't have your looks and her mother knows it."

Zeba didn't feel that much prettier than her cousin. As a matter of fact, she'd felt distinctly less pretty than her and everyone else. It felt good to think she might have been wrong about how her own looks compared to others.

"To think, I spent two days making dumplings for tonight's dinner because she asked me to—not to mention that I cooked for them every day last week while she was ill and bedridden. But your aunt doesn't remember any of that. She's too busy thinking that I sent her brother off into the mountains—as if I had that much control over that man! She doesn't know what she's talking about and should bite her tongue before something else does."

It stung to hear her mother speak about her father so distantly. He'd been gone six years, but Zeba still held out hope that he might return. She dreamed of crossing paths with him in the markets. Would they recognize each other? Would he run to her and kiss her forehead? Zeba had less optimistic thoughts, too. Maybe they'd been within a stone's throw of him already and he'd ducked out of view before they could spot him. There were times when her thoughts drifted further and further in that mournful dejected direction and Zeba's world became colored with loneliness, suspicion, and doubt.

And maybe Gulnaz was right. She did catch Ama Ferei eyeing her and her mother strangely once in a while. Just last week, when she'd dropped off a pot of her mother's soup at their home, Ama Ferei had asked her if her mother was taking good care of her and her brother. Zeba had not mentioned the question when she returned home, shrugging it off as concern, but it was quite possible that there was more to it than she'd realized.

Four weeks later, Zeba sat beside her mother as she chopped a molted snakeskin into tiny flakes and folded a pinch of it into a pot of spinach and leeks simmering over a ringed flame. They cooked in the roofless room at the back of the house, where the smoke and fumes drifted into the outside air. All the while, Gulnaz chatted casually with her daughter, commenting on how pretty Zeba looked that day and that she, as a mother, could not have asked God for a more perfect daughter. Zeba swelled to hear her mother's words and to see the glimmer of pride in her green eyes.

Gulnaz fried some homemade cheese separately and layered it into the spinach when the leaves had melted smooth. She moved the mixture around with a fork to confirm the snakeskin had disappeared completely.

"What will this do, Madar-*jan*?" Zeba had asked her mother as she stared into the pot.

"It will square things with your aunt for trying to skin us with her eyes. This will keep her busy enough that she won't have time to say such awful things about us again."

Gulnaz put the top on the pot and wrapped it in an old wool blanket to keep it warm. She and Zeba delivered it to Ama Ferei.

"Oh, Gulnaz-*jan*, for me? Why did you go to such trouble?" she'd asked, eyeing the small pot carefully.

Zeba wondered if she suspected something. She held her breath.

"You're like a sister to me, Ferei-*jan*. You've been looking quite anemic lately, and I thought some spinach would do you good."

"I have been feeling very weak lately. God save your husband, he would always say that you were quite a doctor with nothing more than vegetables and herbs at your disposal. So tell me. What did you put in this *sabzee*?"

Gulnaz's eyebrows pulled upward.

"Did my husband say that?" she said demurely. "Ah, he was too generous with his words. But to be honest, I added a little fresh ginger. My mother always told me there was nothing ginger couldn't fix."

"I've heard the same thing," Ama Ferei said, nodding. She tried her best to sound playful. "Now, I'm not one for gossip but everyone knows about your tricks, my dear. What else have you put in here?"

Gulnaz put her hands on her narrow hips. Her back straightened and she inhaled sharply.

"Really, Ferei. I thought better of you," she said in a huff. The corner of her blue head scarf fluttered in the breeze.

Ama Ferei laughed easily before turning her attention to Zeba.

"Zeba-*jan*," she said, her voice sweet despite her accusing countenance. "What did your mother really put in this food? You're not going to be deceitful like her, are you? I don't think our family could handle it."

Zeba watched her mother smile gracefully and touch her aunt's forearm gently. Zeba's face flamed red with shame and anger.

"My dear, I know you're not well. There's no reason to say such things, especially in front of my daughter, who's barely a young woman. Feed the spinach to the dogs in the street, if that's how you feel. I was only trying to help."

Gulnaz looped her arm through her daughter's and turned to walk away, leaving Ama Ferei holding the swaddled offering.

"Madar, why would she say—"

"Stop, Zeba. Just let it be." Gulnaz did not allow Zeba to ask any questions.

WHEN THE MOON HAD WAXED INTO A FULL GLOBE, THE EX-tended family gathered once again. Another aunt had delivered a baby over a month ago, and the family convened to mark the infant's fortieth day of life. Zeba and Gulnaz ran into Ama Ferei just outside the home of the cousin who had invited everyone.

Zeba nearly gasped.

Ama Ferei's face looked taut and angry. The skin around her nose and the corners of her mouth were cracked and peeling. Her scalp was littered with tiny white flakes.

They exchanged pleasantries and went inside, Gulnaz and Zeba finding their way to the opposite side of the room.

The roll of fingers on a *tabla* drowned out the chatter. The mood was festive, but Zeba was too distracted to appreciate it much.

For most of the night, Zeba watched Ama Ferei rub and scratch at her arms angrily. She stopped whenever her sister-in-law leaned in to speak to her but resumed just as soon as she turned away. Zeba imagined her aunt's entire body covered in a prickly sheath of scales beneath her cotton dress.

On their walk home that evening, Zeba looked at her mother's face, glowing in the creamy light of the moon. Sometimes, it felt absolutely wondrous to be daughter to the green-eyed sorceress.

CHAPTER 5

YUSUF HAD FLOWN FROM KENNEDY AIRPORT TO DUBAI, THIR-
teen hours pressed against the window of a 747. He checked into a
marble-floored hotel with gaudy chandeliers and plush lounge furniture. Exhausted, he slept for half a day, waking only to wander
through the souk in the evening amid knots of pale-faced tourists
and white-gowned locals. Storeowners were almost uniformly darker-
skinned foreigners, selling goods from India in shops with tentlike
openings. Windows shimmered with sets of bangles and elaborate
necklaces of eighteen-karat yellow gold. Yusuf quickly tired of the
extravagance. He ate kebabs at a sidewalk café and thought of his
long-awaited homecoming.

THE TWO-HOUR FLIGHT TO KABUL PASSED QUICKLY, AND YUSUF
stepped off the plane and into a state of wonder. From here, the land
of his childhood looked unscathed, as if the events of history were
nothing but a bad dream. The mountains were exactly the same as
those in his memories.

It was a short walk from the tarmac to the terminal, with airport
workers in fluorescent green pinnies pointing the way.

Yusuf picked up his luggage from the conveyor belt and met a taxi
at the front of the building. It was a short drive from the airport into

Kabul, and Yusuf's eyes stayed glued to the windows. He caught a glimpse of the airport's main entrance as they drove away.

The wide glass doors were framed by two portraits. On the right was Ahmad Shah Massoud, the martyred Lion of Panjshir who'd led the Northern Alliance in battle against the Taliban. With his flat, round pakol hat perched atop a head of thick, wavy hair, Massoud had been painted looking off into the distance. His mustache and beard were modest, his looks rugged. In this, as in nearly every picture of him ever captured, he looked like he could have been strategizing an attack on the Taliban or turning over verses of poetry, a combination that described the soul of the nation.

On the left was Hamid Karzai, Afghanistan's first president following the ousting of the Taliban in 2001. Karzai's posture, in contrast, was like one from a royal portrait. The traditional *chappan*—stripes of green, gold, and royal blue—was draped over his shoulders, and a peaked lambswool hat sat atop his head. His grayed facial hair was neatly trimmed, and through small but proud eyes, he looked outward, past the people entering the airport and toward the resurrected Kabul.

The taxi driver asked Yusuf why he'd come back. He saw plenty of expats returning, but young men traveling alone were always here for a reason other than visiting family.

"Do you have a business here?" he'd asked.

"No, no business."

"You want to open a business?"

"No, I'm here for a job."

"What kind of work do you do?"

"I'm a lawyer."

"A lawyer? For some foreign company?"

"No, I'm working with an international organization that provides attorneys for Afghans. I'm here to work for the people." Yusuf could feel the driver's curiosity was mixed with something else—skepticism or resentment, perhaps. He knew scores of Afghans had flocked back to Kabul to take advantage of the postwar opportunities. They sold land at inflated prices, built hotels, and grabbed up foreign subcontracting opportunities. Yusuf decided to shift the conversation and asked the driver about the U.S. withdrawal.

"Everyone leaves," the driver said with a dismissive wave. "Why should we expect them to stay? But they'll be back."

"How do you mean?"

"We're going to have bigger problems here as soon as they leave. We all know that. Sometimes you're so worried about getting rid of the ants in your house that you don't notice the mice lying in wait."

"Don't you think it's time for Afghans to look after our own country, though? We have to learn to stand on our own feet."

The driver scoffed, honking his horn as a car nearly sideswiped his vehicle. The roads were jammed with yellow station wagon cabs, Toyotas, wheelbarrows, and pedestrians. Cars were so closely packed on the street that drivers could roll down their windows and reach into the next vehicle.

"Easy for you to say," he muttered. "You don't live here."

"Actually, now I do."

The driver reached for the gear shift and slid into neutral, letting the car drift forward. He didn't say another word.

Yusuf turned his attention to the streets that looked vaguely familiar. On some stretches of road, he was struck with a feeling somewhere between déjà vu and true memory. At a roundabout, Yusuf could almost feel his father's hand holding his. The number of new buildings with shiny steel-framed construction and large glass windows surprised him. Red banners announced slashed prices on home furnishings.

Yusuf asked to be dropped off at a hotel in the upscale part of town, where most foreign nationals stayed. The driver smirked, feeling vindicated.

AFTER OPENING HIS BAGS AND DRINKING THE BOTTLED WATER he'd purchased in the lobby, Yusuf put his feet up and called his mother.

"How was your flight? Have you eaten anything?" Her voice was tense with worry.

"It was fine. Of course I've eaten, Madar-*jan*. I'm here to work, not to go on a diet."

"Don't mention that word to me," she said bitterly. "I've been on a diet for the last fifteen years and have gained twenty pounds."

"Without that diet, you might have gained thirty. Consider it a success," Yusuf offered.

"You can make an argument for anything, can't you? Listen, I know you only have a few days there, so please don't waste time. Go to your Kaka Siar's house as soon as you can. You promised me."

Yusuf groaned.

"I will! I thought you wouldn't mind if I called you before I went looking up our old neighbors."

"This phone call would have been a lot more interesting if you could tell me you'd stopped by their house for a cup of tea."

Kaka Siar was not actually Yusuf's uncle. He and his family had left for Iran around the same time that Yusuf's family had gone to Pakistan. Kaka Siar had three daughters. The youngest had just turned twenty-four years old and was named Meena. As children, Yusuf had looked after Meena while their parents passed plates of food around and discussed the ongoing war—he a school-age boy and she a toddler. Over the years, he never minded her following him around. He'd always been gentle with her, in a way that made his mother and Meena's mother smile with pride.

Yusuf remembered when they'd left Kabul. He'd been a bit more distant from Meena that year, less interested in entertaining a six-year-old when he was eleven and eager to enter adolescence. Still, Meena clung to him like an older brother, and he never could bear to disappoint her. He would sit, cross-legged, and tell her stories or listen to hers. The world outside their homes was harsh, and he felt a sense of duty to make her smile.

"She's a beautiful girl, and they're a wonderful family." Yusuf's mother sighed. She'd repeated this more times than he could count in the four weeks before his departure. "All I'm asking is that you spend some time with her."

Yusuf's mother would only consider his trip to Afghanistan a success if he came back engaged. That was not something he had to infer. She had stated it very clearly, especially after he'd rejected the many prospects she pointed out in their New York community. She accused Yusuf of being too picky and warned him of the dangers of procrastinating.

"Too much makeup, too little schooling, too tall, too short. You need to spend less time finding faults in these girls and more time looking for the right one. You wait too long and there'll be no one left to choose from."

But the Afghan girls in New York didn't seem that much unlike American girls. He'd spoken to many at community events or at student associations and hadn't found anyone who wanted anything to do with Afghanistan. Their idea of cultural identity, he gathered, was putting on a traditional Afghan dress once a year at a wedding and carrying in a tray of henna. Too often, getting to know them involved secretive phone calls and elaborately concocted stories to disguise their whereabouts from their parents, only to find that they had nothing in common.

But Meena was a different story. He'd laughed at his mother's suggestion the first time she'd mentioned it. She'd put her hands on her hips and sternly told him that Meena's mother was not opposed to the idea. Meena was the right age and had recently finished college. She was taking computer classes, and they wanted to see her married to a good person. They knew Yusuf's family and heard that Yusuf had a job as an attorney. He would be a good match for her, Meena's parents decided and hinted as much to Yusuf's mother.

While homeland pulled Yusuf like a magnet, there was a quietly growing curiosity in him about Meena as well. He'd seen a picture of her and knew she was quite beautiful. But there was much he didn't know. So many years had passed since he'd last seen her, her small arms wrapped around his neck as he knelt down to say good-bye to her. He'd wiped the tears from her cheeks, his face flushing to see her so saddened.

"I'll call them in the morning and stop by later in the day. Good enough?" he promised his mother, making it sound like he was only doing this to humor her.

"Fine. Remember, you only have a few days in Kabul before you go out into the provinces. Use that time to get to know her."

YUSUF MADE HIS WAY TO KAKA SIAR'S HOUSE THE NEXT DAY, PASS-ing through swarms of grinning street children with outstretched hands and curious eyes.

"Mister, mister . . . it's good to give!"

"Hello, how are you!" they called, erupting into giggles as they practiced their stiff English. Their clothes were tattered, their fingernails black half-moons. Yusuf wondered if they were orphans or the overflow of an impoverished household.

Yusuf laughed with them, tousling one boy's hair and giving another boy the ballpoint pen he had in his pocket.

"Do you boys go to school?" he asked them.

"I do!"

"Me too!"

They were future pilots, doctors, and professors, they promised him. They were persistent and not in the least bit shy, their confidence boosted by their collective number.

He passed women in *burqas* and others in jeans, teased hair beneath their loose head scarves and platform shoes stretching their height from top and bottom. Some men were dressed in traditional tunics and pantaloons with turbans on their heads. Others wore slim denim

jeans or trousers and Adidas athletic shirts. A man sat on a stool outside his shop, an arc of reed birdcages over his store's entrance. Para-
keets, finches, and canaries sat on thin perches, looking like flittering,
multicolored gems.

Kaka Siar's family members were living in the home one of their
relatives had abandoned. Their own home and the home Yusuf had
grown up in had been reduced to rubble while they were away. Yusuf
knocked on the front gate and waited, nervously, for someone to let
him in. He carried a bag of gifts all picked out by his mother: chocolates, clothes for Kaka Siar, and bottles of perfume for his wife.

It was Kaka Siar who opened the door, shaking his head in disbelief and pulling Yusuf into their courtyard. He'd hugged him tightly
and kissed his cheeks. When he stepped back to get a better look at
the boy he hadn't seen in over twenty years, his wife, Khala Zainab,
came out and hugged him, her palm stroking his cheek with a maternal touch. Yusuf bent and tried to kiss her hands, but she pulled back
and tugged him into the house instead.

"You look just like your father," Khala Zainab said. "How are
they doing? Your brother and sisters are well?"

"Praise Allah, what a fine man you've become! If I'd seen you on
the street, I would not have recognized you," Kaka Siar added.

Their two eldest daughters had married but returned to their parents' house with their husbands and children that evening to see Yusuf.
They were unrecognizable, as was Meena. Yusuf stood when she entered from outside. She'd just returned from her job—something to
do with the United Nations, Yusuf's mother had told him. She was
dressed in black slacks and a long, chartreuse blouse that fell to her
hips. She wore a loose, gauzy head scarf and had a warm smile.

Something about her reminded Yusuf of Elena, but he pushed
that thought aside. Meena took a seat on floor cushions between her
two sisters, a one-year-old niece crawling gleefully onto her lap. Meena
tickled the little girl's stomach and she shook her head in false protest,
her pigtails brushing against Meena's lowered face.

She was lovely, Yusuf admitted, and reminded himself not to stare. He was returning as a family friend and not officially courting her, but the presence of two single people of the same age filled the room with tension. He wished his parents could be here to diffuse the attention. Instead, all eyes and questions were directed to him. A few times during the evening, he caught Meena looking at him, but as soon as he noticed, she would tuck her hair behind her ear and look for a niece or nephew to hold her attention.

They were like two horses with blinders on, standing side by side and pretending not to be aware the other existed. But how was Yusuf going to get to know her if they never spoke? Was he expected to reach some conclusion about the rest of their lives just by eating in the same room?

Meena's older sisters inquired about his own. Though they were closer in age to Yusuf, the presence of children on their laps and husbands at their sides extinguished any impropriety. They could ask questions and joke with him and made a point to do so, obviously hoping to elicit information on their younger sister's behalf.

What does your sister's husband do? Do they live near your parents? And your sisters, what did they study in college?

Yusuf's mother would have been proud to hear him describe how his sister had married a banker and they'd chosen to live close to home. He left out that it was the rent-controlled apartment that kept her and her husband in the same building as his parents. With a baby coming, they couldn't afford to think about moving. His other sister was studying accounting, he told them. He neglected to mention that she had finished in five semesters what others had finished in three and worked part-time as a makeup artist in a department store. For his brother, Yusuf focused on the credentials of the restaurant he managed. It was booked to capacity nearly every night and highly rated.

Kaka Siar nodded in approval. Khala Zainab smiled encouragingly. They were already imagining what their home would feel like without their youngest daughter, picturing her making her way to the United States and being welcomed by Yusuf's parents.

Yusuf attempted to help clear the dinner dishes and take them into the kitchen. He'd been hoping for a chance to interact with Meena in a more casual setting, but Kaka Siar raised a hand and shook his head.

"You are our guest," he said with a gentle smile. "You've come all this way after all these years, and in a few days you'll be headed out of the city to do some good work. Let's not be worried about a few dishes."

It was true. Yusuf had only four more days in Kabul before he would be reporting for duty. He was eager to start working.

Energetic as he wanted to feel, jet lag was creeping in, and Yusuf's eyelids were growing heavy. He bit his tongue to stifle the yawns and, not wanting to be impolite, waited until after the fruit and sweets had been served to excuse himself for the evening.

"How many days do you have here? You'll have to come back." Khala Zainab rested a hand on his forearm as he stood at the door.

He hoped he did not imagine the look of disappointment on Meena's face to see him leave.

CHAPTER 6

THREE POLICE OFFICERS HAD ASSISTED HAKIMI IN ARRESTING Zeba. Those men had been gruff, shoving her into their vehicle for transport to the prison located in the capital of their province. They'd been sad to see her go, knowing true justice would have been served if everyone had simply let Fareed finish what he'd started. Instead, Hakimi had ordered the villagers to pry Kamal's cousin off Zeba, leaving her crumpled on the ground gasping for air. Her children had screamed and shouted, certain they were about to lose a second parent that day.

Once they'd arrived at Chil Mahtab, the officers had turned her over to the prison guards, spitting on the ground as she was led away. Zeba moved through the hallways, her elbow held by a female prison guard, Asma, whose henna-stained red hair was pulled tightly into a low ponytail that made her look stern and decidedly unfriendly. Still, she was a fairy godmother compared to the male officers who'd just left, and Zeba felt her breathing ease.

Asma's overgrown bangs half hid a lazy eye. Her other eye flitted from the open doors of the prison cells to the ugly ring of bruises around the new prisoner's neck. They moved through the wide, tiled corridor. Asma, like most of the guards, treated the incarcerated women decently. There were no smiles or pleasantries exchanged, but nor were there blows or menacing looks.

The guards were all women, dressed in olive-colored jackets belted over shapeless ankle-length skirts or pants. Some wore the uniform proudly, excited by the authority they felt putting it on, the knowledge that they were in control and above someone, anyone. Other guards were uncomfortable in it, which Zeba could better understand. They were friendly and decent for the most part. The female guards seemed to appreciate that even they were one accusing finger away from being thrown in jail alongside the prisoners.

Zeba shared a cell with three women who ogled her freely as she was led into their narrow quarters by a guard. Zeba had grown accustomed, in the last two days, to having all kinds of eyes on her.

"That's your bed. You get the bottom bunk."

Zeba followed their collective gazes and took a seat on a mattress that was as firm as the concrete floor. The cell contained two bunk beds, a small television in the corner, and a United Nations calendar on the wall. The bunk bed opposite Zeba's had a dust ruffle of purple and yellow stripes. On the space of wall over it, her cellmate had hung a pink teddy bear in a protective plastic bag. The top bunk had pages from a magazine plastered on the wall—pictures of women in full makeup, Bollywood actors and actresses, and even one of a cartoon kitten, its eyes wide as saucers, its paws holding a bouquet of sunflowers.

The other women in the cell looked her over, taking stock of her mottled neck and skittish eyes.

"So tell us why you're here. What did you do?"

When the questions began, Zeba shook her head, closed her eyes, and lay down. Her roommates were left to conjure up their own theories. They had hoped a new cellmate would break the monotony of their days. But Zeba, a stone-faced tenant, offered them no reprieve.

They went back to their card game while Zeba lay motionless, listening to their chatter and learning who was who.

There was Nafisa, a sharp-tongued woman in her midthirties whose defiant manner had won her no mercy from the judge. She'd been accused by a relative for an improper relationship with a man, a widower who worked as a blacksmith. Specifically, they'd been seen eating together in a park one evening. Nafisa had never been married, which had not bothered her aging parents until the accusations reached their doorstep. Her three older brothers were furious with her for tarnishing their family's good name. While Nafisa swore it had been nothing more than a quick bite with a platonic friend, few believed her story. That she'd been an obedient and loving daughter and sister all her life did not change a thing. Nafisa's mother, fearing her sons would see no way to restore their honor except by spilling Nafisa's blood, decided to report the crime to the police herself.

With tears streaming down her face and her hands trembling, Nafisa's mother led her belligerent daughter to the police station and turned her in.

I've done nothing, Nafisa had cried out. *I swear to God I've not sinned!*

Take her, her mother had whispered hoarsely. *She's acted dishonorably.*

Nafisa had been convicted of attempted *zina*, or sex outside of marriage. She'd been sentenced to three years.

Her mother visited weekly. Nafisa never blamed her mother, knowing she might not be alive had it not been for her. All her hopes now rested on the slim chance that the widower, a man in his forties, would ask for her hand in marriage. It was true that the meal they'd shared had been the culmination of phone calls and other small flirtations. But it was unclear if the budding connection between them would amount to anything now that Nafisa had been cast as a wanton woman.

But if the man truly wanted her, if he could convince his family to see past this scandal, Nafisa could be released and, more important, her honor might just be recovered.

"I'm not a child. I should be able to eat in the park when I want. And anyway, we weren't doing anything wrong. We were just eating. My mother had made some *bulanee* and I wanted to share it with him," she insisted, her voice unwavering.

"I bet that wasn't all you shared with him," cackled Latifa.

Latifa, who had relinquished the bottom bunk to Zeba, was a brazen twenty-five-year-old with a deep voice and wide body. She looked as if she were snarling even when she was at her most cheerful. Latifa had never really looked like a child, nor had her family ever treated her like one. She'd been beaten and cursed at until the day she'd decided she could take no more. Without much fuss or planning, Latifa slipped a few of her father's cigarettes into her jacket pocket, took her fifteen-year-old sister by the hand, and walked calmly out the front door, never expecting they would be missed. She took the local bus to a larger city and from there she found another bus that would take her to Herat, where she hoped they could escape into Iran. Latifa ran out of money quickly. She was two days' travel from home and needed a place to stay, so she befriended a woman in the market, explaining that she was a widow and passing her sister off as her daughter. The woman reluctantly offered to shelter them for the night.

In the morning, Latifa and her sister returned to the bus station to continue their journey. At a checkpoint, the police questioned her and, seeing the way her sister shifted under their gaze, became suspicious. When they accused her of intending to prostitute her sister, she became indignant. She reported that she'd spent the night in the home of a decent woman, but by then they'd tracked down her family and decided she could be charged with kidnapping and with running away from home. Her sister had been returned to their home and, shortly thereafter, married off to a distant relative. Latifa had then refused an attorney, choosing instead to represent herself before the judge.

It was all my doing, she'd said, tapping her hand over her breastbone and nodding affirmatively. *I decided to flee that miserable home. I wanted to save myself and my sister.*

Latifa had no interest in leaving Chil Mahtab, a place where she was treated better than she'd ever been treated in her life. Had she known what prison would be like, Latifa often thought, she might have marched herself past the barbed-wire fence long ago, turning herself in for some kind of impropriety.

Now she was serving a seven-year sentence for running away from home, kidnapping, and attempted prostitution.

Mezhgan was a doe-eyed nineteen-year-old, half the size of her cellmates and nowhere near as bold. When she'd refused to marry her sister's brother-in-law, her suitor's family had become indignant. Soon, they became aware that she was in love with a boy in her neighborhood and, in retaliation, had pointed their angry fingers and had had her arrested. Two weeks after her arrest, Mezhgan had been taken to a health clinic for a virginity test. Watching her empty the contents of her stomach in the small exam room, the doctor had performed a pregnancy test that only proved Mezhgan's guilt.

She'd cried for days, unsure how those few stolen moments could have possibly led to a child and the undoing of her reputation.

"The worst part is that Haroon is in prison too," she mourned. "I swear I did not do what they say I've done. It was nothing like that."

Mezhgan's parents had pleaded with Haroon's family to allow the two to marry but Haroon's family wanted nothing to do with them.

"I'm sure Haroon is upset. I know he loves me and would do anything he could to get us both out of here. His parents must be refusing to listen to him."

Latifa let out a deep, throaty laugh.

"Ah yes. There could be no other explanation for why he's not asked for your hand in marriage yet."

Mezhgan sighed sharply.

"He has, I'm sure. But his mother, she's impossible. She doesn't like me very much. She said I chased after her son, but that's not true at all. Haroon used to follow me home from school. He really and truly loves me. Did I ever tell you that he even called Radio Sabaa once and talked about how the world was trying to keep us apart?"

"You've told me once a week since you've been here. But no one gives their names on Radio Sabaa. You can't be sure he called. Maybe it was someone else."

"I heard the call, Latifa. He said his beloved was elegant as the letter *alif*, with eyebrows as graceful as the letter *sheen*. Isn't that beautiful?" She sighed, her eyelids fluttering as she tried to regain control of her emotions. "That's just the kind of thing he would say and, besides, I know my love's voice."

"You know a lot more than his voice, little mother," Latifa laughed. "If you ask me, the producers and hosts of Radio Sabaa should be in jail instead of all these women. They're letting people talk about romance and love as if there's a place for it. Some poor girl is going to fall in love because she hears an idiot boy on the radio talk about how he can't live without her. Guess where she's going to wind up? She'll be taking up the last empty bed in Chil Mahtab, that's where."

"People don't fall in love because of something they hear on the radio," Mezhgan contested, her tone steeped in frustration. Her lips pulled into a thoughtful pout. She was early enough in her pregnancy that it had barely changed her figure. She'd also stopped vomiting about a week before Zeba's arrival, which she knew meant she was about three months along. She'd seen her mother through the last two of her pregnancies and knew just what to expect. She put her hands on her flat belly, and her expression turned wistful. "It's about feeling a connection. It's about not being able to sleep without talking to them every day and holding your breath until you can be together again."

"He was that hard to resist, this boy?"

"Oh, Latifa. I'm not a poet. I don't have the words for this. All I know is that from the second I set eyes on him, his dark hair, his handsome eyes . . . I could be dead and buried and I'd still be hot for him!"

Nafisa smiled brightly. Mezhgan spoke for her, too, though she would never dare confess her passions. How could she ever hope to be found innocent if she acted that way?

The words escaped her lips before Zeba could think twice about speaking them:

"Men love for a moment because they are clever
Women are fools because they love forever."

"What did you say?" Nafisa demanded.

"She called you both fools!" Latifa chortled. "Didn't take her long to get to know you!"

Zeba broke her silence, her voice airy and distant. She spoke to the windowless walls and the plastic chairs, the metal frame of the bunk bed, and the rough green carpet under her feet. She had yet to look directly at her cellmates, maybe because it would redefine her as one of them, a prisoner of Chil Mahtab.

"It's just something I do out of habit, something I learned long ago from a woman who had lived in the south. Women would get together in secret, in a house or by the river, and share these short poems, just words. Just ways to empty a heavy chest."

Mezhgan shrugged her shoulders.

"I like it. I suppose that makes you something of a poet."

"Anyone with a heavy chest can be a poet," Zeba said before closing her eyes.

IN THE NEXT FEW WEEKS, ZEBA REMAINED DETACHED. THE women gave up interest in her and went about their business. She was with them but not one of them. Listening to their conversations, she learned the spectrum of criminals housed in Chil Mahtab: petty thieves, drug smugglers, and murderers. Zeba's cellmates, however, were some of the many women imprisoned for crimes of morality—falling in love or running away from home.

The women forgave Zeba's aloofness because of something they saw in her bloodshot eyes, the way she stared off into space. They shared their stories, waiting for the day when they would learn hers.

The prison was a small world. The cells were unlocked for the most part, and women walked through the hallways, gathering in open rooms or in the yard. There was a dark kitchen full of pots deep enough to hold a watermelon, a classroom that consisted of a blackboard and slivers of chalk, and a playroom for the many children who lived in the prison with their mothers. The classroom was a shared space, used sometimes for the women and other times for the children. There was even a beauty salon, a lopsided chair set up in front of a lighted mirror. In front of the mirror were eyeshadow palettes of varied shades, lipsticks in bold hues, and tweezers. Some were purchased through the guards. Some were brought by family members or even the legal aid attorneys to keep up the women's spirits. Crayon graffiti covered the hallways, the canvas for the children of Chil Mahtab.

There was only one good way to battle the ennui of their days. The women sat in their rooms and shared stories, dazzling cellmates with their tales, even as they accused one another of pilfering hair oil or laundry detergent. Some of their stories were as embellished as the women leaving the beauty salon. It was in these halls of gossip, from a woman with brass-colored hair and a crown of treasonous dark roots, that Latifa came to learn Zeba's story.

She whispered the news to the others in the fenced-in yard one afternoon.

"So it's true, what we heard when she first came. They found her husband with a hatchet in his head," she said with deliberate cool. Latifa took a long drag on her cigarette, her eyes narrowed and her head cocked to the side. "I'm surprised she made it here. Where I come from, they would have killed her and made sure the whole village showed up to watch."

"Wow," Nafisa marveled without looking up from her contraband mobile phone. She had just texted a message to her beloved widower and was waiting for a response. "I wouldn't think that just looking at her. Wonder what he did to make her so crazy."

"Maybe he beat her once too often," Latifa offered. "Maybe she caught him with another woman. There's a lot a man can do to deserve something like that."

Mezhgan and Nafisa sighed, thinking dreamily of their lovers, the kind of gallant men who would never deserve a hatchet to the head.

The young women had settled on Latifa's theory that Zeba's husband had somehow deserved his fate, but there were times when they wondered if maybe Zeba was nothing more than a cold-blooded killer. Those thoughts made it difficult to sleep some nights, especially since their mysterious cellmate barely said a word. They shifted uncomfortably when Zeba looked their way. If they dared to return her stare, Zeba's eyes slinked away.

When they did sleep, Zeba stayed awake. The flickering bulbs of Chil Mahtab's hallways cast grotesque shadows across the cell, and the rise and fall of her sleeping cellmates' silhouettes seemed ghostly and strange.

They shared communal meals in their cell. When the others would finish, Zeba would make her way to the cloth spread on the green carpet and pick at the food. She ate enough that her belly did not growl but not so much that she ever felt sated. The food was always cold by the time she got to it, which suited her just fine. She was not here to feast.

She had been told she would meet with her lawyer in a few days. From what the other women in prison said about their attorneys, she had no reason to expect much. But when her thoughts turned to her children, she prayed that God would give her a decent lawyer, for she knew she was in serious trouble.

Her girls. Kareema and Shabnam.

What did he do? She had begged them to answer. *You would have told me, wouldn't you?*

Madar, what has happened? they'd sobbed in bewilderment. Zeba was a gruesome sight, her head scarf crumpled in her hands—hands that looked, at first glance, like they'd been dipped in raw henna. Rima, the baby, was perched on Shabnam's hip. Shabnam bounced her instinctively and kissed her sister's cheek as she'd seen her mother do a thousand times. Rima's petulant cheeks were still flushed from being left alone in the house. Her hands were balled into fists and she had shot her mother alternating looks of resentment and longing.

Basir—how commanding he'd sounded when he spoke with the neighbors. And yet, he'd cringed when she'd touched him. Her chest tightened to remember it, the muscles of his forearm, every fiber hardening into a knot to repel her, his own mother. She'd never seen that look before, at least not on her son's face.

What were they thinking? What did they believe about their mother?

Her arms were empty—there was nothing to hold. Her head spun and her heart pounded.

Rima would be hungry. Zeba wished she could have nursed her once more before she'd been taken away.

Zeba felt her nipples sting. In her first week at Chil Mahtab, she'd stuffed her bra with balled tissues to catch the milk-tears her breasts kept leaking. Her chest had burned and ached until the milk flow dried up.

The girls.

Basir will take care of them. He always does.

It was hard to think of her children and even harder not to. It was hard to block out a cell of women and their inane crimes.

"Your absolute favorite Ahmad Zahir song—what is it?" Latifa asked with the seriousness of a prosecutor.

"That's an easy one." Nafisa laughed. She sang two lines of the song with eyes closed, her upper body swaying in rhythm. "*The taste of your lips lingers on mine, the waves of your passion make my heartbeat sublime.*"

"You shameless thing!" Latifa howled. "Mezhgan, your turn."

"I don't really know his songs that well," she mumbled. She was not the type of girl to answer any question the first time it was asked, believing that would make her seem too outspoken.

"Liar," Nafisa teased. "What did you do in all that time you spent with your boyfriend? He must have sung some love songs to you. How else could he have sweet-talked his way under your dress?"

Mezhgan groaned. She was used to Nafisa's teasing by now.

"My father used to sing those songs," Mezhgan said. Her father was a generation closer to the long-dead pop singer, a man who had set a whole country of broken hearts to song. "I guess I do remember a few of them."

"Let's hear it," Latifa said, clapping.

Mezhgan's voice was high and thin, a shallow echo against the cell walls. *"If this is love that burns within, surely it must be a sin . . . elaaahi elaahahi!"*

"Well done, you harlot!" Nafisa cheered.

"I've got one for both of you," Latifa announced, clearing her throat as she launched into the verse. *"Watch out, my heart, because I have fallen; a gift of heartache has come calling."*

"You're just terrible, Latifa," Nafisa whined. "Wait until you fall in love. You won't be so pessimistic about it then."

"Yes, every night I pray that God curses me with the same affliction you both have."

"At least it gives us hope of getting out of here. A proper marriage and we can appeal to the judge for mercy."

Mezhgan felt pity for Latifa.

"I'm sure there's a way for Latifa to appeal too. You haven't even tried. Maybe you should ask for a lawyer. Why did you refuse one anyway?"

"Because if they sent me back to my family I'd be back here in days charged with murder. I'm doing them a favor by refusing."

Zeba was careful not to react, and the moment passed without her cellmates turning the conversation to her.

Love. Marriage. Freedom.

Zeba's mind floated between melancholy and angry thoughts, a host of colors. A soft melody drifted through the cell, filling the quiet. It was Zeba's voice.

"Alone and free of angst and sorrow
I've bled enough for today and tomorrow
Now it is time for my bud to bloom

I'm a sparrow in love with solitude
All my secrets contained within me
I sing aloud—I'm alone, finally!"

The women howled with delight to hear their cellmate's voice lift in song. They would only realize later the distinct lack of romance in her lyrics and the peculiar mirth with which Zeba sang them.

CHAPTER 7

ZEBA LEANED HER HEAD AGAINST THE COLD WALL, CHIPS OF
paint lifting from the corners and edges. She picked at the flakes with
the insouciance of someone destroying a thing already ruined. In four
days, she'd done nothing but contribute to the slow undoing of these
walls, disappointing the curious women around her. A web of whispers laced through the prison, and with every hushed voice, the account of what Zeba had done changed, sometimes merely by degrees,
but sometimes by great leaps.

*You know she killed her lover—so that her husband wouldn't. Can you imagine
that kind of passion?*

*It wasn't her lover, it was her sister's husband. He was trying to fool around with
her while his wife and her husband weren't looking.*

If she killed him, it must have been for good reason.

*You're such gossips. Besides, I heard she cut off his head and ran through the village
with it.*

Zeba had never gushed or blushed over Kamal before they were
married. She'd never even seen him before their engagement. At her
grandfather's recommendation, her mother and brother had given her
away when she was seventeen. She'd had no say in the arrangement,
a decision made between her grandfather, Safatullah, and Kamal's
grandfather five years before their wedding date. Safatullah was a
well-known *murshid* in their village, and her mother went along with

the decision since Kamal's grandfather was a respected army general. The two grandfathers were good friends who'd played chess together, prayed together, and despised the same people.

As *murshid*, Zeba's grandfather was a spiritual guide, offering invaluable blessings and a connection to the Almighty. Kamal's grandfather brought to the table a more earthly benefit, alliances with all the right people in the new government. Zeba's family owned a great deal of land and needed highly placed friends to secure their hold on it.

In a demonstration of brotherly commitment, the two men orchestrated a marriage, tying their families together with a union that would create common blood.

Zeba's mother, Gulnaz, had protested the marriage, begging her father to reconsider the arrangement. Her husband's family, out of respect for the *murshid*, had agreed to his suggestion years ago and were of no help.

She is young and it is a bad time for a marriage, Gulnaz insisted. *Let us wait a bit more.*

The Soviets had retreated nearly sixteen years ago but in the absence of any real leadership or government, Afghanistan had spiraled into a civil war. Her fate was still unclear.

If you're waiting for the fighting to end, the *murshid* had retorted, *then Zeba may never marry. History has taught us that the fighting won't stop until the last drop of Afghan blood has been spilled.*

Kamal and Zeba were married in 1996 in a part of the country uncontrolled, as of yet, by the Taliban. It was an austere ceremony and celebration, marked by the rhythm of a *dhol* drum and the chiming of the tambourine. The newlyweds knew nothing about each other. Zeba shook her head to think of that first year, living in the family compound with her new husband, wishing desperately to return to her home where her mother lived with Rafi and his bride of one year, a woman Zeba resented for stealing her brother's attentions.

Kamal, when they first married, did what he could to put her at ease. When he saw her tense and shy away, he found ways to endear himself to her. He told jokes. He ate what she cooked and asked for a second plate. He spoke to her about little things and big things and even brought her a gift here and there. A bag of sweets, a pair of shoes. Zeba felt herself relax with the attentions of her new husband. When Kamal was at his best, Zeba felt like she was living out the romantic songs played on the radio. In truth, the last time she'd been so content had been before her father had walked into the horizon and disappeared forever.

Zeba's thoughts drifted to a time long ago when her husband's brother had purchased a television and a DVD player. They'd bragged about it for a month before the women in the family organized an evening where they could get together and watch an Indian movie. Zeba had been invited too, and she'd sat cheerfully with the women, mesmerized by the whirl of colors, women dancing in dazzling saris, arms and exposed bellies gyrating lasciviously. The *bache-film*, the heartthrob of the movie, pounded his fist against his chest as he danced around his beloved, arms spread out in a bold declaration of love. Down on his knees, he thrust himself toward her in a way that made Zeba's pious sister-in-law avert her eyes while the other women cheered with delight. Till the end of his days he would love only her, he sang. The room pulsed with the synchronized heartbeats of a dozen women hungry for a love so dangerously close to sin. Zeba blushed. Kamal had sung this song for her just a few days ago, squeezing her bottom flirtatiously as she passed him in the narrow hallway of their home. Zeba ran her fingers through her son's hair. Basir, just three years old, lay curled at her feet—a small version of his father.

Heady, intoxicating, blasphemous love. The girl smiled coyly, skipping toward him and then away again in a dizzying dance of indecision. The children giggled and imitated the movements. One of the women laughed and slapped her four-year-old daughter on the shoulder.

"Sit down before your father comes in! You think he wants to see a dancer in his house?"

It was the most content Zeba would ever be, but it would not last long.

Their village was thankfully quiet, unlike the rest of the rocket-riddled country, and life was as routine as one could hope for. Zeba was fortunate. Her in-laws, in the years before they'd died, had treated her reasonably well. Only Kamal's sister, Tamina, kept her distance from them. Zeba didn't blame her. She'd acted in the same petulant way toward her own brother's wife.

WHEN ZEBA GAVE BIRTH TO THEIR FIRST CHILD, BASIR, KAMAL had rejoiced. She'd given him a son who would look like him, carry on his father's name, and bring honor to their family. Basir was bright and healthy and smiled readily.

Their next two children hadn't survived and thus began a dark period for Zeba and Kamal. They buried a little girl of just seven months; she had an angelic face that would dance through Zeba's dreams for the rest of her life and make her wake with a tightness in her chest. Two years later, they buried another child. This one was a boy who died the morning after the clan had marked his forty days with a feast and a reading of the Qur'an. Kamal and Zeba didn't speak much after that. It was not an angry silence that hung between them. There was simply nothing to say.

"I won't name her," Zeba had said flatly when her third child was born. She had no reason to believe this child would endure, even after the forty days.

"But, Zeba, she needs a name. If something should happen to her . . . she needs a name."

Zeba knew her husband was right. Even if the child died, she would need a name to be buried. Still, she refused.

"To sleep, to sleep, Little Girl," Zeba sang softly as she rocked her infant daughter.

"Little Girl has started to crawl," Zeba proudly reported to Kamal one day.

Zeba held her breath with every fever, every cold night, and every holiday, waiting for Allah to reclaim her. Only when Shabnam took her first steps did her parents finally choose a name for her, though, out of habit, they called her "Little Girl" until she was old enough to demand they use her real name.

Kareema had been different. Kareema had renewed their confidence. They didn't have to rely on miracles. They could be normal. They would have heartaches and triumphs just like any other couple. This was why Zeba ignored Kamal's mood swings and the times he lashed out at her with a heavy fist. It was a testament, she told herself, to just how normal he was.

Three years ago, they'd taken the children to the river. It was close to Nawruz, the spring equinox and start of the new year. Basir, Shabnam, and Kareema had played in the shallow banks, perched on stones. They'd splashed their hands in the water and soaked their clothes. Kamal had slept on the sheet she'd spread out while she watched the children, water droplets on their earlobes and fingertips catching the sunlight and sparkling like tiny crystals. They had trudged home, clothes heavy with water, but hearts light with the miracle of one joyous day.

In a family photograph taken nearly two years later, Kamal held Shabnam in one arm and Kareema in the other. Basir stood in front of his father, looking up at the lens obediently. Zeba stood demurely behind Kamal, her seated husband hiding the round of her belly, hiding Rima who was yet a few months from joining the family. She remained composed though her heart was ready to burst.

Could anything have been more perfect?

THE CHATTER OF HER CELLMATES BUZZED IN HER EARS, BACK-ground noise to her own thoughts. What were the children doing? Were they terrified? Were they being treated decently? Her only consolation was that they were together.

Zeba's stomach tightened to think of her children as orphans. But Basir, he was the type of boy a mother could have faith in.

Basir had said nothing when they'd taken Zeba away. Zeba had shrieked when they pulled her away, clawing at the air to reach Basir who lifted one arm toward her but hesitantly. A shadow had crossed his face, a darkness Zeba pretended not to see. All the children, especially Basir, were old enough to have known their father for what he was. Still, an angry father was better than a dead father.

Zeba's neck was still sore from Fareed's vengeful grip. Basir had helped two neighbors pull his father's cousin off his mother.

"Let the police take her!" the neighbors had cried and turned Zeba over to Hakimi's wide-eyed custody.

ZEBA FELT THE GUARDS' EYES ON HER, KEYS JANGLING UNCERE-moniously as they strolled the wide hallways. It was a show, mostly. This was a job like any other, and the guards here had received little special training in policing inmates. The government wages were unreliable but better than nothing, and the titillating stories kept the day interesting enough.

Zeba's story was more intriguing than most. Typically, husbands killed wives, not the other way around.

Whispers. Snickers. Eyebrows raised in acknowledgment.

Even the women who spoke in hushed voices were so near to her that Zeba could almost feel their hot breath in her ear. Some voices made her head throb as she pictured her children huddled together, confused.

God help those children. If she's got daughters, they'll probably be given away before her case goes to trial.

You know what they say. You can't kill your husband, even if he's the horned devil himself.

It wasn't clear when the judge would summon her to discuss the charges, but it had to be soon. The children were staying with Kamal's sister, Tamina. Zeba had begged for them to be sent to Rafi's home instead, but Chief Hakimi, recalling Fareed's fiery threats, had scoffed at her request.

"Khanum, I don't think your head is clear. Your husband is dead. Let's not dishonor him further by sending his children to the home of a stranger."

"It didn't have to be this way," she said quietly. "You could have saved us."

Hakimi had not replied, busying himself with paperwork and nodding for another officer to take her into custody. True, Zeba had come to him a month ago, the flesh over her cheekbone purple and blue, warning him that some of the men from the village were praying to a new god, one that lived in a bottle. They spent their evenings in a stupor and returned to their homes in a punishing mood.

God will strike them down for their sins, Zeba had prophesied. *But by then it might be too late.*

Zeba wondered what to tell the judge. When she closed her eyes, the events of that day came slowly into focus, like the flutter of a television on an overcast day.

ZEBA HEARD THE GUARD CALL THAT DINNER WAS READY. DOWN the hall, a heavyset woman in her fifties doled out steaming, cumin-infused rice with stewed potatoes. One woman from each cell would bring back a platter of rice and stew for the cellmates to share. The cellmates sat around a pale yellow tablecloth spread on the floor and mouthed morsels of rice and potatoes from their pinched fingers. Zeba joined them, keeping her somber eyes to herself and wishing she could have fed her own children this well. The women shook their heads but didn't let the presence of their mute cellmate dampen their conversation. They smiled through greasy lips and nodded at stories they'd heard over and over again.

By her second week, Zeba felt sick wondering what Basir thought of her. Her arms ached just thinking of her daughters and the way they had buried their faces against her in the moments before the neighborhood had barged into their home. Day and night, she slept with her face to the wall.

Her cellmates thought her stuck-up.

We're all here for some reason or another, guilty or not. Why not just tell us what you did?

Are you too good to talk to us?

Maybe she's lost her mind.

Come on, if you're going to be living with us for the next God knows how many years, we want to know who you are!

No one in this prison knew Zeba. They knew nothing about her husband or her distraught children. She was miles from home, miles from her village, and thankful for the anonymity. She would meet with the judge in the next week or two, she'd been told. She'd not yet breathed a word about that day's bloody events, the hatchet found in her husband's head, or the trail of footprints leaving their home.

CHAPTER 8

YUSUF SQUINTED HIS EYES, THE HEADLIGHTS OF ONCOMING cars bright in the evening light. A man on a bicycle chimed his handlebar bell. Yusuf stepped to the side to avoid his foot being run over by the cart the bicyclist pulled behind him. He had missed this, though it was remarkably similar to the noise and chaos of the Chinese, Indian, and Afghan neighborhoods of Queens. Had there been an elevated subway train roaring overhead, Yusuf might have felt that he was only a few blocks from home.

He'd spent the day revisiting the city he'd grown up in and trying not to look like a tourist. But between the bottle of water and the iPhone he pulled out to snap photos of the gardens, the monuments, or the dry riverbed, he had little chance of blending into the local crowd.

Another neighborhood, another band of boys in the street.

Kaka, Kaka, a boy had called out. *Uncle, take my picture!* He'd folded his arm across his chest and smiled broadly, revealing two missing teeth. Another child in a baseball cap followed his friend's lead, cocking his head to the side and winking.

He'd taken their photographs and, to their delight, showed the images to them.

You'll take these back to America and show everyone, won't you?

Yusuf had laughed, promising to do just that.

Movie stars! That's what they'll say about us Kabul boys.

He took a sip of water from the bottle he'd purchased and felt his phone vibrate in his pocket. It was his mother.

"You weren't sleeping, were you?"

"No, Madar-*jan*. It's still early in the evening. Is everything all right?"

"Yes, yes. Listen, your Khala Zainab called me just a few moments ago and told me she was so happy to see you. She thanked me for the gifts and said you were so polite and wonderful and . . . well, she praised you so much I didn't know what to say."

"That was nice of her. It was good to see them," Yusuf said.

"Do you have a pen and paper?"

"Why?"

"I'm going to give you Meena's mobile number. You can call her and speak to her. Get to know her."

"Meena's number?" Yusuf was bewildered. "How did you get that?"

"Her mother, of course. She wants you both to talk. Kaka Siar doesn't know about this. It's just between Meena and her mother."

Yusuf debated whether it was ridiculous or progressive of Khala Zainab to call his mother on the other side of the earth with Meena's cell phone number.

"I'm supposed to call her?"

"Yes!" his mother moaned. "She can't really call you, can she? Now, listen. When you call her, ask her what she's interested in. Ask her how many kids she wants to have and if she wants to work or study. Don't do all the talking."

Yusuf tilted his head back and took a deep breath. Was his mother giving him advice on how to talk to a girl?

"Madar-*jan*, I think I know how to have a conversation."

"It's not just a conversation, *bachem*. You have to get to know each other and see if you can spend your lives together. That's a big deal, you know. I wish I'd had a chance to ask your father these questions."

Yusuf could hear his father yell something in the background. His mother laughed and shouted back to him that it wasn't too late to ask now. She turned her attention back to Yusuf.

"Your father thinks everything's a joke. But seriously, Yusuf, call her."

YUSUF HAD WAITED UNTIL THE FOLLOWING DAY, NOT SURE IF HE was being rude or polite in doing so, but it had seemed hasty to call just after hanging up with his mother. Not to mention, he was fairly certain Meena would be home with her parents and that she would be ducking into another room to take his call out of earshot.

"Eh, Meena-*jan*," he'd said, hesitantly when he heard her answer. "It's Yusuf. How are you?"

"Yusuf? I'm . . . good, good. How are you?"

"Good, thanks. I got your number from my mother . . . or your mother, I guess. Hope this isn't a bad time for me to call. I . . ."

"My mother gave you my number?"

Yusuf bit his lip.

"Yes, is that all right?"

The split-second pause before Meena answered told Yusuf that she hadn't known. He closed his eyes and exhaled slowly, shaking his head at the way mothers plotted their children's lives. He struggled for a way to back out of this conversation gracefully—but then Meena spoke up.

"No, this is a great time, actually. I was just taking a break at work. How's your day going?"

Yusuf immediately noticed the confidence in her voice. She did not sound like she was speaking with a hand covering her mouth and receiver. She did not sound like she was checking if anyone was eavesdropping. As a matter of fact, she sounded like she was sitting back with her feet casually stretched out before her.

Their conversation flowed naturally—Yusuf's mother would have been pleased. He asked her about her work and she told him about the United Nations Gender Program. She was an assistant to the director, charged with organizing meetings and coordinating agendas between cooperating departments. Kaka Siar's family had returned to Kabul in 2002, the year the Taliban were ousted and hope for a peaceful Afghanistan flourished. Even while refugees, Meena had continued her studies, including English. Her command of the language, along with the recommendation of an uncle working within the program, had helped her secure the job. She had aspirations to advance in her post and was taking computer classes as well.

"You enjoy the work?" Yusuf asked. It sounded like an impressive job, especially considering that she'd not had much opportunity for stable schooling. It would look great on a résumé, he thought, and she might even have a chance of finding a related job in the United States. He wouldn't say that out loud, of course. It was not as if he'd made any commitment to Meena, nor had he even decided that he wanted to officially seek her hand in marriage. Still, he wanted to consider the logistics carefully.

"I do. I work with some really great people—Afghans and Americans. Even some Europeans. They're all so smart."

"You know, I was thinking . . . you were so young when our family left. Do you even remember me? You were just a little girl then."

"Of course I remember!" Meena cried cheerfully. "I was old enough to realize my best friend was going away. I certainly didn't know how long you'd be gone, though. I remember you being so patient with me. You were the older brother I never had. I think that's why my father liked you so much even then. You were like a son when he didn't have one."

It had been a luxury, in a very difficult time, for the children of each household to feel as if they had two sets of parents. Kaka Siar and Khala Zainab had indeed treated Yusuf like a son, and his parents had done the same for their children. They'd all left just as the Taliban were making their way into the capital, just as both families had realized that there was much, much further for Afghanistan to sink. Yusuf's father had been dreadfully afraid that his sons would be recruited to fight for one side or the other, or caught in the crosshairs.

"You were the only boy in the world willing to put up with a six-year-old girl. I can't believe how patient you were with me. I remember you even braiding my hair and telling me stories, but I can't remember a single one of them now."

"Glad I was so memorable. I was just thankful to know someone shorter than myself," Yusuf joked.

"I'm happy for you," Meena said, her words warm and sincere even through the crackling line. "I'm really glad you've done well for yourself, that your family is healthy and growing and that you're back here. I'm sure you are going to do some great stuff here. We need people like you."

Yusuf ran his fingers through his hair. Was he really doing this? This was not a casual conversation between childhood friends. Every moment they spent on the phone deepened the expectation that it would result in something serious, something that would tie their families together forever. His sisters had teased him about this very prospect before he'd left, but he'd dismissed the possibility, telling them he had serious doubts about Afghan girls, having lived with both of them all his life. He'd been rewarded with a twist of his ear—by his mother.

"You and I are sort of similar in that sense. Don't you think, Meena?"

"Yes," Meena said thoughtfully. Yusuf imagined her tucking a wisp of hair behind her ear with one delicate finger the way she had the other night. He imagined her smiling to hear him flirt with her, words as bold as a profession of love. She was exciting and vibrant, not what he'd imagined for a young woman living in Afghanistan. "Yes, Yusuf. I suppose we are."

CHAPTER 9

EVERY DAY WAS A STEP FURTHER FROM THAT FATEFUL AFTER-
noon. Every day, Zeba was that much more of a widow, that much
more removed from Kamal. There were moments when Zeba felt
light and liberated. She missed her children dearly, but it was hard
not to appreciate the freedom she had. If she did not want to
rise with her cellmates, she could ignore their chatter, roll onto
her side, and sleep through the morning. She had no responsibil-
ities in the kitchen. Her meals came with impressive regularity.
Zeba bathed herself and no one else. She missed Rima's soft cheek
against her own, but there was also a delicious peace in walking
without a baby on her hip, without the tiny fists pounding out the
hot rhythm of a tantrum, without the mouth seeking her bosom
with total disregard for Zeba's needs. How many full bladders
had she held so that the Rima would not go hungry for a moment
longer? And Rima was just the last of them—or at least the last
one to survive, but Zeba would not think about that now. She was
enjoying a moment of lightness.

SHE DID NOT REGRET THE CHILDREN, BUT AT TIMES SHE DID
resent them. All mothers did, didn't they? How could they not bear a
little resentment toward people who took took took all the time? How

could she be expected to feed them all? Where was Kamal when they were sick or tired or unreasonable?

He wasn't the type of father to do much for them. If the children were anything less than perfectly behaved and fed, it was her fault and hers alone.

That she'd wanted the children—that her womb had ached for them—was easy to forget. That her heart had bled for and mourned the two babies she'd lost was a fading memory in recent years when Zeba had grown increasingly tired and angry and worn.

When she was young, there had always been more than one mother in the house. She'd lived in a compound shared with a brood of aunts and older cousins. Zeba had expected something of the same after she married, but when Kamal decided they should move away from the rest of his family, she'd not protested. It was a delicious break to get away from a clan she'd never felt comfortable with. His eldest sister, Mariam, had always been too pushy and intrusive. His youngest sister, Tamina, barely acknowledged Zeba and always found reasons to avoid them. If Kamal's father hadn't died of a heart attack before even a single hair had grayed, there would surely have been more siblings for her to dislike.

Zeba wondered if her mother-in-law didn't sometimes rejoice in her husband's early departure, but it was unlikely. She was loyal to her family and to her husband's memory. Kamal's only brother had been killed by a land mine. He'd lost a sister to a disease that the local physician couldn't even name. Kamal's mother shrank into her skin, fumbling through prayer beads and shaking her head in perpetual mourning.

With his father and brother dead, Kamal became the patriarch of his family, though he still didn't garner the respect he felt he deserved. Day by day, his moods soured. He was bitter toward the children, brushing them away if they dared approach. More often than before, he would send Zeba tumbling to the floor with the back of his hand. She learned to bite her tongue around him and quiet the children with a stern look.

Just keep him happy, she told herself. *It could always be worse.*

Kamal began leaving home and wandering off, returning late and not bothering to explain his whereabouts. Sometimes he disappeared for days. Once, there'd been no word from him for over a week. Zeba was embarrassed to tell anyone. She doubted she would see her husband again but wasn't sure if it was because he was dead or disinterested.

On the ninth day, Zeba worked up the nerve to pay Kamal's eldest sister a visit. Just as she was getting the children ready, Kamal stumbled into the house—his clothes wrinkled, his beard scruffy, and his breath hot and rank.

Zeba steeled herself and asked no questions in front of the children. Instead, she prepared dinner and set it before him even as he scowled.

As things go in villages, people began to talk. Zeba kept away from neighbors and even family. She would pull her head scarf tighter across her face and rush the children inside to keep away the stares.

"Kamal-*jan*," Zeba said cautiously on a winter day when she had stretched the vegetables and yogurt into more meals than she'd thought possible. "The children haven't had a decent dinner in days."

"Don't you think I would bring something home if I could?"

"I just thought . . ."

But he was not interested in her thoughts. He threw his sandal at her, missing her head by a hair.

He jabbed at her, both physically and verbally. He made small, snide remarks under cover of a joke as if daring her to react. Their intimate moments were now abrupt, rough physical interactions. Zeba had changed too. She wasn't the bright-eyed bride she'd once been, but she'd believed their love had a trajectory. There was only supposed to be one direction to their relationship. This was all wrong.

"The war, the years of hardship, they've destroyed him. It's not his fault," Kamal's mother would desperately say in the months before her death—as if she'd known she would not be around to defend him much longer. "Thank God at least he is here with us, alive and healthy."

Zeba would bite her tongue. The Taliban were gone. The West had rediscovered Afghanistan and pale-faced men and even women in thick military gear and helmets roamed the village. There was nothing special about Kamal's suffering. He'd neither been a soldier nor an amputee. They hadn't had much but enough to get by with the work Kamal did as a blacksmith.

No, Zeba decided, *Kamal would have been the same despicable man even if he'd lived through the glory days of kings and progress.*

She cautioned herself to go easy on him. Everything would be worse if Kamal walked out the door and never returned.

But she felt no pity for him. He shamed her in ways she couldn't bring herself to say out loud. Gulnaz would not have tolerated the behavior, but Zeba was not her mother. She was nothing close to it.

She could see the way Kamal's eyes wandered through the market, feasting on the women who had thrown aside their *burqas.* She could see him tracing their silhouettes, undressing them with a greediness that made her face burn. She knew, when he came to her in the night, that he was thinking of a hundred other women—any other woman. He would travel to a nearby city sometimes, disappearing for a day along with money that should have been spent on food for the family. There were some women, everyone knew, who would lie with a man for the price of a meal.

But, to Zeba, the anonymous women were preferable to the vices he took part in in their own village. When Kamal was seen leaving the home of a friend, whispers floated back to Zeba that he was so drunk he could barely set one foot in front of another.

"I just want you to know I'm shocked at what I've heard about Kamal," Fatima, Fareed's wife, had said slyly. "You can trust that I won't be saying a word about it to anyone. Some men are like that. I can't understand it . . . and to think, the rest of the family is so pious and decent. You did know, didn't you? I would *hate* to be the one to break this news to you!"

Zeba had no plan. She'd never thought of an appropriate response to such a comment, believing that her husband's behavior would never be the subject of open conversation within the family. She felt small and dirty, as if it had been her sin instead of his.

The drink made his temper worse. The children knew to avoid him when he came home with glazed eyes. Kareema and Shabnam would pick up Rima and busy themselves pulling the dried laundry off the clothesline. They walked with heads lowered and shoulders hunched, as if they were ducking a blow even before Kamal's temper flared.

People talked about him. Zeba knew it from the way the shop-keepers looked at her. Their eyebrows lifted when she walked in, and their tone was less than respectful. Zeba never smiled. She made her purchases quickly and with her eyes trained on either the flour she was purchasing or the road straight ahead of her. With each time Kamal was spotted drunk in town, he further condemned Zeba to a life of ignominy. She begged him to consider their family, their reputation.

For that, Kamal had broken her nose, her rib, and half their dishes.

His sober interludes were hardly a return to the man he'd once been—they were moments in which an angry Kamal stumbled about the house, shouted at the children to keep out of his way, and grumbled about needing his "medicine." Zeba's couplets soothed her, distilling her fury and despondency into the shortest of verses.

Medicine is what this man calls his liquor
Strange is the remedy that only makes him sicker.

Zeba found it impossible to remember the man who'd whispered tenderly to her in their first days together, whose eyes had welled with tears when she'd given birth to their son. That man had never really existed, Zeba came to believe. He was a creature of her imagination, a way to believe her children had been born of something honorable.

———————

FATIMA STOPPED BY ONE MORNING AND ZEBA HAD RELUCTANTLY invited her in. As she poured a cup of green tea, Fatima explained the reason for her visit.

"Fareed sent me to see if Kamal has the money he owes him. We're not wealthy, you know, and he promised to pay us back months ago. Oh, look at Basir-*jan*. He takes after his father so much now . . ." Fatima's voice droned as she watched Basir pass through their courtyard.

Zeba's stomach tightened. She hated to admit the obvious likeness between Kamal and Basir, because it made her feel things toward her son that she did not want to feel.

Zeba had even tried to find ways to change him so that she wouldn't see Kamal when she looked at him. She buzzed his hair to the scalp. She never let Basir wear his father's clothes. When she kissed him, she would press his face on both sides, his cheeks doubling on themselves and leaving no semblance of Kamal's likeness.

Basir will be different, she promised herself. *He will be better than his father.*

He was her eldest son, the child she should have cherished above all the others. He had done nothing worse than other boys his age, nothing out of the ordinary. But from time to time Zeba saw, or believed she saw, a flash of anger cross his adolescent face, and inside her a dark feeling would bubble up, fear that she had re-created Kamal. Most days, Basir would come home from school and sling his arm around her shoulders and kiss her face. In those moments, Zeba was wholly ashamed of her ghastly betrayal. What kind of mother was she?

Perhaps she could learn to love Kamal again. Perhaps she could find a way to make him sing love songs again.

It took time to despise or love a husband—this much Zeba knew from her conversations with other women. Neither emotion presented itself on the wedding night or on any of the hundred nights that followed. The way a woman ultimately felt about her husband, whether she would spit his name out or whisper it in rapture, this would be decided over the course of years. It would be decided only after thousands of meals had been prepared, after the birth of a few children, after the death of a loved one, after a few nights spent apart and the temperaments had shifted between hot and cold like the seasons.

Marriage was a sport. One point for love, one point for hate. The heart kept score.

His arm around her shoulders in the moonlight. The way he kissed his daughters' foreheads. The smell of sweat and iron on his clothes after a hard day's work. The way he kissed her mother's hands on the holidays. Points for love.

But the passing of each day saw changes in Kamal's many moods, a dial turned to a different frequency.

Yes, she'd been too dependent on him, but what else was a husband for? She would not turn to him as much, she promised herself. She had less and less desire to, anyway. The way he turned away when she undressed, the way he snored through her labor pains, the rage-fueled times he'd called her a fatherless whore—those were all points in the wrong direction. The marriage game was not as close as it should have been.

The poor children, Zeba thought. They were not players, but losing all the same.

She loved them with all her heart, even the ones she'd lost—or perhaps especially the ones she'd lost. They were *good* children. They were her legacy, her creation, even if Kamal had claim over them as well.

So many days, Zeba had woken with a hope their lives could be restored. So many nights, she fell asleep chiding her own naïveté. She thought, *If only Kamal had been the one to die instead of his brother.*

Allah decides the moment of your birth and your death well before you take a breath.

Zeba's father had taught her as much before he disappeared. A smarter Zeba would have inquired further.

What about the moments in between—are they His or mine?

HAD SHE KILLED KAMAL? ZEBA COULDN'T BE SURE. TOO MUCH had happened in the span of a few moments. The images ran through her head too quickly to discern. Truthfully, she was afraid of what she might see if she slowed it down. She would face it eventually, just not today.

And maybe it wasn't all that important to think about it. She could convince herself that she had killed him just as easily as she could insist she would never be capable of such a thing. Wives, mothers, daughters—*women* did not do this sort of thing. They didn't have the stomach for it.

By the time the sun went down, by the time she'd shared another dinner with the three women in her cell, Zeba was one step further from being Kamal's wife. She was one step further from being a resentful and short-tempered mother. She was one step further from being a pawn in God's capricious games.

By morning, Zeba would share a few more words with her cellmates. She would feel a bit more at ease behind these hollow bars. By morning, she would feel her appetite pick up and the dark circles under her eyes would lighten.

By morning, Zeba would be a bit more Zeba—relying on no one to fix the small messes an average day brought. It was one of life's many tragedies that Kamal wasn't around to see it.

CHAPTER 10

ZEBA HAD JUST MET WITH THE WARDEN OF THE PRISON TO GIVE her account of the crime she'd been charged with. The warden, a stout middle-aged woman who spent most of her time behind her desk, was unimpressed and unsurprised by Zeba's poor memory of recent events. She had frowned as she closed the manila folder with Zeba's name on it and nodded for Asma, the red-haired guard, to lead her back to her cell.

Zeba stared at her feet as they shuffled over perfectly square bone-colored tiles. The walls were painted the same color but mostly hidden by the scribbling of children and a few bored women. The cell doors and gates were painted an incongruously cheerful blue.

Two preschool-age boys ran past them, an elbow brushing past Zeba's thigh. Their laughter made Zeba uneasy.

"Slow down!" Asma yelled after them. She shook her head and flicked her veil to the side. "They're just as bad as their mother."

Asma led Zeba past the guard's station, a half-moon glass enclosure in the middle of the prison with views down long corridors in either direction. Inside was a wooden table with a radio, its antenna lying limply on its side, and a small stack of refolded newspapers. Another guard sat inside and looked up as they passed by. Zeba turned her gaze back to her feet.

They turned the corner, and a stairwell led to the second floor. A girl, probably a year older than Rima, sat on the landing between the two floors, a pinwheel in her hands. Her violet dress flared against the concrete. She looked up and smiled beatifically at Zeba. Zeba wanted to smile back at her, but it didn't quite make sense to do so.

Loud voices came from the small room next to the stairwell. Zeba glanced in as they walked by and saw a folding chair placed in front of a vanity. Gaping drawers revealed round and flat hairbrushes, tins full of bobby pins, and tubes of lipstick. A can of hair spray sat atop the counter. One freshly coiffed prisoner sat in the chair, twisting her neck and torso to get a look at the back of her head. Two other women, rust-colored fingertips stained with henna, stood around her, one of them applying rouge to her cheekbones as she stared into a mirror the size of her palm. They didn't bother to look up as Zeba passed by.

"Like they're going to a wedding," Asma muttered, her eyes unlined and her cheeks unrouged. "Boredom is a crime waiting to happen."

Asma took her to the end of the hallway, at the blue door Zeba had come to recognize by the dent where an angry foot had left its mark.

"Zeba, you're back!"

"I thought maybe they'd set you free. You were gone a long time."

Zeba felt herself grow suddenly tired at the sound of her room-mates' voices. One thing about this cramped prison with its wide hall-ways and small rooms—it was nearly impossible to be alone.

"Be nice," Asma chided with one eyebrow raised. "No need to start trouble, right, Latifa?" She scanned the room quickly before her eyes lit on Latifa for effect.

Latifa puffed her cheeks and exhaled in frustration.

"The only difference between us is that uniform, Asma. You know it, too."

"Yeah, that's exactly right, Latifa. That's all there is," Asma agreed sarcastically. She gave Latifa a long, hard look before turning her back and leaving. Zeba figured she could safely assume it had been Latifa's leaden foot against the door that left the dent.

Zeba slipped into the room. She ducked her head to sit on her low bunk.

She was reluctant to engage in conversation with the women, but as Asma had just said, boredom was a crime waiting to happen. Zeba was growing impatient and anxious. She was trying not to imagine spending the rest of her life in this prison but was also having a hard time imagining any alternative. The judge had not yet given her a date for her trial. Her brother was looking for a lawyer. It wouldn't be easy to find one who would want to defend her, she knew.

"You haven't met with the judge yet?" Latifa asked once the sound of Asma's footsteps faded.

"No," Zeba said simply. "Not yet."

"They like to keep people a good, long time before they even start the trial. Keep you in here so long that you and everyone you know start to believe you're guilty for whatever's written in your file."

Latifa sat on a plastic chair facing the television set in the corner of the cell. Mezhgan and Nafisa sat on the floor in front of the bunk bed they shared. They were devout followers of a Turkish soap opera, voices awkwardly dubbed in Dari. Their eyes did not drift from the grainy screen.

"How long were you here before you got your trial?" Zeba asked.

Latifa let out a guffaw before answering.

"I was here two months. Simple case but the prosecutor kept filing extensions. I wasn't even denying that I'd left my family's home or taken my sister. But I know why. I'm sure the judge was hoping my father would sweeten his tea and arranged for the delays."

Two months. Zeba felt a lump in her throat swell. She lowered her head.

"Doesn't mean it will be the same for you, just means that's what he did for me. Isn't that right, Khanum?" Latifa nodded her head in the direction of another guard, a plain woman in her forties with wisps of hair peeking out from under a chestnut head scarf. She'd paused at their doorway, her eyes drawn to the soap opera drama.

"Come on, Latifa. You know I don't listen to anything you say," she said smartly.

Latifa chuckled.

"You're some friend, thanks. How's your daughter, by the way? Is she back to school yet or still having fevers?"

"She's much better, thanks. She went back yesterday, which means I could be here to watch over you instead of her. How lucky am I?"

The mood was light, until the guard asked her next question.

"Nafisa, are you ready for tomorrow?"

Nafisa took a deep breath in and started to squirm on the floor. Mezhgan put a hand on her cellmate's knee.

"You'll be fine," she reassured.

"It's stupid," Latifa declared.

"If you've got nothing to hide, this can help you," the guard said gently.

Latifa noticed the look of confusion on Zeba's face.

"This little girl is going to get examined tomorrow," Latifa sang out, with the theatrics of a radio announcer. "A very wise and all-knowing doctor's going to tell the world if she's a virgin or not. That's what everyone really wants to know. Did she or didn't she? Is she still a girl or is she a harlot? Has she stripped her father of his honor?"

Nafisa's face turned a deep shade of red.

"Shut up, Latifa!" she hissed.

Latifa continued, unfazed.

"Let me prepare you a bit since no one else will. You'll have to take your underpants off and lift your skirt. The doctor's going to use a flashlight to look at every hole in your body to see if a man's been near it. Oh, yes, your backside is part of the exam. But the front is the main story. He'll poke around looking to make sure your woman part still has its modesty veil. If you don't have that little veil they're looking for, you're in big trouble. If you've ever fallen from a window or out of a tree, better mention it before they've got your legs open for a look. That's the only hope you've got to explain what they might find in a way that doesn't condemn you to this place for another decade. Did you fall out of a tree? Think hard, my friend. Surely, you must have fallen from a tree at some point in your life."

Mezhgan clucked her tongue sympathetically.

"Enough, Latifa! You think everything's a joke. She's going to be humiliated enough tomorrow as it is. You don't have to make it worse."

"I'm only trying to prepare her. Look at the poor girl's face. Haven't you noticed that she's barely eaten or slept in the last couple of days? She's a bag of nerves. Not everyone would be as prepared as *you* to have a man sticking his fingers between her legs."

Mezhgan grabbed her hairbrush and threw it at Latifa's head. She ducked just in time. Mezhgan stood and looked as if she might storm out of the cell. She made it to the doorway, where she paused, arms folded across her chest. The guard smiled in amusement.

"I hope her lawyer is better than mine," Latifa said, sighing. "The one assigned to me told me I should be ashamed for leaving my family. He told the judge as much at my hearing and then asked him to have pity on me because I seemed to be repentant—what a defense! There's a woman in here that got examined and the doctor reported that she had been having sex at least once a week with two different men."

"They can tell that from looking at her there?" Nafisa, a lilt of surprise in her voice.

"I'm not a doctor. Maybe the men left their voting cards inside her. Damned if I know."

Nafisa was too nervous to find this amusing.

"What did your test show?" Nafisa asked. In the weeks they'd spent together in the cell, Latifa had never spoken about her exam. She'd not even mentioned that she'd endured one.

"My test? Are you as stupid as they are?" Latifa huffed. "You don't have to ask the flesh between my legs if I've ever had sex with a man. You can just ask me and I'll tell you I haven't, even if the men in my family don't believe it. My brother swore he'd kill me for being a whore."

Latifa then paused, her eyes closed. She wagged her finger in the air as if it were receiving a signal.

"I've got one! I've got one!

"If a man's honor is his highest prize
Why then stash it between a woman's thighs?

"Isn't it brilliant?" Latifa exclaimed. Zeba was too distracted to appreciate the couplet or the fact that she'd inspired a bit of creativity in her cellmate.

"Do they examine everyone?" Zeba asked nervously.

"No," Latifa said as she stood up and shook out her legs. "Only if you're here for adultery or *zina*. And something tells me that's not what you're here for."

Latifa was right. Zeba had hardly desired to have sex within her marriage, much less outside of her marriage.

"So, Zeba, are you going to tell us what happened or are we going to have to guess?"

Zeba met Latifa's stare. She shook her head and took a deep breath.

It was shocking how quickly the smell of blood had filled the air. Ghastly shadows appeared on her husband's face. Was it pain? He'd looked shocked, as if he were staring the devil in the face. He had crumpled, his arms outstretched, half expecting Zeba to catch him. The ground had quaked beneath Zeba and she'd let out a sharp gasp. Darkness, seeping from her husband's head, stained the earth around him and inched toward her. Zeba had stumbled to get back on her feet, never turning her back on him. She'd hobbled backward until her back hit the outhouse wall, then she'd slid to the ground. Zeba lifted her eyes for a second, just long enough to cry out a single word.

Go.

"I have nothing to say." Zeba returned to her cot and buttoned the cuff of her sleeve. The others saw her fingers fumbling, her lips quivering. These moments came from time to time, sudden flashes from that day. It was difficult to have a conversation in those moments. It was sometimes even hard to breathe.

Latifa recognized it but pressed on.

"Nothing at all? Did I get it wrong? Or maybe he just wasn't very handsome. Or," she continued with a doubtful tone, "maybe you are just as lovesick as these girls. Maybe you did find a new man, someone a little less wrinkled. Or with deeper pockets. Please tell me that's it. That would be a story I'd want to hear!"

Kamal's face again. His eyes wild and glaring.

Latifa searched her pockets and took out a crumpled pack of cigarettes. She poked a thick finger inside and felt around, disappointed. She tossed the empty pack on her bed.

Zeba's breaths were shallow. Her fingers tingled.

Go!

Had it come out as a scream or a whisper? It was hard to remember.

"Enough," Nafisa shouted. "Latifa, you're a jackass."

Zeba had melted away by then, her breathing even and her mind empty. This was the third time she'd fainted since she'd arrived. Mezhgan was unnerved by it. She brushed at her skirt nervously and swore she would never let herself be alone in a room with Zeba.

Nafisa put aside her anxieties about her upcoming exam. She would endure it in the name of love. She was a believer in romance, in star-crossed lovers and passion destined by God. How else could she survive the fact that her widower, despite his lusty promises, had not yet approached her family for her hand in marriage? She knew romance well enough to recognize the absence of it in Zeba's face. The prison of Chil Mahtab, Forty Moons, was home to women who'd committed crimes far darker than lust.

"For God's sake, Latifa, are you blind? This isn't love," Nafisa whispered, her eyes on Zeba's trembling hands. "This is something unholy."

CHAPTER 11

ZEBA'S EYELIDS LIFTED SLOWLY, HER VISION FOCUSING ON A metal grid. Her head felt heavy. She lifted a finger. Then a hand. She shifted and felt a bedsheet crumple beneath her sandaled foot. She was on her cot. She had no recollection of being moved, but her cellmates must have repositioned her on the bed with her shoes on. They no longer bothered calling the guards.

Zeba had never fainted before the last couple of weeks. Not as a child when she'd seen rockets fall from the sky. Not when she was pregnant in the hottest, driest months. Not even when she'd cried for her disappeared father. Something in Zeba had changed, and she knew what it was. The darkness was coming for her.

A lifetime had passed since she'd first seen it—so long that she'd nearly forgotten what it was to live without the terror. It came slowly, infrequently in the beginning. It slithered into her house like the smoke of a fire, curled through the gap between the window and the wall, touching Zeba and her children as they slept and making them jerk with fright in their dreams. It clung possessively to her husband, winding its way around his fingers, crawling up his arms and swarming his head with its bitter cloud. The children breathed it in, absorbing it into their innocent bodies, their veins darkening without them knowing. The family slept in one large room together, Zeba listening for the sound of the children breathing in the night, fearing the darkness would wrap itself around their young necks and choke them before the sun rose. The girls woke with a start, more than once, to find their mother's fingertips brushing at their throats anxiously, then patting their shoulders with a hush to urge them back to sleep.

When Zeba did sleep, she dreamed of the darkness. She saw it weaving through their food and knew by dawn there would be evidence of its existence: maggots in the sack of rice, mold on freshly baked bread, and apples covered in bruises. She would wake in the morning and toss the most rotted food to the stray dogs. She would have thrown it all out if she weren't afraid they would have nothing to eat at all. Zeba felt a gray film on their plates and cups and heard the incessant buzzing of flies. She did her best to scrub it off, but she could still taste it. It permeated metal, stone, and skin. It was inescapable.

Zeba's angst grew. The darkness came more often, once a month. Then once a week.

She wished for her mother. Who better than Gulnaz to deal with something as intangible as this? Gulnaz approached darkness with her special kind of science. But Zeba couldn't exactly turn to her now, not after the things Zeba had said.

What do you want, Madar? You want my children to be raised fatherless the way we were? You want me to put them through a life of shame and hurt, too? I won't do it. I'm not you. I don't want people to look at me the way they look at you!

No, her mother had probably not forgiven Zeba for that yet. She would have to find a way to deal with this herself.

She worked up the nerve to tell Kamal about it.

There is something here, Kamal. It is hurting us.

It was blackening their lives, it was a shadow over their home. The first time she brought it up, she was surprised that Kamal bothered to listen to her. When she finished talking, her hands wringing behind her back, he rolled his eyes and shook his head.

"You're imagining things. Don't be like your witch of a mother."

His words stung, but she breathed a little easier. He was confident and concrete, and she could believe in him.

The second time she'd brought up her fears, he had said nothing but twisted her ear so hard that it swelled to a purple mass. She hid it with her hair and head scarf so the children wouldn't ask her what had happened.

"I don't want to be married to one of those stupid women who believe in the unbelievable."

But if she believed in it, how could it be unbelievable?

Zeba bit her lip and went back to her needlework, unconvinced. He did not see what she could see. He didn't understand that they lived in a house with no windows.

She watched the children carefully. She kept them close to her. They went from school to home, where she made sure they played at her feet while she tended to the cooking. She scrubbed at their skin like they were day-old dishes and repeatedly felt their foreheads for fever. The darkness could look like anything, she intuited. Kamal was of no help. It was up to her to protect her family.

Zeba lay awake in the nights, ready to meet the invisible trespasser and thinking of ways to fend it off. Though she could not always see it, she could smell it, like a piece of rotting meat so foul that it turned her stomach. Even the mice stayed away.

When Zeba cooked, she breathed in the fresh cilantro, garlic, cumin, and lemon. She tried to cleanse her senses of the stench that had settled into their walls.

By night, it was back.

The children didn't see what Zeba could see. They acted no differently in the day, as long as their father wasn't around. Basir's laughter echoed through the street behind their home. He came home scraped up from soccer games but not broken. The girls helped each other with the chores around the house. Kareema and Shabnam brought sloshing pails of water from the well, each grabbing on to the warped metal handle. They sang folk songs just like other girls their age. Rima stumbled, crawled, and babbled like any other baby. None of them knew any better. Zeba was baffled by their immunity. Sometimes she was grateful for it. Other times she was angry that she was the only person in her family to feel the weight of the darkness.

ZEBA, TWO DAYS BEFORE THE EID HOLIDAY, STRUNG THE LIVING room carpet up in the courtyard to beat the dust from it. She held the end of her head scarf over her mouth and nose with one hand and thumped at the rug with a thick stick. Her husband had been gone since morning. She hoped he'd gone off to work though it was more than possible he was off drinking and smoking what little money he earned.

She started from one corner and moved across the rectangle systematically. The carpet wobbled pathetically under her blows.

Zeba moved her aim downward and dealt the carpet a few more sharp smacks. When her stick snapped in two, she let out a sharp cry, then picked up a broom handle and took up again where she'd left off. *Thump, thump, thump.* She grunted between blows, puffs of dust rising violently from the tapestry like tubercular coughs.

When she got down to the last square foot of rug, Zeba stopped. She was panting. Her shoulder burned, and she sat on an overturned plastic bucket to catch her breath and let the muscles of her arm rest.

A bitter chill had settled over the village. Even indoors, the children's fingers blanched with cold. She took the carpet inside and spread it out on the floor, its colors no brighter than they were before she'd attacked its wool fibers. This, for some reason she could not put into words, brought tears to her eyes.

Zeba blew on her hands and rubbed them together. She turned when she heard the door clang behind her. Kamal unwound his black scarf and tossed a bag of walnuts and raisins on the table. Zeba smiled weakly at him, thinking his timing could not have been better.

"How perfect," Zeba had declared, reaching for the kettle. "Basir's just brought back some fresh bread. I'll make some tea. It'll warm our bellies."

"It's not for them. They can eat what's left from last night. I bought this for myself," he declared.

Something in Kamal's voice prickled Zeba's skin. She looked up, abruptly. Kamal averted his eyes just as she turned to him. She watched closely as Kamal hung his hat and jacket on a hook in the hallway. She saw the slouch of his shoulders, the defiance in his chin, and the shadows around his eyes. How long had they been there without her seeing? She could barely breathe, her throat thick and tight.

Her voice faltered.

Kamal watched her from the corner of his eye. He did not move toward her or away from her. They stood in measured space, precisely six steps apart from each other, his feet planted firmly on the carpet she'd tried to clean just moments ago. He could see the rare silver threads in her hair. She could almost feel the stubble on his face, the face that had rubbed against hers just last night when Kamal had pressed himself into his wife despite her small pleas of protest. Zeba's dusty fingers flittered to her lips.

But he's my husband. How could this be?

It was in him, that thing she could not name. That thing she could not speak.

"Zeba," he said, turning his broad back to her. "Don't look for trouble."

CHAPTER 12

ZEBA WAS BROUGHT TO A ROOM NEXT TO THE PRISON'S ADMINIS-
trative office, a room just large enough for a table and two chairs. One
large window looked out onto the fenced-in yard and blank walls.
Zeba took a seat across the table from a sable-eyed boy who looked
as if he should be holding a schoolbag instead of a briefcase. He had
short, curly hair and a smooth face.

Oh, Rafi. What were you thinking?

The boy cleared his throat before greeting her. He put a hand on
his chest and nodded his head as he introduced himself.

"Good afternoon. My name is Yusuf and I'll be your attorney. We
have lots to discuss."

Zeba could not believe this was the lawyer her brother had hired.
He looked so young he should be defending nothing more serious
than a goalpost. Her heart fell; she would certainly be hanged before
the end of summer.

"I've read through the arrest registry and the police report. But I'm
here to listen to you. Where do you want to begin?"

Zeba rested her forehead on her palm and stared at the table.
Yusuf was unsure how to interpret this.

"Perhaps I should go first?" he offered.

Yusuf started to pace the small room. He was shocked, he told her, that she wasn't killed immediately by the villagers or by her husband's family.

"It's just not . . . it's not the way things are done. I can't believe they simply shrugged their shoulders and decided to hand you over to the police when we all know who really polices the villages. Completely unexpected and unprecedented, and we have to focus on that because that's important. That's quite critical, actually."

Her village was not being noble or particularly lenient, Zeba thought, but she kept that to herself. This man knew nothing about her husband or her neighbors.

Yusuf described the barriers he'd faced in even getting this far, in setting up a time to meet with her. He had pored over the prison's file and the police reports and decided they were in for a tough fight. He needed to talk with her family and anyone she could think of who would speak on her behalf. There were many procedural codes that hadn't been followed, he emphasized. He slipped a finger into the knot of his tie and tugged at it impatiently, as if it was preventing him from talking as fast as he needed to.

Zeba wondered if there could be some mistake. Was it possible Rafi had hired a different lawyer for her? It would make much more sense if this man were actually assigned to a different inmate, one of the women accused of falling in love, perhaps. He looked like he would be much more suited to the problems of the lovesick.

Yusuf pulled a chair opposite her and met her eyes. Zeba instinctively turned away.

"I need to know what happened. I need to know everything about that day and what kind of man your husband was."

Zeba met his questions with silence. He explained politely, then urgently, why she needed to cooperate with him. Zeba said nothing and wondered which of her cellmates would fall for him first, Mezhgan or Nafisa. Maybe even cool-as-ice Latifa would melt for his boyish charms.

YUSUF RETURNED TWICE MORE AFTER THAT VISIT. ZEBA STILL refused to breathe a word. She moved her attention to the wooden table before her, her eyes tracing the pattern of the grain like a mouse through a maze. Yusuf could read nothing from the expression on her face. He cleaned the dust from his glasses with the end of his tie, waiting for a response.

"I'm here to help you. Do you not understand that? Do you know what will happen to you if—or maybe I should say *when*—you're found guilty of these charges? Khanum, we'll be meeting with the judge sometime soon and you've given me nothing to work with, no way to defend you or . . . or . . . or . . ."

Yusuf threw his hands in the air. He wore his brown suit today, the same one he'd worn the first time he'd visited his client. Zeba had noticed its even stitching, the careful pleats in the front. This was not a suit purchased locally. Yusuf was not dressed like any man from her village. His words, his clothes, the way he looked at her—everything about him smelled of something foreign.

"I have a question," Zeba said flatly. She looked up at Yusuf.

He paused.

"Where are you from?" she asked. Yusuf was silent, confounded by his client's simplicity. Her brother had promised that she was a good woman, that she was a gentle, loving mother. She was not a killer, he promised.

"Khanum, what does it matter where I'm from? Mazar, Kabul, Paghman. What difference would it make?"

"It makes all the difference in the world, young man. If you are not from my village, you don't know what fruits will grow in my soil. You think you can plant an orange tree in my neighborhood? It'll die before you finish wiping the sweat from your forehead. Because you don't know where I come from."

"I'm not talking about planting trees, Khanum. I'm talking about murder and jail and death. I'm talking about ways to defend you from some serious charges." Yusuf was frustrated. Did she not understand the gravity of the situation?

"Defending me? I assume you think there's hope for me to leave this place." Her head nodded in the direction of the wall.

"You don't think so?" Yusuf leaned back in the chair—at least she was talking.

"I'm a woman. I was found with my husband's blood on my hands. My husband's body was behind our house and no one saw what happened to him. I do not know where you are from, *sahib*, but in my village, where I am from, forgiveness is not on the table. This . . . this demands blood."

"Blood."

"Yes," Zeba affirmed.

"But they didn't kill you then. They sent you here."

"Yes," she agreed. The police chief had kept her in handcuffs and seen to her transfer. A husband killer was not someone he wanted to keep in his custody. Good old Hakimi had assigned his best officers to drive her to the prison that very evening, before Kamal's family got wind of it. Hakimi knew how these things worked. If Kamal's family was after her for vengeance, they would find a way to get it.

"And you think I know nothing about where you are from?" Yusuf said coolly.

"If you did, you wouldn't be wasting your time here."

"You have children who are without a mother or father right now. If you don't think you deserve a chance at seeing them again, then, please, tell me to pack my briefcase and leave. Tell your brother he doesn't have to worry about you anymore. Go on, save us all a lot of headache and just say it," he dared.

Zeba pursed her lips. She said nothing. An Afghan who'd lived abroad was worse than a foreigner. They came back thinking they knew everything and were anxious to prove it.

Yusuf stuffed his notebook into his briefcase and snapped it closed before standing.

"All right then. It's time to meet the judge. You've not said much to help me. All I ask is that you cooperate with me once we get in there. Don't make this any harder than it is."

He led her down the hallway and out the building to a smaller structure a few hundred feet from the prison. It was dark inside and smelled of stale ash.

When the judge opened the door and motioned them in, Yusuf gave her one last glare.

Zeba's face remained blank. Her nerves were already frayed, and her lawyer seemed bent on pushing her over the edge.

The judge's office was a narrow, windowless room with a scuffed oak desk at one end. At the other end was a small coffee table and a floral-patterned love seat. Zeba stood by the door while Yusuf took a seat on the sofa. The *qazi*, a thin-faced man in his sixties, frowned at Zeba as he thumbed his way through the beads of a *tasbeh*.

The prosecutor sat on an armchair across from Yusuf. He was in his early forties at least, judging by the flecks of gray in his hair. He looked distinctly more comfortable than Yusuf in the office, which gave Zeba a sinking feeling.

"You and your attorney have had time to consider the charges made against you," the *qazi* said. I hope you appreciate the gravity of the crime here."

Yusuf leaned forward, his haphazard notes in his lap, words connected by lines and circles.

"Your Honor, indeed we do appreciate the gravity of the charges, and it's for that reason that I ask for more time with my client. I have had some challenges getting enough information to adequately represent her and the events of the day in question."

The prosecutor laughed. There was a thin manila folder on the coffee table in front of him with Zeba's name written on it. Zeba tried not to stare at it.

"Challenges? What challenges? You've been able to meet with her freely. Her husband's family has done nothing to get in your way, from what I understand."

The judge shook his head. He was unaccustomed to talk like Yusuf's.

"Indeed, Your Honor, but my client has been understandably grief-stricken by her husband's death and—"

"Grief-stricken?" The judge leaned forward, his eyes narrowing on Zeba and forcing hers to the floor. She shifted her weight from one foot to the other.

The prosecutor said nothing. By the way the judge was reacting, he didn't need to.

"Yes, sir," Yusuf continued, stealing a glance over his shoulder to make sure Zeba was behaving herself. "Respectfully, this woman has lost her husband and she's been taken away from her children. I ask for an extension of thirty days as outlined in . . ."

"That's ridiculous," the prosecutor declared. "There's no need. There's nothing you're going to accomplish in thirty days that can refute what we have here in front of us now. Why would you want to waste our time? You know as well as the rest of us that she's guilty. Do your job and ask for mercy."

The judge's eyes moved from Yusuf's cleanly shaven face to the scribbling on his notebook and the knot of his tie.

"I've not met you before, young man. I don't know where you think you are, but if you want to do this woman a favor, I suggest you get to know how things work around here. You're supposed to help your client express remorse for what she's done. I'll have to agree with the prosecution. Haven't you read the statement she made when the police brought her in? She's guilty as guilty can be. We shouldn't be wasting our time with nonsense."

Yusuf bit his lip.

Yes, he'd read the statement, but it was an obvious sham. It had been written on her behalf by a police officer who claimed she was unable to write herself. At the bottom of the page had been Zeba's blue thumbprint.

"Your Honor, there are problems with the statement."

"What problems with the statement?"

"For one, it wasn't written by this woman. It was written by a police officer when she's literate enough that she should have written it herself."

Zeba kept her gaze lowered, but she could feel the *qazi*'s eyes on her. She focused on the side of the love seat, her eyes staring intently at the blue and gray flowers. The material had once been lustrous, she could tell. It was mostly worn now, its colors faded.

"So they wrote it for her. What difference does it make? Maybe she was too *grief-stricken* to pick up the pen herself," the prosecutor suggested, as he uncrossed and recrossed his legs.

She'd been interviewed for an hour by the police on that first night. Two officers had pressed her with question after question, threatening to beat her or worse for being so uncooperative.

You killed him. Just tell us why.

You're not going to get away with this. It'll be easier on you if you tell the truth.

Your own husband. Your only hope for mercy is if you cooperate.

Zeba had refused to admit anything. She was too scared to say much and kept repeating the same few words.

I didn't kill him.

By the time they slipped the paper in front of her and pressed her blue-inked thumb onto it, she was in tears and shaking. If they'd taken her behind the police station and shot her, she wouldn't have been shocked.

"And second, she's not expressed to me what's written in that so-called confession. It's not a valid statement, Your Honor, and shouldn't be considered as part of the case against her."

"It's a signed confession! They clearly recorded that she said she decided to pick up the hatchet and strike her husband's head because she wanted to kill him. Her thumbprint is on the bottom of the page."

Zeba almost felt sorry for Yusuf, the way the judge spoke to him. It was starting to get to him. She could see it in the set of Yusuf's jaw.

It was funny how she could pick up on something so subtle in a man she barely knew. Why hadn't she detected more in her husband? Had she been always been so blind? What else was she blind to?

"And you, Khanum, do you have anything to add in your defense? The murder of your husband, this is a very heavy charge."

Zeba shook her head, her ears buzzing. The room seemed to dim. She was there again, locked in that moment. She hadn't been able to go near her husband's body though she'd wanted desperately to close his eyes. They were bright and vengeful even as his lips grayed. His mouth had been half open in a look of surprise. Even as she'd backed away, shaking, she'd thought it was terrible that he would die with that dumbfounded, angry look on his face. He'd been such a handsome man once.

The prosecutor was talking, but Zeba wasn't listening. She tried to keep her eyes off the manila folder. It might as well have been a noose.

There were stairs in the hallway. If she could get to the top of the building and jump off, she could end this ordeal now. Would they bury her next to Kamal? Husbands and wives were supposed to be reunited in the afterlife, she'd heard. But God couldn't possibly be that cruel, could He?

You're mine forever, my husband would say
But I'm certain we'll be parted come Judgment Day.

Zeba longed to be that bird of solitude she'd sung about just days ago. The melody replayed in her head and calmed her enough that she remembered to breathe. To be alone was to be free.

KAMAL HAD TRIED TO SAY HER NAME, BUT HE HADN'T BEEN ABLE to get it out. He couldn't even say her name one last time. There was something profoundly sad about that, Zeba thought.

She'd seen the darkness very clearly that day, crisp and stark against the sun's brilliance. Like steam, it seeped out of his pores, a thousand

tiny clouds that merged into one, weaving around his twitching arms
and legs. Slowly, the twitching stopped, and the dark cloud began to
unravel. It uncoiled and traced a path along Kamal's leg, around his
hip, and up to his chest where it coaxed the last breath from Kamal's
lungs. It swarmed around his face. Zeba saw it, so clearly and vividly
she could have grabbed it if she'd dared. Kamal's face began to droop
under the weight of it. As the seconds ticked by, the darkness slid
along the ground and melted into the earth behind the outhouse.

Would it come back for her? For her children?

Rima was crying. Zeba could not rise to her feet. She could not face
her daughter with the splotches of blood on her hands and face. And
although he looked utterly lifeless, Zeba knew now that Kamal was not
a person to be trusted, even in death. She needed to watch over him—
to make sure he did not twitch his way back to life. Rima would have
to wait. Zeba was doing the best she could for her. She could imagine
Rima, alone in the kitchen, crawling around in search of her mother.

Shhh, Zeba had whispered from behind the house. *Sweet girl, don't cry.
Piece of my heart, don't cry. Something terrible has happened but we cannot cry about it.*

Zeba watched for the darkness. She made sure it didn't come
back around the corner and slither back into their home where Rima
bawled, uncomprehending.

Basir's voice rang through the courtyard. He was calling out to
her. Her children were home. He would find her soon enough.

Allah had ninety-nine names. He was the *Merciful*, the *Beneficent*, the
Protector. He was also the *Reckoner*, the *Forgiver*, the *Avenger*. He was the
All-Knowing and the *Witness*.

Zeba bit her tongue. She wouldn't pray to Him until she knew
which of those names to choose from. But if she couldn't pray, was she
not already damned?

"KHANUM? KHANUM! ARE YOU LISTENING TO ME?"

Zeba's breaths shortened, sharpened. Her legs felt like lead, and the walls of the judge's office seemed to bend inward as if they were being pushed from the outside. How was that possible?

Something rose in her chest, clawing its way to the surface, hungry for air. She tightened every muscle and tried to push it back down, to bury it for just a little while longer, but it refused to be tamed.

"Khanum, did you hear what I said? Have you anything to . . ."

Zeba's head lifted. Yusuf's mouth slipped open in a dumbfounded stare reminiscent of Kamal's last moments. The prosecutor put down his cup of tea and watched through narrowed eyes.

A tingling sensation crept up from the tips of Zeba's fingers to her hands. By the time it reached her shoulders, Zeba was no longer in control. She opened her mouth and a piercing howl erupted, quite indecorously, in the *qazi's* office.

CHAPTER 13

ZEBA WAS FORCIBLY RESTRAINED AND LED BACK TO HER CELL AT the women's prison. Nafisa had stuffed her cell phone into her pillow-case at the sound of the door opening, not wanting it to be confiscated again. Zeba's cellmates gawked at the sight of the guards dragging her limp frame onto the bed, where she curled up on her side and faced the wall, shutting her eyes to their stares and falling into a deep slumber. She slept all afternoon, through the evening, and into morning. She did not waken for breakfast or lunch. Nafisa and Mezhgan sat on the edge of the bed and whispered about her. Latifa's round face loomed just inches from Zeba's, peering at her with irreverent curiosity.

"What are you doing? Get away from her face!"

"I want to see if she's breathing. A dead cellmate will stink this place up really quickly," Latifa whispered.

"She's sleeping, you goat," Nafisa hissed. "Let her sleep as long as she wants. She's not much different when she's awake. The judge thinks she's a little crazy. That's what the guard said."

In the evening, just as her cellmates were finishing dinner, Zeba opened her eyes. Her limbs and neck felt stiff. Zeba sat up slowly, feeling her head spin.

Latifa scoffed.

"Our roommate has risen from the dead. A little late for dinner but I'm not complaining," she declared and slid another ball of rice into her mouth. "You're back just in time to hear the big news. Our darling Nafisa passed her test! Her purity has been confirmed!" Latifa threw a heavy arm around Nafisa's shoulders while the poor girl's face turned a splotchy red.

"Latifa!" she protested, throwing the arm off her and turning away. "I don't want to talk about it."

Mezhgan shook her head.

"You're a bully, Latifa. Leave the girl alone. She's been through enough, spreading her legs for that stupid doctor."

Latifa grinned but said nothing more.

"I'm happy for you, Nafisa." Zeba's voice was somber.

"Yes," Mezhgan said sweetly. "You've got your honor. There's hope for you now. And, Khanum Zeba, you will enjoy this. I even wrote a couplet for her!

*"Innocence is a word that can only be spoken
If your womanly veil has yet to be broken."*

Zeba felt her lips lift in smile. Her couplets had always been a solitary habit, a private escape. It was surprisingly enjoyable to hear someone else join in.

"Well, don't get too comfortable," Latifa warned. "Who knows? The doctor might have taken your honor while he was in there."

Nafisa's eyes watered. She would forever be the tramp who'd been imprisoned for premarital sex, regardless of the doctor's final statement in her case file. Would the widower want her as a wife after a flashlight had been shone on the place only one man was meant to claim? She flopped onto her bed and buried her face in a balled-up blanket. The women listened to her cry, mourning along with her.

YUSUF RETURNED THE NEXT DAY.

Women and their hysterics, one of the guards had muttered as she checked him in. When Yusuf looked up at her with a distinctly unamused expression, she picked up a pen and turned away to adjust the belt on her olive jacket.

Everyone knew about Zeba's outburst. She had raged for nearly a half hour, her fingers digging into her scalp and tearing at her dress.

Yusuf had jumped to his feet when Zeba had created that scene. He would have been more embarrassed had he not seen the *qazi* and the prosecutor look just as bewildered by his client's explosion.

Zeba could see a change in him. Yusuf's voice was controlled. He chose his words carefully.

"What are you not telling me?"

Zeba brought her hand to her forehead and closed her eyes. She would scream her story for all to hear if she thought anything good would come of it.

"Khanum, with all due respect, you have to tell me what happened that day. Tell me what kind of man your husband was. Did he beat you? Did he try to kill you? Did he beat the children? Was he a drug addict?"

How hopeful you sound, thought Zeba.

"Don't look at me like a child. Don't tell me I'm a foreigner. I was born in this country too. I come from the same land, the same people. I know how things go. For anyone, *anyone* to have come forward and said anything in your defense is some kind of miracle. Talk to me so I can defend you or tell me there's nothing to defend so I can explain that to your brother and walk away."

Yusuf held his breath. The more time he spent around Zeba, the more bizarre her behavior, the more he believed that she was worth defending. And that, more than anything, was what made Zeba look on him as a child *and* a foreigner.

"My brother?" Zeba said absently.

"Yes, your brother, Rafi. He told me you were wronged. From what I can see, it's hard to understand why he would say that. I've heard the description of the scene, and you offer no other explanation for being found next to your husband's body. Maybe Rafi doesn't want to see anything happen to his youngest sister, but it looks like he's going to be *very* disappointed *very* soon."

Rafi was five years older than her. When their father had wandered off, Rafi became a father figure to his younger sister. Their mother came to rely on him for everything from putting food in their bellies to representing their family at funerals. Rafi went along with his grandfather Safatullah's plan for Zeba to marry Kamal. He saw no real reason to object.

"Was my mother there too?"

"Who?"

"My mother. Did she come with Rafi?"

"No, why?"

Zeba said nothing. She closed her eyes and pictured her mother's soft face, her incredible golden-green eyes, and the way the corners of her mouth lifted just slightly when she spoke. Zeba felt a sudden yearning to be at her mother's side, to fall at her feet and press her face against her mother's hands.

"Who came?" Zeba asked. "You said someone came from my village. Who was it?"

"I don't know. The *qazi* didn't give me a name. He didn't tell me if there was any connection to you either. It could be a neighbor, a friend, a family member. Maybe you have an idea who it might have been."

Zeba didn't.

"All the judge would tell me was that the person said you were innocent. That your husband met an unfortunate fate and that your children needed their mother returned to them."

Zeba winced at the mention of her children.

"Have you heard anything about my children?"

Yusuf shrugged and shook his head. At least she was talking.

"Not much, unfortunately. I know they are with relatives. I wish I could tell you more."

Kamal's sister. The family was undoubtedly plotting her death and turning her children against her. The prison didn't allow any children over seven years of age. Regardless, Kamal's family would have claimed the children, and she, even as mother, couldn't contest their claim.

"I want to see them."

"I don't know if that's possible. I have no way of reaching out to them."

Zeba knew just how impossible it was. Every day she became more certain it was useless to argue for her innocence. It would be better to relent and accept whatever punishment the *qazi* issued. Without her children, there was nothing left for her. Her husband's family would surely kill her even if she were freed.

"Why are you here? Do you really think there's a way to defend me?" Zeba was oddly calm as she posed the question to Yusuf.

"I'm here because the answer to that question is yes. We've got everything stacked against us to be very honest. But I still think there's a chance if you'll just talk to me about the day your husband died."

Zeba stared at the table; she shook her head.

The day your husband died.

Zeba noticed, as Yusuf hoped she would, that he had not assumed her guilt.

"You come here with your briefcase, pieces of paper . . . forms filled out. You have a notebook you can't seem to live without, eyeglasses that are from another country. Maybe you've seen things in your young life, something that makes you think all *that* can do something. Makes you think there's something more than the *qazi*, more than the Qur'an, more than the people around us. There is nothing more. There is nothing in your bag that can change what happened. The village saw my husband with a hatchet to his head. They saw his blood on *my* hands, sir."

Yusuf stared at Zeba. Her shoulders had straightened. She was sitting upright on the edge of her chair. Her chin trembled slightly though her voice was steeled.

Yusuf felt his designer-brand titanium frames pinch the bridge of his nose. He resisted the urge to take them off and rub away their imprint. He also kept his eyes off his notepad. For now, he would just listen.

"I lost my children the day I was taken away, the day my husband . . . They are with his family now. They will be fed and clothed and told of their mother's sins. Am I to tear them apart with my claims? Curious eyes are on them now. They are orphans. *Orphans.* Am I to turn them against the only people looking after them now? Am I to make my children targets just because I'm desperate for them? They deserve better from their mother. The only thing I can do for them now is to let them go. My son is strong and wise. God will lead him."

Zeba slumped back into her chair, exhausted. She'd spent moonlit hours twisting and turning the situation around in her mind, exploring every angle, every potential end to the tragic story of Zeba and Kamal and their children. Zeba prayed, not with the usual ritual of prostrations and cupped hands, but with a desperate stillness.

Oh merciful Allah—their fates are in your hands. My fate is in your hands. Everything is in your hands, dear God, isn't it? But then . . . are your hands not bloody, oh all-knowing Allah?

Zeba shook her head. Was she stupid? Had she learned nothing from her years as Gulnaz's daughter? As the granddaughter of the pious *murshid*?

Yusuf watched her face. He saw her mind, saw her for the first time not as a client or a defendant. He'd been exasperated by her lack of fight, baffled by her submission, as if she was content to live her life in this prison or even be executed for the crime she probably did commit. But he saw now that she *was* fighting, probably harder than any client he'd ever had. Yusuf saw the flame in her eye. His mind churned.

"You're not going to help me defend you."

Zeba's breathing was steady, resolute.

If Yusuf was going to defend this woman, he was going to have to do it on his own.

"I did not ask you here. You can tell Rafi that I did not cooperate. He can save his money."

Yusuf remembered his last conversation with Rafi. He didn't have much money and knew that his sister's case was dismal. Yusuf had reassured him. The legal aid organization would take on her defense. There was still hope.

He leaned in.

"Then why not make it simple? Why not plead guilty to the crime? Just one visit with the *qazi* and you'll save us all a lot of trouble."

His tone was not antagonizing or patronizing, nor did he look ready to walk away. He was curious.

Zeba met his stare. He was asking the question Zeba asked herself a thousand times over. Why not take the final step and declare herself guilty before the *qazi* did? Why prolong this misery?

"Well?"

Zeba looked at Yusuf, his bright eyes and thick hair. She saw decency in him. She saw an earnestness that she'd never seen in anyone before and didn't understand. That was what felt so foreign about him, along with his thin framed lenses.

She couldn't answer that question. Was it because confessing to this crime felt wrong? Was it because she didn't want her children to hear the words? Maybe it was because she secretly hoped Yusuf would find a way to help her. The questions were too much. She turned away.

"You're not ready to give up," Yusuf concluded, nodding his head. He was digging his heels into this case when every attorney at the office was telling him not to waste his time. "I don't know the reason. Maybe it's a simple one. Or maybe it's complicated. But you don't want to say you're guilty. And that's all I need right now. I can work with this."

Yusuf's mind raced. He would have to be creative. His foot pressed against the floor as if it were an accelerator.

Zeba closed her eyes. What was she doing to this boy? Was it wrong to pull him into this mess? He was so young, too young to share in this bloody mess. It would surely ruin him, and she would be the one to blame.

CHAPTER 14

GULNAZ KNEW HE'D SEEN HER COMING UP THE HILL. HIS CHAIR was positioned under the shade of the chinar tree, a position that put him right in the way of visitors to the shrine. The *ziyarat*, tall and majestic, loomed over his humble desk, a slab of wood on a crate. When she got close enough that he could be sure his eyes were not deceiving him, he put his teacup down, interested. He'd expected her to walk past his open-air studio without a pause in her step.

Jawad watched her careful steps, her generous head scarf hiding her hair and delicate shoulders. The rest of the world could decay and crumble, and much of it had, but time dared not touch Gulnaz.

Gulnaz was still a beautiful woman, even with her fifty-some years. Jawad's chest tightened to think of her milk white complexion and bewitching green eyes. He shook his head and, for the thousandth time in his life, regretted that he lacked the power to make his own wishes come true.

Jawad pulled three tiny squares of paper from his leather pouch. Just like the others, Gulnaz was seeking something.

"*Salaam-ulaikum,*" she said, trying not to sound as breathless as she was. Her back was straight and confident, but her kohl-rimmed eyes darted behind her occasionally. No doubt, her son had no idea where she was.

"*Wa-alaikum al-salaam,*" he replied. Gulnaz hadn't called on his services in years. Jawad was curious what dilemma might have brought in the town's most beguiling widow. The breeze teased wisps of jet black hair out from beneath her head scarf.

It was midmorning, a time between prayers. A few people wandered through the arched porticoes and coiled pilasters. No one noticed Gulnaz, daughter of their beloved spiritual leader. Jawad knew the *murshid* well and was one of the few people in town not utterly devoted to him. He smiled to think what the great Safatullah would say to see his daughter calling on him.

"What can I do for you, Khanum?"

The turquoise tiles of the mosque glimmered in the sunlight. Gulnaz shielded her eyes from the glare. She pretended not to notice the way Jawad looked at her.

"I have come to ask for something."

"Of course. Tell this simple man how he can be of help to you."

Gulnaz tried to sound formal, as if this were their first conversation.

"I am in need of a *taweez*," she said carefully. She didn't want to stray from the script she'd rehearsed on her way up the hill.

"And what kind of *taweez* do you need exactly?" Jawad was the town's most notable talisman maker. He had crafted a talisman for nearly every villager at some point or another, not to mention the visitors who came to pray at the *ziyarat*. The hope that a *taweez* offered was hard to resist, and his were known well beyond the town's borders for their potency. That was why, after so many years, Gulnaz was again standing before him, in a place so holy people said every seventh pigeon carried a spirit and that gray pigeons would turn white within forty days of joining the flock.

"Protection."

Jawad paused.

"Protection," he repeated. Jawad was intrigued. He squinted up at Gulnaz, his wrinkled face tanned from years of hilltop sun. He was somewhere between sixty and sixty-five years old but had not a single gray hair. He'd been writing *taweez* for as long as he could remember and had clashed with Safatullah on more than one occasion.

Safatullah Kazimi was the most renowned *murshid* of their province. Safatullah had, from a young age, garnered attention for his mystic devotion to Allah, for his ability to lift the prayers of those around him to Allah's ears. By the age of twenty-five, his hair had turned completely white, which everyone took as a testament to his divinity and wisdom.

Safatullah's family lived a kilometer away from the edge of the *ziyarat*, the tomb of a beloved mystic. Maybe it was the hallowed ground or maybe it was the flocks of devout travelers—but something made Safatullah into a figure larger than life. His reputation grew as he saved children from fatal illnesses, restored sight to the blind, and gave barren families precious babies. He took no money for his work though people brought him whatever gifts they could. Even when wishes weren't granted, people left with solace and understanding. He steadied their spirits and affirmed their beliefs.

The work Jawad did was similar. For a fee, he offered people recourse when prayers weren't enough. His skills weren't mentioned in the Qur'an, and though nearly everyone sought him out, no one talked about their *taweez*. It was something private, between the seeker and Jawad, who would carefully etch the letters and numbers on the tiny squares of paper.

On more than one occasion, Safatullah had advised his followers against using Jawad's services. There was nothing that a talisman could say better than a devoted heart. He didn't like that Jawad charged a fee for his service and felt Jawad wasn't pious enough to be writing amulets. Jawad had said, loudly enough for his words to reach Safatullah's ears, that charging a small fee was more honest than expecting a lamb from the poorest family.

Jawad had also accused Safatullah of following in his father's footsteps and serving as a spy for the British. The previous *murshid*, Safatullah's father, was rumored to have helped overthrow King Amanullah, the monarch who sought to free Afghanistan from Britain's reins. Though Safatullah was still in diapers when King Amanullah had been forced to abdicate, it was a suspicion that stuck with him like the smell of garlic on fingers.

Then again, Safatullah, as the son of a grand *murshid*, was part of the light, part of the righteous, and Jawad was outside of Islam, a purveyor of the secrets and tricks people used when their faith became sullied with desperation.

"Protection, Jawad-*jan*. No family is above misfortune. As you said, our family is very much respected. There are eyes of every color upon us, and I have to look after the ones I love. I need to protect them."

"I understand. And what does Safatullah-*sahib* say on the matter?" Jawad took out three pens, green, black, and red. He held them up and examined their tips and then looked past them, refocusing on Gulnaz's stoic face. She was not going to feed the feud between these two men.

"I have come for a *taweez*, Jawad-*jan*. Nothing else."

Jawad chuckled. Jawad-*jan*, she'd called him. Was that out of respect or affection?

"Good," he said, flattening the first paper square with his fingertip. "Who exactly is it that is being threatened?"

"Make me a good *taweez* so you and the rest of the village can never know."

He paused for a moment, his eyes closed and his head bowed. As bewitching as she was, not every man could stomach a woman like Gulnaz. She was a bit too bold and much too clever for most. Maybe that was why her husband had disappeared. The village had a hundred stories to explain his vanishing. Jawad's position outside the *masjid* put him in earshot of both the town's synchronized prayers as well as their unsynchronized rumors. Folks couldn't even settle on whether he was alive or dead. Jawad was relieved when he heard the first person refer to Gulnaz as a widow. It was easier on his soul to lust after the wife of a dead man.

That Gulnaz was too clever for most only excited Jawad. His life's work, after all, had been overcoming obstacles. With his fingertip still on the square, he dragged the bit of paper to the center of the table. "I must concentrate."

Gulnaz watched him choose the green pen. The colors of the ink were critical as were the other details that only Jawad knew. This was part of what people came for—the focus, the deliberately placed letters, the undecipherable method by which Jawad filled the tiny squares with a verse, a symbol, or a set of numbers. There was method to his magic.

Fifteen minutes later, Gulnaz, daughter to a man who despised amulets, handed a folded stack of bills to Jawad and accepted the *taweez* he'd written for her daughter. She tucked it into the pocket of her dress and nodded in appreciation. She felt Jawad's smug eyes following her hips as she made her way down the hill and smiled to think she could still, after all these years, make a man look at her in that way. The hour of prayer was nearing. Gulnaz quickened her step. She hoped Safatullah wouldn't hear about this, though she realized there was a possibility he might.

A mother can take no chances, she told herself.

CHAPTER 15

BASIR WANDERED DOWN BY THE STREAM, A BUBBLING RUNOFF OF the town's waste. He watched the small fish dart about in the water and wondered how they managed to survive in such filth. The waters here were much worse than the smaller streams by his family's home. He imagined the minnows choking on pieces of trash, getting trapped in plastic bottles, and succumbing to the diseases that festered in those murky waters. From his perch on a rock, he could make out their faint shapes, just a few inches below the surface of the water. There were more than he expected.

Basir picked up a pebble and hurled it at the fish.

In the weeks since he and his sisters had been taken to Ama Tamina's home, his father's sister hadn't said much about the murder or the arrest. She seemed too distraught to say much of anything. Her husband, Kaka Mateen, seemed more outraged at the crime than she did.

While Ama Tamina dabbed at her eyes, Kaka Mateen had talked up a fury on behalf of his brother-in-law. Basir listened with his head hung low. His uncle's fervor was surprising to Basir, who could remember more angry exchanges between Kaka Mateen and his father than pleasant ones. They'd fought over money, politics, and even card games.

Basir felt a twinge of guilt that he wasn't as outraged as Kaka Mateen, a man who was only related to his father by marriage. Basir had been the one to stumble upon the gruesome scene first. It had been his home and his family that had been torn apart. Basir hadn't seen or spoken with his mother since she'd been dragged away. She'd looked at him, pleading with him to understand but not daring to say a word. If the neighbors hadn't been there, Kaka Fareed would have killed her. Basir didn't know if he would have been able to stop him.

His sisters were melancholy. Shabnam and Kareema stayed close together and said nothing when relatives cursed their mother. Rima, the baby, whimpered for her mother's breast in the night. Sleeping at Ama Tamina's side, though, she got nothing more than a pat on the back to return to sleep. Ama Tamina had four children of her own, none of them infants.

Judgment is for God alone, she told Basir when no one else was listening.

Ama Tamina was patient and didn't seem to resent the children. This surprised Basir. He knew Zeba had always thought Tamina did not care for her. Visits to Tamina's home were short and infrequent and Tamina's visits to their home were even shorter, formalities really, so that the world could not say the families had become estranged from each other.

Basir's older aunt, Ama Mariam, stopped by often. She was much more vocal about her brother's murder and lamented his death enough to make up for Ama Tamina's restraint.

"Has she forgotten what I did when you were born? I brought her food for the forty days when she was *zacha* and not supposed to lift a finger. I was there to take care of her and her home. I showed her how to swaddle you. I made tiny mittens so you wouldn't scratch your face. She didn't know how to do any of these things! And this is how she shows her gratitude after all our family did for her?"

Basir couldn't find the words to defend his mother, nor was he sure he wanted to.

"Leave the kids out of it, Mariam," Tamina implored. "They've been through enough."

"They should know what she's done!" Mariam would say, the words firing from her mouth like artillery. "She's destroyed their lives! They're going to have to live with that. I hope they hang her!"

Basir was thankful his father had decided to move his family into a different part of town after he'd quarreled with a few relatives, including Kaka Mateen.

The village was large enough that families could grow apart but small enough that everyone in town would talk about it if they did. People came to know Kamal as the troublesome brother, the one who could be spotted around town intoxicated from time to time. He was the stain on their family name, though Ama Mariam would defend him if anyone should dare speak of his trespasses.

Still, even she kept her distance.

Basir had heard his mother mumble about something she called the darkness, but he didn't believe in it. He knew only that his family was different. He heard foul whispers about the kind of man his father was and wondered if the stink of it stuck to his skin. He watched his mother out of the corner of his eye, saw the way she examined their vegetables with distrust. He knew she hovered over him in the night, brushing at his chest and pretending to smooth his blanket when he stirred. He saw the way she fussed over his sisters, washing their skin until they were red and raw, then apologetically slathering them in soothing oils. He saw the way she watched his father, her eyes skirting over his clothes, checking for something she never talked about. Though her behavior was peculiar, Basir loved his mother deeply. When his father raged, she made herself wide as a tapestry so that his hands would strike only her.

When Basir was eleven years old, he'd gone with his father to a nearby farm to get a freshly slaughtered lamb. It was Eid, the holiday that marked Abraham's willingness to sacrifice his son for God and the ransoming of a lamb in his son's place. He watched the farmer drag a lamb by its two hind legs toward the slaughterhouse, a shed with metal hooks hanging from a horizontal beam, a butcher's knife thick with dried blood and an earth floor that had been a killing field. As if the lamb knew precisely what lay ahead, its eyes bulged from its cottony head like soap bubbles. The lamb bleated loudly, its two front legs raking at the ground in futile protest.

Nearly every day was a sacrifice in their home.

Basir's throat had felt thick and his hands clammy. He'd scurried off to an outhouse and emptied his stomach behind it. His father barely noticed he'd left.

Basir knew what his mother did for them. She was the reason he could laugh and eat and look after his sisters. She hid her bruises and scars.

On those days when Zeba's resolve wore thin, she startled easily. She stared off into the fire of their clay oven in a way that made Basir nervous to leave her alone. When his father left the house, they all relaxed. When he was gone a bit too long, the house grew taut with nervous expectation.

Basir's dilemma was that, as much as he wanted to despise his father, he still found himself drawn to him. He saw Kamal as strong and capable. He listened to his father's stories of his own boyhood mischief, wishing time could bend and make him his father's childhood friend. Basir compared himself to his father, wondering if his own feet would ever be so big and grounding, if his beard would be as full or if his comings and goings would be so free.

If his mother seemed to forgive his father's outbursts, why shouldn't he? If she'd been so upset about the kind of man he was, why hadn't she said something? Why didn't she ever scream out or strike back? She'd done nothing to say things should be any different. She'd always carried on as if his father had been exactly the type of husband she'd expected.

Basir hurled another rock at the stream. The fish darted back and forth in no particular direction, which angered Basir inexplicably.

He hated staying with Ama Tamina and Kaka Mateen. He hated hearing all the things people said about his mother. Each time someone proclaimed she was damned or that she should be executed, he would grind his teeth and stifle a scream.

One morning, after Kaka Mateen had left the house, Basir pulled his sisters aside.

"Don't listen to anything you hear them saying about our mother, okay?" he whispered to Shabnam and Kareema. "They don't know what they're talking about. Madar-*jan* is going to be just fine and until she comes back, I'm looking after you all. There's nothing to worry about."

He said it not because he believed it, but because he believed they needed to hear it.

His sisters were young and frightened and stayed on their best behavior. Shabnam tried to look after Rima as much as she could. She was used to helping Madar-*jan* at home and hummed the same soothing tunes, watching lovingly as Rima's eyelids grew heavy. Kareema kept the few clothes they'd brought neatly folded in a corner of the room they shared with their five cousins. They stayed close by Ama Tamina's side and offered to help with whatever she was doing.

Basir sat on a flat rock and pulled his knees to his chest. The sun was sinking into a sky of purple and orange ribbons. He should be getting back before dinner or Kaka Mateen would be angry. Basir hated feeling controlled. He hated that he wasn't allowed to visit his mother. He heard that she had a lawyer now. When he'd asked if she had gone before a judge yet, his aunt and uncle stopped talking about his mother's case altogether. It was no use asking anything else. He would only be told what they wanted to say anyway.

As he looked at the earth under him, Basir dug his fingers into the dirt, feeling the grains embed under his fingernails and liking the way it stung. He scraped his fingers against the ground, lifting it and letting it drift through his fingers. How many handfuls of dirt covered his father?

Basir tried to picture him, his corpse sheathed in white. His uncles had insisted that he help wash his father's body for the burial.

Kaka Fareed held nothing back.

"Look! Look what your mother's done! This man should be alive. Your father should be standing next to me. But here I am washing his dead body because your damned mother took a hatchet to his head."

Kamal's eyes were shut and his jaw was closed with a strip of white cotton wrapped around his face, below his chin and knotted at the top of his head. There was contempt in the downward turn of his lips. Basir couldn't bear to see that scorn, wondering if it was directed at his mother or at someone else. Basir had picked up his father's hand and, feeling the stiff fingers against his own, had dropped it as one would a hot coal. He'd taken two abrupt steps backward, his father's cousins staring at him with a mixture of disappointment and understanding. They'd said nothing when he sat slouched forward with his head in his hands.

Did my mother really do this?

He could not imagine it. Nor could he imagine another plausible explanation for the scene he'd found at home that day. The blood, the look on his father's face, the way his mother quavered when she told him to take the girls inside.

Basir had dug a small hole, the size of an apple. He clenched his hand into a fist and pressed his knuckles into the dirt, moving his hand back and forth and letting the friction burn his skin. His chest heaved with one deep breath.

Maybe he didn't know his mother as well as he thought he did. Maybe his father had strayed from home for a reason.

Basir's head ached at the thought of having to choose between two parents, especially since one of them was dead. He didn't know who to blame. All he could wish for was for his mother to stay alive.

Any parent, his mother had told him once, is better than no parent at all.

CHAPTER 16

GULNAZ STRETCHED HER LEGS ON THE FLOOR CUSHION AND leaned her head against the wall. She'd spent all day avoiding everyone. She wanted to speak with Rafi, but he wasn't yet back from town. His wife, Shokria, watched her nervously. Gulnaz scowled and kept her green eyes averted. On more than one occasion, Shokria had whispered to her sister that her mother-in-law's emerald eyes bored into her so intensely she could feel her muscles knot.

Gulnaz knew what people thought of her. As daughter of the powerful *murshid*, people had always treated her with cautious respect. And when they caught a glimpse of her green eyes, she could see them hesitate to take their next breath, as if she might have cursed the very air around them. Even as a young girl, her aunts and cousins had thrown accusing looks her way when things went wrong, as if it were her fault they'd oversalted the stew or tripped on a stone in the courtyard. No one else in the family had green eyes, which made them all the more striking. By the time she was two, the family had concluded she'd been born with a twisted form of the *murshid*'s powers, not the kind that drew people in hopes of blessings and good fortune, but the kind that could bring on a toothache or destroy a field of crops.

Gulnaz was an only child, another oddity attributed to her mysterious powers.

She must have cast a nazar *on her mother's womb in the nine months she was in there. Not a single child after her! Allah have mercy!*

When Gulnaz was born, Afghanistan had been flirting with madness. The Soviets had just helped build an airport in Kabul. They poured money into the small country, showering her with compliments and adorning her wrists and ears with jewelry.

In hard times, when the *murshid* seemed to have lost his connection to the Almighty, onion fields remained fallow. Horses fell ill and died. Prayers went unanswered. Rumors spread that the *murshid* was a spy for outside nations. He was selling out his own Afghans, they said. He was an emissary for the Russians, the Americans, or the British, depending on who was asked, feeding them information about the local officials and the movements of the mujahideen. Any bottle of perfume, any ink pen, any nickel-plated teakettle in his home was evidence of his duplicity.

But when people were desperate enough, they'd turn even to a suspected spy if it meant putting food back on their tables or saving the life of a child.

Gulnaz had watched her father puff from the attention of the townspeople. Visitors would come to their home, arms laden with gifts, and cry their woes to the *murshid*. He would listen to them, cup his hands in supplication with them. And then, as if a broken pipe had been soldered back together, the *murshid*'s prayers would restore life and hope.

It was not surprising that his body aged at a different pace than those around him. The unending pleas from neighbors, the scandalizing rumors, and the strife within the family compound weighed heavily on him. Prestige was a blessing and a beast.

Her father had never believed that people actually gave weight to the superstitions about green eyes. He would smile softly and brush his daughter's hair from her eyes.

"These eyes? How could anyone think these eyes would bring anything but joy? *Nazar* is born from a lack of faith. It is something that exists where God does not. Your eyes are not the source of *nazar*, Gulnaz. Everyone in our village should know better than to think that."

But they didn't know better. Gulnaz and her mother kept out of sight when visitors called upon the *murshid*, which they did nearly daily. Gulnaz would hide in the courtyard of their home and watch as his magic unfolded. When she was nine or ten, she became more curious as to what her father did that had people leave looking so comforted, as if a burden had been lifted from their shoulders.

She followed one visitor to find out. A man with a basket of eggs was escorted by one of Gulnaz's cousins, led through the compound at a leisurely stroll, making small talk along the way. In the meantime, another cousin darted around the back of the house, with Gulnaz close behind. He made his way to the room where Safatullah received guests. Breathless, he told the *murshid* about the visitor, the basket of eggs he had brought and his ailing wife.

The man was announced, entering the room with his head bowed and a hand over his heart in respect. The *murshid* extended a hand in greeting and kissed his guest's cheeks. From the hallway behind the sitting room, Gulnaz could hear her father clear his throat.

"It is wonderful to see you, my friend, though I wish you would have come under happier circumstances. I sense something troubles you deeply."

"You're most right, Safatullah-*sahib*," the man said, his voice gravelly with emotion.

"And what weighs on your mind most doesn't seem to be what troubles lesser men. You are not here to ask God for more food or more land. No, your heart has no greed. You are here about something far more important."

"Oh, good *murshid*! My soul is bare to you!"

"Your eyes tell your pain. How is your dear wife doing?"

"She is not well, *sahib*. She grows weaker by the day. The fevers come and go. Her skin and eyes have yellowed. I beg her to eat, but she can't bring anything to her lips. I fear the children will soon be without a mother, and I don't know what else to do. We've tried all the remedies my elders recommended for us."

"You must have faith. Allah knows best for you. He will not allow her to suffer this way, not when you have both been such devout people. God is merciful, my dear friend. Let's make a prayer together . . ."

With hands cupped, heads bowed, and shoulders swaying side to side, the men would pray. Gulnaz's cousin caught a glimpse of her peeking into the room and shooed her away.

Gulnaz was struck by the way her father had spoken, a voice so different from what she was accustomed to. The voice of the *murshid* was patient, soothing. Her father's voice was harsher, sometimes angry, other times jovial. It was as if he were two different men, one for his family and one for the townspeople who called upon him for miracles. Gulnaz started to learn from him then. She would hide and listen carefully, her back to the wall and her ears straining to catch every word. She learned the right tone of voice, the right words, when to pause. Some things she added on her own, the tilt of her head, the clasp of her hands. She practiced when no one was around, whispering prayers in the dark before she went to sleep as if she were rehearsing for a day when she would take her father's place. Only her mother noticed, and she was more amused than anything else.

The more Gulnaz watched her father, the more intrigued she became by the amount of respect he garnered for his simple efforts. People often came back, praising him with more gifts when their prayers had been answered. For those who were not so fortunate, the *murshid* offered gentle explanations and guided them through their sadness. The poor man with the basket of eggs came back devastated when his wife succumbed to her illness.

"You see, my friend. Allah did not allow her to suffer. Allah knows best and will take care of your children. Let's pray together for your children now . . ."

And in that way, disquieted hearts were calmed. People found solace. The *murshid* remained beloved and needed, a pillar of the community. Gulnaz became hungry for the same adoration, the same power. She asked her father if she could sit with him while he received his visitors but he refused. She asked him to teach her how he performed his miracles, how he raised the people's prayers to God's ears.

"It's not a thing that should be taken lightly," he said, shaking his head. "What I do is not to entertain myself or others. It is not because I want people bowing at my feet. It's because people are in need of help. They need something that I can offer, and Allah has pointed to me to fill this need. It is not something I chose. It was chosen for me."

Gulnaz knew he was speaking from his heart. She knew because his voice was abrupt and sharp—it was her father's voice, not the placating voice of the *murshid*.

When she tried to pray out loud and within her family compound, she was met with cynical looks from her cousins, aunts, and uncles. They questioned her motives and shook their heads at her attention-seeking. In their skeptical eyes, she wasn't devout. She was playing with fire.

But Gulnaz wanted to be good. She wanted to look after people the way her father did. She copied his prayers, she mimicked his words. She would pop in and tell relatives that she had prayed for them or for their children.

But when a family refused to give their daughter's hand in marriage, when a son broke his leg playing soccer, when a woman's face broke out in hives—they would remember that Gulnaz had stopped by that morning, that week, or even a month ago. She was turned away, politely by some and forcefully by others.

These were the same people who would kiss the *murshid*'s hands in gratitude for a simple *dua*. Gulnaz could not understand why her benevolent gestures were met with such resistance.

"It has nothing to do with your faith," her mother had explained. "It has everything to do with theirs."

Gulnaz, at ten years old, had become embittered. It felt as if everything that went wrong was thrown at her feet, even when she kept to herself. Outside her family's compound, she was not the beloved daughter of the *murshid*. She was Gulnaz with the dangerous green eyes.

She was meant to do bigger things. She was meant to affect people, she knew. Why couldn't they see it?

Safatullah told her not to distress herself. Sometimes people needed time to understand what was best for them.

Disappointed, Gulnaz bottled the gifts she believed she'd inherited from her father. But inside of her, they began to boil over and transform into a very different energy. She could not hold it in.

She decided to live up to the image they'd created of her. When the mood struck her, she could make their narrowed eyes quiver with fright.

Gulnaz liked how powerful she felt. She was in control.

By the time she was an adolescent, Gulnaz had harnessed the effect her green eyes had on others. With a few careful, sweet words, she could manipulate situations to suit her mood. For Gulnaz, it became a sport. Since she'd never known a time when people saw her as innocent, she didn't feel guilty about it in the least. They'd created this Gulnaz, this young woman who drew strength from their suspicions, from their fears. Her extended family treated her delicately, loving her at arm's length and burning *espand* seeds in her wake to smoke away the effect of her gaze. Her mother resented how the family treated Gulnaz and was proud that her daughter had learned to use their fears against them. It was much better than being their victim.

Gulnaz loved her father, the *murshid*, as any daughter would, but she was utterly devoted to her mother. Her mother understood her and loved her wholly, unconditionally. From the moment she opened her eyes in the morning, she could feel her mother's watchful gaze. She would see her whispering prayers and blowing blessings her way. Because of her mother, Gulnaz could walk tall through the compound regardless of the mood of the rest of the family.

"My daughter, keep your tricks to yourself for now. You're a young woman, and this is not the time to show off the things you can do. Those are a woman's talents, not a girl's."

Gulnaz understood her mother was preparing her for marriage. She came from a much respected family and was unquestionably beautiful, but if word trickled out into the rest of town that she could wreak havoc on a household with a pinch of spice and a ball of clay, no family would even consider courting her for their son.

Gulnaz didn't think much of marriage, but out of respect for her mother, she did as she was told. Her mother casually mentioned that Gulnaz had outgrown her make-believe powers. Gulnaz, doing her part, kept her eyes safely downcast. She kept a neutral smile on her face and pretended to be a demure girl. By the time two years had passed, the family had grown considerably more welcoming toward her. Gulnaz missed the way she could send ripples through family gatherings but took solace in the knowledge that she'd simply reined in her powers. That, too, was a manifestation of her control.

WHEN GULNAZ TURNED FIFTEEN, HER MOTHER BEGAN TO TAKE her to festivals and gatherings. She was old enough to sit with the women and be seen at her mother's side. Her looks were quite striking, and the women took notice. She could feel eyes on her, checking the fullness of her eyebrows, the straightness of her teeth, the promising curve of her hips. The boys in town became intrigued by the excited descriptions their mothers shared with them.

Remember to act like a lady, her mother would warn her before they left the house. *Answer questions politely and kiss the hands of the gray haired. Keep your voice and words soft. We're the* murshid's *family and people expect more of us.*

Gulnaz would nod her head. She'd been hearing the same instructions since she'd been a little girl and knew perfectly well how to carry herself.

It was fall and just a few months from Gulnaz's sixteenth birthday. The *murshid*'s family had been invited to a wedding. The groom belonged to one of the more well-to-do families in town, who had expressly invited Safatullah, grateful for the blessings he'd given their son before his engagement, and insisted that his wife and daughter accompany him for the celebration.

Gulnaz was excited. She'd never attended a wedding before. The promise of music, dancing, and lavish dresses tickled her curiosity.

Her dress was picked out months before the party. Just before leaving the house, Gulnaz's mother retrieved a pair of eighteen-karat gold filigree earrings from her jewelry box and placed them in her daughter's palm. Gulnaz put them on and swiveled her head side to side to feel them dangle from her lobes. She felt positively exquisite, considering her usual unadorned attire.

When she and her mother entered the women's hall, Gulnaz's mouth dropped. The music was so loud, she could almost feel the rhythm of the *tabla* beating within her chest. Thin vases holding red roses sat atop round tables draped with pink tablecloths. The large banquet hall had been partitioned by a heavy curtain that ran the length of the room. The women, protected from the view of the men, shook their shoulders and let their hips undulate to the dance music, the quick tempo carrying them across the dance floor, spinning them and bringing them to a halt as if it were an actual dance partner. Giddy faces glistened with sweat. They laughed and squealed at each other's moves.

The older women and bashful adolescents stayed in their seats and clapped in encouragement or looked on with interest. Mothers of young men watched with a keen eye, looking for a girl who was beautiful but not too haughty, someone who danced well but not too suggestively, a girl who glowed with innocence and virtue and fertility.

Gulnaz and her mother wove through the maze of tables and chairs to join their relatives, seated far enough away from a cluster of vibrating speakers that they could have some conversation. The sharp sound of the electronic keyboard, a synthesizer blending familiar beats, and the melody of the up-tempo song echoed through the room.

Gulnaz's eyes scanned the hall, drinking in the sounds, so much louder than anything she could remember. She brushed wisps of hair from her forehead, enjoying the clink of the bangles, the feel of the cool metal against her wrist. She felt her mother's hand against her back, guiding her to the table. Gulnaz kept her eyes lowered, playing her part to her mother's satisfaction.

Her dress was the color of a peacock's feathers, blended together in an exotic and rich cotton. Narrow sleeves ended just below her elbow and the narrow waistline opened into a long, generous skirt that billowed as she walked. A panel of gold embroidery and small mirrors covered her budding chest. The regal stitching swirled from the shoulders to the cuffs, which were lined in a satin of the deepest emerald green. The dress was extravagant but, on some holidays, the *murshid* chose to spoil his daughter.

Gulnaz crossed the room, heads turning as she placed one foot in front of the other. Her dark hair fell gently against her shoulders, her eyes vibrant and striking. Gulnaz's lips curled into a shy, barely noticeable smile. By the time she reached her table, Gulnaz had become acutely aware that her beauty was magnetic, unmatched, and, most important, powerful.

IN THE THREE WEEKS AFTER THE WEDDING, SAFATULLAH'S HOME was visited by a flood of callers, unusual even for the esteemed *murshid*. What was most peculiar was that it was women knocking on the gates and that they were asking to see the *murshid*'s wife. Gulnaz's mother would push her amused daughter into the next room or out of the house while women showered her with platitudes.

Gulnaz would smile coyly from behind a closed door or with an ear pressed to the clay wall. She giggled at the flattery, the way the mothers lauded their sons' good looks, intelligence, and sense of honor. Sometimes she would slip past the room just to tempt them with a glimpse. Why bother with magic when she could make grown women bend and jump just by showing a sliver of her face?

The suitors were plentiful and persistent. Gulnaz's dark reputation was a thing of the past, a childish phase, a distraction to keep the suitors at bay. A few of Gulnaz's aunts and cousins watched the wave of interest with suspicion. They explained the phenomenon in whispers and knowing glances: Gulnaz had bewitched the village.

Gulnaz became the most sought after young woman in town, and her parents felt compelled to wed her soon lest that desirability backfire. Surely, those who had been turned away would be disappointed, and spiteful tongues could make Gulnaz out to be a heartbreaker or a temptress.

Gulnaz's mother spoke to her about the suitors. She described their families, the work each boy was able to do to provide for a family. Gulnaz would shrug her shoulders. She had little interest in a man who would come home with hands calloused by metalwork or one who aspired to follow in the devout footsteps of her father, the *murshid*. She scowled at the proposition of a boy who was intent on becoming an army general. She had no use for a man who liked to shout orders all day long.

Gulnaz's mother grew impatient with her nay-saying. They had turned away too many families, and she was growing anxious.

The tailor's family didn't think they stood a chance. They were nowhere near as well-to-do as others in town. Their eldest son, a young man of twenty years, had been blessed with handsome features but was soft-spoken and didn't know what to do with his hands when he wasn't holding a needle and thread. His mother had come alone twice already. When she came with her son, Gulnaz went outside the house to steal a glance through the living room window. The boy's mother had her back to the cinched lace curtains and didn't see Gulnaz's emerald irises peering curiously through the dust-spackled pane. Gulnaz's mother, on the other hand, was duly horrified to see her daughter's face in the glass. She refilled the teacups for her guests, praying that they wouldn't turn their heads and spot the onlooker. The boy sat at an angle, staring appropriately at the carpet before him and appearing like the well-mannered young man his mother promised he would be.

He was actually fairly handsome, Gulnaz decided. She liked the softness in his voice and the way his fingers toyed with the teacup in his hands. He was gentle. He would not tell her what to be.

Look at me, Gulnaz willed. *Let me see your eyes.*

Gulnaz's mother's shoulders were stiff. She nodded her head politely as the boy's mother spoke, though barely a word of what she was saying registered. She was preoccupied with how she would explain her daughter's behavior should the tailor's wife turn her head round.

Gulnaz pressed her fingertips to the glass.

Come on, now. Do you really want to be my husband for all our days? Let me see who you are.

The boy's back straightened. His chin lifted slightly.

Gulnaz's eyes widened.

Look this way. Here I am if you want to see me. Tell me you will treat me like a queen and I will nod my head and give myself to you.

Why was she doing this? He wasn't the most handsome man to come courting. He was not the boldest or most accomplished, either. But she was taken by his demeanor and the patience it took to thread a needle, to measure fabric by the centimeter, to stitch a perfect hem. He was the type of man who would appreciate her. He would let Gulnaz be Gulnaz.

Gulnaz sighed. She needed to look into his eyes to know. She needed him to listen now if she were to believe he would listen any other day.

Am I what you want with your whole heart? Do you believe it's our kismet to be man and wife? Look at me if we're meant to be.

The man of thread was pulled by an invisible one that led to the window, to the unimaginably beautiful young woman beckoning him to prove his devotion. His eyes lifted from the carpet, his hands relaxed, and he looked over his mother's shoulder.

Gulnaz gasped and put a hand over her mouth, as if she'd been speaking her bold thoughts out loud.

When he smiled, Gulnaz whirled away from the window and pressed her back to the wall of the house. Her breathing quickened as she inched back to the glass to peek in again. His eyes! They were as kind as Gulnaz had hoped, but they also shone with something Gulnaz couldn't name, and Gulnaz had a weakness for mystery.

Gulnaz's mother was wringing her hands and doing her best to keep the boy's mother looking straight ahead. This behavior was unforgivable.

The boy's eyes were again downcast, but there was a glimmer of mischief on his face.

Yes, Gulnaz thought. *You, I accept. I will be your beloved, your fiancée, your jewel.*

Within six months, the *murshid*'s daughter was engaged and married to a promising young tailor who would later prance out of her life irreverently, leaving her with two children and plenty of reasons to hate the world around her.

CHAPTER 17

ZEBA FELT THE HOLLOW ACHE IN HER STOMACH BUT COULDN'T bring herself to eat anything. Her cellmates had nudged her for breakfast and lunch, but she'd ignored them, barely grunting a reply to their concern. By this evening, they were indifferent. She was a grown woman and if she didn't have enough sense to eat, they would gladly split her share.

Yusuf was young and inexperienced, she knew. He had noble intentions, the noblest intentions Zeba had ever seen, but intentions accomplished little in Afghanistan. Guns, money, power, pride—these were the currencies of this country. That glint in his eye the last time they'd spoken had only made him look pathetic to his client—like a child who'd spotted a toy in a minefield.

Zeba couldn't save him. She could barely save herself.

She thought of her mother. The notorious Gulnaz. It was a full year ago that Gulnaz had come knocking on her door, her piercing eyes scanning their home. She told Zeba she'd sensed something was awry. She'd been having terrible dreams, images of the children rolling off the roof and falling to the ground, of Basir's foot being run over by a car and Kareema being kidnapped by a caravan of *kuchi* nomads. She was waking up in the middle of the night with a terrible feeling.

"Madar-*jan*, I'm a grown woman. I won't be scared by your nightmares anymore," Zeba said, though mother and daughter both knew she didn't mean it. Zeba hadn't been raised in any ordinary family. She'd been raised in the shadow of Gulnaz, the *jadugar*, and Safatullah, the great *murshid*. Nightmares weren't just bad dreams—they were omens. Feelings were divinings. These were gifts of knowledge, and ignoring them constituted a sin.

Gulnaz had opened the purse strings on a pouch and let a handful of *espand* fall into her palm.

"Let me *espand* these children . . . and you. At least let me do that much for my grandchildren."

Zeba had watched complacently as her mother tossed the seeds into a small pot and held it over a fire until a curl of smoke rose from the lip of the vessel. Gulnaz moved the seeds around with a stick, giving them all a chance to smolder into incense. The smoke grew denser and the pungent smell of the seeds filled the back room of the house and drifted into the courtyard.

"Do you see?" Gulnaz had said, clucking her tongue in exasperation. "Look at how thick the smoke is! Just think how much evil eye has been cast upon your home and your children."

The smoke was a precise measure to Gulnaz, who could almost assign a weight in ounces to *nazar*.

"Look at that!" She'd pointed, her finger piercing a rising plume. "See the way the smoke bends and curls? It's the letter *beh*, I swear. There's a *kof* for Kareema. And a *meem*."

Gulnaz had found enough letters from the children's names that she was convinced her *espand* was speaking volumes, proving just how much evil eye had been directed at her grandchildren.

"Madar, this is ridiculous. It's only *espand*," Zeba had protested.

"You're being stubborn. I'm only trying to help you. I know something's wrong. I can *feel* it in my blood. I'm trying to warn you for your own sake, for my grandchildren's sake."

"There's nothing going on here. We're fine. The children are fine. What can I do anyway? What do you want me to do about your dreams, Madar-*jan*?"

Zeba shook her head. As a young child, Zeba had seen her mother as a magical being. She could do things that no one else could do. When her brother had gotten bad marks from his math teacher, one visit to the school by Gulnaz brought his numbers right up. When she overheard a neighbor's wife speaking ill of her family, Gulnaz sprinkled a line of dried, crushed pepper at their gate. When the neighbor's cow was found lifeless the next morning, Zeba felt protected and safe.

Zeba had watched her mother, squatted by the kitchen fire as she heated the herb leaves they'd gathered together. She'd stood by as her mother smeared a person's photograph with ashes from the fire. Gulnaz had no book of recipes; none of her tricks were written down. She never formally taught Zeba any of her spells. She made Zeba curious by grumbling about the evil and whispering about the magic. She made it enticing enough that Zeba came to her, begging to be let in to this secret and powerful world.

When they were with the rest of the family, Zeba could sense that the other women bit their tongues around Gulnaz. Politely enough, they smiled and offered her and Rafi sweets. Gulnaz would shake her head on her way home and mutter that she could see right through their pleasantries and that she was no fool. A little sugar sweetened a child, she knew, which was why she stirred a spoonful into their milk. Too much, though, had the opposite effect and would sour a character forever.

Zeba thought her mother so insightful. People really were trying to ruin them. She would remember this as she laid a handful of wild flowers at someone's door, smiling to think of the dog urine she and her mother had dipped them in that morning.

After Zeba's father disappeared, Gulnaz became even more consumed with her sorcery. Before long, it seemed more important than anything Zeba or her siblings were doing. When Gulnaz's husband vanished, her suspicions about others casting evil eyes upon them were confirmed. And worse was the realization she'd failed to protect her home. Zeba recalled lingering in the corner of the kitchen while her mother chopped fingernail trimmings into tiny little pieces, so incredibly angry at her sister-in-law. She fumed as she mixed the trimmings into a bowl of ground beef, onions, and spices. It was Zeba who carried the meatballs to her aunt's house, ashamed to look her aunt in the eye but also afraid to disobey her mother's instructions. She had a terrible feeling in the pit of her belly as she walked away, imagining her aunt eating bites of tainted meatballs between squares of folded bread.

Zeba couldn't begin to understand what her father's disappearance had done to her mother. She had no way of knowing how much her mother and father had once loved each other or how she worried about him in the days, weeks, months, and years after he left. Her mother had grieved quietly, the only thing she'd ever done quietly, not knowing if her husband was alive or dead. Zeba had asked Gulnaz only once about her father.

"It was the work of someone with an eye more evil than mine," Gulnaz had hissed. She'd stopped slicing the crowns off the eggplants. She held her sharpest kitchen knife in her hand, its blade reflecting the afternoon sunlight.

"But Madar-*jan*, was he acting strange before he left? Khala Meeri said that he'd been saying odd things . . ."

"May God blind your Khala Meeri for speaking of him that way! She had her own reasons for hating to see us happy. She couldn't take it! She just wants me to suffer the way she has. That woman—oh, the things I could do to her if I wanted to. I've shown her mercy but sometimes I wonder why. Ten years I've lived without a husband. And she . . . she lives with your overbearing uncle in that house with those children that run around like street urchins and don't even bother to say hello."

By the time Zeba was an adolescent, she had had enough of her mother's trickeries. She knew Gulnaz's reputation and resented that she was made part of her evil spells. She was angry that people were starting to look at her as an extension of her mother, as her mother's accomplice. Zeba didn't want to be feared or shunned, as her mother was. Zeba wanted to be ordinary. She wanted to be part of the rest of the family. If only her mother would stop looking at the world through such suspicious eyes, Zeba had thought, they might stand a chance.

I am nothing like my mother, she would tell her adolescent self.

She turned away when her mother busied herself with new trickery. The first time she stood up to her mother, Zeba's voice shook. She had never been a disobedient child, and defiance did not come easy to her.

"I won't . . . I won't, Madar-*jan*! If you want to send those cookies to Khala Ferooz, then you'll have to take them yourself . . ." she said, her voice trailing off so it wouldn't break completely.

"Zeba! Take these cookies over to their house right now. Stop with this nonsense!"

"I will not do it, Madar-*jan*. I don't want to be part of this. I can't stand it, all this evil!"

Zeba wished her father would walk through the door. If he would only come home, her mother might stop spinning sandstorms. It was sad to think, but her behavior might very well have been the reason he'd chosen to leave and join the fighting.

"Evil? You think I'm evil? Have you no idea what evil goes on out there, really? Have you not seen enough to understand?"

Their relationship never recovered. Zeba knew her mother no longer trusted her. Gulnaz would watch her daughter from the corner of her eye, chewing her lip. Zeba could feel the angry heat between them, and while she had no doubt her mother loved her, she couldn't help but wonder if her mother would ever turn the magic against her. When Safatullah, her maternal grandfather, and her father's family joined together to announce Zeba's engagement, she was not as infuriated as Gulnaz. As much as she loved Rafi, it was difficult to live in the shadowy world her mother created. Marriage would be an escape.

NOW ZEBA MISSED HER MOTHER. SHE COULD FEEL THE COILS OF the prison cot pressing against her ribs, nudging her to admit what lurked in her mind.

Have you no idea what evil goes on out there, really? I'm trying to warn you for your own sake, for my grandchildren's sake.

She'd pushed Gulnaz away. Zeba felt her chest tighten with regret.

When her mother had seen the darkness, Zeba had been haughty, determined not to drive her husband away the way Gulnaz had. She would not wind up a woman alone, without the respectability of a widow or a wife. She remembered very clearly those days when whispers kept her mother shuttered in their stifling home. Zeba refused to become that woman.

But in the wake of her mother's visit, the darkness slipped its long, opportunistic fingers around her neck. If only Zeba hadn't closed the door on her mother.

Zeba couldn't bring herself to shift on the cot. She wanted to feel uncomfortable, to feel something pierce her skin. She pressed her temple against the mattress, tightening the muscles of her back and neck to dig her head as far in as she could.

She'd only wanted to be part of an ordinary family. Her only wish had been to be loved, not feared or despised. She'd learned all she'd needed from her mother, from the treacherous Gulnaz with the dazzling green eyes.

She should have acted. Maybe she still could.

Zeba sat up suddenly, her pulse throbbing a new, upbeat tempo.

CHAPTER 18

"MY MOTHER IS COMING TODAY," ZEBA ANNOUNCED OVER A breakfast of bread and sweet tea.

Nafisa looked up with interest. She was fascinated by the transformation she'd seen Zeba undergo in the last two days. Zeba was a different woman. She joined her cellmates for meals and smiled warmly. There was no explanation for the shift. It had been sudden and gave the cellmates plenty to speculate about.

"Your mother? You've never mentioned your mother before. Where is she coming from?" Nafisa shot a quick glance at Mezhgan, who tried not to look too intrigued.

"She lives with my brother, about a half day's travel from here. She's . . . different . . . my mother. Not like most other women," Zeba admitted hesitantly. She wondered what it would be like to see her mother now, in this place.

"What do you mean? What is she like?" Latifa's hair was pulled back in a tight bun, which exaggerated her heavy facial features. She had been least impressed by Zeba's abrupt recovery from hysteria. She had declared Zeba a charlatan who wanted to make fools of them all.

"She's . . . she's a strong woman. Very strong-willed."

"Is that all?" Latifa huffed, shaking her head. Every time she gave Zeba a chance to redeem herself, Zeba disappointed.

"No, it's not that simple," Zeba said softly. "She has her own special ways of doing things. Things she's learned along the years."

"What does she do?"

Zeba wasn't quite sure how her cellmates would react to her mother's talents. She tread carefully.

"Since I was a young girl my mother was always mixing up herbs and things. She knows all about concoctions to . . . to help people get what they're looking for."

"A *jadugar!*" Latifa exclaimed, slapping her hand against her thigh. Her eyebrows lifted and her face broke into a smile. "She's one of those women who can curse an enemy to choke on her food or set a husband and wife into a bitter fight!"

Mezhgan's and Nafisa's eyes widened.

"No, no. It's not like that. The things she used to do . . . she never made anyone choke. What she did was different." Zeba struggled to find the right words because they didn't exist.

"Does she use dead pigeons? Oh, I've heard of things like this!"

"Is that what your mother does?" Nafisa asked in awe.

Their suspicions were raised, and Zeba became all that much more interesting to them—because of her mother.

WHEN ZEBA'S CELLMATES SAW GULNAZ, THEIR THEORIES WERE confirmed. She was an impressive silhouette, sitting on the other side of the prison yard's metal fence. The ends of her eggplant-colored head scarf draped elegantly across her chest, and her back was straight as a schoolchild's. Her skin was smooth, with barely a crinkle at the corner of her eyes and no evidence of years she'd spent mourning her husband or glowering over the things said about her. Even across the yard, the green of her eyes caught the sunlight and shimmered like gemstones.

Zeba spotted her as soon as the women entered the courtyard. Her cellmates did their best and tried not to stare too directly. Latifa

watched from the corner of her eye and raised her eyebrows instead
of saying what she thought. It was her way of demonstrating restraint.

Zeba left her roommates behind, walking toward her mother instead of running only because there was a world around her that still
expected her to behave a certain way. Her cellmates would sit at a
wooden table with benches, Zeba knew without turning around, casting glances over their shoulders.

Gulnaz watched her daughter approach, her heart sore from
longing.

It was thirty-five years ago and Gulnaz was nervously touching
the soft spot on the top of Zeba's newborn head. She blinked and
it was a year later, Zeba toddling on pudgy legs, holding on to low
tables, and bouncing as her father clapped his hands. A flash. A pig-
tailed Zeba was on her lap, singing songs and mixing up the lyrics.
She was five and holding her tooth in a warm palm, showing off her
gap-toothed grin with pride. A single heartbeat. Zeba was eight and
her wide, brown eyes looked up at her mother, begging for a story. A
candle flickered. Zeba was twelve and whispering to her mother that
the old woman beside her in the *fateha* had just passed gas. Gulnaz
had stifled her laughter as best she could and hid her face behind a
handkerchief as if she were overwhelmed by the sadness of the funeral.

Zeba sat facing her mother, the two women separated by a mesh
fence and the river of good intentions that flowed between them.

"*Salaam,* Madar."

"*Salaam, bachem.*"

"You came a long way."

"I would have come farther."

Zeba lowered her head. Gulnaz watched her daughter's face. She
looked tired, much older than the last time she'd seen her. The past
few weeks in this prison, away from her beloved children, had cast
dark circles under her daughter's eyes. Zeba looked as if she'd been the
one traveling all day, not Gulnaz.

"Have you heard anything about my grandchildren?"

Zeba shook her head. She felt glass shards in her throat. If she spoke, her voice would break.

Gulnaz spoke for her.

"Basir's always been levelheaded and mature," Gulnaz said. "Nothing like his father."

Zeba's fingers laced through the fence. She'd been longing for someone, for anyone, to give her a reassuring word about her children. She let out a tight sigh.

"Last I heard they were well. Basir is looking after the girls. They are together and that's all I can ask for now."

"It's a good start," Gulnaz said as she touched her daughter's fingers. She let her own fingers rest upon them lightly. She was relieved her daughter did not pull away. "Tell me what happened, Zeba."

Zeba looked up and met her mother's eyes.

"What difference does it make?"

"It makes all the difference."

"It was an ugly scene."

"This much everyone knows."

Zeba didn't move her hand from the fence. It felt more comforting than she would have thought to have her mother here, touching her. She felt like a child.

"Madar-*jan*, I don't know how this happened."

"Tell me what you do know."

Zeba looked at the ground. She'd rehearsed this conversation in her mind. Each time it went a little differently. Each time she was a little more honest.

"I know that when you came to me and warned me that something was wrong, I wasn't ready to hear you. I thought I could protect my home better than you protected yours. I wanted to stay away from all . . . all that. But it was there. I started to see it. I could feel it walking through my house and laughing at me while I slept. That day, I finally saw it for what it was. Standing in our own courtyard, the worst kind of evil. The kind that people whisper about when they think you're not listening. The kind that keeps mothers awake at night. The kind that turns your insides black with rot to even think how close you've been to it. I don't remember much from that afternoon. I just know that when I opened my eyes again, it was gone. And I found myself here, without my children, and I'm not honestly sure if I should worry about them more or less now."

"Zeba—"

"The one thing that I think again and again is that I should have turned to you," Zeba said flatly. Gulnaz's eyes softened and misted. She brought her other hand to the fence, reaching two fingers through the wires. Zeba held them tightly. "That's all I can think. Maybe things would have worked out differently then. I thought what you did, all those things you did for so many years, I thought it was so dark and evil, but I know now what evil really is. Forgive me, Madar-*jan*."

Gulnaz wanted to put her arms around her daughter, to feel her face against her own. She wished she could have done more too. She knew she should have pushed harder, found out what her troubling dreams meant and followed her instincts. There were so many things she could have done.

"Zeba," Gulnaz said with a heavy sigh. "I've held so many grudges, I'm surprised I can still get up and walk. I'm not going to hold one against my own daughter. Anyway, this isn't the right time for pity or blame. You did what you thought was the best thing for your family, just as I did."

Zeba nodded. The tightness in her throat began to release.

"You're in a whole lot of trouble, Zeba. Murder is no small charge. Let's keep our eyes forward, eh? You've met with the lawyer Rafi sent for you?"

"Yes," Zeba said.

"And?"

"God bless my brother," Zeba said shaking her head. "I know he feels he needs to look after me because I'm his sister and now I'm . . . I'm a widow. The lawyer he hired is a boy, a young, naïve boy who thinks he can save me. But the stones of retribution will come my way. It's just a matter of time."

"Rafi said good things about this lawyer. They both want to help you, but they are men, and men can often only see what they can hold in their hands. The world is made of rocks and wood and meat for them. It's not their fault; it's how they were designed." Gulnaz sighed. "We cannot leave everything in the hands of men. I made that mistake once, and I won't make it again."

Zeba looked back. She saw Latifa lean across the table and say something to the two younger women. She could imagine the wild speculations they were making about Gulnaz. She turned back to her mother.

"And women?" she asked thoughtfully. "What is the world to us?"

Gulnaz offered a meek smile.

"Do you not know, my daughter? Our world is the spaces between the rocks and meat. We see the face that should but doesn't smile, the sliver of sun between dead tree branches. Time passes differently through a woman's body. We are haunted by all the hours of yesterday and teased by a few moments of tomorrow. That is how we live—torn between what has already happened and what is yet to come."

Zeba's eyes glazed. Her mother's voice soothed her as it probably had when Zeba could still be cradled and rocked to sleep. She would save these words, she knew, and consider them more carefully at another time. Zeba's mind darted back to something else Gulnaz had said just a moment ago.

"What did you mean before? What mistake did you make?"

Gulnaz's face was drawn, solemn. She looked at her daughter squarely.

"I have no reason to hide anything from you. You're not a child any longer."

Zeba waited.

"Your father. When we were first married, he knew about my habits, the things I could do to bend the winds. He found it endearing. He would smile and watch, but in truth, he thought my concerns were exaggerated. He told me I was smelling smoke when there was not even a glint of fire."

Zeba felt uncomfortable, hearing about the conversations between her parents as husband and wife. It felt inappropriate.

"I was young, of course. I wanted to make your father happy. And maybe part of me was tired of keeping up such a guard. I let my walls come down. We spent more time with the family, with friends. Things were bad at that time, of course. War and bloodshed and scarcity all over the country. We were not that different. We struggled just like everyone else. You remember, I'm sure. We couldn't hide the ugliness from you and your brother.

"I told myself a lot of bad things were happening to everyone, not just us. I tried talking myself out of thinking I was the target of any evil thoughts. I tried very hard."

Zeba stared at her mother's hands. Her fingernails were peeling at the tips and there were tea-colored spots where Zeba didn't remember seeing any before. The years that did not show on Gulnaz's face were quite obvious on her hands. It pained Zeba to see it.

"In truth, we were no worse off than anyone else. If you and Rafi were hungry, other children were surely starving or dead. I was beginning to think maybe your father was right. Maybe I was overly sensitive and creating my own problems. I put all my *jadu* aside and felt, for once, as if the weight of a thousand stones had been lifted from my shoulders. Even when my own mother died, I did not falter. I did not blame anyone. I told myself she was on in her years and that was the road for all of us, sooner or later. I lived that way, my eyes blinded by your father who saw nothing, least of all that which was in front of him."

Zeba was surprised to hear there had been a time when her mother had turned away from *jadu*.

"Madar-*jan*, I cannot remember a single day when I did not see you busy with some kind of spell. It was with you from the moment you woke up in the morning."

"Not always. I did what I did only when I needed to."

Zeba grew pensive.

"Why did my father go off to fight? No one else in the family did."

Gulnaz clucked her tongue and looked away. Her eyelids fluttered at the memory of that time. She spoke about him not as one speaks of the dead, but also not as one speaks of the living. That was the purgatory Zeba's father had always lain in.

"I cannot explain your father's thoughts. He didn't really share them with me. That man—wherever he is may he be at peace—was an unreasonable man. He followed his own compass. I had no hand in swaying him. He used to listen to that old Russian radio, that block of wood with the brass dials, and curse into the night. Then, one day, he just left. He walked out the door and never came back."

Zeba sat motionless.

"Did he not say where he was going or who he was going to fight with? Did no one ever say they had seen him in the fighting? So many dead were returned to be buried near their families."

"And plenty more were absorbed by the land they fought for. We'll never know, Zeba, and it's useless to think about it now. You have much more important matters you should be concentrating on."

"Did you not ever think he might come back?"

Gulnaz scowled.

"I used to expect him to walk through the door. Maybe next Friday, to return for *Jumaa* prayers. Or maybe in two weeks. Then I thought he might return for the Eid holiday, thinned from a month of fighting and fasting. Then the Russians were gone. I waited again, but there was no sign of him. And then the fighting started again, and I told myself he'd dug himself back into it."

The civil war had meant there would be no peace even after the Russians had retreated. How could there be when the ethnic diversity of Afghanistan—barbed-wire distinctions and deep-rooted resentments—resurfaced? It was as if Afghanistan had been folded up into itself at the borders. Without a common outside enemy, they turned on one another.

"Finally, I wondered if he would come before Rafi was married. I told myself that if he didn't return by Rafi's wedding, then he was surely dead. War or no war, how could a father not be present for his son's wedding?"

"But if he hadn't known about the wedding . . ."

"By then I was tired of making excuses. I counted him among the dead and so did you."

It was true. When she cupped her hands in prayer, she always asked God to keep her father in heaven's gardens. It had been the safest assumption given the war's death toll.

"I kept his clothes at the house. There was always a place for him in case he did return. And I wept sometimes to see the emptiness where your father should have been, but they were bad times for us, too, and I had to think of you. I had two children to feed and only my sewing kept us alive. Your uncles hinted at me marrying one of them, but I told them I wouldn't marry again until your father's body was brought home."

Zeba cringed at the thought.

"You never told me this."

"There was no reason to tell you."

Zeba let her fingers drop from the fence. Her arms were beginning to ache. It was hard to hold on for too long.

"Rafi knew?"

"Rafi was old enough and wise enough to see what was happening, but he only saw bits and pieces. I didn't want either of you to know."

Zeba understood completely. How could she blame her mother for keeping this secret when she now wanted to spare her own children the shame of the truth she'd just learned?

"Did you go to my grandfather?"

Gulnaz shook her head.

"What could he have done for me? He was an old man by then,

and people had become convinced that he was a spy for the British. I grew up in that home, and I knew he was not as powerful as he would have had people believe. To this day he won't admit it, but I can tell you—that man was full of tricks."

Zeba turned her gaze to the ground.

"Zeba-*jan*, there's a special kind of hurt in learning that your parents are not the angels or saviors you wish them to be. I know it well."

Zeba wanted to speak. She wanted to tell her mother that she hadn't been resentful or disappointed in her, but the words wouldn't take shape in her mouth.

"We survive it. We all survive learning the truth about our parents because you can't stay a child forever."

A light breeze blew between them, lifting wisps of Zeba's hair and tickling the dampness behind her neck. Gulnaz shifted her weight and brushed at her skirt.

"You couldn't save my father," Zeba said blankly. Her legs were tucked under her, her hands fidgeting with the hem of her once-white pantaloons. "What makes you think you can help me now?"

"You are my daughter, Zeba. Just as I watched your grandfather practice his craft, you stood in my kitchen and watched everything I did. You know just how strong we were together. You saw what happened to those people who wished us harm. I kept you and your brother safe from the evil eye, and there were many around us. Whether or not you want to admit it, you know all my tricks. You know my secrets better than anyone, even if you turned your back to it. Nothing has changed. It's all at your feet."

Zeba's head pounded. Her temples tightened under the sun's glare, but somehow, Gulnaz was barely squinting. There was so much about her mother that Zeba still didn't understand.

"I've brought you something," Gulnaz whispered. "Not much, but at least a beginning." With two fingers she reached into the inside of her dress sleeve, just past the cuff. She gave a slight tug and pulled out something Zeba recognized immediately, a *taweez*.

"Is this from Jawad?" Zeba let the folded blessing fall into the palm of her hand. Her fingers closed around it. She felt the years melt away. She was a child again, in awe of her mother who found ways to control the stars. This was precisely what she'd wanted. She'd wanted her mother to come and save her, to bend the winds in her favor this one time. If she were to dare to have hope, this was the form her hope would take.

"Of course it's from Jawad. I wanted a *taweez*, not a scrap of paper. Jawad is the only one with real talent."

Zeba closed her eyes and pictured Jawad. Even when Zeba had become a young woman, Jawad had looked right past her to Gulnaz. Zeba could picture him, his back hunched over a tiny square, his pen marks deliberate. Every *taweez* he created infuriated Zeba's grandfather, Safatullah. Jawad was black magic while the *murshid* was God's light.

"You believe in his talismans."

"Because I've seen them work. It's his craft. Your grandfather has his and I have mine. You can choose to believe in one or all of our methods but believing in something makes it a whole lot easier to rise in the morning."

"My grandfather wouldn't be happy . . ."

"Your grandfather hasn't been happy in years. Once people started to doubt him, his heart grew weak and never recovered. I'm a respectful daughter so I keep my activities quiet, but I am also your mother. Doing what I can for you—that is all I need to be concerned with now."

"Madar-*jan*, I'm grateful. But I don't want to feel . . . I mean, there's no reason for this to work," Zeba said cautiously, eyeing her mother's face to gauge her reaction.

Gulnaz brought her face so close to the fence Zeba could feel her mother's breath on her cheek. They were together again, the feel of her mother's touch lingering on Zeba's skin. It was time moving forward and backward all at once.

"Tell me, my dear daughter, what have you got to lose?"

CHAPTER 19

YOU'RE GOING TO READ YOURSELF BLIND.

Yusuf took off his glasses, the echo of his mother's voice in his mind. Reading in the dim light of the evenings did strain his eyes. He knew full well even as he rubbed them that he was only making matters worse.

His apartment was on the third floor of a three-story building. Off the living room was a balcony big enough to fit one folding chair. It boasted an unenticing view of another apartment building with curtained windows and clotheslines strung from balcony to balcony. There was a galley kitchen tucked to one side and a bedroom behind that. The bathroom was functional and simple. For Yusuf, who'd spent years with his siblings and parents in a cramped, two-bedroom Flushing apartment, these quarters were more than he needed.

Yusuf had set up a small table with two chairs in a corner of the living room. The set doubled as his kitchen table and home office. His living room had a glass coffee table and a threadbare sofa. The walls were bare except for a plastic framed picture of Mecca that had come with the apartment.

Kind of like hotel Bibles, thought Yusuf when he'd first seen it and not because he had any disdain for his religion. Rather, he believed, he'd developed a certain objectivity to the world around him because he'd lived elsewhere.

He pulled a leather toiletry bag from the hall closet.

There were four bottles of eyedrops left. He cursed himself for not bringing more. He hadn't anticipated the effect the wind-spun dust would have on his eyes.

So much for being a native.

He shook the tiny white bottle and decided to save what remained. It would be months before he returned to the United States, and the air wasn't going to get any better.

Yusuf was accustomed to bouts of insomnia. Big cases kept him up, and he would go weeks at a time, sleeping just three hours a night. That was Yusuf's way. He made lists of precedents to look up, holes in his arguments, and research he still needed to complete. Statute by statute, point by point—it was a meticulous process, like extracting pomegranate seeds one by one. His restlessness was not entirely because of Zeba, though. Yesterday's conversation with Meena had taken him by surprise. He was doing his best to put it out of his mind and focus on the work at hand.

Yusuf poured himself another cup of black tea. Tea replaced coffee here, not because coffee couldn't be found but because the Afghan taste for tea had come back to him quickly.

A much needed draft slipped in through a half-open window. It carried the faint smell of blood from the butcher shop below the apartments.

Yusuf was only fifteen minutes away from the prison by taxi. Just fifteen minutes between him and Zeba, his reticent client. He was close enough that he could see her on a daily basis if he chose to, but he didn't bother. He thought that if he pulled back, she might realize how badly she needed his help. He wasn't usually a fan of playing games, but defending Zeba required creativity on all fronts. Her chances of beating the charges were slim, at best.

Since he wasn't with his client very often, Yusuf spent his days digging up what statutes he could and poring over law books. Afghanistan's legal infrastructure had been destroyed over the years, but a team of international players had taken on the rebuilding of it. They'd created a reasonable set of laws for the country—a playbook he understood. The real justice system, though, was much different. People didn't play by the rules. Even some of the higher courts judged without jurisprudence. Outside of the major cities, there was no true rule of law.

Yusuf's colleagues in the main office understood his frustration, though they had little patience for it. Sometimes, his huffing incited anger in those who had been diligently doing this work before he showed up. Aneesa was the head of the legal aid group. She was a bold woman in her early forties who had lived in Australia for the worst years of the war. She'd returned after the fall of the Taliban, determined to put her foreign law degree to good use. Yusuf had been immediately impressed by her when they'd first met.

"Yusuf-*jan*," Aneesa began firmly, "the justice system, if you can even call it that, is as twisted as a mullah's turban. There are ways to work with what we have, but it takes creativity and patience. You cannot expect this country to have its house in perfect order the moment you decided to walk through the door. There's a lot to be done. And even more to be undone. Yes, in many places the authority of the white beard prevails. What the elders say is law. Lucky for you that your client is facing a judge, not a community trial. And from what I've heard about the judge overseeing your case, you should be very thankful. You could be at the mercy of someone much, much worse."

Yusuf thought of the *qazi*. Maybe Aneesa was right. The judge hadn't yet brought up execution. Others probably would have by now. He flipped to a new page on his notepad and made a reminder to learn what he could about the judge. There could be an angle he could use to his advantage.

YUSUF WAS IN THE OFFICE BY NINE O'CLOCK THE FOLLOWING morning, earlier than everyone except Aneesa. When he entered, she waved to him from her desk and adjusted her head scarf, a thin mocha-colored veil in perfect harmony with her pantsuit. Aneesa had quietly pleasant features, soft brown eyes, and a delicate chin. She pursed her lips just slightly when she was thinking. She had a sharp legal mind, Yusuf had learned quickly. Well versed in both Sharia and constitutional law, she could glide between Dari and Pashto and had built a reputation as one of the city's most formidable lawyers since her return to Afghanistan. Yusuf could only imagine what kind of force she'd been in Australia, the salary she must have turned her back on to return to her homeland.

Yusuf greeted her and sat at his desk on the opposite side of the office. They were separated by two putty-colored filing cabinets.

Aneesa took a hard look at him—hard enough to make Yusuf uncomfortable.

"Have you been sleeping?"

He nodded.

"I'm fine. The dust here, it's . . . I'm fine."

"How's the case going?" She spoke to him in English, a faint Aussie accent that somehow made the conversation feel more casual.

"It's not," Yusuf admitted. He ran his fingers through his hair just so he wouldn't rub his eyes. "I'm defending a woman who doesn't want to be defended. She thinks it's better for her children if she doesn't put up a fight. When she's not screaming like a lunatic, she doesn't talk. She's given me nothing to go on. How am I supposed to make a case out of that?"

"We work with what we have," Aneesa said matter-of-factly. "Why don't you tell me what you've learned about the case against this woman? Maybe we can come up with something together," she suggested. She pulled a chair over and propped her elbows on the desk. It shifted. Without a word, Aneesa tore a page off a newspaper lying nearby, folded it, and wedged it under the lopsided leg. Yusuf pretended not to notice. He'd been meaning to do the same. He cleared his throat and began laying out what he'd learned thus far about the day of the murder.

"Did the police note any bruises on Zeba? Did she say anything about him beating her?"

Yusuf shook his head.

"Some bruises on her neck but someone had tried to choke her just before she was arrested. I know what you're getting at. I was hoping to somehow use that defense, but she's not even hinted that her husband had done something awful to her. I know there's something there, though." Yusuf pictured Zeba, her face solemn as a tombstone. She was always so careful with her words. "I can't believe this woman would slam an ax into her husband's head without reason. She doesn't strike me as that type of person. She's too controlled for that."

"Controlled? The woman who screamed her head off in the judge's office and then slept for two days?"

"That might not have been her most controlled moment," Yusuf conceded. "But I'm telling you, this is not a woman who loses it so easily."

"Maybe. What has her family said? What did they think of her husband?"

"Her family hasn't been around. Her brother, Rafi, hasn't said much about Zeba's husband, just that he wished his sister had never been married off to him. It's obvious he feels guilty for letting her marry that man. He wouldn't say anything specific. 'Talk to my sister,' he kept saying. 'She knew him better than anyone.' He did say his sister did not deserve to be in prison—that her children needed her and wouldn't fare well living with their father's family. I believe him."

"And no one else from the family is coming forward?"

"There's nothing recorded in the arrest register," Yusuf said, tapping his pen against the notepad. "The chief of police said only that there were no witnesses to the murder, but then nearly the entire neighborhood was there to see the body and Zeba sitting there, covered in blood. There doesn't seem to be much room for doubt."

"Talk to the neighbors. Someone must know something. The sun cannot be hidden behind two fingers."

Yusuf bit his lip. He'd taken the arrest report at face value, but Aneesa was right. He had no choice but to make a trip to Zeba's village. *Why not,* he thought, looking at his cell phone and seeing that no one had called.

THE QUIET OF HIS APARTMENT WAS BROKEN BY THE SOUNDS OF traffic and daily life filtering through the window. Mischievous boys chased after a dog in the alley, just as Yusuf had done as a child. The bustle of the market had settled as the skies turned hazy and aromas from food carts swirled into the evening air. Yusuf considered shutting his window to block the noise, but he found that the passing voices both comforted him and helped him focus.

What were Zeba's children thinking? Her son was old enough that he would have known if something was amiss at home. Would he be willing to speak about his father? Was it at all possible that Zeba hadn't killed her husband? Yusuf closed his eyes, trying to imagine his client burying a hatchet in the back of her husband's head. How tall had her husband been? Was he thin and wiry or heavyset? How close was the nearest neighbor's house?

Yusuf began to pace. Aneesa had given him some ideas today, some direction. He would need to see Zeba. They had much to talk about.

He pulled out his yellow pad and made a few notes. He circled some thoughts, scratched out others. He rubbed his eyes.

His phone rang. He looked at the number and saw Meena's name flash on the screen. Should he answer? They'd spoken on the phone several times, each conversation more comfortable than the last. Three days ago, though, Meena had surprised him. Her tone had been polite and reserved. When Yusuf asked her what was wrong, she'd told him she was not honestly sure if they should continue their phone calls. Yusuf had been taken aback and abruptly asked her why. He wondered if she was uncomfortable spending so much time on the phone with him. Maybe she wanted confirmation of his intentions. But Meena had hesitated, leaving his question unanswered but promising to call him in a few days.

He pressed the talk button.

"YUSUF," SHE STARTED, HER VOICE SMALL AND SERIOUS. "I DON'T want you to think badly of me. I didn't know my mother had given my number to you. She likes you so much . . . both my parents do. My whole family loves yours, actually."

"Meena, what's going on?"

"I need to tell you something. I've been trying to find a way around it, but I can't come up with anything and I feel like you deserve the truth."

Yusuf leaned forward, elbows on his thighs.

"Go ahead, Meena-*qand*," he urged, wondering if he was going too far by using endearments. "Tell me what it is."

"I . . . I've been in love with someone for the last year. My parents are not happy about it because they don't like his family but . . . but that doesn't change anything for him or me. I'm so embarrassed to tell you this."

In love with someone else. Yusuf blinked rapidly. He'd thought Meena had pulled away because she wanted more from him when the truth was that she wanted less.

"Oh, I see," he said, wavering between anger and sadness.

"I'm really sorry. I didn't mean to make it seem like . . ."

"Listen, Meena, you don't have to explain."

"My mother was hoping that seeing you . . . talking to you . . . the possibility of going to America . . . that it would change me. You know what I mean?"

He'd been a ploy—an unwitting pawn in Khala Zainab's strategy.

"Listen, Meena. You should follow your heart," Yusuf replied curtly. "No hard feelings. Thanks for letting me know. I've got lots of work to do here so . . . good night, okay?"

"Oh, sure. Sorry, I didn't mean to interrupt your work. I just . . . yes, good night."

With a click, it was over, and Yusuf was more disappointed than he should have been. They'd only spoken on the phone for a couple of weeks. They'd never held hands or talked over a cup of tea or brushed shoulders as they walked down the street. Why should he feel like he'd lost the girl he was meant to be with?

Yusuf groaned angrily, rolled onto his belly, and buried his face in his pillow. Maybe his mother was right. Maybe he did need to get married.

CHAPTER 20

MEZHGAN SAT CROSS-LEGGED IN FRONT OF ZEBA'S BED. SHE rarely woke this early in the morning, but she'd been particularly restless since Gulnaz's visit.

"Zeba-*jan*, I want to ask you something."

Zeba did not respond.

"Please. I know you're awake. I can tell by the way you're breathing."

Zeba moaned, quietly enough that Mezhgan didn't hear it. She sat up and yawned, wondering what could be so urgent that it had the girl rising with the sun.

"When is your mother coming back? Maybe you can ask her to help my situation. Would she do it?"

"My mother would tell you that this is your own mess and that you've got to deal with it. She would tell you it was a mistake to fall in love with a man before his family fell in love with you."

Mezhgan was unperturbed. She blinked rapidly and pressed her palms against the small round of her belly and looked thoughtful.

"I bet you can help me. I bet you know how she does it anyway. You've got to tell me everything you know. Surely she must have done something similar in the past? Is there something I should eat? Maybe something I should feed my fiancé's mother?"

"Fiancé?" Latifa laughed, awake now. She stood up and stretched her arms over her head. "If he were your fiancé, you wouldn't be here. You want Zeba's mother to wave a magic feather around so your movie star boyfriend will go running to your parents and beg for your hand in marriage. Psht, maybe if she does too good a job with it, you'll have a whole crew of boys asking your father for your hand in marriage. Wouldn't that be nice? You and your *harami* baby can choose a man together."

"Don't say that, Latifa. He *wants* to marry me but his parents . . . they just haven't agreed yet. You probably don't know anything about *jadu*, but I know it can work. My uncle is married to a hideous-looking woman he wouldn't otherwise have looked at, and my whole family knows it's because she cast a spell on him. He wanted nothing to do with her one day and by the next week he was begging his parents to ask for her hand. *Jadu*, for certain."

Latifa sat back down on her cot and rolled her eyes.

"Your uncle sounds an awful lot like a pregnant girl."

"You're curious, too," Nafisa said, inserting herself into the conversation. "You nearly climbed the fence to get a better look at her when she came to visit!"

"What else is there to do here? I've been in this chicken coop with the same women for months and I'm tired of hearing all your stories. If Judgment Day comes and God has any questions about either of you, He should call me first. I'll fill Him in with what you did with whom and when," Latifa joked.

Nafisa and Mezhgan covered their mouths and squealed.

"Latifa! Watch what you say! God forgive you." Nafisa sat up and let her legs dangle over the side of her bed, the one above Latifa's.

"It's true," Latifa insisted. She pushed Nafisa's legs aside and stood. "Come on, Zeba. Tell this poor girl what she wants to hear. Give her the secret recipe and help her find her way back to a respectable life. Spare the world the shame of another *harami* baby, will you, please?"

Mezhgan bit her lip.

"Shut your ugly mouth, Latifa," Nafisa shot back. There was much she could tolerate from Latifa, but she drew the line when her cellmate referred to an unborn child as a bastard. "Stop calling the poor girl's baby *harami*! It's not like you've got much to be proud of. Are you here because you were just too honorable for your family?"

The air was thick with tension. Mezhgan kept her gaze on Zeba's bedsheet, fearful that anything she said would invite more insults. Nafisa looked down at Latifa from the top bunk, her arms folded across her chest defiantly.

Zeba broke the quiet with a couplet:

"Life's made your heart as tense as a blister
Don't spill its pus on your innocent sister."

Latifa tapped her foot, annoyed.

"Fine, I won't call him that," she finally conceded, before her face broke into a smile. "And you're right. My family's not in the least proud of what I've done. But at least my belly's not growing the evidence of my crime."

Mezhgan smiled weakly and Nafisa's shoulders relaxed. The banter between them filled the otherwise drab days.

"No, your belly is just growing, my chubby friend!"

Latifa chuckled and rubbed her belly as a gesture of truce. Heavyset to start with, she'd rounded considerably in her time in the prison. Her pumpkin-colored dress strained at the waist. Her face had grown fuller, like a waxing moon. At every meal, Latifa ate as if she'd received news that she would return to the world of scarcity tomorrow.

"Your friend is avoiding your question, Mezhgan. Looks like Khanum Zeba's not interested in helping you," Latifa teased.

Mezhgan sensed truth in Latifa's words. She turned her attention back to Zeba.

"You will help me, won't you? It would be the noble thing to do—to bring two families together with a respectable marriage.

Think what a blessing it would be for this child. How could you possibly refuse?"

Zeba was nervous. These girls knew nothing about the *jadu* she'd learned from Gulnaz. They couldn't possibly imagine the things she'd helped her mother do. Zeba felt ashamed to think of the concoctions she'd carried, the illnesses she'd delivered, the malice she'd stirred. Was it possible to use the tricks she'd learned without causing harm?

It must be possible, Zeba thought. She thought of the way her mother had stared off into the distance as they'd talked. She imagined how long her mother must have traveled just to slip two fingers through a metal fence. There was good in her that was surely not new. It was only that Zeba was seeing her mother in a new light. She had the darkness to thank for this new insight.

"My mother's *jadu* is unmatched," Zeba stated with confidence. "She's started and ended love affairs. She's pulled people out of their deathbeds and thrown others in. She's made minds hot with anger and others soft with love. From the time I was a young girl, I stood at her side and learned every potion, every unfathomable combination, and I know better than anyone what her spells are capable of. You want to marry this boy, Mezhgan? A problem as simple as yours can be fixed in the time it takes to bring a pot of water to boil."

Zeba exhaled sharply. There was pride in her voice, more than even she had expected to hear. The women in the cell listened carefully; she'd commanded their attention. They watched her eyes glisten, her cheeks draw in, and her neck straighten. Latifa was not snickering or mocking her. Mezhgan and Nafisa absorbed every word. Zeba could taste the respect in the air. She was reluctant to break the silence and spoil the moment.

Mezhgan spoke first.

"I believe it, Khanum Zeba," she affirmed, her voice trembling with young hope. "I beg of you to help me. Tell me what I should do!"

"I don't know if I should be getting mixed up in your troubles," Zeba said quietly. It was true.

"Please, Zeba. I swear to you he's my beloved and I am his. We are destined to be together. We need only someone to unlock our fates."

Across the room, Nafisa's eyebrows rose a degree.

Was I ever so naïve? Zeba wondered. She felt like Gulnaz, a seer amid the blind. But she couldn't bring herself to disappoint the girl sitting before her, waiting for her help so earnestly it was heartbreaking. Zeba thought of the many hours between now and tomorrow. Then she thought of the many days ahead of her. She leaned back, her palms flat against the thin mattress of her prison bed.

My bed, Zeba thought. *This is where I'll be sleeping for God knows how many nights. Maybe all the nights of my life, however many that may be.*

If she did not find a way to claim the cold walls around her, they would close in on her. Zeba looked around the room. The other women had hung up pictures, magazine cutouts, or family photos on the rectangular spaces above their beds. Nafisa had cross-stitched a geometric border in red thread on her white blanket. Latifa had set a vase of artificial roses at the foot of her bed.

To survive, they had to adapt. They could adapt themselves or they could adapt the space they occupied, Zeba realized. If she were to be a prisoner of Chil Mahtab, she would have to do the same. She looked at her cellmates. She could do it with their help. She could settle into this place if she could *become* someone here.

"Listen carefully," Zeba began, knowing that the women would hang on every word that came out of her mouth. She knew, too, that this would be a test for them all. It would test their faith in Zeba and test the sorcery skills she'd inherited from her mother. It would test Mezhgan's patience while she waited for the spell to sway her beloved's parents.

Zeba shared with Mezhgan, in painstaking detail, how the hearts of her lover's parents would be softened toward her. She told her about the string of red, about the seven knots and the three drops of blood. She described the cloth it would be folded in and how it would be thrown over the walls of her lover's home, along with three feathers from a freshly killed chicken. She did not forget to tell Mezhgan about the thread that would be tied around her own wrist with the same seven knots to bind her to her lover.

Mezhgan listened intently, her fingers tying knots in an invisible thread even as Zeba spoke. She nodded with every instruction and dared not interrupt.

"That is all that needs to be done," Zeba declared. "But it must be done quickly, before their resolve grows too hard for the spell to break it."

"How long will it take to work?"

"I can't tell you that," Zeba said. "It depends on how precisely the instructions are carried out. *Jadu* is a fickle creature. You're at its mercy once you call on it."

Mezhgan threw her arms around Zeba's neck. Zeba stood still, resting her hands on the young girl's back hesitantly. Mezhgan's embrace made Zeba's eyes well with tears. Would her daughters one day be as foolish as this girl? She brushed the thought aside and enjoyed the weight of another person, even as it anchored her to the prison floor.

MEZHGAN'S DISGRACED MOTHER CAME TO VISIT HER DAUGHTER one week later. Mezhgan relayed to her Zeba's very specific instructions. She impressed upon her mother the importance of following the road map precisely. Yes, the thread had to be red. No, the blood did not have to be fresh nor did it have to be Mezhgan's. Yes, the tiny packet had to be thrown over the wall of her beloved's home for the magic to be effective.

Mezhgan's mother listened, doubtful, but willing to try anything to lift the dishonor her doe-eyed daughter had brought upon their family. Mezhgan's father hadn't left the house in three weeks, too ashamed to meet his neighbors' eyes. It made for a very tense home.

The mother made the long walk back to her home, stopping on

the way and buying a spool of red wool thread from the seamstress. By the light of an oil lantern, her knobby fingers knotted the thread. She whispered a prayer over it too, for good measure. When she'd carried out all the directions, she returned to her living room and clutched a cup of freshly steeped tea in her hands. She held the cup to her chin, letting the steam mist her skin. Her husband did not lift his head to ask where she'd been, a small blessing.

Either this magic would work, she thought, or her daughter had made a fool out of her for a second time.

ELEVEN DAYS LATER, MEZHGAN'S MOTHER RETURNED TO THE prison.

Mezhgan's fingers gripped the metal rings of the fence so tightly they turned white. Her cellmates watched from enough distance to feign privacy.

Though they could not hear a single word, they could see the excitement pass through the latticework of the fence. Mezhgan's head fell back in elation. She clapped her hands once, twice, three times and twirled on her foot. She drew her shoulders up and covered her grin with her cupped hands. Her mother wiped away a tear of joy.

"Either her head lice spread to the rest of her body or she's gotten some good news," Latifa quipped. She stole a sidelong glance at Zeba.

Nafisa could not take her eyes off Mezhgan. Her buoyant mood was infectious, even across the dismal prison yard.

Mezhgan came running over, the ends of her lilac head scarf dancing in the breeze. Zeba braced herself. Until this very moment, she still harbored doubts as to what she could do on her own; it had been so many years since she'd last toyed with Gulnaz's craft.

"Zeba-*jan*, you did it! His mother's come to ask for my hand in marriage! I knew he loved me. You unlocked my *naseeb*. How can I possibly thank you for bringing my darling to me?"

Mezhgan, with her hands clasped together, shot Latifa a coy look.

"Latifa, you were wrong to poke fun! Zeba's spell worked faster and cost far less than buying off a hardheaded judge!"

Mezhgan crouched down to kiss Zeba's hands in gratitude. Zeba's eyes fluttered in surprise, and she pulled her hands away.

"That's not necessary," she said abruptly. "I'm glad the boy's family has come around. For you and your baby."

Mezhgan's eyes twinkled. From behind the fence, her mother called her name and waved her over. She shook her head at her daughter's giddiness. There was much that still needed to happen. There had to be a formal *nikkah*. Until her daughter was married in the eyes of Islam, she should not rejoice. A premature celebration would only invite misfortune.

Mezhgan wasted no time. Her mother left the prison that day with even stricter instructions directed, this time, by her own daughter. She needed a proper wedding dress. The clothes she'd been wearing in the prison would not do for such a momentous occasion. When she and her lover, Haroon, visited the judge to update him on the status of their relationship, she pushed closer to him, whispering honey-coated words of devotion.

"I knew we were meant to be together. I've been thinking of nothing but you," she cooed. "And now we need to plan our engagement."

Her shackled fiancé was sent off with a list of supplies needed to mark this momentous occasion behind bars. He would need to relay the list to his parents, who should deliver the items as promptly as possible so that Mezhgan could make plans. She handed him a folded sheet of notebook paper that bore her childish scrawl: chocolates for the guests, sugared almonds, pink lipstick, and money to her mother for any other expenses.

Mezhgan walked with the confidence of a woman adorned in gold. Latifa looked bored. The promise of a *nikkah* took all the sport out of their banter.

Haroon's mother and father, along with Mezhgan's anxious parents, arrived on the day the young couple were to sign their *nikkah*. They nodded at one another briefly but said nothing else. Mezhgan's father was still too angry and ashamed to string more than two words together, and her mother was afraid she would be confronted for what she'd done with the thread and the feather. She pulled at her sleeves, a nervous twitch.

The parents, bride, and groom were led into a small courtroom with three rows of wooden chairs. The groom, wearing white pantaloons and a tunic, was escorted by two guards with distinctly unfestive handguns on their hips. Mezhgan, early in her second trimester, beamed in a silver brocade head scarf and a billowy emerald dress that she'd cinched at her still delicate waist. The hem of the dress fell to her calves and covered her ivory, satin pantaloons. She smiled coyly at her new fiancé. Her reluctant mother-in-law turned away. She'd agreed to this arrangement but only because she'd not wanted her son to serve the remaining eighteen months of his sentence.

How disappointed she was to have raised a fool for a son.

The young couple had their handcuffs released so that they could sign their names on the *nikkah* contract that bound him and Mezhgan as husband and wife. It was the most important piece of paper Mezhgan had ever touched, and she took her time penning the curves and dashes of her name. Before he was led away by the guards, Mezhgan dreamily exclaimed they would have a beautiful wedding party once they were released. He shook his head and sighed with amusement. Her eyebrows shot up as he was led away. His dainty bride had not been joking.

IN THE PRISON, NEWS OF MEZHGAN'S *NIKKAH* BROUGHT A BUZZ OF activity. It passed from cell to cell in whispers, nods, and exaggerated stories. Some scoffed, some giggled, and some were just a bit fearful. But each and every woman behind those locked doors wondered if the rumors of a sorceress among them might just be true. Soon they were lining up at the dented door of Zeba's cell, their newly found hope stoking the wildfire she'd set off within the cold walls of Chil Mahtab.

CHAPTER 21

GULNAZ STOOD BY THE FRONT DOOR OF THE PRISON AND watched as a young man slid his legs out of the backseat of a taxi, struggling to keep the strap of a bag on his shoulder as he slipped the driver a few bills.

He was in a rush to get to the prison—as if his hurrying would save something more than a moment of time. He pushed the taxi door closed and raised his hand in thanks to the driver who had already turned his attention back to the radio dial.

Oh, Rafi. Did you find a lawyer to defend your sister or a playmate for your sons?

Gulnaz wished she'd paid closer attention to Rafi when he was younger. He meant well, but his efforts were childish.

The man was walking quickly, his messenger bag bouncing playfully against his hip. He checked his watch, and Gulnaz sighed with renewed disappointment.

Time is not the problem, child. Time is all we have.

This was the baby-faced lawyer Zeba had told her about—the one whose expensive cologne and crisp clothes could not mask the scent of inexperience. Zeba had been right to hang her head.

When he reached the shaded entrance, Gulnaz took a step forward. Yusuf put a hand on his chest and nodded in respectful greeting. He reached for the door's handle.

"You are my daughter's lawyer," Gulnaz declared.

Yusuf paused, caught off guard.

"Excuse me?"

"You are Zeba's lawyer."

"Yes, I am," he said cautiously, his hand still resting on the metal handle. "I'm very sorry. You are . . ."

"Mother of the prisoner."

He stopped abruptly, retreating a step and turning to face Gulnaz. He felt himself pulled by the crystalline green of her eyes.

How exotic, he thought, feeling fully Western as it occurred to him. These were the kinds of eyes that foreign photographers would plaster on magazine covers. His Afghan senses returned, and the sparkle of Gulnaz's eyes also brought a chill to his bones.

Bewitching. His mother would have been muttering prayers under her breath if she were caught under the gaze of such eyes.

Yusuf reined in his thoughts.

"Pleasure to meet you. You're here to visit your daughter?"

"I sat with her for a time."

"How is she doing today?" It felt like the right thing to ask though he wasn't clear why he was spending time with pleasantries. Surely there were more pressing things to ask Zeba's mother.

Gulnaz must have agreed. She ignored his question and asked a more relevant one.

"Has she spoken much with you?"

"Well, she's been reluctant to say much of anything so far," Yusuf replied slowly. The family wasn't paying a lot for his services, but they were paying something. He had disappointingly little to show for the case thus far.

"She knows better," her mother confirmed. "My son-in-law's body was found in his home. That means only that he's dead—not that she killed him. Tell me your plans."

Yusuf shifted his weight and moved the strap of his bag to his left shoulder.

"Well, for one, I'm going to be traveling to her village. I need to speak with the neighbors, people who knew her and her husband. I've got to see where it happened, especially since she's not saying much. I'm going to do my job, Khanum. Your daughter seems to think she's a lost cause, but I don't see it that way. There's always a way to . . ."

"People don't speak badly of the dead. Do you really think you'll find the truth there?"

"It is a starting point."

"You don't have a plan," Gulnaz surmised.

"This is a complicated case, mostly because of how uncomplicated it looks. It's not going to be simple to argue for her innocence." Yusuf sounded defensive and he knew it.

"Innocence is a luxury not everyone can afford."

Whether Gulnaz was referring to prisoners bribing their way out of convictions or her daughter's role in Kamal's death, Yusuf could not tell.

Gulnaz lifted the ends of her black-and-green head scarf, crossed them in front of her, and let them drape over her shoulders in one fluid motion.

"I need you to do something for me," she said as the sound of a diesel engine rumbled past the prison. "I need you to tell the *qazi* that Safatullah's daughter wishes to see him."

"I see. May I ask, who is Safatullah?"

"My father."

"I'm sorry I don't recognize your father's name. Should I?"

"No," Gulnaz said without elaborating.

Yusuf's eyebrows lifted slightly.

"Do you know this judge?"

"I have no business knowing judges here," Gulnaz replied flatly.

"No, I suppose you wouldn't."

They weighed each other's words for a moment.

"I'll speak to the *qazi*," Yusuf offered. "But how about you and I sit down and speak for a moment? Maybe we could go inside and find a place to talk."

"I prefer not to be in a prison. We can speak here." Gulnaz took a few steps away from the building. Yusuf had no choice but to follow. "What is it you want to speak about?"

"In order to defend Zeba, I've got to understand her. I need to know what kind of person she is. I need to know what kind of mother she is. I need to know about her relationship with her husband."

Gulnaz had never been one to speak of private matters. The daughter of the *murshid* had been raised in a world of discretion. People could not know how the *murshid* knew the things he seemed to know. They could not find out that the family compound was a network of observers, scouts, runners, and messengers. Safatullah was the *murshid*, but without his family, he would have been deaf and blind and impotent.

Discretion served Gulnaz well later in her life, too. People asked lots of uncomfortable questions when Gulnaz's husband disappeared.

She didn't tell anyone, not even their children, that she'd watched him fill a flask with tea and tuck a rusted gun into the coiled hat on his head. In a small bag, he'd packed one of Gulnaz's old housedresses and a few sets of clothing. He'd kissed his wife on the cheek and told her the entire world had turned into a battlefield.

The determination on his face told Gulnaz it would not be useful to argue.

He went off to end the war, she maintained over the years, wondering if maybe that weren't some form of the truth.

"MY DAUGHTER DOES NOT SPEAK TO ME ABOUT HER HUSBAND. She never has." Why should she? Zeba had matched her mother's reticence in the last few years. It was a punishment.

"Tell me what she was like when she was younger," Yusuf suggested. There had to be some kind of useful information she could offer.

Gulnaz looked back toward the prison, squinting in the midday sun. Zeba as a girl. Nothing brought Gulnaz as much joy as thinking about her daughter as a child. Before she could stop herself, she was reminiscing.

"Zeba twinkled like a star. She laughed often and followed her brother around everywhere he went. I kept her close at my side and taught her everything I could about managing a household. We were a pious home and Zeba grew up saying her prayers, honoring her family. She was a good girl, always obedient."

"What was her relationship like with her father?" Yusuf asked gently.

"She was in his arms from the moment she was born. He would pick her up and toss her into the air. They were very close up until he was gone."

"Gone?"

"He went off to fight the Russians," Gulnaz continued with rehearsed ease. "He never came back."

Yusuf sighed empathetically.

"A brave man. You've not heard from him since then?"

"Not a word, not a letter."

"How did Zeba react to his absence? It must have been hard on her."

"It was hard on all of us. That was not a time that passed easily." Gulnaz turned her gaze back to Yusuf. "She was only six years old then. She cried. She asked for him often. But people move on and Zeba did too. He was not a warrior. I knew she would never see him again. My husband's family, they wanted to hold on to hope. They wanted to believe he would walk through the front door at any moment and tell grand stories of war."

"You didn't think there was even a chance he would return?"

"If he could have returned, he would have. But he didn't, which is how I knew he was dead."

"I see. Of course."

He couldn't possibly see, Gulnaz thought. Every family was a mystery to outsiders. There was no way to understand a father and his children or a husband and wife by sitting with them and asking a few questions.

"Tell me about her marriage."

"It was meant to be a happy marriage."

"Aren't they all," Yusuf said, chuckling, though Gulnaz thought it an odd thing for someone so young to say.

"Kamal's grandfather was an army general, a very respected man. He was good friends with my father. They sat together one day and, over a cup of tea, decided that Zeba and Kamal should be husband and wife. They tied themselves to each other through their grandchildren."

"Did you approve of the match?"

"No one bothered to ask me."

"Did you object?"

Gulnaz shot him an impatient look.

"It was much bigger than me."

Yusuf thought of his sister. His parents had always imagined her marrying the son of their good friend, but she'd foiled their plans by falling in love with their neighbor. He was young when she was married, but he remembered the shouting, his sister slamming her door so hard it rattled the walls of their apartment. Would Yusuf have stood up for his sister if they'd insisted she follow their wishes or would her problems have been bigger than him, too?

"How did Zeba feel about the marriage? She must have been young."

"She was seventeen and ready to live her life. She was less of a child than others her age . . . probably because she'd lost her father."

"So she was content."

"As content as any new bride can be." Gulnaz drifted briefly to the first weeks of her own marriage to Zeba's father. Her new husband had showered her with gifts and gazed at her in such a way that, even in the privacy of their home, she used her head scarf to cover the flush in her cheeks. Gulnaz had begun to warm to him when the comments began. Her husband had gushed about her so often with his family that, drop by drop, he'd created a river of jealousy toward her.

"We thought Kamal was a decent man. Zeba did not complain to me, but I did not see her much. When they were first married, she lived with his family. I did not want to interfere, and Kamal kept to himself. He didn't want anything to do with his wife's family. He and my son, Rafi, never had much of anything to say to each other."

"But Zeba and Kamal moved away from his family at some point. When did that happen?"

"They moved after the second child was born. Little Girl, at least that's what they called her at the time."

"Was there a reason they moved?"

Gulnaz shook her head.

"If there was, I don't know it. No one knew anything about him. He couldn't be trusted—that was all I knew."

"What makes you say that?"

"One time Kamal brought Zeba and the children over on their way to visit one of his cousins. I'd made mushroom stew, a recipe I learned from my own mother, God rest her soul. I'd also made rice and meatballs. Rafi's wife, Shokria, had just given birth and was in her resting period. She needed to eat well so I'd been cooking fresh food all day. Kamal sat back and didn't touch a bite of it. He sniffed at the spread and turned up his nose. Everyone else was starving, especially the children. We begged him to try at least a little, that it wouldn't feel right for us to eat if he didn't join us. It was the rudest thing I've ever seen."

"Perhaps he had just eaten," Yusuf agreed, not sure what the point of this story was.

Gulnaz stared off into the distance.

"Then, exactly two months later, we were invited to the wedding of Kamal's sister. It was a summer evening, hot and dry. Kamal nodded at me and barely acknowledged Rafi. Rafi went out of his way to strike up a conversation with Kamal, as a brother-in-law should. 'Come visit us again. We don't see you often enough.' Rafi is that way. He wouldn't turn the devil away if he came knocking on our door."

"What did Kamal say?"

"He said he wouldn't step foot in a house that had treated him like a dog. He said we'd disrespected him by eating in front of him and offering him nothing. Before we could argue, he had shoved Zeba to get her away from us. Half his family heard what he'd said. We left. There was no reason for us to stay after that." Gulnaz's face betrayed no emotion.

"I don't mean any disrespect, Khanum, but it's a big jump to get from there to a reason for his murder."

Gulnaz let her eyes close for a second.

"Maybe you're right," she agreed softly. "And maybe you've got a lot more investigating to do."

CHAPTER 22

THE *QAZI* HAD AGREED TO SEE GULNAZ, A HIGHLY UNUSUAL turn of events, but Gulnaz had expected nothing less. The judge had shown great restraint when Yusuf made the request, careful not to let his face twitch at the mention of Safatullah's daughter. Safatullah's daughter—meaning the woman that young lawyer had brought into his office was Safatullah's granddaughter. It was the *murshid*'s granddaughter who'd been dragged out, screaming and limp, by the guards.

Unimaginable.

Qazi Najeeb shook his head to think of what his elders would have said about such a scene, but the elders from their village were long dead.

The *qazi* hadn't seen Zeba since that episode, and he was, truthfully, not anxious to summon her back.

When the guards led Gulnaz into his office, Qazi Najeeb stood instinctively. He was unaccustomed to having women ask for an audience with him, much less one like Gulnaz. She'd been a near legend in their town even as a young woman. There were rumors of her powers, too, that she could cast spells and sway minds with a mere glance. Najeeb remembered the women in his family talking about her when she was only an adolescent.

Qazi Najeeb had seen Gulnaz only once. He'd gone to the home of Safatullah with his father, who needed the *murshid*'s prayers for his ailing youngest son. Najeeb was intrigued by the prospect of seeing Gulnaz, the girl who made all the other girls pout with envy. It was Najeeb who had knocked on the plank door of their compound, his father's arms heavy with warm rosewater cake, homemade cheese, and freshly picked tomatoes.

Two young boys had answered the door, unloading the gifts from his father's arms and leading them both into the expansive courtyard, meticulously kept with fruit trees and flowering bushes. The *murshid's* home was made of the same materials as every other home in town, but it was somehow different. The wooden beams looked sturdier, the plaster smoother, the glass windows more crystalline. Najeeb's father shot him a look that told him to take heed; the aesthetics of the home were a validation of sorts. If anyone could help the ailing boy they'd left back home, it was the man who lived within these blessed walls.

Najeeb followed the young boy who led them to the *murshid's* living room, a simple chamber with sitting cushions on opposite ends and an intricate burgundy carpet on the floor, octagonal elephants' feet patterned into the weave in white and black knots. The *murshid* sat on a floor cushion, positioned such that, through the room's only window, a soft beam of sunlight fell directly upon him, illuminating his face and leaving his guests in relative darkness. There were glass bowls of golden raisins, walnuts, and pine nuts on the floor—set just out of reach of the guests. Najeeb and his father greeted the *murshid*, bowing their heads and kissing his hand. Safatullah was gracious. He touched his hand to his own chest and kissed the top of Najeeb's head.

Najeeb's father made his pleas. He explained the situation at home and described his youngest son's belly pains and fevered restlessness. The *murshid* listened patiently, then nodded his head and thanked them for bringing such generous gifts.

"Your tomatoes are the only ones to have survived this dry weather," Safatullah commented. "That you've shared them with my family is evidence of your generous spirit."

Najeeb and his father wondered how the *murshid* knew they'd brought tomatoes since they'd given the basket to the young boy at the front door, but it was a question that would go unanswered.

The *murshid* cleared his throat and, motioning for Najeeb and his father to join him, raised his hands in a prayer. The tenor and vibrato in his supplications was artful—his voice was calligraphy. Najeeb watched his father's face, eyes pinched closed and forehead wrinkled in concentration. His head bobbed rhythmically from side to side, as did his body in a sway that matched the rhythm of the *murshid*'s prayers.

Najeeb watched, his head lowered just enough to appear deferential.

The *murshid* prayed with head bowed as well, and the words rolled off his tongue as if he'd said them a thousand times before.

Najeeb lifted his head an inch.

The *murshid* scratched his ear furiously and scowled. In a second, he was back to his graceful swaying.

It was nothing. Najeeb should not have seen it. But he had. His illustrious words had been interrupted by something as banal as an itch. How much could he revere a man who itched and scratched as the rest of the world did?

He followed his father out of the *murshid*'s sitting room, an obsequious back-stepping with lowered heads and shoulders and hands splayed across chests.

"Thank you for your time, Agha Safatullah. Your kindness is much appreciated."

"I will continue to pray for your son. *Inshallah*, he will recover soon and grow to be as strong and healthy as the boy who has accompanied you today."

They were escorted back to the front door and had nearly left when Najeeb realized he'd dropped his hat somewhere between the front door and Safatullah's receiving room. He raced back into the compound while his father waited outside. As he turned the corner around one of the smaller houses, he nearly ran straight into a young woman. He'd been within an inch of her face before he backed up, startled.

Had her eyes not met his and rendered him speechless, he would have politely apologized for nearly knocking her over.

What color is that? So purely green, the very color of Islam, and yet something about them seems perilously unholy. What is it like to see the world through eyes like those?

This was Gulnaz, he knew, by the quickening in his heart. She took a step back but did not look away from him.

Najeeb drew a breath.

"You were here to pray for your brother," she said softly.

He wanted so badly to answer her, but his tongue had suddenly been replaced by a brick. He nodded.

"I will pray for him, too. I always pray for the young and innocent. I will pray that he lives a long and fruitful life."

Gulnaz slipped away without waiting for a response.

Najeeb left the compound without his hat. His brother recovered in three days, regaining his strength and appetite. His father praised the *murshid*'s prayers. Najeeb bit his tongue then and again six months later when his sisters brought news of Gulnaz's engagement. He would not see Gulnaz again until a lifetime later, when she appeared in his office and he stood before her, a grayed but important man.

DOES SHE REMEMBER ME? WOULD IT BE TOO PRESUMPTIVE OF ME TO think she might?

"Thank you for agreeing to see me," Gulnaz said. Her tone was perfunctory. There was no room for reminiscing or wistfulness.

"I don't usually speak privately with mothers of the accused." This was only partly true and came out sounding much more scandalous than Qazi Najeeb had meant it to. The judge took his seat as Gulnaz took hers. He poured a cup of tea and placed it on the nesting table before her. "I cannot offer you anything much. A judge's quarters are not known for their lavishness."

"That depends on the judge," Gulnaz said, plopping a sugar cube into her cup and watching it sink to the bottom. Qazi Najeeb stared at her downcast eyes, the graceful arches of her cheekbones.

Dear God, he thought. *Now, that's how a woman should age.*

"Very true," he agreed. "You did not bring Yusuf with you. Why?"

"He had his turn to speak with you. This is mine."

"I see," the judge nodded.

"Qazi-*sahib*," she began. "I am here because of my daughter. You are the judge presiding over her case. Since I'm the one who gave her her first breath, I thought it only fitting I should speak with the man who might sentence her to death. You and I share a connection, in that respect, that is undeniable. Wouldn't you agree?"

Qazi Najeeb's eyebrows pulled together in surprise.

"Well, indeed, though that is certainly an odd way of looking at the situation."

"It's an odd situation to look at."

"Well, not as much as you would think. She's not the only woman in Chil Mahtab to have killed her husband. Men have to watch their backs these days."

"How awful," Gulnaz said glibly.

The judge leaned back, preoccupied with thoughts of long ago.

Did you save my brother's life? Because I think you did. Oh, I've been wanting to ask this question for years.

"Qazi-*sahib.*"

"Yes?" Najeeb cleared his throat and took a sip from his teacup. He heard she'd been widowed while her children were still young and wondered what had happened to her husband.

"As I was saying, my daughter is not a murderer. I'm asking that you show mercy on her. She is a pious woman and a devoted mother. Her children need her."

"Did she kill him?"

Gulnaz blinked twice. Slow, deliberate blinks meant to give him time to regret his question.

"Okay, a simpler question. I notice that you said nothing about what kind of wife she was. Was she a good wife to him?"

A man would ask such a stupid question, thought Gulnaz.

"I'm her mother, Qazi-*sahib.* What makes you think my answer to that question would be at all useful to you? I was not there to see what happened. And if I had been, for the sake of this discussion, and I had seen Zeba kill her husband with her own hands, I'm only one woman. As far as I know, there isn't another woman who will come forward and complete my testimony."

It was true, and the judge nodded in agreement. A woman's account carried only half the weight of that of a man's. That was not his decision. It was how they'd always measured a woman's word.

"A moot point, Khanum, as I know you were not there at the time her husband was killed."

"Nor was anyone else, though the world is ready to condemn her."

"We have to look at the situation. She was at the house with him and was found with blood on her hands and clothes."

"He was her husband. She could have held him as he died."

"Which still leaves the question of who killed him."

"I can tell you one thing, Qazi Najeeb, since you are a God-fearing person. If you'd known the man, you might have killed him yourself."

"Why?" Qazi Najeeb leaned forward. "Why do you say that?"

Gulnaz shook her head.

"My daughter had not been well in the months before her husband died. I'd been to see her a few times, but she would barely open the door for me."

"For her own mother?"

"The truth is, Qazi Najeeb, that while tradition states a woman's word is only worth half a man's, a mother's word is the full story. I am telling you that Zeba was deeply troubled, and that man had everything to do with it."

"What do you think is wrong with her?"

"It is hard to say. But I am afraid that he may have caused her to be unwell in her mind."

"I see," the judge said, leaning back in his seat. "A deranged woman kills her husband? Is that what you think happened?"

"I don't think she killed him, nor did I say that. I want for her situation to be investigated. I ask that you take into consideration what kind of husband he was to her. I can tell you I did not see her often, but when I did, I could tell she feared for her life."

Najeeb nodded.

"How about some more tea?" he suggested, pointing to the nickel-plated kettle on the red-coiled electric burner beside his chair.

Gulnaz laid her hand over her untouched cup.

There was a pause. Each waited for the other to speak.

It was Qazi Najeeb who broke the silence. His wife would have cursed him if she'd been here to see the way he behaved. At this age, it was admittedly shameful.

"Any information we receive will be discussed when the trial comes together formally. But even if he'd raised his hand against his wife, that still doesn't justify murdering him and her village knows that. Those people, her neighbors and Kamal's family, are surely anxious to see a verdict."

"Of course they are. The man's body may be cold and buried, but his family is alive and well. I'm sure they're filling my grandchildren's heads with hateful lies."

"Khanum, I may be nothing but a man in your eyes, but I know a few truths, too, and here's one I will share with you: children always forgive their mothers. That's the way God's designed them. He gives them two arms, two legs, and a heart that will cry 'mother' until the day it stops beating. Your daughter can grow horns on her head, but her children will think it's a crown."

Gulnaz looked at the judge; her skin prickled. What did he know of forgiveness? She remembered Zeba's face, meshed by prison fencing. She thought of the way her fingers had reached through the metal rings to touch Gulnaz. Was that forgiveness or desperation? Had she sought her mother's touch only because she was in Chil Mahtab?

"With all due respect, Qazi, plenty of children are born without arms or legs."

The judge chuckled.

"Very true. But none are born without a heart. I stand by what I've said. A mother is a mother until the very end."

Gulnaz straightened her back. She hadn't noticed that a half-raised nail in the chair was digging into her leg. She shifted, but it seemed to follow her.

When Gulnaz stood to leave, Najeeb told himself to look away as she turned toward the door. He was acting like a schoolboy. Then again, he hadn't asked her to saunter into his office asking him for private favors. What kind of women dared be so bold, anyway?

"Khanum Gulnaz," he began, feeling as if the boundaries of propriety had already been blurred. "It's been a pleasure speaking with you. I'm glad you asked your lawyer to arrange for this."

Gulnaz looked at him, the same fearless stare that she'd given him when they'd been face-to-face in Safatullah's decorated courtyard.

"I came for the sake of justice," Gulnaz explained pointedly. "True justice, which is as rare as a seashell in this country. I can only hope you'll come to see that she's not responsible for Kamal's death, just as she was not responsible for his life."

She was on her feet, her back to him. It was the end of their conversation. Najeeb felt his chest tighten to think that this very moment she would walk out of his office and never return. What did she think of him? He still couldn't tell by the way she spoke.

Gulnaz paused, her hand resting on the door frame. Her finger tapped once, twice before she turned around and asked one more casual question.

"By the way, Qazi-*sahib*. It would be rude of me to leave without asking. How is your younger brother doing these days?"

CHAPTER 23

WHEN BASIR WAS TEN YEARS OLD, HE MADE AN IMPORTANT discovery—the adults he'd always trusted could lie. In fact, it was not as much of a possibility as it was a proclivity. They were just as dishonest about small, insignificant details as they were about life-changing truths. When Basir detected the first lie, he vowed to keep his eyes open for a second. By the time he noticed the third and fourth deceit, he decided it was impossible to trust much of anything that came out of the mouths of adults.

Kaka Mateen claimed he'd gone to fight in the war, but he'd actually run off to Iran. Khala Shokria swore she'd made fried potato flatbreads just for him, but he knew she'd bought them from the street vendor. His mother claimed to love all her children equally, but Basir could see that Shabnam claimed more of her heart than the rest of them.

Basir didn't point out the lies. He knew better than to contradict his relatives. He simply nodded and tightened his lips so nothing disrespectful would slip out.

This decision to distrust complicated Basir's life. Everything that was told to him had to be tested. Sometimes he wished he could be more accepting, but when he sensed holes in a story, he could not rest until he'd put his eye to each tiny opening and made sure he saw all that there was to see. Truth became an obsession, and vetting became a compulsion. That compulsion was what brought him to keep a secret box within the grove of trees in Ama Tamina and Kaka Fareed's small yard.

Months before he'd walked into his house to find his father's head cracked open, Basir had heard from a friend that scorpion mothers ate their young. For Basir, who had seen dogs nuzzle their pups and mother hens coddling newborn chicks, this seemed unnatural. Scorpions were admittedly nasty creatures but that didn't quite explain why they would disrupt the God-ordained order of things. Mothers spent their energy creating and caring for babies. Even scorpion mothers shouldn't consume their offspring. It was backward and couldn't be true.

Basir set out to unearth the truth for himself.

After nine days of turning over rocks, he found a pregnant, tawny-colored scorpion and nudged her into a box. Her tail curled up as she darted left and right, but there was nowhere to go. Basir had put a heavy rock over the top of the box so she wouldn't be able to escape and kept it behind the outhouse of his home, where no one in his family would dare to look. It was dangerous, he knew, but his curiosity demanded he take the risk.

He threw scraps of food into the box every couple of days and used a long stick to poke at the scorpion from a safe distance. She hated him for keeping her captive. Basir could see it in the poise of her tail, the vindictive posture she assumed when he lifted the box cover.

She would kill him if he gave her the slightest chance. But her own babies? Basir was still skeptical.

Day after day, he would check on his captive. Every time he was done with his observations, he would shut the lid of the box and replace the heavy stone that kept the scorpion trapped within. The box itself lay well out of sight, in an ignored corner of the lot. Still, its presence made him nervous and he wished the insect would hurry her babies along so he could bring his experiment to a close.

When he'd walked into their courtyard that day, Basir had

thought for the shortest of seconds that his scorpion might have been responsible for the gory scene. It was as if he'd half expected that his need to test something as dangerous as a scorpion would, one day, cost him the life of someone in his family. Basir walked into his home and smelled death and destruction that day. He'd nearly fallen to his knees with the weight of it, believing it to be his own doing—until he'd seen the hatchet.

When Basir and his sisters had been sent to live with Ama Tamina, Basir's scorpion was still in her box.

Basir walked out of Ama Tamina's house one evening and without explicitly planning to, his feet plodded their way back to his family's home. It was nearly dark, and no one noticed the slight young boy slip through his front gate.

He stood in the front yard, motionless. He half expected his mother or father to emerge from the doorway of the house, sipping tea and chastising him for being out after dark. No one came out. Basir stepped over the threshold and was met with the pungent smell of rotting onions. It felt oddly comforting to a boy who was likely expecting to detect something far worse. His mother's brass mortar and pestle lay on a square of newspaper, a small mound of cardamom beside it. Rima's pink knit blanket lay crumpled by the wall.

Basir took a few more steps into the home. For years, he'd been told to stay within these walls, scolded for staying away too long in the afternoons. Now it felt wrong to stand here. He peered into the small room his parents had once shared. His father's wool hat and scarf lay on the dresser that was missing one knob. Their sleeping cushions lay on the cold floor, their pillows marking their places like tombstones.

He stared at the space as if it were an old photograph. Why did they decide to live away from the rest of the family? Basir had heard his parents argue. He'd heard his father's rage and seen the way his mother had reeled from his blows. Basir had believed his mother to be meek but devoted, exasperating but well-meaning. His father had a violent temper, but why couldn't his mother, after all their years of marriage, avoid triggering his fury? Had his cowed mother finally had enough? Had she stood her ground in one grand gesture of defiance?

Basir hadn't really known his parents all that well, he admitted to himself.

He stepped through the back door and into the yard, two meters away from where his father's body had lain, the earth still darkened where his head had been. The neglected pot of peppermint stalks and the chili pepper plant had dried, leaves curled and browned and scattered in half circles at their bases. The dried red peppers looked like tiny, crinkled daggers. His mother's rosebush, in the corner of the yard, was the sole survivor. It seemed oblivious to all that had transpired in its presence.

Cocking his ear to the sky, Basir strained to hear anything. There was only the distant sound of the neighbor's television. He imagined them watching their favorite programs, drinking tea, snacking on almonds, and playing cards—as if nothing had happened. Had they heard anything that day? Did they know more about his family's undoing than he did?

Basir moved toward the outhouse, careful the soles of his shoes did not tread where his father had fallen. Tucked behind the back wall of the outhouse was the small box. Basir removed the stone anchoring its lid. He lifted the box and listened for signs of life.

All was still.

He took the box to the center of the courtyard where the glow of a full moon fell upon it. He lifted the top and gasped.

The mother scorpion was very much alive, her back heavy with baby scorplings, two dozen pale beetle-ish creatures. Basir broke off a twig from the rosebush and poked at the mother. Her pincers snapped and she moved to the side of the box, her tail curled in readiness.

No, Basir thought, even the babies of scorpions could rest assured they had their mother's love.

He should have destroyed the whole lot. There was no room for mercy when it came to creatures who could kill grown men with a twitch of the tail. Basir should have doused the mother and her babies with cooking oil and thrown a matchstick at them. It was an effective means of eliminating scorpions and provided decent entertainment for most children, listening to the pops and snaps of a scorpion's shell cracking in the flames.

But Basir felt a bit of guilt. He'd kept her locked up and cornered for months only because he'd suspected that she just might go against all that seemed natural and consume her own young. He'd been wrong. Even scorpions knew how to mother.

He made the long walk back to Ama Tamina's house with the box, hiding it in a grove behind the clay walls so that his cousins wouldn't stumble upon it. It was riskier to keep it here. He would take the box to the edge of the village in the morning where there was nothing but rocky expanse and free them there.

Kaka Fareed was waiting for him in the courtyard. He'd made a habit of stopping by Ama Tamina's house to ask for updates on Zeba's case.

"Where have you been?"

Basir felt a heat rising in his chest. It took a great deal of strength not to run back out the front gate. He could still picture Kaka Fareed's fingers around his mother's neck.

"I was out for a walk," he mumbled.

"Why didn't your ama know where you were? You're living in this house. You don't come and go as you please."

"I'll apologize to her," Basir said as he stepped toward the door. He wanted to leave before Kaka Fareed said anything more. This was the third time he'd dropped by since Basir and his sisters had come to their aunt's home. Even she breathed a sigh of exasperation when he showed up.

Last time he was here, he'd called Zeba a thief and a murderer. Kamal had owed him money, he swore, and Zeba had probably killed him so she could pocket it all.

Basir didn't need to do much investigating to know this was a lie.

When Kaka Fareed called his mother a cheat, Basir bit his lip. It was on the tip of his tongue to scream out that she was no such thing, but that's not what came out. All he could do was shout for Kaka Fareed to stop talking about her.

"Where were you?" Kaka Fareed asked again. He sucked at his teeth and cocked his head.

"Nowhere, Kaka-*jan*. I was just walking. I wanted to get some air."

"You're as bad a liar as your mother," he said snidely.

Basir bit his tongue so hard he tasted blood. Fareed began to rant, as if his anger had been mounting while he waited for Basir to return to the house.

"Just like your mother. Lies, lies, lies. Watch yourself or you'll end up a criminal like her. That whore deserves to die. God help us with these judges and courts that sit on their asses all day instead of doing anything. We used to have real justice in this country. It's gone now, and that bitch is getting fat in a prison while we look after orphans. She killed him. I should have killed her when I had the chance."

Until now, Basir had done nothing more than leave the room when his father's cousin went on tirades about his mother's character. He and his sisters were dependent on their father's family and Basir harbored a fear that they might be turned out onto the street if they spoke up on their mother's behalf.

It was hard enough to hear Kaka Fareed call his mother a cheat or a murderer. It was quite another to hear her called a whore. Basir's young pride rose up in defiance.

"Eat shit," Basir said quietly but precisely, his body trembling. Kaka Fareed, without a second's hesitation, landed a backhanded slap across Basir's face.

"You son of a whore!"

Ama Tamina burst into the courtyard at the sound of her cousin's booming voice. She saw Basir on the ground, his hands covering his face. She saw Fareed's red-rimmed eyes glowering over him, ready to strike again. She stepped between them and flicked the end of her head scarf over her shoulder.

"Fareed, what's happened?"

Kaka Fareed ignored her questions and kept his eyes trained on Basir.

"Both Kamal and his wife cheated me out of money. Now their freeloading kids are here, and this one has the nerve to talk back to me. I'll teach you a lesson!"

Fareed lunged at Basir.

Ama Tamina stepped in front of him, her outstretched hands in protest.

"You will not touch him!" she shrieked.

Fareed was furious. Basir scrambled to get to his feet. His aunt was only half Fareed's size.

"Cousin, move out of my way! This is between me and Kamal's boy. Are you forgetting that they killed your brother?"

Ama Tamina's voice shook, but she did not budge.

"You're not here to defend Kamal's honor. You hated him. The two of you couldn't be in the same room together unless you were both too drunk to see straight."

"Shut up!"

"It's the truth. You come here now and want to recover some century-old debt from his children? Get out of my house. I don't care if you are my cousin. I'm not going to let a drunk torture my nephew!"

Fareed brought himself within an inch of Ama Tamina's face. It took every ounce of resolve she could muster not to step back.

"You crazy woman," he said slowly. "You can't talk to me like that!"

Basir stood next to his aunt. All this felt too familiar. It was the same tension he'd experienced in his own home on a thousand occasions.

"It's my home and I'll talk as I please!" Tamina responded.

What Fareed would have done next would remain unknown, for

at that precise moment, Kaka Mateen emerged from the house. He'd heard the shouting and seen the way Fareed towered threateningly over his wife's slight frame. He grabbed Fareed by the back of the neck and shoved him toward the door.

"What are you—" Fareed blurted.

"Get out of our house!" Mateen roared. Fareed threw his hands up in defeat.

"You deserve these children of dogs."

Basir had never missed his mother as much as he did in that moment, in his aunt's dark courtyard, the air thick with resentment and anger.

Fareed was gone. The girls were peering out the door, half faces looking out to see what had happened.

Ama Tamina cleared her throat.

"Girls, get back inside. It's late and you should have been in bed already. Let's go." She shooed them back into the house. "There's nothing more out here."

"I . . . I'm sorry, Ama-*jan*," Basir said hesitantly.

His father's sister turned to face him, her lips drawn tight in anger. She had every reason to hate them. Kaka Fareed was right. She had lost her brother and their mother had been locked up for his murder. How could she not resent Zeba's children?

"Stop," she groaned. "That's enough for tonight."

Kaka Mateen put his hands on his hips.

"What was he so worked up about anyway?"

"This boy," Tamina said quietly. "Coming in at this time of night and not saying where he's been."

"I . . . I just wanted to go for a walk," he mumbled. "I should have told you, but I didn't want to disturb anyone."

"Fareed hated Kamal, and he's taking out his anger on the rest of us now." Tamina sighed. Her voice had steadied some.

Basir felt the urge to say something. His aunt had stepped forward on his behalf and he needed her to know that he appreciated that. If she decided to see him and his sisters as Zeba's children and not her nieces and nephew, they would be in dire straits. He could not provide for his siblings. "Ama Tamina-*jan*, I . . . I just wanted to say sorry. I'm sorry this happened because of me. I know you're upset with my mother but . . ."

"You don't know anything," Ama Tamina blurted in frustration. "You think it's that simple but it's not!"

Basir took a step back. It was exactly as he feared. Ama Tamina was the only person who'd offered to take them in, but even her kindness would have limits.

Kaka Mateen put a hand on his wife's shoulder.

"Don't get so worked up about it, Tamina. I'm going inside."

The girls in the doorway parted so that he could pass. He barely looked at Shabnam and Kareema, touching only his daughters' heads before telling them all to go to bed.

"You don't understand," Ama Tamina said in a voice that Basir heard only because the courtyard was stone silent. "You couldn't possibly understand what your mother has done."

Basir waited. Even when Ama Tamina had disappeared into the house, he stood unmoved. She would return, he anticipated, and tell them all to leave. Or maybe she was waiting for him inside the house. Maybe she was bundling their two sets of clothes by the light of a lantern so that she could rid herself of their presence by morning.

Basir sat on one of two plastic chairs.

What was Madar-*jan* doing now? Was she thinking of him and the girls? Did she have any idea how tenuous their situation was?

*Why didn't you tell everyone what happened, Madar-*jan*? There has to be a truth that will explain all this.*

Truth. Basir knew more truths about his father than he cared to admit.

They tried to save each other, mother and son, but their mutinous efforts were rewarded with broader bruises, louder shouts, and harsher curses. Recalling the futility of it, Basir sometimes chose to shrink away when he felt the chilling wind of his father's presence entering their home. It may not have felt like the most honorable action to take, but it did minimize the damage.

In the year before his father had been killed, Basir had tried new tactics. Instead of allying himself with his mother, he began to reach out to his father. If his mother couldn't figure out how not to rile his father's anger, perhaps he could show her. Basir took it upon himself to dust off his father's shoes in the morning, as if he were going to a city office instead of a blacksmith's shop. He would bring his father a cup of tea and scrounge up whatever he could from the kitchen to place before Kamal as soon as he came home.

And Basir's plan worked. Though he was barely an adolescent, he celebrated each peaceful day as a general would celebrate a strategic victory. He would smile at his mother and could not understand why she did not mirror his cheer. She looked wary. They did not talk about the delicate balance of power in their small home. It was the same in so many other homes dominated by heavy-handed fathers. Periods of peace were calms between storms.

It never lasted very long. Kamal was one of those men who needed to exert his strength to reassure himself he was capable of something. He needed to see his wife and children react to his presence to confirm he was in command. A man's might was right because no one had ever told him otherwise. And Kamal had secrets, filthy shameful secrets. When he was inebriated or angry or preoccupied, he was quite able to forgive his sins. But there were rare moments, small awakenings of a deeper conscience he didn't much care to face. In those moments, Kamal's face would flush with shame, his spine would hunch with horror. It was unbearable. Kamal could not tolerate anyone pointing out even the smallest of his shortcomings because he sensed that it would undo him completely, in the way that pulling on a stray piece of yarn just so can turn a sweater back into a pile of string.

Kamal was not an easy father to love, Basir admitted. *But he might have changed. Maybe things would have gotten better.*

BASIR WAS UP AT FIRST LIGHT, SHAFTS OF YELLOW BREAKING through a hazy, purple sky. He sat cross-legged in the living room where he slept at night, away from his sisters and cousins. The house still breathed collectively, a slumbering clan. He could almost feel the walls bend and bow like the rise and fall of a chest.

Basir remembered his box, the experiment he'd left outside. He thought of his little cousins and his sisters and decided it would be best to get rid of the scorpion immediately, before it or its babies found a way out of their cage. Basir slipped out the front door and made his way to the back of the home. He would let the scorpions free before someone stumbled upon them.

The box was precisely where he'd left it just a few hours ago. With the tip of his sandaled foot, Basir kicked aside the rock he'd placed on the lid and then used a twig to lift the top. Basir the captor jumped back, his foot knocking the box onto its side. He gasped with disproportionate horror as he learned a bitter truth.

Out ran the unencumbered scorpion, leaving two dozen half-eaten, lifeless young in her wake.

CHAPTER 24

ZEBA STARED AT HER MOTHER.

"And what did the judge say?"

"Not much. But he won't be your biggest problem."

"What did you do?" Zeba asked, feeling an old anxiety rise within her.

"Nothing. We talked mostly about your children needing you." Before Zeba could ask any more questions, Gulnaz gave a quick nod in the direction of the yard. "Why are those girls staring?"

Zeba glanced over her shoulder. Latifa looked away abruptly. Nafisa pretended to point at something in the distance. No wonder she was in jail. The girl couldn't lie to save her life.

"Probably because I told them about you," Zeba admitted. "You're the kind of person women love to hear about—especially women with big problems."

"Oh, is that so? How nice to know that at this age, I can still be interesting." Gulnaz's eyebrows lifted in amusement.

"Of course. You always have been. Even when your daughter's accused of murder, you're the more interesting person."

"Are you sure it's me they're staring at?"

"Positive."

Gulnaz sensed a difference in her daughter. Her back was a little straighter, her eyes a bit less downcast. Gulnaz pursed her lips.

"You've done something," she declared.

Zeba hid a sheepish smile. Gulnaz's intuition was confirmed.

"What did you do?" she pressed.

Zeba shook her head, but there was an undeniable twinkle in her eye.

"Zeba!" Gulnaz whispered brightly.

"Okay, Madar-*jan*, I'll tell you," Zeba whispered with halfhearted reluctance. "There was a girl here—a dumb, pregnant, lovesick girl. Though I have to admit she was clever in some ways. She managed to get herself and her boyfriend thrown into jail by turning herself in. For him to get released, he had to marry her."

"You're joking."

"Not at all," Zeba said cheerfully. "She needed his family to propose and they did."

"If only they had a prison for couples," Gulnaz said. "Though I suppose that's what marriage is, isn't it?"

Zeba didn't flinch. In the years since her father had disappeared, she'd not really seen her mother lament his death the way other widows had. She'd almost seemed relieved, actually.

"Tell me what you did," Gulnaz said, intrigued.

Zeba bit her lower lip. She suddenly felt like a child caught trying to walk in her mother's shoes.

"I told her about the string and the chicken feathers."

"You did?"

"I did."

Gulnaz looked puzzled.

"Where did you learn that from?"

"From you, of course. You made me pluck the chicken feathers myself when we did it for Nooria-*jan*."

"Oh, I'd forgotten about her." Gulnaz looked off into the distance. There was a haze in the air, as if the day might bring rain. "There was no way Latif would've married her if we hadn't helped out. The rumors in town about her sneaking around with him *and* his cousin were pretty bad."

"If it were today, she would have been my cellmate. Ten years for *zina*. Lucky for her she chose to be immoral in a better time. How is she doing, anyway? She must have grandchildren by now," Zeba mused.

"She died years ago. Her devoted husband remarried three months later."

"Three whole months. Love is beautiful, isn't it?" Zeba smirked.

Gulnaz smiled faintly. When had Zeba become so sarcastic? What had happened to her docile daughter, the girl who had been tearful even as she closed the door on her mother?

"Anyway, my roommate and her mother did everything I told them to do. I was surprised, to tell you the truth, when we heard his family had gone to her home to ask for her hand. I didn't know if it would really work."

"Seven knots?"

"Seven knots," Zeba confirmed. Gulnaz smiled smugly.

"Then there was no way it wouldn't work."

"It had to. She's too young to have her life ruined like this. Not to mention the baby."

"And her life would've been ruined for sure if you hadn't pulled her ass from the fire. Imagine a girl choosing to go through all this," Gulnaz said softly. "For one awkward moment in the dark."

"The girl puts on a good show, Madar-*jan*," Zeba said in a low tone. Gulnaz looked at her with raised brows. "But I highly doubt it was one moment, and it was surely not in the dark."

Gulnaz laughed, an unbridled, carefree laugh. Her eyes closed, and her head tilted back a degree.

She had to catch her breath. There was no fence. There was no jail. There was only a mother and a daughter, gossiping in the warm glow of the sun. The ache of Gulnaz's bones eased and the knotted muscle in her neck released just enough for her to chuckle without pain. The blood pulsed to her toes and fingers, turning her nailbeds pink. She was, in that one trivial moment, more alive than she'd been in years.

Watching her mother, Zeba was overcome. She giggled like a schoolgirl.

Gulnaz's eyes welled with happy, wistful tears.

Relishing the sound of lost laughter, mother and daughter looked at each other. The world around them dissolved.

"Madar, are you all right?" Zeba asked hesitantly.

"Ah, Zeba, you are my daughter after all, aren't you?"

Six months ago, Zeba would have resented the comment. But now, surprisingly, Zeba felt a twinge of pride. She blinked and uncrossed her legs. The grounds of the prison were pebbly, and Zeba hadn't brought out a blanket to sit on.

"I've spoken with your judge and your lawyer. The lawyer is off in the village now, trying to find out if anyone believes you could be innocent or if anyone knows anything helpful."

"No one will talk to him."

"Probably not, but it's a possibility. And Yusuf looks like the type of man who goes wild when he smells a possibility. That could be a good thing for you."

"There are worse traits, I suppose."

"Are you ready to tell me what happened?" Gulnaz prodded gently. "I might be able to better help you if I know."

"You sound like my lawyer." Zeba sighed.

"I suppose I do," Gulnaz said. She reached into her pocket and pulled out three chocolates wrapped in red foil. "I brought something for you. Something to sweeten your tongue in this sour place."

She slipped the chocolates through the fence. Zeba took them from her mother's fingers, wishing she could pull her mother's whole hand and arm and body through the latticework as well.

Gulnaz leaned forward, pressing her forehead against the warm metal of the fence.

"I know you, Zeba. You might not think I do, but you're my blood. Your soul talks to me even when your mouth doesn't. It always has."

Zeba looked up. Why did her mother always say such peculiar

things? Why was her whole family bent on being holier or craftier than everyone else?

"I don't know what you're talking about, Madar. I tell you what I'm thinking and there's no more to it. Whatever rings in your ears is your own—it doesn't come from me."

Zeba unwrapped one chocolate and popped the entire round candy, half softened by the warmth of Gulnaz's body, into her mouth. She crumpled the foil in her palm and felt the chocolate melt against the inside of her cheek.

"Zeba, I'm here to work out what I can for you. Trust me that I know best."

Her mother was wrong. She'd never listened to Zeba. Why should she when Gulnaz knew best? Gulnaz made all the decisions and, out of paranoia, had driven away every single family member who'd ever looked upon Zeba with kindness.

"You always have, haven't you?" Zeba said sarcastically.

Gulnaz bit her lip. Zeba was too tightly wound. Where had Gulnaz gone wrong? Why did she have to tread carefully in speaking with her own child?

"Zeba, I didn't come here to argue with you."

"Then what did you come here for, Madar? Are you here because you don't want to see me in prison or because you, the infamous Gulnaz, want to be the one to get me out with your powerful *jadu*?"

Gulnaz took a deep breath.

"I went to speak to the judge, Zeba, because I have spoken with him before. I met him years ago, before you were born. He came to call upon the great Safatullah once with his father. They were desperate for his younger brother to recover from a crippling illness. The boy was near death, from what I remember."

Zeba seethed. It was hard to listen to Gulnaz when thirty years of resentment was boiling to the surface.

"His younger brother believed he was saved by your grandfather, the *murshid*."

"What does this have to do with me?" Zeba asked through tight lips.

"A life was saved. People don't forget about that kind of thing."

Zeba looked back at the yard, half listening to Gulnaz. Latifa sat on the ground with her back resting against the wall of the prison. An unlit cigarette dangled between her fingers, her way of making her stash last longer. Latifa's eyes were closed to the half-hidden sun, and she looked to be asleep. Had she ever been so at peace in her life? The way she described her family, probably not.

Zeba had the urge to get up and walk over to Latifa—to sit beside her, shoulders touching, faces to the sky.

Maybe Zeba could give her mother one more chance. She unwrapped a second chocolate. They tasted stale and she wasn't really hungry for them, but it was easier than deciding whether or not to share them with her cellmates later.

Gulnaz laced her fingers through the metal links. Zeba was stubborn as a corpse. There was a grim possibility that was exactly what she would be if the fingers remained crooked in her direction.

My poor grandchildren, Gulnaz thought. *They'll never see their mother again.*

"Your father and I were a bad pair," she said hesitantly.

Zeba was silent.

"Early on, we were decent together. We were both young, and it felt important and new to be a married person. I didn't mind him and he didn't mind me. We did what we thought husbands and wives were supposed to do. I cooked. He worked. We visited our elders for the Eid holiday. But we were different people. We argued. We argued about our arguments. We found ways to make each other angry.

"If I knew he wanted rice for dinner, I made soup. He would leave walnut shells on the floor only because I'd asked him not to. It got to the point that I couldn't stand the smell of your father, to tell you the truth. We were a breath away from choking each other at all times. These are awful things to say now, but it's the truth."

Zeba's anger abated. The timbre of her mother's voice was different than she'd ever before heard.

"Why did you hate each other so much? Had he done something?"

Gulnaz shrugged her shoulders.

"I never hated him for anything in particular. And I don't know which of us started disliking the other first, but once it started, there was no turning back. When I look at other husbands and wives around me, I see so many people who were just like us—snapping at each other, sitting on opposite sides of the room. That's how we were, but bolder. We could admit we were bad together."

"Do you think he chose to fight in the war because of your arguing?"

"Who knows?"

"You must have some idea. There must be something you're not telling me."

"Now you, of all people, think I'm not sharing enough of the story?" Gulnaz snapped.

Zeba bit her tongue.

"Why did you never tell me about him before now?"

"What good would it have done? The man was gone. He wasn't a bad father to you in those early years, though. But after that, you really didn't have a father, so there was nothing to talk about."

"But you call him my father."

"Better for me to call him a father than to have others call you a bastard."

Zeba knew it to be true, though she didn't dare agree. Long ago she'd denied her mother's wisdom. Recovery would be slow.

Zeba arched her back. Her body felt stiff. Why was Gulnaz able to look so comfortable for so long? Did the pebbles not press into her flesh the way they did for Zeba?

"You couldn't fix things with him?" Zeba asked, thinking of Kamal as much as she was thinking of her father. "When I was a little girl, I believed you could fix everything."

A passing cloud cast a shadow over Gulnaz's face. Zeba's question pushed on an old but tender wound. Why hadn't Gulnaz done anything about the way they'd argued? She'd started to once. She'd snipped locks of his hair while he slept and torn a pair of his underwear into shreds. A bit of ash, a bit of blood, and he could have been a different man.

But she did not go beyond those first simple steps. Instead, she let him go. It had been as simple as releasing the string on a wind-borne kite. All she had to do was nothing.

"Our minds are wild beasts. We tame them with fear of God or punishment, but sometimes they refuse to cower. That's when things turn ugly."

Zeba understood her mother precisely. In the last few months she shared with her husband, she'd begun to feel exceptionally ugly.

CHAPTER 25

IT WAS MIDAFTERNOON IN CHIL MAHTAB AND JUST DAYS AWAY from the Eid holiday. The temperature within the prison had climbed to over a hundred degrees. Women who should have been home preparing to celebrate the holiday of sacrifice were wilting within the prison's high walls instead. The heat should have rendered the women immobile . . . but it hadn't.

Zeba's success with Mezhgan had set the women's prison alight with hope.

A steady stream of women moved through the cell Zeba shared with the others. The guards had, at first, tried to prevent the women from congregating but they quickly gave up. The women were persistent and the guards curious.

"Would you let me speak? You've had your chance!" Bibi Shireen, a woman old enough to be Zeba's grandmother, pushed her way to the front of the line. "Zeba-*jan*, you're a mother. You've got to understand. My son was in love with a girl and when they ran off together, the girl's brothers found them and killed him. They've locked me up because my son is dead and someone's got to be blamed. And they want my daughter to be married to one of the killers, in retribution for my son's transgression. I've been here three years and have another twenty-seven to go. Do you see my hair—white as a garlic clove? I will die here! What can you do for me?"

"What idiots. Bibi Shireen, I had no idea you had another twenty-seven years still. That's a disgrace," Latifa remarked with blatant disgust. She sat on the edge of her bed and watched over the pleas. She was learning things about her fellow prisoners that she hadn't learned in her eighteen months in Chil Mahtab.

"Tell me, Zeba-*jan*. What should I do? I once heard something about the feathers of a white pigeon bringing mercy, but I don't trust the person who told me. Whatever you say, I'll do it."

Zeba listened in silence. She had not intended to create such a maelstrom. It had been an exercise really, a way for her to prove to herself that she could do something, even if it meant dipping her feet into murky waters.

"Bibi-*jan*," she said respectfully. "I will think carefully about your situation."

The women came in two or three at a time with all kinds of requests. Zeba quickly became accustomed to the ones in need of recipes to make families accept their beloved. But the prison housed women accused of more than being star-crossed lovers. Because of their various improprieties, many had been convicted of the broad crime of *zina*, sex outside of marriage. Some were convicted of attempted *zina* or imprisoned for assisting another woman to commit *zina*. An eighteen-year-old girl had run away from her elderly husband. A wife had left a husband after he sold their ten- and twelve-year-old daughters into marriage. Another had been arrested when a stranger reported seeing her leaving a man's private office.

They all begged Zeba for help. They needed the judge's mercy. They needed their families to be understanding. They needed their husbands to grant them divorces. The prison was teeming with stories of sex, love, and violence.

Zina. Zina. Zina.

Two women came to Zeba together.

"Go on, you tell her," said the older of the two, the soles of her feet stained with henna. Zeba thought them to be mother and daughter at first but soon realized she was mistaken.

"Our husband was killed by his cousins, but the family pointed their fingers at us. They're free while we're in here. We did nothing, but no one seems to care. What should we do?"

"You were both married to him?"

"Yes," explained the older woman. "I was his first wife. Then he took her. He was a decent man. He had land that his cousins had been eyeing for years. They wanted it and finally killed him for it. Three of them came into our home and strangled him. Blaming the two of us only made it easier for them to claim his lot."

Zeba bit her lip.

"Let me think about it," Zeba said. "I'm not sure what would be best . . ."

Actually, she didn't know at all. Gulnaz had never tackled dilemmas of this ilk, which was not to say that she could not have managed them. The opportunity just hadn't presented itself.

Madar, you would have the time of your life in this place.

Zeba cobbled together recipes from her childhood, recalling what Gulnaz had done in similar situations.

"This place, these crimes—it is an injustice what's being done here," Zeba declared. A chorus of agreement rang through the small cell. "What a burden it is to be born a woman."

What she could not articulate sometimes came more naturally to her in rhyme.

"Men treasure their manhood as God's greatest gift
Because without it, justice is brutal and swift."

There was an outburst of laughter.

"What did she say?" Like links on a chain, the women passed Zeba's couplet from the cell into the hallway, the beauty salon, and beyond. They repeated it to themselves, not wanting to forget the two lines that should have hung like a slogan beneath the prison's name.

"Zeba, you'll never have to wash your clothes again. I'll do your laundry and use my own detergent if you'll help me."

The woman before her had two wide-eyed children at her side. They looked like baby birds hidden under their mother's wings. Zeba noticed the bandages on her left wrist. She'd seen this woman undoing and redoing the strip of cotton a day earlier in the washroom, her back turned for privacy. Zeba could still picture the neat row of scabbed-over slice marks that ran from the middle of her forearm to the end of her wrist.

"My clothes?" Zeba asked with surprise.

"Now, that's an offer worth considering. I'd move her request, whatever it is, to the top of the list. But that's just me," Latifa said. She was standing at the television, turning the dial to flip through the channels. When she came to the TOLO channel, she stopped abruptly and clapped her hands together. Zeba and the three women still waiting to talk to her all turned their attention to the television.

"It's the finals! They're going to announce the winner today," she exclaimed. "How could I have forgotten?"

Two young men stood on a stage, microphones clutched in their nervous hands as they shifted their weight from foot to foot. They were being judged by a colorful panel of three men and one woman, some of Afghanistan's biggest names in the music world. One man wore a tuxedo, the two other men wore butterfly-collared dress shirts under jackets, their necks adorned with bold silver jewelry, the kind only musicians could pull off. The woman, with heavily darkened eyes, wore a beige, glimmery long-sleeved shirt and layers of thin gold necklaces. Her inky, black locks cascaded over her shoulders and acted as a backdrop for her dangling gold earrings.

Her name was Fariha and she was everything the women in prison were not. She was bejeweled, sitting in a room full of men. The audience revered her voice. She leaned back in her chair with the comfort of an unchallenged ruler, sparkling as she congratulated both contestants on their tone, emotion, and range. Rubbing her hands together and lowering her smoky eyelids, she announced: "I choose . . . Isah-*jan* as the winner!"

The camera panned to Isah, a young man with curly hair and a sheepish smile. The host of the show lifted Isah's left hand into the air triumphantly. The audience, young men in their twenties, stood and clapped wildly.

"Isah!" Latifa cried. "I knew he would win. He's the best by far. You know he's from the same town as my mother."

"Oh really? My congratulations to your whole family, then," Nafisa mumbled. She sat cross-legged in front of her bed, flipping through a beauty magazine.

"Zeba-*jan*," the woman went on. "As I said, I'll take care of your laundry if you can help me get out of here before my boys turn seven and they're taken away from me."

Somehow, the fact that they were twins made them seem even more forlorn.

"How old are they now?" Zeba asked, touching the top of one boy's head. The prison was home to enough children that walking through its halls sometimes reminded Zeba of an elementary school.

"Six, and the guards have already started talking about sending them to the orphanage with the others," the woman said, her voice cracking. "I can't be away from them. I've only survived this long because they've been here with me."

"You've been here seven years?"

She nodded. She was younger than Zeba and had the freshness of an adolescent. But judging by the ages of her boys, she had to be in her early twenties.

"Why are you here?"

Latifa was glued to the television. The winner of the competition, Isah, was singing his victory song. The audience was clapping in time, cheering him on. Fariha moved her shoulders to the rhythm and nodded in approval.

The young mother looked at her boys and then around the room.

She spoke so softly that even Zeba had to lean in and pay close attention to make out her painful story.

"I was attacked by my cousin at my home. He cornered me in a room and told me he would kill me if I screamed. My family didn't believe me and when I went to the police, they arrested me."

"They arrested you?"

"No one had seen or heard what had happened. The police said if it had been forced, I would have screamed. Since I hadn't shouted, they arrested me for *zina*. I was already in prison when I realized I was pregnant. Once my family found out about that, I never heard from them again."

The boys were watching Zeba, looking for her reaction. She forced a quick smile their way. They'd heard the story before, she could see.

"Because you didn't scream . . ." she echoed. The words rattled her. "But you didn't scream because you were scared?"

"He had a knife," she said plainly. Zeba sensed these were words she'd said a thousand times before to no avail.

Zeba rubbed at her eyes. The stories were too much for her. There was no way her *jadu* would free a prison full of condemned women. No spell would change the fact that a woman's worth was measured, with scientific diligence, in blood. A woman was only as good as the drops that fell on her wedding night, the ounces she bled with the turns of the moon, and the small river she shed giving her husband children. Some women were judged most ultimately, having their veins emptied to atone for their sins or for the sins of others.

"You've said nothing about wanting to be released," Zeba remarked. "You just want the boys to stay with you?"

"Released?" She laughed lightly and shook her head. "Not at all. I don't know what I would do if I were turned out. My family will not take me back. I have no friends to take me in. I have two boys and a story no one wants to hear or believe. The boys will be sent out when they're seven, and even though they are what they are, I can't . . . I can't imagine being in here without them."

The boys flinched. Their mother's lower lip quivered.

Latifa was flipping the channels again. Nafisa pretended to turn a page but was looking past the magazine at the woman with her two boys. She looked relieved not to be in her place. Zeba hated sending every woman away with nothing but a promise, so she undid the *taweez* she had safety-pinned to the breast pocket of her dress. The needle pricked her finger and drew a spot of blood. Zeba wiped it on her own skirt and pinned the *taweez* her mother had gotten from Jawad to the inside of the young mother's collar.

"Take this for now. I will think very carefully about what can be done," Zeba promised. Even as she spoke the words, she could hear how hollow they sounded.

THE NEXT TWO DAYS BROUGHT MORE OF THE SAME. THE STREAM of women grew steadier. They followed Zeba into her cell or found her in the yard or approached her in the hallways. Zeba was not accustomed to so much attention. They clasped her hands between their own. They brought her small hand mirrors or tubes of lipstick. They offered to wash her hair or to allow her to use their contraband mobile phones, which wouldn't have done her any good. Kamal's sister did not have a phone and, even if she had, likely would not have answered her call. Zeba tried to refuse the gifts and favors though some were left anonymously on her bed or done before she could protest. If bribery was practiced in the outside world, it was perfected in the prison.

"I HAVE A SIMILAR PROBLEM, BUT IT INVOLVES MY HUSBAND AND his new bride. He had me locked up in here so he could get married without me in the way. Tonight's their wedding, and I want to do something to make him limp as a noodle."

Another woman was elbowing her way into the room.

"I'm not trying to ruin anyone's life. I have a simple request. My hair's been falling out in clumps since I've been here. Look here, sister. Just look at this!"

She lowered her head before Zeba and let her head scarf slip down to her neck. She raked her fingers through her hair, showing large patches of white scalp.

"I've tried washing it with red mud. I've tried rubbing raw eggs on my head. My sister even brought me a bottle of hair oil from India, but nothing's worked. You must know something that will help my hair—please!"

Zeba turned to Latifa and sighed heavily.

Latifa had become Zeba's agent. She would sit at her side and appoint each visitor a turn. When Zeba grew too fatigued to even listen to their requests, she had only to look at Latifa. With a nod, Latifa would shepherd the women out of the cell.

"Time to go!" Latifa announced with a clap of her thick hands. She turned the television off and guided the woman to the door with a hand on her back. "God created head scarves for situations like yours. How wise of Him, no? Khanum Zeba's not a doctor or a pharmacy. If you ask me, I'd say you should really stop gossiping so much. The things you said about your own cellmates—shame on you. Someone's probably cast a spell on your hair. Did you ever think about that?"

The woman scowled at Latifa and pushed her hand away.

Zeba wanted to help them all, but there were so many pleas and not even Gulnaz's *jadu* worked all the time. Sometimes it was overpowered by another spell, Gulnaz had explained, and sometimes it was struck down by God. Zeba also knew that she was not Gulnaz. Zeba's eyes were a dull brown, her skin showed its age, her convictions were weakened by doubt. She was an apprentice when what these women really needed was the master.

Latifa closed the door to the cell.

"Thank you," Zeba said gently.

Latifa shrugged her shoulders. She was quite content with the informal position she'd been given. Zeba knew that Latifa had also been showered with gifts by women hoping to have Zeba's ear. Prison guards, police officers, and judges had their palms greased all the time. For Latifa, having her turn at it meant she was rising in the ranks.

"I need to get out of this room for a bit," Zeba said, fanning herself with a rumpled magazine. The electric fan in their cell had stopped working a week ago. "I need some air."

"Sure," Latifa said. "I'm going to go down to the beauty parlor and see what the women are up to."

She was probably trying to drum up more business for tomorrow, Zeba realized with a sinking feeling as soon as she stepped out of the cell. She didn't have the energy to fight it.

She wanted so much to help each and every one, to open the doors and set them free or promise them that their children would stay with them forever. But Zeba was neither a lawyer nor a judge. She could do nothing with the bribes she'd been given, nor could she even know if her own children would ever see her again. This prison, with its beauty salon and televisions and crayon-scribbled walls, was a dungeon. The injustice inside it leached all the energy from her body. Zeba ran her hand along the red oily scrawl left by a child just learning the alphabet. The children here made her most sad.

"Madar-*jan!*"

Zeba spun around. Shabnam? Kareema?

"Madar!"

The echo of a child's voice through the cold hallway made Zeba weak, even when it belonged to another woman's child. She turned each and every time, though it had been so long since anyone had called to her.

A six-year-old girl with plastic sandals and a brightly colored dress came racing down the hallway. The hems of her hand-me-down pantaloons looked like they would catch between her feet.

"Slowly, slowly!" Zeba cautioned.

The little girl slowed her step and looked at Zeba curiously. The roundness of her eyes, the drift of her bangs, the dimple in her chin called to mind Kareema. Zeba's eyes watered.

"You sweet thing. Why are you calling your mother? Do you miss her?"

"No, I . . . uh . . . I just needed her."

Zeba's head spun slightly. She'd not had a chance to eat lunch with all the women coming to see her. Latifa had brought her water, but she'd left it untouched.

"Your dress is so pretty."

Kareema had been wearing a dress just like this little girl's dress on the day Kamal had died. It had been Shabnam's until just a few months ago. The girls would have grown since she'd been away. Rima must have learned a few more words by now. Maybe she was running.

There were thoughts that Zeba couldn't push out of her head. Did Tamina really look after them? If Rima cried at night, did anyone soothe her? Were the girls being used as house servants or would they be married off as revenge for their father's murder? They were only children. She prayed, with the fervor of the most devout believer, that Kamal's family was not blaming them for Kamal's death.

She remembered the faces of the twin boys, the way they'd flinched on hearing the crime committed against their mother. Tiny shoulders bore a lot of blame.

Zeba was on her knees. She was holding the startled girl's hands in her own, turning them over and staring at the pink of her palms.

Children had such perfect hands—so soft and eager to hold on to someone who would love them. Was Rima holding her aunt's hands? Did she try to nestle against her aunt's bosom? And when she did, was she pulled in so she would forget Zeba or was she pushed away and left to wonder why?

A little boy came along. By the way he took the little girl's hand from Zeba and moved close enough that their shoulders were touching, she guessed he must have been her brother though he couldn't have been more than a year older.

"What a good brother you are! So good of you to take care of your sister. God will reward you for being such a caring brother. What is your name?"

The two children exchanged looks.

"My name is Bashir," he answered slowly.

Zeba threw her head back and laughed. She wiped her tears away and leaned in to share her story.

"My son's name is Basir! Did you know that? He's older than you. He's such a good boy, too. When he was your age, he used to take care of his little sisters. Your mother must love you both very much. You should never leave her, understand me? No matter what people say about her, you should never believe it. Even if they call her a whore or a liar or a murderer or a . . ."

The two children were looking past Zeba at the warden and Yusuf. They stood behind her, listening to her wild rant.

Zeba didn't hear them calling her name.

"People don't know. They say terrible things, but they don't really know what's happened."

The children took one step backward, then two.

"Are you afraid of me? Please, please don't be afraid of me! I'm nothing to be scared of! I'm so sorry. I only wanted to talk to you!"

There were hands on her elbows, bringing her to her feet.

"Why are you running from me!" she shrieked. "I'm not the person you should be running from! I promise I am not that person!"

There were shouts, calls for guards to help, more hands on her even as she kicked. Her head scarf fell to the floor.

"Let me go! Let me go! I didn't kill him!"

Latifa loomed over her.

"Shut up, Zeba! You're scaring these children! Look what you've done!"

But Zeba hadn't done anything. Why couldn't anyone see that? Why did everyone continue to blame her?

"Zeba," Yusuf said. Asma and another guard were holding Zeba up by the elbows. Her knees were bent, and she was writhing in their grasp. "Control yourself!"

Latifa grabbed Zeba's face with her hands—thick, manly hands that made Zeba's feet kick out, striking Latifa in the shin. Latifa let go and scowled sharply.

Zeba's head ached. She felt the urge to slam her skull against the wall and release the poison. *Human skulls are nothing more than eggshells anyway,* she thought. *And even a child can crack eggs.*

"Get your hands off me! You brought that filth into our home. I could smell it and taste it and feel it and you told me it was nothing! I should have killed you long ago!"

"Khanum Zeba, please, stop screaming . . ."

"Take her to the interview room and watch over her until she calms down. She's not going to get away with acting like this in my prison," the director said, her arms folded across her chest. Her words cut through the shouts and made Zeba go still. Her legs straightened, and she was standing on her own.

"This is not prison. Prison is out there," said Zeba in a throaty, singsong voice. "I'm no one's slave. I'm no one's prisoner. God as my witness, I'm unshackled!"

"Not for long, I'm sure. My God, Zeba. You're as crazy as we always thought you were," Latifa shouted from far enough away that Zeba's foot couldn't reach her.

Yusuf watched carefully as his client was led down the hallway, her back now straight with a dignity that only an insane person could feel. Maybe Latifa was right, he thought.

Maybe, just maybe, Zeba was as crazy as she seemed to be.

CHAPTER 26

YUSUF STOOD WITH CHIEF HAKIMI AT THE DOOR TO ZEBA'S home. Hakimi pushed the door in.

"This is the scene of the crime," he announced dramatically. "I gathered what evidence I could. It was obvious she had killed her husband."

They stepped into the courtyard. The absence of life hit Yusuf harder than the shadow of death. This had been a home, and the ghosts of its inhabitants seemed to be present. Yusuf could almost hear the echoes of an everyday existence in the courtyard: the scrape of a spatula against an aluminum pot, the pungent smell of seared garlic and onions, the soft giggles of sisters sharing secrets, the hum of a mother with her children at her feet.

They were gone.

"Where was Khanum Zeba when you got here?"

"Right there," Hakimi said, pointing to the front wall of the house. "She was sitting on the ground, and all the neighbors had gathered around her. Her children—they were shaken up. She was a bad sight. The blood on her hands was already dry. The baby was crying. I don't know how long she'd been sitting like that. She wasn't saying much."

Thank goodness for that, Yusuf thought.

"People were very upset. They didn't know what to think. Nothing like this should have happened in our town. The women couldn't believe she would have done such a thing, but it happens."

"What happens?" Yusuf said without turning to the police chief. He sensed that looking this man in the eye made him uncomfortable, and he wanted to hear Hakimi's unfiltered thoughts.

"Women lose their minds. Maybe he did something to make her that way. I don't know. I didn't know either of them very well, but I know the rest of his family. This has been very hard on them."

"So you think Khanum Zeba flew into a rage and killed her husband?"

"Yes, that's . . . well, then why else would I arrest her?" Hakimi replied defensively.

"Of course. Anyone in your shoes would have done the same," Yusuf reassured. He kept his tone casual and friendly. "As you described it, there was no obvious reason to think Khanum Zeba *hadn't* been the one to kill her husband. But let me ask you this. While you were here with the neighbors and friends, did anyone come forward to say they'd heard any shouting or that they'd seen anything unusual that day? Maybe someone else entering or leaving the home? I'm not saying you did the wrong thing, but I'm just curious if there were any other sides to the story that need to be investigated."

But Hakimi's shoulders stiffened.

"I don't need you to tell me I did the right thing. I know I did the right thing. I'm the police chief here. What you need to be asking is what your darling Khanum Zeba did—not what I did! Where are you from, anyway?"

It was Yusuf's turn to tense.

"I am not questioning you. This is a misunderstanding. I'm only trying to make sure I know the full story so that I can do my job and provide Khanum Zeba with a reasonable defense."

"Do what you need to do then. I will wait here for you to finish," Hakimi huffed and turned to take a seat in an upturned plastic chair in the courtyard. "Don't touch anything. I'll be watching."

"Of course. I'll just be a few moments."

Yusuf took a deep breath. How had this conversation gone so wrong? He'd meant to befriend Hakimi, to make him an ally. He strolled through the house. There was nothing unusual about it. There was the usual sparse kitchen area with a few items spread out, as if someone would walk in any moment and pick up where they'd left off. The rooms were small and simple with floor cushions and a single wooden-armed sofa. A thermos sat on the living room floor next to a glass teacup stained with a series of brown rings. There was a brown-and-yellow tapestry nailed to the wall, a geometric print that echoed the pattern of the carpet. He walked through the back door and into the yard behind the house. He recognized the layout from what Rafi had described to him and from the police report. The outhouse was right where he expected it to be, as was the pear tree. The solitary rose-bush sat off to the side, almost as if it were retreating from the home.

Was that where Kamal's body had been? Yusuf could almost believe that the ground still carried the stain of blood though it was now several weeks and quite a few rains since Kamal's murder.

"That's all there is to see."

Hakimi's voice startled Yusuf, who had crouched on the ground over where Kamal's body had been.

"Yes, there is nothing surprising. I just wanted to see with my own eyes."

"Let's go then. I don't need the neighbors thinking the chief of police is giving Zeba's lawyer extra help."

"Of course. But I believe she's innocent and in order for me to defend her, it's important for me to gather information. You're a fair person—I can tell."

"I am," Hakimi agreed, his hands on his hips. "And that's why I have this title. It's a big responsibility, but I take it seriously. Most people in my position don't and that's the problem."

"I'm sure of that," Yusuf said, nodding. "One question, Hakimi-*sahib*. What position was the husband's body in when you found him?"

"He wasn't moving. He was just dead."

Hakimi's tone made his unimpressed opinion of Yusuf quite clear.

"I know he was dead when you found him, but what position was his body in? He was here, correct?"

Hakimi pulled at his chin and squinted.

"He was . . . he was on his belly. His head was turned to the side and facing us."

"Where was the hatchet?"

"Over there," Hakimi motioned to the back wall of the house, not far from the door Yusuf had just come through.

"And was there any other evidence? Anything else found here or in the house that seemed out of place?"

"It looked just like this. What you see here now is the same thing I saw that day, except for the dead husband, the wife, and the hatchet. You can't make a simple thing into a complicated one just by asking a lot of questions."

"That's not what I'm trying to do. I don't have the benefit of having seen it with my own eyes so I'm asking you. Was there blood inside the house?"

"No," Hakimi said, though the truth was that he hadn't checked. What difference would it have made? If Zeba had tracked blood through the house, would that have made her any more or less guilty?

Yusuf sighed.

Forensic science had a long way to go in Afghanistan. Yusuf knew he wouldn't have the luxury of DNA tests. Fingerprints might have been a possibility, but no one had bothered taking any.

"What's been going on with the children? I know they're living with their uncle. Have you heard anything from them?"

"What's to hear? Poor kids lost their father and their mother, really. At least they had somewhere to go. Not every family would have taken in the children of a killer."

"But they're of the same blood."

"Yes, but the circumstances are different."

"I'd like to be able to talk to Khanum Zeba's children. They're the only ones who know what things were like between their mother and father. How can I get to them?"

Hakimi laughed lightly and shook his head, ushering Yusuf toward the door.

"You're being ridiculous. They're only children. They don't know anything about their parents, and they weren't there when their father was killed—thank God they were spared that much. There's no way that Fareed is going to let you near his nephew and nieces. You'd better find someone else to talk to."

ONCE HAKIMI HAD LEFT HIM, YUSUF DECIDED TO CONTINUE HIS investigation. He knocked on the door of the house to the left of Zeba's. There was the patter of small feet before the door swung open. A young boy, no more than six years old, peered at Yusuf.

"*Salaam!*" he said brightly.

"*Wa-alaikum salaam,*" Yusuf replied, burying a smile. The sight of young boys had had a surprising effect on him since his return, as if he were stepping back in time and seeing himself as a child.

"Who are you?" the boy asked. It was unusual to have strangers at the door.

"My name is Yusuf. Is your father home?"

"No, he's working," he answered. Just then his mother appeared behind him, sliding her head scarf over her forehead.

"Sorry, who are you? What do you need?" she said abruptly, pulling her son aside and closing the door just slightly.

Yusuf took two steps back.

"Forgive me, Khanum. I am looking into the terrible tragedy that happened next door to you. I was wondering if you or your husband wouldn't mind helping me. I just have a few questions and won't take much of your time."

The woman's eyes narrowed.

"No, I have nothing to say about it. This is something for the police to take care of," she replied as she gently closed the door on Yusuf.

The next four homes gave him the same response. The fifth refused to open the door. Yusuf was beginning to wonder if he'd wasted his time in coming out to the village. He'd learned nothing from visiting the house. Why was everyone so reluctant to talk about Zeba's family? Where was the gossip mill when he needed it?

Two blocks away from Zeba's home, Yusuf's luck changed.

She was a sprightly, gray-haired woman who shouldn't have come to the door herself but she'd been in the courtyard picking peppermint leaves and was probably happy to have someone to talk to. Yusuf crooked his neck to speak to her.

"Yes, I knew that family. For God's sake, we all know that family! We almost live close enough to know when they've burned their dinner."

Yusuf smiled brightly.

"What was Khanum Zeba like? Did you speak to her often?"

"Who are you? You're not a police officer. Why are you asking so many peculiar questions?"

"No, and forgive me for not introducing myself properly. My name is Yusuf. I'm a lawyer working on the case."

Yusuf found it better not to say, straight off, whose interest he represented.

"Oh, a lawyer. You're not from the city, then," she deduced, taking a closer look at him. "Good for you. Are you married? Where is your family from?"

Yusuf felt his potential being assessed. He half expected a dark-haired young woman to emerge from the house and bat her eyes at him. Had he imagined it or had the window curtains just fluttered?

"You're a kind woman. You remind me so much of my aunt," Yusuf interjected in an effort to redirect the conversation. "She was always friendly with the neighbors as well. Everyone loves her."

"Is she dead?"

"No, no . . . God forbid. She's very well." Yusuf was thrown by her comment.

"Oh, that's good."

"Why?"

"The way you talk about her. People only say nice things about the dead, so you never know what the truth is. You can be a brute in life, but the moment you die, all is forgiven. It used to make me mad, but now that I'm old and know what people say about me, I'm glad for it."

"I'm sure people have only kind things to say about you," Yusuf offered politely. "But what did you think about Khanum Zeba—since she's still alive—was she a good person?"

"I saw her from time to time. Enough to know she was a good woman—always polite. She knew God."

"And what about her husband?"

"Eh, he was a man. Nothing special about him."

"Do you know if they fought? If he beat her?"

The woman let out a sarcastic chuckle.

"Young man, I came out here to pick mint leaves," she said, waving a fistful of greens in Yusuf's face. "Do you see this? Half of this is weeds because my eyes can't see the difference. Even if I'd seen those two with their arms around each other, I couldn't tell if they'd been wild with passion or about to kill each other."

"I suppose every family has its secrets."

"Of course. And that man was up to no good. Even with these tired old eyes, I could see that."

"What makes you say that?" Yusuf asked, intrigued.

"First of all, they moved to this neighborhood to get away from his family. They never said that was the reason, but I know it because I used to know his mother. My daughter-in-law's sister is friends with his sister. No one in his family could stand him."

"Do you know why?"

She shook her head and waved a hand in the air dismissively.

"Siblings are supposed to love each other but some people are so busy being jerks that they forget who their siblings are. They start being a jerk to everyone around them. I've raised my children differently, thank God. My own sons and daughters get along very well. When they were young, I used to tell them . . ."

"I'm sure your children are quite different," Yusuf gently interrupted. "How was Zeba when they moved into the neighborhood? Did you ever speak with her then?"

"That was years ago. She was friendly, actually. She was always very polite to me. She told me once that I reminded her of her mother."

"Really?" Yusuf did not see a bit of resemblance between this woman and Gulnaz.

"Yes, and the way she said it, I almost thought her mother might be dead. But I met her once when she came to visit her daughter and grandchildren. Her mother's much younger than me. And I think her vision is just fine. Both of us have lost our husbands, though. Maybe that reminded her of me. I can't imagine what else."

"I've had the pleasure of meeting her and she's an admirable woman, just like yourself."

"I see. You're one of those young men who knows all the right things to say," she said with a smirk. "I like that."

Yusuf laughed lightly.

"I hope I can ask the right questions as well," he said, trying to stay on track. "When did you notice a change in Khanum Zeba? Did something happen?"

The old woman's smile turned quickly into a scowl.

"She couldn't take anymore, that's what happened. Her husband would barely say hello to my sons when they passed him in the street. He would pretend as if he hadn't seen them, but I would watch him from here and he would stare as soon as their backs were turned. He did the same with anyone on the street, especially the young girls. No decency. No, that man was not a good man, and I know the difference because I was married to a good man. Thirty-two years we spent together until God took him from me. Everyone in town knew him and he knew everyone. He would have hated Zeba's husband. He told me once if a wife doesn't love her husband, there's a good reason for it."

"Your husband, God rest his soul, sounds like he was a wise man," Yusuf offered.

"He was."

"What do you think was going on between Zeba and her husband?"

"Hmph." The woman folded her thin arms across her chest. "You know, God made turtles with a hard shell. They're born expecting to need that shell. Women are not born that way. A husband like Kamal can destroy them. He was a beast. Lately, I didn't see her as much, and when I did see her, she was scurrying back home, afraid she'd been gone too long. She was nervous a lot. And her husband . . ."

But before Yusuf could ask his next question, a voice boomed from inside the house.

"Madar, who are you talking to?"

Her son entered the courtyard and looked at Yusuf with suspicion. Yusuf stuck out his hand, hoping to defuse the situation before he lost this opportunity.

"*Salaam*, brother. My name is Yusuf and I was just speaking with your dear mother—"

In a moment, Yusuf was back on the street, listening to the son admonish his mother for letting in a foreign spy.

With heavy feet, Yusuf headed down the street. He couldn't bring himself to knock on any more doors—not for now. No, Yusuf was done for the day. He walked past the school Zeba's daughters attended and opted not to stop the man pushing a wagon of fresh fruits and plump, enticing raisins.

CHAPTER 27

THE NEXT DAY, YUSUF STEPPED INTO THE VILLAGE MAIN STREET. The acrid smell of diesel mixed with the aroma of freshly baked bread. There was the clink of soft drink bottles in a crate as a man in a gray tunic and pantaloons set up his kiosk.

The young lawyer breathed it in, dust and all. It was the smell of opportunity, rebirth, and hope. He'd dreamed of this moment for years, imagined walking through streets just like this one and struggling to practice law here the way thrill-seeking doctors travel to field hospitals in Africa to test their skills.

It was stripping the profession down to its core. It was all guts. It was all glory.

He'd imagined drafting arguments and constructing defenses and finding ways to make the well-intentioned Afghan penal code live up to its potential. He would plow through the weeds of injustice and corruption and let righteousness see the light of day.

His time in Afghanistan had been nothing like what he'd imagined. He tried not to dwell on it. These were the obstacles that would make it all worthwhile in the end. These were the challenges that made him want to come to Afghanistan in the first place. If it had been easy, someone else could have done it. The lawyers here could have managed.

It wasn't easy. That's why Zeba needed him. That's why this place called out to him.

Yusuf wanted to make a name for himself and he wanted to do that in Afghanistan. Was that vanity? No, he promised himself. Vanity was wanting a tailored pin-striped suit or a corner office in a skyscraper.

This was honor and legacy. This would give his mother something to boast about to her friends. This is what would save him from looking as disappointed as his father at the way life had turned out.

Still, Yusuf had to admit that this visit to the village was not as productive as he'd hoped. He'd confirmed that the police hadn't gathered any evidence, something he could use in his defense argument though he could already imagine the *qazi* shaking his head.

The police didn't have the time or resources to gather evidence, Aneesa had told him as he'd pored over the arrest registry for Zeba. As long as the officers had obtained a statement from the arrested person, there really was no need to waste time with evidence that probably didn't exist or couldn't be scientifically interpreted.

Zeba's prosecutor had probably heard by now that Yusuf had gone to the village to poke around. He was doubtless entertained by Yusuf's naïve efforts. The prosecution could write his case up on toilet paper and unfurl it in the *qazi*'s office—it would still be stronger than Yusuf's defense.

Two men passed Yusuf walking in the opposite direction. One, who had a white beard and a triangular karakul hat, reminded Yusuf of his grandfather. The other had a stubbly chin and walked with his two hands knotted behind him. Their unhurried pace gave them ample opportunity to take in Yusuf's incongruous appearance.

"*Salaam-ulaikum,*" Yusuf said with a nod.

They returned his greeting and continued to look at him unabashedly.

Yusuf wanted to return to Zeba's neighborhood today. If he could just find a person who had actually been in their home that day when they'd all descended upon the murder scene, he might have a chance of learning something. There had to be information he could use.

Yusuf was lost in thought and barely noticed the rickety sound of uneven wheels approaching. It was the woody scent of fresh almonds that caught his attention and caused him to stop short. A three-wheeled cart had rolled up close enough to tempt him with its stock.

"Agha, wait. Let me see what you have," he called out.

The man stopped his cart but kept his hands wrapped around the two handles, his elbows bent and tucked close to his sides. He wore a round wool hat that did little to block the sun from his face. It was only late morning, but his forehead already glistened with a light sheen of sweat.

Yusuf took a few steps toward the cart, leaning over it to inspect the stock in each of the tall, thick plastic bags that made up the load. Dried chickpeas, long green raisins, almonds, and walnuts.

"*Salaam-ulaikum.*" Yusuf felt the man's eyes on him.

"*Wa-alaikum,*" the man replied. There was a pause before he spoke again. "These raisins are so sweet, you'll think they've been sugared. You've not had anything like them, I promise you."

"Very well." Yusuf nodded. "I'll take them and some of the almonds as well."

The vendor flipped open a paper bag and scooped almonds into it. His tawny hands and face had been weathered by many days under the unforgiving sun. It was hard to judge his age. He looked to be in his midforties, but Yusuf had come to realize that everyone in Afghanistan looked ten to twenty years older than they actually were, and few could expect to live past sixty-five. It was as if life was in fast-forward, though it did not seem to give anyone a sense of urgency to do more in the abbreviated time he or she had. The vendor grabbed a second bag and was about to flip it open when he paused.

"Where are you from?" he asked curiously.

"I'm visiting from town," Yusuf said, hoping to skirt the question. He could tell people where in Afghanistan he'd been born, but he knew that wasn't what they were asking.

"What have you come here for?" The man squinted as he looked at Yusuf, whose back was to the sun. He was also a good six inches taller than the fruit vendor.

"I've come to ask some questions," Yusuf said, being unnecessarily careful with his words. "I'm sure you know that a man was found dead in his home not too long ago."

"Mm."

"I'm trying to find out what might have happened to him. People say his wife killed him, but no one saw it happen."

The man scratched his beard.

"They call me Walid."

"Good to meet you, Walid-*jan*," Yusuf replied. Walid was not much older than himself, he realized with a closer look. "My name is Yusuf."

Yusuf stuck out his hand. Walid met it with his, calloused and gritty.

"You're not a police officer," Walid remarked. "Why are you asking questions?"

"No, I'm not a police officer. But I want to be sure we find the truth so that justice can be done."

"The government sent you?"

"Not really. An organization. We work for justice."

Another dodge.

"Has anyone told you what happened?"

Yusuf shook his head and frowned.

"Not yet. If you have something to share, I'd be very interested to hear it. Did you know the man who was killed or his wife?"

"I know everyone who eats almonds and raisins."

"I'm sure you do. What did you think of him? God forgive his soul," Yusuf added to play it fair.

"Yes, God forgive his soul," Walid echoed, blankly. "He was a lucky man. He had a wife and children. His eldest son is a good boy—looks after the family even now that the mother is gone."

"You've seen the children lately?"

Walid nodded.

"I saw them two weeks ago. They're with their father's family. They look well enough."

Yusuf could pass this along to Zeba. It wasn't much, but he was certain she would be grateful for any news about her children.

"That's good. They've been through a lot, those poor children. They're missing two parents now."

The raisin vendor nodded and gripped the handles of his cart. He leaned in as if about to push off then thought of something else and stopped.

"What kind of truth are you looking for?" he asked.

Yusuf was surprised by the question.

"Just the truth. I want to know if she was really responsible for killing him. I want to know if she deserves the punishment that she'll get if the judge believes she's guilty."

"They'll kill her, won't they?"

"Maybe."

"How can you say maybe? Why wouldn't they kill her?"

"There's always a possibility she didn't do it, I suppose. And even if she did do it, maybe there was a reason that we're not aware of."

"A reason."

"Yes, a reason."

"What reason do you think?"

"I think I came all this way to ask questions because I don't have all the answers."

A street mutt scampered past them. The sound of boys playing rose from the distance. The dog's ears perked and he ran off in the opposite direction with the fearful look of the abused. Yusuf was getting the distinct feeling that he was not in control of the conversation.

"Of course you have questions. Everyone does. No one can imagine why a decent woman would do such a thing," Walid said, shifting his weight on his feet.

"Exactly."

"What did her neighbors have to say about it?"

"I'm surprised you don't know what her neighbors are saying about it."

"I don't hear everything," he admitted as if it were a personal shortcoming.

"They didn't say much. Seems that no one wants to talk about it."

"I'm sure you found someone to talk to. The old woman down the road from them always has something to say, even if it has nothing to do with anything."

Yusuf felt a tickle on the back of his neck.

"You saw me yesterday." It was a question disguised as a statement.

Walid was silent. He held Yusuf's gaze, which was all the confirmation he needed. Yusuf opened the paper bag, peered inside, and shook it slightly to rearrange the almonds. He plucked two out and held them in his palm.

"She said Zeba was a nice woman. She seemed to think it was a shame when family matters spilled into the street."

"Spilled into the street?"

"Yes."

"I think the street spilled into their home, to tell you the truth," Walid quickly replied. There was the hint of indignation in his tone.

"What do you mean by that?"

Walid took a deep breath and straightened a bag of walnuts that was threatening to topple over.

"Akh, nothing. Just that . . . nothing really. But there were so many people in that home after the shouting. Everyone came running over to see what had happened."

"Were you there that day?"

"In their home?"

"Yes. I hear lots of people rushed in. Were you one of them?"

Walid shook his head.

"I didn't go in. My job is in the street so I stay in the street. I know my place."

"Weren't you curious to find out what had happened?"

Walid wiped his forehead with the back of his hand.

"I'd heard enough."

"Enough that you didn't need to see it with your own eyes," Yusuf surmised.

Walid squinted. The two men were figuring each other out.

"You don't sound like you think she's a killer. Your questions are different. Are you her lawyer?"

Yusuf casually tossed the two almonds into his mouth. Toasted by the sun, they were indeed delectable.

"I am," he admitted.

"I heard she confessed to killing him."

"I wouldn't say that."

"What would you say?"

"That there are lots of things that don't make sense and there is something about her that makes me very concerned. She's not been well since she's been in the prison."

"Not well?"

"My friend, sometimes people under a great deal of stress become fragile. Sometimes they start to come undone."

"What does that matter? If she killed him, she killed him. Who cares if she's upset?"

Walid was becoming tense. His breathing was laborious, nostrils flaring a bit.

"Well, I don't think she's in her right state of mind, right now. And I'm also wondering if she wasn't in her right state of mind at the time that her husband was killed."

"So you do think she killed him."

Yusuf smiled and shook his head.

"No, I didn't say that. Even if she did, it's not right and it's not legal to convict someone of murder if she's crazy."

Walid looked at him skeptically.

"The things you're saying. You're not making any sense."

"It's the law," Yusuf explained. "The law of this country states that she can't be guilty of a crime if she was insane at the time it happened."

"That can't be true."

"It's true. It's written into the judicial codes that govern this country. We have to respect that. But tell me, Agha Walid, tell me about the man who was killed. Did he prefer walnuts or almonds?"

Walid snickered, both at the notion that a single set of codes could govern this whole country and at the young lawyer's odd question. His snickers turned into a rattling cough. Yusuf waited for him to catch his breath and continue.

"He was a man with peculiar tastes—nothing I could offer him."

"What do you mean by peculiar?"

Walid shrugged his shoulders.

"Since he didn't care much for what I had to sell, I don't know."

Walid looked down the road. A mother carried a little girl in her arms. The child was probably old enough to walk but not quickly enough to keep up with her mother's pace. For now, she would be carried safely.

TALKING ABOUT WHAT HE'D SEEN WOULDN'T DO ANY GOOD, Walid knew. The best thing for that poor little girl would be for no one to know what had happened, not even her parents. Walid had five children of his own, two of them girls. They were much younger than the girl he'd seen that day, but it still gave him chills.

If only he'd chosen a different route that day—he'd be a much happier man right now. As it was, he hadn't been sleeping very well lately. His wife, after hearing him recount that day's events, shook her head and looked at him with disappointment. She'd pulled their two- and four-year-old daughters closer to her, a gesture that had angered him. Was she pulling them away from him? He wasn't the dangerous one.

What was I supposed to do? He was just talking to her!

Walid. She was just a girl. And now that poor woman . . .

Walid was smart enough to know what he was and what he wasn't. He was a simple man who sold nuts and fruits. He worked with his

back and his hands to make barely enough to feed his family. He was
no oracle. He was no authority figure. He resented his wife for implying he could have done something more even when that very thought
had nagged at him since that awful day. If he hadn't known what was
to happen, why had the hairs on the back of his neck stood at attention to hear that man speak to the girl?

If Walid hadn't known, why had he turned away so quickly? Why
had he pushed his cart back down the street in such a hurry, his eyes
glued to the nuts and raisins as if they were the ones that needed
saving? God shouldn't have put him on that street that day. There was
no reason for him to be there. He'd barely sold more than a few handfuls of anything there in months. It had been a mistake.

YUSUF WAS WATCHING HIM, PATIENTLY WAITING FOR WALID TO
break the silence, a silence that had gone on so long it was obvious
he had something to say. The streets were unexpectedly empty, and
the sun hung high in the sky, undimmed by the wispy clouds. There
wasn't even the faintest stir of dust.

"I can tell you this . . ."

But what could he say? He didn't need to say which girl it was.
He didn't need to lead Yusuf back to her house to dig up things that
shouldn't see the light of day. The woman. How could he help that
woman?

"Kamal, God rest his soul," Walid said awkwardly, "was not a
right man. I knew that. Other people knew that. I'm sure his wife
knew it, too."

Yusuf felt something pull at his stomach. He tried not to appear
too excited. He nodded, a small gesture but one that Walid seemed
to need in order to continue. Like an exhalation, a breeze drifted
through, causing the dust to rise and settle around their ankles. It was
there, under the gaze of the round and brilliant sun, that Walid began
to unravel the story of Zeba and Kamal.

CHAPTER 28

MEZHGAN, IN A FLURRY OF HUGS AND KISSES AND PROMISES TO reunite beyond the prison's bars, had been returned to her family. They would have a real wedding in a month, but for now, the judge had been appeased by the formal union between her and her beloved. Before she'd gone, she'd pressed her cheek against Zeba's and tried to kiss her hands though Zeba had pulled away.

"I can't begin to tell you how grateful I am," she'd said. "And just to show you how much you mean to me, I want to show you what I've done."

She rolled up the sleeve of her dress and Zeba gasped. On the pale flesh was a fresh tattoo, black writing raised from the skin and haloed in red. It was as clumsy as a child's scrawl but clear enough to read—*Zeba*. Zeba couldn't believe the girl's foolishness, to sit while another prisoner had pierced her flesh with a pin, dripping melted rubber thinned with shampoo into each divot, to embed the letters of her name into her young body.

"Mezhgan, why?" Zeba had been baffled. "Why would you put that on your arm?"

Plenty of women had tattoos in Chil Mahtab—names of lovers, hearts, and other symbols. But Zeba had never expected to see her own name carved into another person's flesh.

"I've never met a woman as strong as you," Mezhgan had professed. "There's something special about you. I knew that from the day they brought you into the cell. You have magic. You're powerful. Just look what you've done for me! And I know that whatever you did to your husband, you did with God on your side. Every woman in here agrees with me. Every single one."

ZEBA WATCHED HER TWO REMAINING ROOMMATES SITTING cross-legged on the floor of their cell. It was morning and an odd time for a game of cards, but Mezhgan's absence left a void none of them had anticipated and there were few ways to fill emptiness in prison. Latifa had borrowed a deck of cards from a woman whose cell was on the second floor. She'd been jailed for leaving the husband who had stabbed her in the belly. Her neighbor, a girl she'd known for a few years, had been jailed as well for helping her to escape.

"There's absolutely no way I'm letting you deal the cards again," Nafisa declared with exasperation.

Latifa's eyebrows shot up jovially. The cell was stifling and hot.

"Accusing me of cheating? Don't flatter yourself. I don't need to cheat to beat you at this game. You're even worse than Mezhgan was."

Nafisa held her fan of cards over her heart and looked wistfully at Mezhgan's vacant bed.

"I am so happy for her," she said. "She's going to be married soon to her sweetheart. I do miss her, though."

Latifa threw a queen of hearts onto Nafisa's nine of hearts.

"Killed that one, too," she said smugly before slapping a jack of diamonds in front of her frustrated cellmate. "Don't bother missing her. I doubt she's wasted a second thinking about us."

"What a spiteful thing to say!" Nafisa snapped.

"But it's true! What would you do if you were released today? I'll tell you what you would do," Latifa said with the conviction of a politician. "You would turn your back on this place and everyone in it. You would never let the name Chil Mahtab cross your lips again.

You would deny you'd ever been here, just as you deny what got you sent here in the first place."

"I would not!" Nafisa huffed, with equal conviction. "I would never turn my back on you, Latifa. And if you were a nice person, I would write to you and visit you, maybe even bring you chocolates from my *shirnee* whenever that happens. I wouldn't want to forget you, even if you do cheat like a thief."

Latifa scoffed and shifted her hips on the ground. She kept her eyes on her cards, but her face had softened.

This early game of cards was not as relaxing as Latifa had promised it would be—not when there was still a prison full of women looking to Zeba for help she couldn't provide. If she were all that powerful, she should have been able to do some good for herself. The women of Chil Mahtab were not bothered by that small point, though. Their need to believe in Zeba loomed so large that it eclipsed all skepticism. Zeba thought, again, of her name carved on Mezhgan's young forearm like a blood tribute.

When Asma, the guard, came rapping at their door, Zeba was not at all disappointed.

"Zeba, come. Your lawyer's here to meet with you."

Zeba wasn't expecting Yusuf back so soon, less than a week since he'd last been to see her. Each time they met, he left appearing frustrated but determined. She did not know what he did in the intervals between their visits and wasn't sure if she wanted to ask.

"My lawyer? Are you sure?"

Asma laughed.

"Get up, Zeba. No reason to keep the handsome gentleman waiting."

YUSUF WAS PACING THE ROOM WHEN ZEBA ENTERED. HIS BAG hung from the back of the chair, and there was his yellow notepad with his indecipherable scribbling. The top page looked softly crin-

kled and Zeba would have bet anything at that moment that Yusuf
had fallen asleep with his face pressed to it.

He looked at her, grim-faced.

"We've got to talk, Khanum Zeba. We've got to talk."

Zeba slid into the chair across from Yusuf's bag. Asma lingered
at the door until Yusuf sharply thanked her for bringing Zeba in for
the meeting.

Asma's ears perked at the tone of his voice, but she closed the door
behind her and took a few steps down the hall. Zeba watched her walk
away from the glass-enclosed interview room and turned her attention
back to Yusuf. He had shadows under his eyes.

"What's going on? Has something happened?"

Yusuf shot her a look of annoyance.

"I've asked only that you be open with me. I told you from the
beginning that if you let me in, if you shared everything with me,
I might be able to help you. You could have saved us both a lot of
trouble if you would've just trusted me from the beginning. That's the
only way this"—he waved a finger back and forth between him and
Zeba—"can work."

"Say what you want to say."

Yusuf stopped short. Zeba breathed a little easier. His pacing
always made her nervous. Yusuf pulled the chair back quickly, its legs
scraping against the floor tiles. His bag slipped off the back, but he
didn't bother to pick it up.

"I went to your village," he said, looking straight at her.

Zeba felt a knot in her stomach. She waited.

"I went to your town and I went to your house. I knocked on your
neighbors' doors. There's a lovely woman down the street from you
who's watched you walk past her house while she tends to her plants."

Zeba knew precisely who Yusuf had spoken to. On two occasions,
Zeba had herded her children out of the house rather abruptly. Those
were days when Kamal had come home with red-rimmed eyes and
heavy feet. He'd been violent but in a directionless way that made

Zeba frightened for the children. The drink gave Kamal bursts of energy followed by bouts of exhaustion. Knowing he would not bother to chase after them, she'd thrown a head scarf on and scurried past that woman's house, tears streaming down her face as she anxiously looked over her shoulder. She'd seen the woman looking out into the street as if she'd been waiting for just such a curious sight to come by.

"There's more," Yusuf said. "I talked to a man who was outside your house the day Kamal was killed. He was just outside your door that afternoon. He says he knows what happened."

A man. Zeba thought back to that day. What could a man have seen or heard from outside their walls? He couldn't have seen the hatchet go into Kamal's head.

"What man? Is he saying I killed Kamal?" Zeba was on the brink of rage, a sudden boiling anger at the thought that a man would step forward to further condemn her. "I don't know who he is, but he's a liar!"

"The man saw something. He saw someone go into your home, Khanum Zeba."

Zeba remained in her seat, her lips pressed together into a thin, pink line. Had a man really seen her? Had he told anyone else? All the days she'd spent away from her children and all the days ahead that she would fester here without them—all this could not be for nothing. She could not let Yusuf or this man, whoever he was, render her sacrifice meaningless.

By the severe look on Zeba's face, Yusuf felt any doubt he'd harbored in Walid's story melt away.

"I don't really feel like talking now," Zeba said with quiet resolve. She crossed her legs at the ankle and kept her fingers tightly intertwined, an effort to prevent any part of her body from revealing more than had already been revealed. If only Yusuf could understand how badly she wanted to tell him. But it seemed the truth would be of little benefit—not to people who deemed her testimony worth only a fraction of a man's. In a flicker of despondency, the lines came to her:

"What good is a woman's telling of truth
When nothing she says will be taken as proof?"

Yusuf looked at her quizzically.

"Where did you hear that?"

"The words are mine," she said, emboldened. "But every woman knows them."

She was right, he admitted to himself. A woman's word held little value here. Women themselves seemed to hold little value here. But Yusuf couldn't stop now. He would press her because he wanted to get to the heart of the story. This would be the moment that redefined the case. Zeba would break down and be completely honest with him and he would put together a magnificent defense, the likes of which had never been seen in this town, maybe in this country.

"Listen, this is a whole new case now. I've got—"

Zeba's head lifted suddenly. Urgently.

"Did you see him?"

"Who?"

"My son, Basir. Did you see him?" She was leaning across the table, her palms pressing onto its wooden surface.

"No, I didn't see him. Did you hear what I said?"

"Did you hear anything about him? Are they all right? Did anyone tell you about him and the girls? You said you talked to people. People must know how they're doing."

Yusuf took a deep breath in and exhaled slowly. She was entitled to inquire about her children, even if that meant diverting his questions.

"I'm sorry, but I think Kamal's family is keeping them at home. I didn't get much information from anyone, but no one said anything worrisome either. I'm sure they're as well as they possibly could be given the circumstances."

"Yes, they're probably fine," she mumbled.

"Khanum Zeba, it's really important for us to focus on you now," he said gently. "I think there's a way to defend you."

It occurred to Zeba that just a few moments ago she had been watching a stupid card game. How could she have gone from that moment to this one without much warning?

"I know about the girl."

Zeba stared at the table until the grain of the wood blurred. She leaped ahead, skipping his questions and arriving at the inevitable conclusion.

"Even if I am released from here, I won't get my children back. If I cannot have my children, there is no reason for me to leave this place."

Yusuf leaned back in his chair. She was right. The odds of Kamal's family returning the children to their mother if she were released were slim. Yusuf spoke again.

"Khanum, I said I know about the girl."

The girl. All this because of a little girl who had been stupid enough to get within reach of Kamal. Zeba didn't know how he'd lured her into their yard but he had. The poor thing had been so frightened. Zeba could still see her eyes, wild and round with shame. She had looked so much like her own daughters. It could have been Shabnam or Kareema. Feeling took so much less time and energy than thinking. Zeba hadn't paused to ask questions. She'd seen everything she needed to on the girl's face, the desperate way she clutched her pants in her hand.

And Kamal. Kamal had stood before her, his back to the afternoon sun. He'd been nothing but a silhouette, the dark shape of a man she hardly recognized. He'd dusted his shirt off. He'd been flustered, nothing more. He'd started mumbling something, but Zeba couldn't hear him over the roaring in her ears, loud enough to drown out any reasons he might have offered for her to ignore the gruesome scene she'd just stumbled upon.

Kamal wanted her to be something she wasn't. He wanted her to be the woman who would look away forever.

But she'd seen everything. And Rima was only a few meters away. How could she explain this to the girls? She would never explain it to them. It would be buried with her.

So much had been decided in the space of seconds, in a span of time too short to accommodate thoughts but with only enough room for reflexes.

When had she picked up the hatchet? Zeba closed her eyes. She couldn't say for certain. She didn't even remember seeing it leaning against the side of the house. Kamal must have left it there, though Zeba couldn't remember the last time she'd seen him hold it. How often had she asked him to put it away so that the children wouldn't hurt themselves with it?

Yusuf watched his client withdraw. He let her be, hoping that her thoughts would lead her to a place of use to him.

"The girl, Khanum. She was the reason for all this."

Was he asking her or seeking confirmation?

She was too young to be so damaged. Had she been the first one? It was too late to ask Kamal. Was that the first time he'd hurt that girl? By the look on her face, Zeba would guess so.

"There was no girl," Zeba said flatly.

"There was no girl?"

"There was no girl," Zeba said, each word steeped in resolve.

Yusuf sat directly across from her. Their eyes met, each daring the other to back down.

"But there was, and that girl changes everything."

"Did you talk with anyone else?"

"What do you mean?"

"Did you talk with anyone else in my village?"

Yusuf tapped a finger on the table, the ticking of a metronome.

"I didn't talk to the girl's family, if that's what you're asking me."

Zeba hoped, for the sake of the girl, that it was humanly possible to forget something so horrible and pretend it had never happened. She needed that to be true.

"Why don't you want to let the judge know what happened? This girl could be the way for you to—"

Zeba's face hardened. She stared directly at Yusuf and spoke with absolute clarity.

"She is just a girl and I won't do that to her. Listen to what I'm saying, Yusuf. There was no girl."

Yusuf lowered his voice. He understood, somewhat, that Zeba was trying to protect the girl, but he couldn't let her sacrifice herself unnecessarily.

"I'm sure we can do this in a way that won't bring attention to her or cause her any problems. We may not even need to talk to her. But we've got to share some of this information if we're going to make any kind of reasonable defense for you. There's no other way to get you out of here. A man was killed."

Zeba scowled.

"Anything I say will ruin her. I don't know if her family knows. What if they don't know? What if she's okay now? That possibility is everything to me. I know what they might do to her if they find out. You may not, but I do. Every woman in Chil Mahtab knows. Every woman and girl in Afghanistan knows!"

Yusuf bit his lip. Zeba was right about that. It was a truth he understood the moment his foot hit this soil. It was all about honor. Honor was a boulder that men placed on the shoulders of their daughters, their sisters, and their wives. The many stories in Chil Mahtab were evidence of that fact. This girl had lost her father's honor in Zeba's courtyard. If he knew that something had happened to her—the details hardly mattered—she might not be forgiven, even though she was an innocent child.

Whatever Kamal had done to that girl might have been just the beginning of her woes.

Zeba's eyes drifted off. A guard was slowly walking past the interview room, with a step so heavy that it had to be deliberate. Zeba watched her, her eyes going glassy again. The path was simple to her. She looked utterly unconflicted in that moment.

"Do you think Kamal was the only person killed that day?" she asked in a hollow and monotonous voice. "He wasn't. I was dead the moment his blood spilled. That girl was dead the moment she was alone with him. There were three dead bodies in my home, though only one had a decent burial and mourners to pray for his soul. They prayed for him. They are still praying for him. They have marked the fortieth day of his passing as if he were some decent soul to be missed. They will shake their heads and talk about what a shame it was to lose their brother, their cousin, their uncle. They don't know what shame is, nor do they know that there are lots of ways to take a life."

Yusuf was silent. The guard outside had disappeared around the corner for a few moments only to return. She glanced into the room and continued to stroll past them, stopping briefly to adjust the belt on her uniform.

Yusuf could not argue that defiled girls were worth very little. If something were to happen to that young girl, Yusuf did not want to be responsible either. But there was the possibility this girl's family would be different.

"Did you hear about the nine-year-old girl who was raped by their local mullah about a year ago? Her parents were paying him to instruct her on how to read Qur'an. Her parents tied him to a chair and cut off his nose and ears. Then there was the case in Kunduz. That ten-year-old girl testified before a judge, and her rapist was sentenced to twenty years in prison. Not every family considers this a shame they can't recover from. There can be justice."

"You're talking to me about two cases in a land of millions. How can I burden that girl with such a risk?"

Yusuf stood, frustrated. He walked the short length of the room and returned helplessly to his seat.

"I don't know how else to defend you," he admitted. He ran his fingers through his hair brusquely, feeling his professionalism slip away from him. Maybe Aneesa had been right to warn him against taking this case. He'd pushed it further than anyone else probably would have, and all that had gotten him was information he couldn't use.

"I did nothing for too long," Zeba whispered. "I lived with my eyes and ears closed when I should have been paying attention. I should have known sooner. But I was not vigilant. If I did nothing then, I can do nothing now. I will do nothing and I will say nothing. I refuse to bring any more shame to my children."

Yusuf's elbows sat on the table, the cuffs of his sleeves rolled back. She wouldn't budge, he knew, but he wasn't quite ready to give up on her altogether. Knowing about the girl only made him want to defend her more. He could only imagine what the little girl had been through. Too bad the world wouldn't stand and applaud Zeba for what she'd done.

"Are you saying to me that you killed your husband?"

"Looks that way, doesn't it? Why would you doubt it if everyone says it's so? I've even confessed to it according to my arrest record. You should drop this case."

"I won't do that," Yusuf said defiantly. "I've got to find a defense that will stand up to the prosecution's case."

"God is great and you are young, Yusuf-*jan*," Zeba said as she pushed her chair back and stood to leave. "There are plenty of innocent people to defend. Stop wasting your time on the guilty."

CHAPTER 29

"A DEFENDANT'S MOTHER HAS NEVER BEEN PRESENT FOR THESE proceedings," the *qazi* said. He rubbed his palms on the end of his tunic and wondered why they were so sweaty. The prosecutor shot him a curious look.

Gulnaz sat with her back as straight as the chair itself. Her eyes were lightly lined in kohl, which made Qazi Najeeb want to touch her cheek as he stared into their green depths. He cleared his throat and reached for the *tasbeh*, the string of amber prayer beads on his desk.

"I am sure I am not the first mother to be concerned about her daughter's case," Gulnaz said as she set her purse on the floor next to her.

"No, you are not," the prosecutor agreed, reaching for a biscuit from the table in the middle of the room. He bit in and felt the buttery cookie crumble in his mouth. By the nod of his head, Gulnaz could tell the taste of it agreed with him.

"These are delicious, Khanum," the prosecutor declared.

"Yusuf-*jan*, you haven't tried one yet, have you?" Gulnaz asked gently.

Yusuf shook his head.

"No, Khanum, I've just eaten, but thank you," he said tightly. A plate full of biscuits was a far cry from bribery if that's what Gulnaz was trying to accomplish.

"Maybe later then," Gulnaz suggested.

"You don't have to ask me," Qazi Najeeb said before Gulnaz even offered the cookies. The prosecutor held the plate out and watched as the judge took two and placed them on a napkin before him. "When I was a boy, there was nothing I enjoyed more during Ramadan. Before the sun came up, my mother would make me a mug of sweet tea and cream and let me eat as many of her homemade biscuits as I could stuff into my stomach. Part of me looked forward to Ramadan for that very reason."

"I made these for my family during Ramadan as well. They would tell me it would have been difficult to survive the hours without these."

Gulnaz had asked for nothing more than to be present for the discussion, especially since it had become clear that Zeba could not be. Hearing of her recent collapse in the prison hallway, the judge had decided to leave her out of the proceedings.

"I hope that Zeba will be back to herself soon. We'll have to continue in her absence, and I don't think anyone wants to delay this case any longer."

"She wanted to be here," Yusuf offered. "But she hasn't spoken in two days. I checked on her again this morning, and she is not improved at all. She's actually gotten worse, in my opinion. The director of the prison told me that she's been moaning and rocking in her cell. Her roommates complain that they wake to find her whispering to herself and they are frightened."

"What are they frightened of?" asked the judge as he brushed crumbs off his desk.

Yusuf had watched Zeba leave the interview room the day he'd confronted her about the girl. She'd walked as if each step had been a great effort. She'd drifted to the wall and leaned against it, her fingers looking for something to grip on to. Again and again, Yusuf had asked her to talk to him, but her eyes had gone wild. Her words were incomprehensible, and those that he could make out didn't make sense anyway. Her roommates had been quite shaken up at the sight of her.

"They're frightened because she's unstable. I was there, sir, and I can tell you that she is not in her right mind. I'm sure I don't have to remind you of what happened when she was last here in your office. If you think that was bad, you would be horrified to see her now."

Yusuf stole a quick glance at Gulnaz, who had drawn her lips together tightly as she listened. Her eyes were lowered, staring at the floral motif of the small rug beneath their feet. She seemed neither shocked nor saddened to hear of her daughter's condition.

"It makes no difference. We can continue with the case, as the *qazi* has said," the prosecutor agreed with a wave of his hand. "It shouldn't take long anyway. We have a signed statement from the day of her arrest and we've got a dead husband. Let's wrap this up, and we can move on to the sentencing."

"I don't think it's that simple," Yusuf said. He braced himself for the reaction he was about to get. "I don't think Khanum Zeba is in her right state of mind and, thus, is incapable of standing trial."

"What are you talking about? What do her senses have to do with anything?" The prosecutor was incredulous. The *qazi* leaned forward as if he may have misheard Yusuf's words.

"Are you suggesting we delay this again?"

"Qazi-*sahib,* I am simply stating that she's not competent to stand trial, which means we cannot try this case now. It's not really a postponement as much as it is allowing for a proper procedure to be followed."

"Proper procedure? What you're suggesting is anything but proper procedure," the prosecutor roared.

"She's upset," the *qazi* agreed. "But that doesn't mean that we can ignore what happened."

"She's more than upset," Yusuf explained. "From what I have seen, she is suffering from mental disease, and I do believe this mental incapacitation began before she was brought to Chil Mahtab. I believe it existed in her well before the day her husband was killed. I think she was not in her right state of mind, and we can all see that she is not in her right state of mind now, either. I think she should undergo a formal evaluation and obtain treatment for her condition. That's what the law prescribes for situations like this one."

The truth was Yusuf wasn't fully convinced of Zeba's insanity. He'd made a case for it, but given what she'd been through, he imagined the way she'd been acting to be almost rational. She'd been living with a man who drank and beat her. She'd raised four children with him lording over them. She'd walked into her own backyard to find her husband violating a child in the worst way imaginable. Maybe this wasn't the first time. And their three daughters—had he violated them as well? Two of them were close in age to the girl the raisin vendor described. If the thought crossed Yusuf's mind, it must have boiled with horror in Zeba's.

In all honesty, she probably had killed him. Yusuf had to admit that given her motive and the scene of the crime, little else made sense. She would have been out of her mind to do nothing. Yusuf, had he been in her shoes, would have gladly slammed the hatchet into the man's skull.

It was his job to defend her, and he didn't have much in his arsenal to use. If this was a stretch, so be it.

Gulnaz watched the men's faces. They all seemed to have forgotten she was in the room, which was fine by her. She only needed to hear what they were saying.

"The law? Listen, I haven't objected to much until now, but it's clear that you've come here with some kind of American agenda."

Yusuf gritted his teeth. The prosecutor's case was a handful of handwritten documents, composed mostly of Zeba's "confession," which had been written by a police officer. It wasn't a case at all. Anywhere else in the world, the prosecutor wouldn't be able to call himself a lawyer, and yet here, sitting in a ridiculous armchair, he could accuse Yusuf of representing foreign interests.

"I'm here to defend a woman who's been accused of a horrible crime and had her children taken away. I'm here because if we want the

Afghan judicial system to have any kind of integrity, we have to follow the procedural code and give accused individuals their due process. I know you don't care much for due process but it's important."

"I do my job. You have no right to question my professionalism."

"Don't I? My job is to question how well you do yours. And I have lots of questions for you." Yusuf's voice cut through the room like the sound of glass breaking. Even Gulnaz was impressed.

"What questions?"

The prosecutor was still in the armchair but barely. He had both hands on the armrests with elbows bent, as if he were about to lift off the seat. He looked at Qazi Najeeb who sat back in his chair and crossed his legs.

"I'm interested to know what questions you have as well," he said quietly.

Expecting the judge to intervene and squash the discussion, the prosecutor huffed with annoyance.

"To start, I wonder if you conducted any kind of real investigation. Article 145 of the Criminal Procedure Code states: 'Investigation is required for all felony and misdemeanor crimes and it is performed in the presence of the accused person's defense lawyer by the prosecutor in accordance with the provisions of this law.'"

"Investigation? We have a signed statement from Khanum Zeba!" the prosecutor insisted, waving a folded piece of paper in the air.

"She did not write that statement. She's a literate woman—her mother can attest to that and she can prove it herself. If that were her statement, it should have been written by her own hand."

"From what I was told, she was hysterical and so the police officer making the arrest did his job and transcribed what she recounted to him. That's her thumbprint on the bottom of the page," he shouted, his finger jabbing at a blot of blue ink. "Why would she sign it if it weren't her statement?"

"She was hysterical when she was arrested? By hysterical do you mean crazy? That's exactly my point, friend. I'm glad you agree."

"That's not what I said. You're trying to put words in my mouth!"

"Let me continue. Article 145 talks about a few more requirements for an investigation. Did the police go to the scene of the crime to collect evidence? Did the police interview any one of their neighbors? Did you try to ascertain if there was any possible motive for this crime? Did you have any experts speak with Khanum Zeba to assess her mental status? Has he, Qazi Najeeb?"

"If anyone's mental status needs to be assessed, it's yours. The police are the ones who conduct discoveries. It's a simple, black-and-white case, and I'm sure Qazi Najeeb will tell you that."

"I'll speak for myself!" Qazi Najeeb interjected. He hadn't expected today's trial proceedings to be so animated, especially with Gulnaz present. Gulnaz, as far as he could tell, did not seem bothered by the shouting match. She remained composed, listening intently.

The judge continued. "Let's move on. There was as much investigation as there typically is for a case like this. Your client's been charged with the crime. We know the crime happened. We've got a written statement in which she confesses to killing her husband."

"Your Honor, on that piece of paper is a confession of a woman who hit her husband on top of his head with a hatchet."

"Yes?"

"Kamal died from a hatchet wound to the back of the head, low enough that it was near his neck. If she did confess, she would know where his wound was, wouldn't she?"

"On top of the head . . . back of the head . . . you're really reaching."

"Why are we wasting our time on this?" the prosecutor asked.

"I don't consider it a waste of time to do my job," Yusuf shot back. "Maybe you should ask yourself if you're doing yours."

Qazi Najeeb stroked his short beard and felt a few crumbs between his fingers. Of course, a case involving the *murshid*'s daughter would not be straightforward. He could let these two lawyers take cheap shots at each other but he had to do it in a way that would save face for him.

"Go ahead, Yusuf."

The prosecutor huffed and sat back in his chair with his arms folded across his chest.

"This is what happens when we let foreigners stick their noses in our affairs," he muttered.

"Article sixty-seven of the penal code of Afghanistan states," Yusuf recited with his eyes set on the prosecutor, "that 'a person who while committing a crime lacks his senses and intelligence due to insanity or other mental disease has no penal responsibility and shall not be punished.' "

"I've never heard of such a thing," the prosecutor said, chuckling.

Both the judge and Yusuf noticed Gulnaz square her gaze on him.

"And I've never had such a case," Qazi Najeeb explained. "Yusuf, this is not the type of defense I was expecting to hear. Maybe you want to reconsider. Khanum Zeba is obviously distressed, but that could be because she's thinking about the day she plunged a hatchet into her husband's head. Women have gone mad over much smaller matters, I'm sure we can all agree."

The *qazi* took a sip of his tea. The biscuits, though delicious, were dry and seemed to have caught on the inside of his throat. Still, he found himself reaching for another.

"These are delicious, Khanum," he said absently. "My own mother's biscuits were not this good, God rest her soul. What did you put in these?"

"May you eat in good health, Qazi-*sahib*," Gulnaz replied politely. "They are nothing but flour, butter, and sugar."

"Mm, delicious." The *qazi* wiped the crumbs from his mouth before he spoke again. "I have an idea that might help us in this odd situation. I have a good friend who provides treatment for the insane. He's been quite successful curing some very seriously affected people. Maybe we can ask him to evaluate Khanum Zeba. Why not follow the letter of the law in this case? We might make a name for ourselves here."

"Make a name for ourselves? Your Honor, I thought we'd have this case decided today or in the next week. If he were asking for mercy because she's a mother or if she stated her husband tried to kill her, then maybe there would be something worth talking about but this . . . this . . . insanity excuse . . ."

"It's the law," the judge said with amusement. "We cannot argue with that."

The prosecutor was astounded. Qazi Najeeb had a reputation for being objective and difficult—though not impossible—to bribe. Still, this was unexpected behavior.

"Qazi-*sahib*, this is a great idea!" Yusuf said excitedly. If Zeba remained in her current state, the evaluation would provide a quick answer in their favor. "Your friend is a doctor? Is he at the hospital in the city?"

"He's better than a doctor," Qazi Najeeb said proudly. "Doctors can't do anything for the poor people who've lost their minds. They can barely fix a broken leg. He's a mullah with a special talent for healing the insane. I met him years ago when I was living closer to my father's home."

"I don't understand."

"Don't worry. He's the best person for this." The judge looked quite pleased with himself, as if he'd personally solved the mystery of who had murdered Kamal.

"With all due respect, Qazi-*sahib*, this is not something that requires evaluation. Was she crazy? She killed her husband in their own home—of course she's crazy! But that doesn't mean that she isn't guilty." The prosecutor turned his attention to Yusuf. "And if you're saying she's crazy, are you saying that she did kill her husband or are you still maintaining that she didn't?"

Yusuf took a deep breath. That was the question he had been hoping the prosecutor wouldn't ask. The judge intervened just as he opened his mouth to try to answer.

"It's been too long since I last spoke with my friend. I believe this is a sign that I should reach out to him. God is great, my friends. We will reach a conclusion soon. I know the victim's family is waiting and trusting that we will make the right decision."

"Exactly!" exclaimed the prosecutor. "What are we supposed to tell them? That the murderess might have had a temper? That some djinn had taken control of her body and turned her into a bloodthirsty husband killer?"

"We won't tell them anything," said the judge. "We'll take Khanum Zeba to the shrine and have the mullah look at her. If he thinks she's not crazy, there's nothing more to it. She'll be brought back to Chil Mahtab and we'll decide on her guilt based on what we have here."

Yusuf fanned himself with his notepad. The opinion of some shaman was not what he'd been hoping to pin his defense on.

"What about a hospital? There are mental health professionals that we can work with. With all due respect, Your Honor, there are doctors in this country to tell us what we need to know."

"We've never done anything like this before, Agha-*jan*," the judge explained with a hint of condescension. "The nearest hospital is nearly two days' travel from here and is always filled to capacity. The community trusts this mullah. We'll get his expert opinion quickly."

Yusuf feared pressing the judge too much and losing this narrow opening. He had to bend, he realized, if he wanted Zeba to have any chance at all.

"Khanum Gulnaz, did your daughter have any mental problems as a child?"

Gulnaz rubbed her hands together. Dust had clung to her skin on the long journey from home to the *qazi*'s office.

She thought of all the things she could say. Zeba talked to herself as a small child. She'd once woken in the night screaming that she'd seen a djinn in her bedroom. She'd claimed to see letters in the flames that licked at an aluminum pot. She could've used everything Gulnaz had taught her over the years, but she chose to live without power. Even now, she would not say exactly what had happened in that courtyard. Were these not the signs of a mentally defective person?

"She was a plain and ordinary child, Your Honor," she said mournfully. "But she is not the same now. Something terrible has happened to my daughter and I cannot imagine what it is. It's as if her mind was poisoned."

"I can't believe we're actually considering this. Tell me, what happens if she is deemed crazy?" the prosecutor asked.

Gulnaz looked at the judge and spoke before he could.

"But this is wrong. Let her go to a hospital. My father would tell you what some of those mullahs do in the name of treatment is un-Islamic."

The judge met Gulnaz's eyes and felt the moisture of his palms again, the tickle at the back of his neck.

"The mullah is a remarkable healer and I trust his assessment. Zeba would be in good hands."

"And if she is crazy and he is able to heal her, then she can be tried and found guilty. Fine. You can let me know when you want to reconvene," the prosecutor said impatiently. "Whether it's today or next month, Zeba will be found guilty."

Yusuf and the prosecutor stood. Gulnaz picked her handbag off the floor and brought the strap over her arm. The judge felt his face warm to watch her, as if he'd spied her slipping a dress over her bare shoulder instead.

Did a man ever grow too gray and wrinkled to have such thoughts? He was helpless.

Qazi Najeeb picked up his *tasbeh* and began thumbing; the beads felt cool and reassuring against his clammy palm. He would think of her later, he knew, when he met his wife's dull eyes and ready scowl. How different his story would have been, he thought, had Gulnaz become his bride all those years ago. They would have been content as husband and wife. She, the daughter of a respected *murshid* and he, the ambitious son of a hardworking man. The judge uncrossed his legs and stole a glance at the clock on the wall, the second hand ticking ever forward. There was no way to go back in time.

Despite all his efforts, there wasn't much justice in this world.

CHAPTER 30

"RAISINS, WALNUTS, ALMONDS! THE RAISINS ARE GOOD FOR YOUR diabetes, the walnuts will cure rheumatism, and the almonds will cool your wife's temper! Pine nuts, roasted chickpeas, and dried apricots! Pine nuts so fresh you'll be knocking on my door in the middle of the night asking for more!"

Walid's throat felt gritty. He coughed a bit and took a sip of water from a crumpled plastic bottle he kept tucked next to the bags of walnuts. He shouted the same pitch he'd been using for years, and it no longer drew the smiles it once had. People didn't chuckle or make conversation. It seemed everyone was too tired for any of that anymore.

Walid walked in a cloud of dust, spun into the air by the wheels of his cart and a light wind coming down from the mountains to the west. He was nearing their block for the third time today. Usually, he only passed through a street once.

"Ramadan is coming! Don't go hungry a day before you're sup-posed to!"

Two school-age boys raced by him, passing an underinflated soccer ball back and forth. Walid brought his sleeve to his nose and mouth. He'd always had bad lungs. His mother told him it was because she'd been caught in one of the worst dust storms in history while she was pregnant with him. He'd grown accustomed to feeling like he was sucking air through a straw, but today was particularly hard.

He set his cart down and placed his hands squarely on his hips. He was in front of their house. Where was the little girl? Was she in school? Was she just a few feet away from—close enough to hear him call?

Walid coughed and felt something loosen in his chest. The dust settled a bit, and he took a long breath through pursed lips.

Why had he, a wheezing street vendor, been charged to hold her secrets? He could barely feed his own family. He was a man of faults. He had gossiped and cursed. He had been short-tempered with his wife and children. He had done nothing when his sister begged him to talk to her abusive husband on her behalf. He had cheated nearly everyone in the village at one time or another, charging some more than others when he didn't like the way they looked at him or if they hadn't purchased anything from him in a long time. He lied about where his walnuts came from and how fresh they were. When he'd found maggots crawling between them, he'd simply plucked the intruders out and returned the lot to the cart, thinking of the many hungry bellies waiting on his return at home. He prayed and taught his children to do the same. He was not a very learned man and feared his family suffered for it. He was nothing of use.

His wife cried at times, heartbroken for a girl she'd never met. The girl was not their child. Why should they bother themselves with this? Had they not enough to worry about under their small, patchwork roof?

"Raisins, golden ones the color of a *pari*'s hair and just as enticing! Green ones so perfect your husband will forget his troubles! Black ones to give you the figure of a movie star!"

His voice was raspy. He'd thought of bringing one of his children with him. If he could teach his son to sound the call into the streets, he could save his breath for pushing the cart around. But the boy was young yet, and Walid wanted him to go to school. If they could read and write, they might stand a chance, and he would need them to care for him in his old age, which seemed to be fast approaching. Judgment Day.

Walid would have much to answer for on Judgment Day. What would the most righteous person do with this? Could he do better than standing outside the poor girl's door and reminding her of the raisins that had ruined her?

He would stay away from this block. He would never hawk his raisins or nuts on this street again. He would lower his voice even one block away so she wouldn't be tortured by his ridiculous chants. He would leave the poor girl in peace. It wouldn't be great, but it would be better.

Walid heard the creak of metal behind him.

He should have rejoiced. He'd spent years walking up and down these streets, hoping to hear that creak, the sign that he would sell a sack of walnuts or a half kilo of raisins. He would laugh and smile and watch walnuts tumble into a brown paper bag. He would take a few bills and know that there would be rice, tomatoes, and onions for tomorrow or the day after. He would have a reason to wake up in the morning and bring his goods through the streets again. The sound of a door opening was, usually, a blessing.

He knew, without looking, that someone stood in that doorway. Someone was staring at his back and waiting for him to turn around.

The door scraped again, slowly and deliberately. Walid breathed a sigh of relief to hear it close. He'd been released. There would not be a conversation today, and he had promised himself a thousand times, in the few weighted seconds that had just passed, that he would never dare to roll his cart down this block again.

Walid picked up the handles of his cart, his shoulder blades pulling together with resolve. *Leave the family to their private matters,* he told himself. It was the only respectable thing to do. His wife would understand. She would stop looking from their daughters to him with those dark, castigating eyes.

The wheels had not yet made one full rotation before Walid was stopped short.

"Agha-*sahib*, don't go."

He took a deep breath and turned around. The metal door wasn't closed at all. It was open, so narrowly that Walid could not see the speaker's face but wide enough that a mother's heart could spill its caged sorrows into the unpaved street.

CHAPTER 31

YUSUF FELT THE CAR'S SUSPENSION STRUGGLE WITH THE ROUGH road. With every jostle, he was further convinced that coming to the shrine was an even worse idea than he'd originally thought.

The car had puttered down the long dirt road leading to a small one-story clay-and-mud building with blue window frames and an arched doorway. A man emerged just as they parked the car.

Zeba stared out the window and moaned softly. "Yusuf, why did you let them bring me here?"

"I didn't have much choice," he mumbled. If they'd been assigned to any other judge, they wouldn't be here, Yusuf noted. Then again, with any other judge, Zeba might have been convicted long ago.

"Welcome," the man said as Yusuf, Zeba, the prosecutor, and one male prison guard stepped out of the car. "I am Mullah Habibullah. Welcome to the shrine."

Zeba's ankles had been chained together. Yusuf, distracted by the surroundings, did not notice her shuffle her feet to position herself closer to him than the male prison guard.

The prosecutor shook Habibullah's hands and put a hand on his elbow.

"Thank you, Mullah-*sahib*. I'm sure your esteemed friend, Qazi Najeeb, explained the situation to you. We're here to have this woman evaluated," he said, nodding his head in Zeba's direction. "She's killed her husband and has been acting erratically. We need your opinion on whether or not she's insane."

Yusuf stepped toward Habibullah with an outstretched hand that Habibullah shook firmly.

"I'm this woman's defense lawyer," Yusuf explained.

"I thought you might be," Habibullah said with a hint of a smile. He turned his attention to Zeba, studying her while she kept her eyes to the ground. He was a slight man, dressed in a beige tunic and pantaloons. Over his tunic, he wore a military green vest with zippered pockets. The end of a small turban dangled past his left ear and hung as low as his salt-and-pepper beard.

"Forgive me, Mullah-*sahib*, but how long do you think you'll need to evaluate this woman? I want to be back in the office in the afternoon."

For once, Yusuf and the prosecutor were on the same page. Yusuf had promised to report back to Aneesa, who had seemed entertained by the prospect of his client being evaluated at the local shrine.

He'll find her insane only if he thinks he can save her, she'd predicted. *But I still don't think the judge is going to stand by any insanity defense. It's a reach, even for someone as optimistic as you.*

"Gentleman, I can sense your uncertainty. Let me show you around, and I'm sure you'll feel more reassured."

Habibullah walked, his fingers casually intertwined behind his back, toward a small stand-alone structure that stood in the shade of a looming acacia tree.

The lawyers shot each other a look before following.

"Bring her," the mullah called out without turning his head. The prison guard let out a heavy sigh. He crouched down and undid the shackles from Zeba's ankles, replacing them on her wrists. When he was done, he motioned for her to follow the others.

They bowed their heads as they stepped through the low door frame. Inside the mausoleum, the ceilings were elevated, and one side of the room had a small bench built into the clay wall. In the center of the room was a concrete tomb, over which neatly lay a green cloth with gold-embroidered Qur'anic scripture. The room was barely large enough for all of them to fit inside. A narrow shaft of daylight entered through a rectangular window and shone onto the green flag, on a patch it had faded over time.

Zeba turned away from the tomb. There was too much death in this small room for her liking. Her eyes fell on a few handwritten messages scrawled on the walls.

There is no God but Allah.

Allah, the All-Knowing and the Beneficent.

"This tomb, my friends, is the tomb of Hazrat Rahman. He was a wise and learned man, a true disciple of the Qur'an. He traveled to Mecca twenty times in his life, and it's widely known that he was the founder of this village."

Yusuf looked at Zeba, who had moved from the corner toward the small window. She was staring out at the chain-link fence with ribbons of every color tied to the latticework, loose ends flapping hopefully in the soft breeze. Just beyond the fence was an open yard with an L-shaped structure on one end. Yusuf saw Zeba's eyes narrow in on the long flat-roofed structure, barely tall enough for a man to stand in. He could see her breathing quicken.

"What's that building over there, Mullah-*sahib*? The one past the fence . . ."

The mullah pointed to the door.

"Let's step outside and I will tell you."

Zeba was glad to be back out of the stifling room.

"That's where I've treated some people who have come to me with very serious problems of mind and soul," he explained, his voice rich with pride. "This shrine is stronger than any medication, when one believes."

"What kind of treatments do you provide?" Yusuf asked, nearly choking on the word "treatments."

Too many people, Yusuf thought, put faith in talismans, trinkets, and superstitions. But Yusuf was also hesitant to criticize. He'd suffered breathing problems as a child. When he was two years old, he'd had an attack so severe that his mother and father had feared he wouldn't survive. His mother had taken him to a doctor, but the elixir he'd prescribed had done very little for Yusuf. His mother, watching her son's stomach heave and chest rattle with cough, had then taken him to a shrine in Kabul where a mullah had prayed for him and another man had written a talisman. It was a tiny folded piece of paper wrapped in cloth that Yusuf's mother had pinned to the inside of his shirt, just over his left chest. In two days, his shortness of breath had resolved, and in the following years, his asthmatic attacks came much less often and were much milder. His mother had been convinced that the talisman, not the doctor's prescription, had done the trick. Yusuf, having heard the story a few dozen times growing up, had accepted it as truth.

"Our prayers are more powerful than any tool, any drug, any weapon. I pray for the poor individuals who come here to Hazrat Rahman's tomb and those who tie their wishes to the fence. God is listening, always, to those who believe."

"And what's over there?" Yusuf said, shielding his eyes from the sun with a hand. He pointed to the structure Zeba had noticed from inside the mausoleum. He could make out what looked like a row of honeycomb cells, open to the fenced-in courtyard.

Zeba walked to a large rock and sat on it. She let her head fall toward her knees. The prison guard eyed her with suspicion but let her be.

"That's where I treat some of the more serious cases," the mullah said with his head cocked to the side. "Not everyone's illness can be cured with a simple prayer. Sometimes, it takes a period of cleansing the mind and body. Sometimes those who are ill need to be confined in a place of solitude where their energies can be channeled into conquering their maladies. This is that place."

"You have people in there?"

"I do," Mullah Habibullah stated. "Sometimes they wander through the yard. Most of the time they sleep or talk to themselves."

"What about food and drink?" Yusuf asked. The prosecutor listened in. He was familiar with this shrine, though he'd never been here personally.

"They are fed bread and black pepper along with plenty of water. These are the foods that we've learned treat the ailments of the mind. Other foods can poison the healing process or delay their recovery. This is the best way to get true relief."

"Bread and black pepper? That's all they're fed?" Yusuf was incredulous. How could such a place actually exist? There were hospitals in every major city, and the nearest one was not that far from this shrine. Why wouldn't families take their loved ones there instead?"

"For every patient those hospitals treat, there are a hundred more waiting to be seen. You're skeptical of this idea, but that's only because you haven't seen what this place can do. I assure you, if you speak to the patients who have passed through this shrine, they will tell you how grateful they are for having been cured here."

Yusuf bit his tongue.

"Mullah-*sahib*," the prosecutor said politely. "I'm very glad to have seen the shrine and hear about your work. The judge spoke highly of your skills and we are eager to hear your assessment of this woman. What do you need to do to evaluate her?"

"Yes, the woman." The mullah turned his attention to Zeba, who looked up at the circle of men standing a few feet away. "Let me speak with her. Let us go inside, and my son will serve you a cup of tea to revive your spirits."

Yusuf stole one last glance at the cells beyond the fence, wondering if he could spy one of the patients the mullah was treating, but there was not even a shadow of movement. *The mullah could be blowing smoke*, he thought. *There might not be a single soul in those cells.*

They went into the building where a burgundy carpet with an elephant foot motif lay on the floor. There were two floor cushions with wool-covered pillows resting against the wall.

The prosecutor took a seat on the cushions and a boy, no more than ten years old, came in from a back room with a silver tray holding four small cups of tea. He placed a cup before each of the lawyers and took the other two to the plastic table and chairs outside where Mullah Habibullah sat facing Zeba. The prison guard stood a few feet away, talking quietly on his mobile phone.

"What do you think of this place?" the mullah asked.

Zeba refused to meet his gaze. She stared at the branches of the acacia tree. The mullah's eyebrows lifted with interest.

"What crime have you been arrested for?" The mullah's eyes were soft and reassuring.

Zeba's voice was raspy. The dusty air had dried her throat, but she refused to take even a sip of the steamy amber tea.

"What do you want from me?"

Mullah Habibullah was taken aback by her acidic tone. Not even the most insane patient had been so insolent.

"Why do you ask?"

Zeba looked away, as if she'd already lost interest in her own question.

"Why are you in jail?" the mullah repeated.

"He must have told you."

"I want to hear it from you."

Zeba smirked.

"Because God intended for me to go to prison and I am His disciple. Because some men can talk from both corners of their mouths at the same time. Because my lawyer thinks he is going to save my life when my mother and grandfather, with all the tricks they have between them, could not do a thing for me."

The mullah's eyes narrowed.

"Your mother and your grandfather?"

He leaned in closer, staring so hard that Zeba turned in her chair and kept her shoulder toward him. She lowered her eyes.

"Who is your grandfather?"

"My grandfather, Safatullah, is a *murshid*. He's not known here. This is too far from our village."

The mullah nodded slowly.

"I see," he whispered. He stood and wandered a few steps away. His back was to Zeba as he stared at the spreading branches of the acacia tree.

"They say you killed your husband. Did you?"

Zeba laughed.

"Everyone wants to talk about my dead husband—except me."

"Was he a bad man?"

"I said I don't want to talk about him. Listen, Mullah-*sahib*, I'm not crazy. There's no reason for me to be here. If they think I should be in prison, then send me back there, please."

The mullah cleared his throat before turning again to face Zeba.

"You must know what happened to your husband. Have you told your family anything? Your . . . your mother or your grandfather?"

"There's nothing for me to say. They have their police reports."

"I heard as much," he said, returning to his chair. He pulled it a few inches closer to Zeba before settling in. Zeba tried not to recoil too visibly at his closeness. Yusuf and the prosecutor were just inside, she reminded herself.

"What has your family said about this? Do they believe in your innocence?"

"My mother . . ." Zeba began. She was surprised to hear her voice quaver with emotion at the mention of her mother. "She has always believed in my innocence. There is no mother like her. My brother found me a lawyer. They are my family. I have no one else."

"Your grandfather?"

"Whether he believes in my innocence or not doesn't matter. He can do nothing for me."

"Is that hatred in your voice?"

"For my grandfather?" Zeba was taken aback at the mullah's comment.

"No, not your grandfather. Your husband," he said pensively. "The wrong spouse can make a person crazy. Or can at least make a person do crazy things."

"I told you," Zeba said through gritted teeth. "I'm not crazy."

Crazy was a river. It swept some away, drowning them even as they clawed for a rocky hold. If she let herself think too long on what had happened to Kamal or what Kamal had done or what had become of her children or what might have already happened to her children, Zeba felt the unmistakable rush of water between her toes, then lapping at her calves, cold and threatening.

Zeba fought it off.

"Like an emerald ring," she muttered.

"What did you say?" Mullah Habibullah asked.

"Do you know that if you feed an emerald to a chicken, it will pass through its belly and come out the other side without a mark—once you wipe the shit away, of course. All you have to do is be patient and trust the entrails of the chicken to return the truth to you. Then you know it's really emerald."

The mullah frowned to hear her curse.

"Are you suggesting I pass you through the bowels of a chicken? Would you come out unblemished?"

The thought of being squeezed through the guts of a hen made Zeba's lips curl with amusement. She drew her head scarf across her face to hide her mouth. This was how she kept the floodwaters at bay. She found reasons to smile, even as she sat a few meters away from what looked like a row of crypts.

The mullah noticed the crinkling at the corners of her eyes. He peered at her with curiosity.

"You can't tell by looking at me? You really don't know?" Zeba jeered as she thrust her chair back. "Mullah-*sahib*, I've already slithered through the bowels of a beast. There's no reason to test me anymore."

The mullah picked up the thermos his son had left on the table and refilled his cup. A swirl of black leaves slipped out, a thousand unfurled flags. The leaves had yet to settle when the sound of a rattling chain made Zeba turn her head away from the hills and toward the desiccated honeycomb. The mullah followed her gaze, then traced his path back to her face and the shadows below her eyes. Her face was the shape of an owl's, with round, inky eyes and a prominent widow's peak. Her olive skin was smooth, but the last few weeks had sapped any natural flush from her cheeks.

There was a shout, a man's voice. Zeba couldn't quite make it out at first. She strained her eyes and spotted a flutter at the mouth of the cavelike cell, so subtle that she wondered if she had imagined it. The voice came again, a loud, slow moan.

"God, oh God, what have I done to deserve this? Help me! Someone please help me!"

Another voice followed—it, too, dragged to the mouth of the cave by a chain.

"Shut up, shut up, shut up! God doesn't love you!"

But he wouldn't shut up, whoever the man was. He sat just at the brink of his cell, close enough that daylight fell upon a sliver of his body. Zeba could make out the curved shape of a defeated spine, one gaunt arm, and a cowed head.

"I don't want to be alone! Please don't leave me alone any longer! I swear to you I've been cured! Please let me out . . . I'm going to die here!" It was human but reminded Zeba of the bleating of a sheep being dragged to slaughter, its front legs dragging in the dirt and an instinctive dread vibrating in its soon-to-be-sliced throat.

Zeba's breaths quickened. She bit her tongue.

The mullah took a sip of his tea, drawing it through his pursed lips in an obnoxious slurp that made Zeba want to hurl his cup against the trunk of the acacia tree.

"He is a sick man. When his family brought him to me, he spoke only to demons that no one else could see. He could not even answer his mother or father. But in the twenty-nine days he's spent here, he's shown remarkable improvement. This is what I do," he said, with a regal wave of his hand. "It's my calling. I have given up . . . so much to devote myself to this work. Sometimes we have to make sacrifices to find our true *naseeb*, do you understand? God has instructed me to do this work, and it is for me to obey. I make people well here."

Zeba felt her stomach tighten into a knot. The hairs on her arms prickled. Within those cells was the purest of solitude. From the openings, the ill could see the jagged line of mountains that separated this world from the next.

Zeba could see in the mullah's eyes that he'd already reached his conclusion. Anything she said at this point made no difference. Yusuf would be surprised, but Zeba was not. That was the problem with Yusuf. He devised plans and expected the rest of the world to fall into place.

The lines came to her in a flash:

A woman indignant must suffer from madness.
That ignorant guess is the cause of our sadness!

Yusuf and the prosecutor were at the doorway. They'd grown impatient, and small talk was a chore, especially while the mullah's son sat mutely in the corner of the room.

The prosecutor cleared his throat.

"Mullah-*sahib*, I don't mean to interrupt, but . . ."

The mullah glanced in their direction and took another loud slurp of his tea.

"Gentlemen," he said with his eyes on Zeba. "You are free to return to the prison, but this woman is staying here with me."

CHAPTER 32

"BUT . . . BUT . . . BUT FORTY DAYS?" YUSUF STAMMERED. "AFTER forty days, we'll be dragging her corpse out of that place! Is this your plan for sentencing her?"

Qazi Najeeb was nonplussed. He scratched at the back of his neck and looked, distractedly, at a land deed on his desk. He squinted his eyes to get a better look at the list of signatures on the bottom. He needed to settle this property dispute in the next few days or he could safely anticipate another murder being committed.

"Young man, you're out of line speaking to me that way."

It had been one week since they'd taken Zeba to the shrine. For seven days, Yusuf had been pacing outside the judge's office. The guards, two lanky men in their twenties with holstered guns on their hips, watched him in amusement as he intercepted the judge on his way in. There were no other judges to beseech, and the chances of bumping this particular plea to an appellate court were next to nothing. Yusuf softened his tone.

"Please, Your Honor. I'm asking you to consider her well-being. We cannot conduct a fair trial if she is going to be starved and chained for forty days."

"Forty days is the standard treatment period. Mullah Habibullah surely explained to you that Zeba is not his first patient. He's been treating people there for years and has a very good reputation in the area." The judge was matter-of-fact about the situation, as if he'd not been surprised at all to hear the mullah had decided to keep Zeba for treatment.

The prosecutor scoffed.

"This is exactly what you wanted, isn't it?" he accused from the comfort of the floral armchair. He uncrossed and recrossed his thin legs, his knees jutting out like beaks as he leaned forward to toss his manila file on the coffee table. "You wanted someone to say that she was crazy and you got it. Now she's getting treatment for it, just as you said she would if she were a defendant in America. If anyone should be upset with what's happened here, it's me."

Yusuf couldn't believe the turn this case had taken. As if the justice system wasn't bad enough, now he had to contend with the opinion of the town shaman. He huffed, hands on his hips and his necktie loosened.

Gulnaz had accompanied Yusuf in this visit to the judge. While Yusuf had dreaded telling her what the mullah and the judge had decided to do with Zeba, Gulnaz had taken the news better than he'd expected. They'd been in the interview room of the prison and she'd put both hands on her temples and lowered her head. When she finally looked up, Yusuf saw no tears—merely grim determination.

"God help her," Gulnaz had hissed before leaving the room, implying surely that no one else had.

She was more talkative today.

"Qazi-*sahib*, what exactly did this . . . this . . . mullah say about my daughter's condition?"

The judge turned his attention to Gulnaz. He wondered if she might have taken extra care to dress for this meeting. Had she thought of him as she slipped on her brassiere? Her brows drew close ever so slightly, so the judge cleared his throat and mind, worried she might have just read his thoughts.

"Since interviewing her that first day, he's spent time observing her. What he explained to me, he's also written in this report that was sent over here by a messenger." By "report," the judge meant a paragraph scrawled on a sheet of a schoolboy's notebook and by "messenger," he meant the mullah's own son, the same boy who had served the lawyers tea. "In his professional opinion, she is suffering from a very deep mental illness and he thinks it's unlikely she was in her right mind at the time her husband was killed. The good news is that he believes he can help her heal."

Yusuf sat back down in his chair and breathed deeply. How could he get Zeba out of that dungeon without tossing the entire case into the prosecutor's hands?

"With all due respect, Your Honor, he is not a physician and can't really make that assessment. I wanted to get a person with a medical degree to evaluate her. The hospital is not that far away. If we can have her sent over there, they have two physicians on staff who are qualified and have been treating people suffering from all kinds of mental problems. They even have an inpatient unit where they keep people and provide recognized treatment—"

Gulnaz interrupted her daughter's lawyer.

"Unlike this young lawyer, I don't doubt Mullah-*sahib*'s qualifications." Her voice was firm and unwavering. She looked directly at the judge. "In fact, I am so confident in his skills that I believe he will be able to manage her condition in less than forty days. You will please pass along my thoughts to him. I've heard she's the only woman being held at the shrine right now and, as you can imagine, I'm concerned about her welfare there. Those are uneasy conditions for a female."

"The conditions are designed to be what is necessary for the treatment of the patient," the *qazi* explained gently. "It's been a safe treatment for many, and he will keep a close eye on her."

"So what does this mean for her case, then? We've already reviewed the penal code. If she's been declared insane by a source you trust, then she cannot be convicted of this crime," Yusuf insisted.

"For now," corrected the prosecutor. "This is just as you said. Get her treatment and then she can be tried and convicted. And she will be despite this delay."

"My friends, we are making history," Qazi Najeeb said proudly. He looked around the room with the glow of a chemist who'd just synthesized a novel compound. "We are carrying out true justice as it has been delineated in the procedural code. This is a new age for the judicial system, young men. I never thought I would see it in my lifetime. We are leaders, we three!"

Gulnaz listened intently and thought back to the biscuits she'd brought in for their last meeting. The judge was a thin man, and she hadn't expected him to eat so many. She'd come empty-handed today and wondered if that had been a wise decision.

"There's something else we need to discuss," the judge said, leaning forward in his chair. His elbows rested on his desk and he stroked his beard twice before continuing. "I've received a report from the chief of police in Khanum Zeba's village. Several people have provided statements to the police chief, Hakimi, about Zeba."

Yusuf felt the hairs on the back of his neck stand. Gulnaz's left eye twitched once, which she took to be a good omen.

"What statements?" asked the prosecutor.

"There are quite a few, actually, but they are from various people who bear no relation to the defendant. They are comments about her behavior in the weeks before her husband was killed, and I must say, they are quite interesting."

"What do they say?" Yusuf asked cautiously.

"I will read parts to you," offered the judge, nudging his eyeglasses to the bridge of his nose as he pulled a handful of papers from a folder. "Here's the first. It's from a woman who lives not far from the defendant. She states, 'I noticed this woman following me home several times. I paid attention since I am alone with my children in the home and my husband died a few years ago. She tried to see through a crack in my gate and I witnessed her doing the same to my neighbors' homes. She looked to be speaking to herself, and when I asked her to leave, she did not seem to hear me.'"

Yusuf was baffled for a moment.

"Another reads, 'I did not know this woman very well as she lived a few blocks from my home, but I had seen her from time to time in the market. More than once, I saw her whispering to cans of cooking oil and bags of flour in shops. She didn't know I was watching and I didn't mean to snoop but she has a daughter the same age as mine. I could not help but notice.'"

"This cannot seriously be considered part of the case," the prosecutor lamented.

"But why not? If we are going to be part of a legitimate process, these must be included as evidence. This is part of the investigation. This is witness testimony. This is how things will be done in the Afghanistan of tomorrow and we will start it here, today!"

The judge felt years younger, as if he were at the beginning of a career instead of winding down the end of one. Gulnaz raised an eyebrow. Qazi Najeeb's chest puffed a bit, interpreting her reaction optimistically.

"This one is most interesting. 'I saw Khanum Zeba twice on my route selling things throughout the town. Both times it was just before her husband was killed. She was walking down our street, and after every few feet, she would stop and pick up a small rock or a handful of dirt and put it into her mouth. I asked her why she was doing that, but she only growled at me like a stray dog and hurried off before I could ask anything else. I could see the crazy in her eyes that day. You would have to be a blind man not to see it.'"

"So they're all saying that she was insane?" Yusuf asked. What had happened in that village? He thought back to his conversations and wondered why so many people could be volunteering accounts of Zeba's bizarre behavior.

Gulnaz took out a handkerchief and dabbed at her forehead. The air in the judge's office was stifling. It was no wonder her daughter had shrieked her head off in here.

"That's what a lot of people are saying. And the police chief,

Hakimi, told me that each of these witnesses came to him on his own. Some were nervous, he said. Others said they felt badly that this woman should be in prison at all since it didn't seem like she was in her right mind at all. And, what's more, people didn't have anything good to say about her husband, which is odd given that he was murdered. No one likes to speak ill of the dead, but some even called him a cheater, a liar, or a godless man."

"That doesn't mean she should have killed him," the prosecutor insisted, more out of obligation than anything else.

Gulnaz shot Yusuf a look. The young lawyer had gone to the village and knocked on doors. He'd walked through her daughter's home and met with Hakimi himself. What had he done there? All these people saying Zeba was madder than a sandstorm . . . could this be his doing? Or could these accounts actually be true?

Gulnaz lowered her gaze to the floor. Her shoes blurred through her teary eyes.

The pain of watching her husband walk away had never left her. She'd wanted so much for Zeba to have a life free of dark curses. Secretly, she'd been glad Zeba had turned away from the *jadu* she practiced at home. When Zeba had grown resentful of her mother, Gulnaz had not faulted her. Zeba had believed her mother to be angry with her for the distance she'd put between them, but it was not true. Gulnaz had only ever been angry with herself.

It was heavy, the weight of all the troubles she'd caused and the revenge she'd sought. Gulnaz never fell asleep until well into the night and then only after she'd taken a mental inventory of her children's heartaches and all the things she could not change. When it was most quiet, she found herself at the window of the room she kept in her son's small home, her ear to the night listening for the sound of something intended only for her—a laugh, a howl, a heartfelt apology.

She sat now, with knees stiff and shoulders hunched, listening to people speak of her daughter's demons. Was this all she was meant to see on this earth? And, more important, was this her own doing? Had she been trying to make her daughter stronger or had she been looking for a way to prove herself?

She'd meant only to do right, with every step she'd taken in her life. She'd meant only to thwart someone's evil eye or prevent a marriage that wasn't intended or to punish someone who'd wronged her family. Even now, she meant only to save her daughter. She was nothing without her *jadu*, Gulnaz knew. Like a pulse, its persistence gave her life.

Qazi Najeeb was determined to make history with her daughter's case. Men were always so frightened by their mortality that they obsessed over ways to live forever: sons to carry on their work, grandsons to carry on their name, their legacies in books, on streets, or in newspapers. Some became more desperate as their black hairs turned silver.

Yusuf seemed hesitant to say what he was thinking. This was a game of chess to him as he, too, hungered for a moment of glory. Was Gulnaz doing the same? Was she using her daughter's plight to test her sorcery once more?

Sometimes you just don't know when to stop, Gulnaz told herself. Gulnaz drew in a deep breath. She had much to worry about and barely enough strength.

There was no air in the office.

Gulnaz stood and picked her handbag up off the floor. The men turned and waited for her to speak, but she did not. Without a word of explanation, Gulnaz walked out of Qazi Najeeb's office.

"Khanum? Khanum, where are you going? Are you all right?" the judge called out after her.

Yusuf wasn't surprised that she did not turn or answer. Zeba and her mother, he'd surmised long ago, were cut from the same unruly cloth.

CHAPTER 33

DURING THE DAY, ZEBA WOULD WATCH THE THICK CLOUDS DRIFT across the sky, like a flock being coaxed home by a shepherd with a *tula*, a wooden flute. For the first two nights, Zeba did not sleep. She would watch for the scorpion that walked past her cave, pausing to eye her with his tail curved in the air, as graceful as calligraphy. It distracted her from the meals of bread (which was often stale), black pepper, and water. The black pepper made her sneeze, five or six gunfire convulsions of her body in the span of seconds. They were like small exorcisms, each of them. The water was pumped from a well that, Zeba assumed, must have plunged deep into the ground because it was sweet with minerals, percolated through layers of rich earth. The water brought to mind her cousin.

He was her father's nephew, a good spread of years between them. Zeba remembered carrying him on her hip as a girl. As a young man, he traveled to the city and worked for a month digging wells. He died, just a foot from water, when the earth's gases overcame him. Zeba had cried for the boy, wondering how it must have felt to reach the core of the earth and tap into its life-giving fluid, only to realize he would never live to taste it.

At his funeral, women consoled his wailing mother with lofty promises.

"He died bringing water to people. There is *sawaab* in the work he was doing, and he will be rewarded in *janaat*."

It was the kind thing to say, much better than saying he died for no good reason.

In the afternoons, Zeba listened to the mullah pray over each person. He sat at their cells and recited verses in a soft and gentle voice. He asked each man to speak of his troubles, to describe the visions or voices, to seek peace in the scripture. He brought cool water his son had drawn from the well to wash down their meals of dry bread and gritty black pepper.

I suppose the mullah, too, seeks sawaab for his work in this world, Zeba thought.

The first night had not been as difficult as it should have been. The cell was the length of two people but the roof was low, and the mullah had to crouch to pass through it. Zeba spent her time curled on a small rug Habibullah had brought her.

One man called out with a howl that reminded Zeba of a mullah's *azaan* ringing out from a minaret. As if it truly were a call to prayer, the others followed. Moans, sobs, and laughter mingled anonymously in the moonlit courtyard. Zeba couldn't guess at their numbers and presumed no other women were present. Hers was the last cell in the row, and the nearest patient was more than three empty cells away, an arrangement she preferred.

She was almost relieved to be out of Chil Mahtab, having grown wary that her *jadu* was a watered-down version of her mother's. Those women needed so much more than Zeba could give.

Her gnawing hunger pains reminded Zeba of Ramadan, the holy month she'd always welcomed with open arms. It was a chance for her to demonstrate her strength, to fast from sunrise to sunset without letting so much as a single drop of water cross her lips. She took pride in knowing she'd never once faltered, even as a teenager. The moments she spent in this cell were a different kind of Ramadan, but brought the same burning hollow in her stomach. She craved the feeling of real thirst and hunger, for it kept her mind from wandering into the dangerous realm of self-pity. Fasting felt holy and necessary and just.

She pressed her forehead to the cold earth and prayed her time at the shrine would sanctify her—if that were even possible.

Every day she'd tolerated his drink and heavy hand had been an admission that she'd been powerless.

That girl could have been her daughter. The truth was, when Zeba had walked into the courtyard, she'd seen her Little Girl. Her jade head scarf, her flailing legs, her balled-up fists—Zeba had believed them all to be parts of her own daughter. She was horrified, thinking she was seeing her Little Girl's honor ravaged by a man she'd fed, excused, and obeyed. She'd seen a scarlet trickle of shame run down the small, pale leg.

By the time Zeba had seen her face, it was too late. There was no going back. She and Kamal were finished the moment her fingers had wrapped around the wooden handle. Kamal had seen his wife anew in that moment, staring at the curl of her lips under the weight of the raised hatchet and realizing, for the first time, that Zeba had teeth, too.

The sound of urgent whispers shook Zeba from her thoughts.

"He's here! I saw him! Get away from me!"

She shook her head to think of her haunted neighbors.

"Please don't . . . please don't take me away. I'm waiting here for Judgment Day. I can't go with you!"

While most of the nights were still and peaceful, there were occasional outbursts. The yelling, on top of the persistent gnawing of her stomach, made the drums in her head pound harder and harder.

"Please, Satan! Not me! Don't take me to hell!"

"Shut up shut up shut up!" roared another patient, whose illness was of a different kind. Some patients were paranoid and carried on conversations with people that no one else could hear or see. Others were so depressed that they cried and slept most of the day. Zeba believed there were six men in total at the shrine with her, though she'd never spoken to them.

"If he comes for you, do us all a favor and go with him," a man hollered. Wild laughter echoed in the dark.

She groaned and rolled onto her side, the carpet rough against her cheek. Every joint and every muscle felt stiff. She rubbed the long muscles of her neck. She'd lost enough weight in these eleven days that she could feel the ropy muscles and ligaments beneath her skin. Even her belly, which had softened with each pregnancy, had shrunken in on itself like a raisin. The satiny streaks she'd grown with each baby disappeared into the folds.

The mullah prayed over her just as he did the others. He'd warned her, as he'd fastened the chain to her ankle, to stay in her cell. The rest of the patients were men and she should not mingle with them.

"Judgment Day is coming. Allah help me, I'm ready for it. Send the winds, the hail, and the fires. I'm waiting for it! Just keep that devil away from me!"

"*Imshab ba qisa-e dil-e-man goosh mekonee . . .*" Zeba sang softly, hoping to drown out the moaning of her neighbor and the angry shouts for him to keep quiet. "*Farda, man-ra chu qisa feramoosh mekonee . . .*"

Tonight, you will listen to the sorrows of my soul, the lyrics went. *Though tomorrow, you will forget all that has been told.*

The slow melody sounded even more sorrowful against the backdrop of rattling chains and low sobbing.

Forty days, the mullah had declared. Forty days until her treatment was complete and she could be returned to the prison for whatever awaited her there. That she'd managed to survive eleven days gave her little hope for the remaining twenty-nine.

The mullah had peered into her cell earlier in the day, hands clasped together behind his back as he stared at her as if she were a new species of animal in his zoo.

"Dear girl, so troubled. Where does your mind take you?" he'd asked.

"Where can my mind take me?" she'd replied. "I am heavier than that mountain over your shoulder. My mind cannot move me."

He'd considered her answer for a moment before asking another question.

"Zeba, are you miserable here? I've brought you food. I know the bread is not much to go on and you should keep up your strength. Here, take this *bulanee*. It is still warm."

Zeba had chuckled, amused by the mullah's sudden desire to make her comfortable. No, she decided, she would not take anything from this man—not when he'd been the one to lock the shackles on her legs.

"I will leave it here for you," he'd said quietly so the others would not hear. He'd passed the stuffed flatbread into her cell inside a page of newspaper.

"Take it out of here!" Zeba had hissed, though the smell of the spiced potatoes and fried dough made her salivate.

"Why are you being so stubborn?" he'd asked, exasperated. "I know it is not the most comfortable place, but I'm doing this all for your own good. If you could see that, you'd be grateful."

"I am grateful," she said, "that someone had the great wisdom to divide time into days and days into hours and hours into minutes because without knowing that the seconds were passing I would likely die waiting for these forty days to pass."

He'd left her after a moment of silence, whether it was because she had made perfect sense or none at all, Zeba did not care to guess. She'd said what was on her mind, which brought her some small peace.

The mullah moved on to his other wards, praying over each man and dispensing the daily dose of bread and pepper. He listened to their mental wanderings, to their weeping and to their angry rants. He spoke to them of peace, though he did not undo their shackles. He spent long days with them but returned to his home with his wife and children most evenings. It was then that the patients were left alone, with the mullah's quarters empty and only the entombed patron of the shrine to watch over them.

Zeba drifted into a hum, her eyes growing heavy, and unable to remember the rest of the lyrics. The sting of black pepper lingered on her tongue. She would drink more water tomorrow, she decided.

She'd not had enough today and regretted it. The night air was hot and stifling. Zeba felt the moisture in her armpits and her groin when she moved. She sat up with her back to the wall and stretched her legs out before her. A single bead of perspiration trickled down the nape of her neck and slid down her cotton dress.

"I saw him! I saw him! He's coming for me!" The man was still crying out though his shouts were quieter. He sounded defeated. "Mullah-*sahib*, where are you? Help me!"

When Zeba was a young girl, her family would gather on festive nights—aunts and uncles, cousins and close friends. Her uncle had taught himself to play the harmonium. She could still feel the puff of air released from the holes on the back of the polished wooden box. Her uncle's left hand would pull and release the bellows as the fingers of his right hand would tickle the forty-two black and white keys, coaxing songs out of those around him and filling in lyrics when they faltered. The synchrony of their voices disguised the truth that not one of them could carry a tune.

Zeba's eldest cousin had learned to play the *tabla*, one stout drum and one taller drum, with bent fingers rapping against stretched goat skin. He would beat out rhythms that were thousands of years old. Zeba would watch his fingers fly, doing something she could not dream of doing. It excited her to see him thrum against the unblinking black eye on the tabla surface.

Zeba's aunt played the *daira*, a tambourine twice as big as her head, with its tiny pairs of cymbals clapping along the round of the disc. The country was at war then, and the mujahideen had taken to the mountains to fight back the Russian soldiers and tanks. The soil of Afghanistan was slowly filling with martyrs. It made it all the more important to dance and laugh, knowing the war would touch them sometime soon. Her father smiled more on those nights than any other.

Sing, Zeba-jan! Don't be as grim-faced as your mother. Sing from your heart!

I don't know the words to the song, Zeba had whispered to her father.

You know how to clap, don't you? he'd replied with a twinkle. *You don't need much to make music.*

She'd sat next to him and clapped until her palms were red and stinging, swaying side to side as the others did in a movement not unlike prayer. There wasn't enough music in her head to bring about that kind of peace.

If I make it back to the prison, I will make the women sing. I will sit them in a circle and we'll find ourselves a daira, *even if it means skinning a goat myself to do it.*

Zeba paused. Was that the sound of footsteps in the yard? She listened carefully and heard the crunch of dirt beneath a leather sandal. Solitude had sharpened her senses and she didn't need to see to perceive her surroundings. It wasn't the mullah. His step was slower, heavy with righteousness and conviction. It wasn't one of the other prisoners, either. Their steps were timid and unsure—and it didn't seem likely that any of the men could unshackle themselves from the chains around their ankles.

Picking up the pail in the corner of her cell, Zeba gripped its handle in her hands.

Two more steps, closer this time. This foot was lighter even. Zeba wondered if it was a small animal. Perhaps one of the fanged deer had come down from the mountain to see what mysterious creatures disturbed the silence of the night with their shrieks and moans.

"Go and never come back, Satan!" screamed the man meters away. Zeba's heart pounded. His silence had been deceiving. He was still unnerved, probably because he hadn't slept in days.

The footsteps had stopped. Had the man scared him off? Zeba didn't know if she should be afraid or relieved.

She closed her eyes and inhaled deeply, dragging hot, night air into her body and breathing it out even hotter. If only she could be alone again with her music, she thought wistfully.

When she opened her eyes, she gasped at the figure standing before her. Wreathed in moonlight, she could not make out his face. Still, she knew his shape well enough that she needed no other confirmation.

How insane, she thought, *for even a crazy man to think this was Satan.*

"You! What are *you* doing here?" she whispered frantically into the darkness.

CHAPTER 34

"I HAD TO SEE YOU," BASIR WHISPERED. HE WAS AT THE OPENING of her cell and, though there were no bars or doors between them, he looked hesitant to cross the invisible threshold.

"How did you get here?" Zeba asked. She inched closer to him, the clanging of her chains causing her to stop short. She hadn't seen her son in months. Being apart from her children had brought her so much pain, despite the lengths she'd gone to to numb herself. She knew how wretched she must look, her hair unkempt and unwashed, her clothes filthy. She could not have imagined a more humiliating reunion.

"I found my way," Basir said with a shrug of his shoulders.

"But it's so late and so far from home!" Zeba lamented, thinking of what he must have done to travel from his aunt's house to the shrine. "Did someone drive you here? The buses don't come near this place . . ."

"I'm here, Madar. Just leave it."

There was an edge to his voice that made Zeba inclined to do just that.

"I'm sorry you have to see me like this."

"Me too," Basir agreed quietly. He hunched his back and stepped into her cell as moonlight lit on his face. Zeba could even see the whispers of hair on his upper lip. She leaned forward, forgetting the condition she was in.

"I've missed you so much," she cried softly. "You and your sisters. Are they all right? Has something happened to them? Is that why you're here?"

"Nothing's happened to them. They're fine."

"Are you sure? You wouldn't lie to me, would you?"

Basir's face drew tight. Zeba winced to see him look at her in that way.

"What a thing to say, Madar."

"I'm sorry." Zeba shifted her legs. In eleven days, this was the most uncomfortable she'd been and it had nothing to do with the pebbly earth or the heat. Her son looked tired, but she had nothing to offer him. "My son, what a blessing to lay eyes on you."

Basir looked away sharply.

When he looked up, his teary eyes glistened in the moonlight.

"We've missed you so much, Madar," he said, his voice cracking. Basir fell into his mother's arms. Zeba cried out, her hand covering her mouth to muffle the sound. She didn't want the mullah coming out to find Basir with her, and her neighbors had already been restless tonight.

Basir's arms were wrapped around his mother's trunk, his head was buried in her stomach. Zeba touched his face with one hand and pressed her cheek so tightly against his back that she could feel the bones of his spine.

Zeba pulled his face up toward her and wiped his tears.

"This has been so hard on you, I know," she murmured. She didn't know where to begin. Did he hate her? Had he forgiven her? She couldn't be sure, even as he clung to her in the night.

Basir pulled himself upright, sniffled, and cleared his throat. He looked away for a second to regroup then spoke in a very matter-of-fact tone. He'd shifted, Zeba observed.

"I've brought some food," he said as he reached for a small plastic bag just outside her cell. "There's some rosewater cake, two tomatoes, and a tin of rice."

"You brought food?"

Basir shrugged his shoulders awkwardly.

"I heard what they do here. I would have brought other food, but I couldn't find much that I could pack . . ." he explained.

"No, no, no," Zeba said, shaking her head. "*Bachem,* I'm so grateful to you. Really. I just can't believe you came all this way and thought to bring food with you. You're just . . . you're just . . . I don't know what to tell you."

Basir's lips tightened.

"I heard you weren't allowed any food here, but I didn't know if you wanted something." He placed the bag in front of her and watched as she took out one tomato, turned it over in her palm, and smelled its earthy ripeness. She could almost taste its juice, feel it running down her chin without having taken a bite. Zeba put it back in the bag and took out the round tin. She twisted the top off the stainless-steel container and breathed in the scent of rice browned with caramelized sugar and generously seasoned with coriander, cinnamon, and cloves. The rice was cold but Zeba imagined it warm as she sank her fingers into the tin and spooned it into her mouth.

No, she decided, she did not believe in the powers of the shrine. Not when her own son had carried food all this way.

The rice was delicious. Tamina had always been gifted in the kitchen.

"Your ama's rice," Zeba said, her head leaning back, "has always been better than anyone else's but this . . . this is the best it's ever tasted."

"Too bad I can't pass along the compliments."

Zeba swallowed hard.

"How are things with your ama? Is she treating you well?"

"She's been nothing but kind to us."

Zeba wondered if Basir was lying. Surely the family was convinced that Zeba had killed Kamal. Could they possibly be so generous hearted to see that the children had no part in this mess?

"Has she . . . has she said anything about me?"

Basir shook his head.

"No, she doesn't talk about you at all."

Zeba was surprised.

"Where do you sleep? They only have three rooms. Has she made space for you?"

"She keeps Rima in her room with her. Shabnam and Kareema sleep in a room with her girls—most of the time. Sometimes they want to stay close to me, but Ama Tamina doesn't like that. I sleep in the living room alone."

"And she feeds you?"

"We eat with them. No more, no less than the others."

Thank God, Zeba thought, breathing a sigh of relief.

"I've been waiting for her to tell us to leave," Basir said quietly. "I don't know why she hasn't."

Zeba touched her son's forearm. It occurred to Zeba that she might have just crossed the line into complete madness, and the boy in front of her might be an invention of her mind. Somehow that seemed more likely than Basir leaving his aunt's generous arms to find his murderess mother in a shrine for the insane.

Basir pulled his arm away.

"You should eat more, Madar. You look terrible."

Zeba attempted a light laugh.

"Appetite is a funny thing," she said casually. "It comes and goes in this place. Are you hungry? You must be. You've traveled so far."

Zeba proffered the tin, but Basir held up a hand. It was a polite gesture, too polite for an exchange between a mother and her son. It broke Zeba's heart to see it, but she bit her tongue and put the lid back on the round tin.

"Are you going to tell me what happened to my father?" Basir said, his voice taut and dry.

In the months Zeba had been imprisoned, she had asked herself that question a thousand times and had come up with a thousand different answers. She would tell her children everything. She would tell them nothing. She would tell only Basir that his father had been a monster. She would tell only the girls. She would make up an explanation for what had happened that day. She would tell them that Kamal had tried to kill her or that he had slipped and fallen on the ax. This was all a horrible mistake, an accident, and that their father had been a good and decent man.

"Well?"

Zeba looked at the cloudless night sky. Where could she turn for answers?

"*Bachem*, our family has been torn apart. Never have I wanted to do anything that would hurt you or your sisters."

If Basir was breathing, Zeba could not see it. He sat perfectly still, his gaze focused on the dark space between his crossed legs.

"That day . . . that day was terrible for all of us. I don't know why we've been struck like this, but we all know that fate is decided by God."

"Are you going to answer my question or are you going to keep talking shit?"

"Basir!" Zeba shot back. He had never cursed in her presence before.

"I came here to ask you what happened. Are you going to tell me or not? Because if you're not, then I'll just have to guess for myself."

"Basir. *Janem*, there are some things that are between adults and I don't want to—"

"This wasn't just between adults, Madar."

Zeba's back straightened sharply.

"What do you mean?"

"This wasn't between adults. I saw him. I saw what . . . what . . . what had happened to him. He wasn't some stranger. I washed the blood off his body and wrapped him in a white sheet. I buried my father, and now I listen to my sisters cry at night. Whatever happened, it happened to all of us, so please don't tell me that this is between adults."

He was right. He deserved to know, but Zeba had wrestled with what might happen to him if he heard the truth. Would he try to find out who the girl was? Would he think his mother was a liar and despise her even more? Would he be so ashamed of his father that he could never recover? Or would he slip and tell someone else about the shame that had been perpetrated in their own home? He had the anger of a man but not the understanding or judgment of one.

How much easier this would be if she were as starkly mad as her neighbors!

Her heart pounded. In a moment, she would either tell Basir everything or nothing. And in a moment he would either hate her or cry for her.

Had the mountain grown since she'd last looked at it? It seemed to stand taller in the backdrop, as if it were inching its way toward the moon.

The song returned.

Tonight, you will listen to the sorrows of my soul. Though tomorrow, you will forget all that has been told.

Zeba heard the faint roll of a tabla drum in the night, its unblinking eye gawking at her. The funereal whine of the harmonium followed, and a puff of stale air tickled Zeba's face.

Then came the crash of the *daira* and a chorus of applause.

If she lost her son, her children, she would have nothing. Had she loved them enough to survive this? Her son sat poised, looking at her as if she were a scorpion about to strike. The babies she'd mourned told her they'd had enough of her tears. Her daughters' hurt eyes bored into her, telling her that she'd built that house of sin, that she was just as vile as Kamal.

"Are you going to answer me?" Basir asked.

He deserved better. He was a good son.

Zeba filled her lungs with the hot, night air and made a decision she was certain she would regret.

CHAPTER 35

"I DON'T KNOW WHAT TO THINK," HAKIMI SAID. HE WAS TRULY baffled. The man before him was the fifth person to come in for the same reason. And since when did people feel it necessary to report a neighbor's crazy behavior? His own neighbor kept no fewer than twenty-five gray pigeons on his roof and had named each and every one. Hakimi had argued with him that it was impossible to tell one bird from another but the man insisted that he could recognize them just as well as Hakimi could recognize his children.

"It's the truth," the man said, rubbing his hands together and shrugging his shoulders. "I didn't think anything of it at the time and I didn't want to intrude into a family's private life. But now . . ."

"Yes, what makes you come here now to tell me this?" Hakimi asked, leaning across his desk to hear the man's response.

"Well, now, it's that so many things have been said and I'm not sure what's true. I know the judge will want to know everything about her before he makes a decision, I suppose. Yes, and if he wants to make a decision, then he can only do that if he knows what I've seen."

"Fine. Tell me what you've seen. I don't know how much the *qazi* is going to care, but you can start by telling me. We'll go from there."

Hakimi pulled out a notebook and a ballpoint pen. He scribbled in the corner of the page, which produced only inkless depressions. He made an O with his lips and stuck the pen into the hollow of his mouth. He huffed hot air onto its tip, then licked it with the tip of his tongue before touching it to the page again. This time his scribble was visible, a reluctant, incomplete twirl of blue.

He turned to a fresh page. He'd kept a file of the other reports he'd recorded. Whether the judge would consider them in Zeba's defense or toss them aside without reading was impossible to say. Hakimi didn't really care either way. It felt good to be doing this, as if he were gathering evidence of his authority in this town instead of evidence related to the case.

"Now, tell me what it is you saw."

"I . . . er . . . I didn't know her name. We're not related to the family, of course. But they lived close enough that I'd seen the wife a few times. I can't recall what day it was, but there was a day when I was going to work and just as I stepped out into the street, I heard a noise. I turned around and there she was. Her head scarf had fallen away from her face so I could see who she was. As soon as she saw me she pulled it back over and looked away."

"What was she doing?"

"She . . . she was digging behind the door of a neighbor's house—with her fingers. It was like . . . it was like something really important to her was buried there. She looked like she wanted to get to it really fast."

"Bizarre. Did she say anything to you?"

"No, she didn't. She just . . . she just looked at me the way a stray dog looks at a gang of schoolboys. She looked ready to claw at me if I got close to her. I didn't."

"Of course you didn't." Hakimi nodded. "Did you stay to watch her or did you leave her there?"

"I stayed for a bit. I mean, I actually asked her what she was doing and if she was all right. She looked wild . . . not like a right person. She was digging at the earth with her fingers. When she didn't respond to me, I asked her if her husband knew where she was. I assumed she had a family."

"What did she say?"

"She . . . uh . . . she didn't say much of anything. She just stuffed a handful of dirt into her mouth and ran off like she'd stolen something."

"She stuffed dirt in her mouth?" Hakimi repeated incredulously. If only every day were like this. If only he could wake every morning to record crazy stories about people in his village, putting ink to the page to turn hearsay into official evidence. It was a powerful feeling, just as good as the glint of his badge or the weight of his pistol. "She didn't just wipe her mouth with a dirty hand?"

"No, no. She took a mouthful as if it were . . . as if it were rice."

Hakimi eyes widened with interest.

"That is very concerning behavior. And you watched her run off?"

"Yes, I did."

"Which direction did she run in?"

"I don't remember."

Hakimi inhaled through pursed lips. He leaned back in his chair and tapped his pen against the page.

"Well, if you don't remember, then I don't know if I can . . ."

"Ah yes, she ran toward the shoemaker's shop and away from the school. I remember now because I was going to work and had to pass the school."

"I see," Hakimi said slowly, as if this detail changed everything. He added a line to the record, his penmanship meticulous. He hadn't quite graduated from high school but there were other ways, he'd realized, to feel like a learned man. He took pride in these details. One could tell by the way he shined his own shoes, not trusting his children to do a good enough job. It was a task beneath most men with any kind of position, but Hakimi believed the end result would more than make up for that.

"I'll be sharing this information with the judge," he said. "Now, unless you have something else that you haven't yet mentioned . . ."

"No, that's all that I know. Just that she was definitely an afflicted person in the mind. And that was at least a couple of weeks before the man was killed."

"Understood. Well, thank you for coming in—" Hakimi said, ripping the page off the notepad and paper-clipping it to a stack of similar sheets.

"*Sahib,* if I could ask one question—out of curiosity. Have you had others comment about that woman's husband? I didn't know him really."

"You mean the murdered man? God rest his soul. No, no one seems to have anything to say about him—not that I've been asking. If there's one thing that's clear in this case, it's that he was the victim."

"Of course," Timur mumbled and before he could second-guess himself, he went on talking. It was unplanned and risky, but he was like a shaken soda bottle. In a small way, this was the moment he was uncapped. "But I'm surprised you didn't hear the rumors about him."

"Rumors? What rumors?" Hakimi said, with one eye squinted.

"I probably shouldn't say anything. I didn't witness it myself, but I heard from others. This was a few months ago, and it was so terrible that I didn't want to believe it myself."

"Tell me what you heard. It's my job to sift truth from rumor."

Timur said nothing, knowing Hakimi wasn't capable of sifting rubies from desert sand.

"It was an ugly thing that I heard, so terrible that it hurts me to even repeat it."

"Out with it, brother. I do have other work to do." Hakimi was growing impatient.

"Of course. It was pretty well known that he was a man of sin and that he had, in a rage, set a page of the Holy Qur'an on fire."

Hakimi abruptly sat up in his chair, both palms pressing onto the desk. This was shocking news, even if it were only a rumor.

"Set it on fire? God forbid! Why would he do such a thing?"

Timur shook his head. His palms were moist. He rubbed them on his pantaloons out of Hakimi's view.

"I have no idea. As a man who loves the Qur'an with all his heart, I can't imagine what would bring a man to do something so ghastly. I told you it was bad."

"Bad? This is well beyond bad. This is the highest form of blasphemy! And he's not even alive for us to inquire about this or to punish him. What am I supposed to do with this information? Who can confirm this?"

"I . . . I don't know who can confirm it. As I said, it was about four months ago in the market and I cannot recall who I heard this from, though I do believe it was more than one person who shared this story with me. I went home that day having forgotten what I'd gone to purchase—that's how upset I was by what I'd heard."

"Who wouldn't be?" Hakimi had his elbows on the desk now. He was fidgeting, his arms and legs trying to find a position that made sense when the information didn't. A thought suddenly occurred to him. "Did his wife know about this?"

"His wife?" Timur shrugged weakly. "I don't know. I suppose she could have known. She might have even seen him do it. How disgraceful it must have been for her and her children. For their sake, I'm glad the whole town didn't hear about it."

"This is bad. This is very bad."

Such blasphemy was not tolerated in Afghanistan. Both men were thinking of the young woman who had, only eighteen months prior, been accused of setting aflame a page of the Qur'an in a Kabul mosque. A single accusing finger had ignited a frenzied mob of mostly men, who viciously attacked her with beams of wood, rocks the size of watermelons, and angry boots. They drove a car over her body before throwing her into a dry riverbed and torching her remains. Immediately after, an investigation was launched. The purpose of the investigation—to determine whether the woman had indeed burned a page of the holy book.

The accusation proved to be a false one and the men who were arrested and convicted of murder were, over months, quietly released or had their sentences dramatically reduced. The results were clear. There was excusability for those who took on blasphemers and defended the Qur'an. Was it possible that Zeba had been angered by her husband's actions? Hakimi had heard much about Kamal's love for the drink. It wasn't that common in their town, but a few men had fallen for the bottle. It was a sin, no doubt, but one that paled in comparison to this new accusation. What kind of man had Kamal really been?

"This is terrible news. I understand your hesitation in coming forward with this. I don't think we should say a word about it to anyone else, though. It could make a lot of people angry, including the family of the deceased."

Timur shifted in his chair.

"I wouldn't want to upset them further, but don't you think that the judge should know? It's possible his wife . . . I mean, I can't say for sure, but isn't it possible that she knew about this and . . ."

"Possible, yes. But let's leave her fate to the court." This was more than Hakimi wanted to handle. He shook his head, reassuring himself that he was making the right decision. "We cannot risk the reaction to this rumor. And it is only a rumor, right?"

"I suppose it is only a rumor. Though I heard it from more than one person."

"You said that already."

"Of course I did," Timur said through a parched mouth. "I'm sorry. I just find it hard to let something like this be—as a Muslim. I felt like I had a duty to say something. Someone who stands up against a crime so terrible should be respected in this life as well as the next, I think."

Hakimi said nothing. He contemplated Timur's words. "I . . . I understand completely. I feel the same responsibility. I suppose I could get a message to the judge quietly."

"I leave it to your judgment," Timur said deferentially. "I'm thankful the responsibility for this doesn't rest on my shoulders."

Hakimi let out a sigh and glanced around the small police station under his watch. It was true, he thought, that no one in this town fully understood the burden of his position.

"I've taken enough of your time, Hakimi-*sahib*. But I do have a question if you don't mind. What about the woman . . . his wife. Have others mentioned noticing any odd behavior? I was just wondering if I was the only one who'd seen it."

"Not at all," Hakimi chuckled, relieved to have moved on to lighter details. "You're the fifth person to come forward in the last week. I suppose it all makes sense. The woman must have been a lunatic to drive a hatchet into her husband's head. The poor guy, Allah rest his soul. I wonder if he knew what kind of crazy his wife was or if she just snuck up on him. Women are odd creatures, you know. Awfully good at hiding things. You just never know what they've got tucked in the folds of their skirts. That's what my father told me."

Timur smiled politely, relieved to hear others had come forward before him, just as Walid had promised.

"Yes," he said, nodding in agreement as he pushed his chair back and pulled down the ends of his linen vest. This would be the first good piece of news to cross their threshold in a long time. That they'd survived this long after what had happened to Laylee was all because Zeba had kept Laylee's secret. Nargis reminded Timur each time he'd changed his mind about coming forward with this story about seeing Zeba eat dirt. "They certainly are surprising creatures."

Timur's heart pounded as he walked home, unsure if there was wisdom in heeding the entreaties of a broken girl and her mother.

CHAPTER 36

"ZEBA! ZEBA!"

It was a trick of slumber, she thought, to hear her mother calling her in this place. Her head felt lighter than it had the first few nights.

"I'm looking for my daughter!"

Zeba sat up with a gasp. She looked down and realized a small, round pillow had been tucked under her head. Had the mullah placed it there while she slept? She shuddered to think his hands had lifted her head to slide it beneath her. How could she not have waken to the touch of a stranger?

"Is there anyone here?"

Zeba crawled to the mouth of her cell no differently, she thought briefly, than the way Rima would crawl to her.

"Here! I'm here, Madar!" she shouted timidly. It was the first time she'd raised her voice above a whisper in this cell. She knew the others would be riled to hear her, a woman, but to answer her mother's call was an irresistible instinct.

"Zeba? Is that you?"

Zeba craned her neck past the lip of her cell. There were two men in the center yard looking curiously toward the shrine and the mullah's quarters. Local devotees would go directly to the shrine, steering clear of the valley of the insane.

Zeba waved her arm, squinting against the sunlight that stung her retinas.

"Here! Madar-*jan*, I'm here!"

By the shift in her mother's posture, she could see that she'd caught her attention. Her mother started toward her with a brisk pace. When the voices began to call out, Zeba's stomach reeled.

"Madar? Is that you, Madar?" shouted one wisp of a man. His voice cracked as he yelled toward Gulnaz. "Have you come for me after all this time?"

"She's not just your mother. She's here for all of us. She's come to take care of us," cried another man in joy.

"Fools!" called a third morosely. "A desperate man can see the ocean in the desert."

Gulnaz ignored them all and stayed clear of their cells, her face stern as she neared the last vault—the one that contained her daughter.

"Who are these women?" A chain rattled, but the moan remained faceless.

Zeba saw the mullah burst through the doors of his quarters with his son at his side. Though she couldn't make out the expression on his face, he looked flummoxed. He nudged the boy back into the building and watched without moving, as if an invisible chain tethered him to his house.

"Zeba, are you all right? What have they done to you? Dear Allah, look at this place!" Gulnaz had crawled into the cell without a second's thought. She threw her arms around her daughter then drew back, patting down the frazzled puffs of hair that hid her face.

"Madar . . . Madar . . ." Zeba sobbed. She buried her face in her mother's shoulder. When she came up for air, she pulled her mother's hands to her face and kissed her palms, closed her eyes, and held them against her cheeks. Gulnaz brushed her daughter's tears away with the pads of her thumbs.

"I'm not crazy, Madar-*jan*," she whispered. "He says I'm crazy but I'm not!"

"You will be if they keep you in here," Gulnaz said in an icy tone.

Zeba sniffled and nodded. She fidgeted with her hair, suddenly aware that in these days without a proper place to wash, she likely looked quite insane.

"You're right. I don't know why he kept me. I didn't say or do anything out of the ordinary. I . . . I . . ."

"Of course not. I know how these people work. It's God's work they claim to do but for a good price." The words came out of her mouth like gunfire. "Someone must be paying him to keep you. Did the lawyers say anything about money when they brought you here?"

Zeba shook her head.

"Uff! I can't believe that Yusuf let this happen. What is wrong with that boy?" Gulnaz pressed the heels of her palms to her forehead as if to push her teeming thoughts back into her head. When she looked up, she'd regained her composure, looking more like the mother from Zeba's childhood. "I'm going to talk to the mullah myself."

"Do you think he'll listen to you?"

Gulnaz reached into her handbag and pulled out a piece of soft flatbread folded in half and stuffed with *halwa*.

"Eat this, *janem*," she whispered. "You've got to keep up your strength."

Zeba's head fell to the side, and she exhaled deeply. She took the pocket from her mother's hands and brought it to her lips. The flour and sugar glistened with grease. Her mother had scooped parts from the bottom of the pot, a toasted deeper brown. Those had always been Zeba's favorite pieces. It shouldn't have surprised her that her mother remembered but it did.

She swallowed hard, her throat dry.

Gulnaz pulled a small bottle of orange soda from her bag as well and placed it on the ground next to Zeba.

"I didn't know what else to bring. Should I open it for you?" she asked.

Zeba nodded quickly.

Gulnaz gave the cap a quick twist and the bottle fizzed, a soft, carbonated whistle rising from the lip. Zeba took a long sip, the bubbles sending a tingle to her nostrils as they passed through her mouth.

"Thank you, Madar," she said breathlessly. Her stomach was more grateful than she could express. She'd refused the mullah's offer, but it hadn't been easy. "Basir was here two days ago. I thought I'd imagined him. Sometimes I still think I imagined him, actually."

"He was?" Gulnaz felt her throat tighten at the thought of her grandson braving the journey to this distant place to see his mother. She wished she could have brought him here herself.

"What did he say?"

"He said they were well enough. I can only pray he wasn't hiding anything from me. He . . . he brought me food," Zeba said, her voice cracking.

You are not your father, Zeba had told him, immediately regretting her words. Basir's whole body had jerked in response as if the thought hadn't crossed his mind until his mother had said it. It had been her fear, not his.

How could you be sure? he'd demanded. *You could have been wrong! Who are you to judge?*

She'd floundered, searching for the right words and wondering if they even existed.

Gulnaz clucked her tongue and sighed.

"God save him."

"Have you heard anything about the children, Madar? Has anyone sent word from Tamina's house?"

Gulnaz let her gaze fall to the ground.

"I've called my friend Fahima who lives not far from them, but she said she hasn't seen or spoken to Tamina since the *fateha,* when she went to pay her respects. She says Tamina's been holed up in mourning. I told her that we were . . . that we were very worried about the children. I asked her if she could walk past their home and listen for anything. She promised she would and I haven't heard from her. I think that means she hasn't seen anything to worry about. I'm sure they're all right."

Zeba wasn't certain of anything and resented her mother's thin re-assurances. The absence of screams was not evidence that all was well, but she lacked the energy to point that out. She'd finished the *halwa* and bread and decided against wiping the grease from her chapped lips.

"*Janem*, let me speak with the mullah. I'll see if I can reason with him to send you back. This is no place for a mother of four children. This is no place for anyone, actually." Gulnaz put her hands and knees on the unforgiving earth. She pushed herself to stand, wincing.

Zeba wanted to pull her back and make her stay but she didn't. She merely watched as her mother set off to pull Zeba from the quicksand she'd fallen into. Gulnaz marched defiantly toward the figure standing on the hill. She clutched her handbag close at her side and snuck side-long glances at the other cells. Seeing her coming, the mullah swiveled his head in either direction. He put one foot behind the other and re-treated, halfheartedly, toward the house. Was he trying to avoid a con-versation with Gulnaz? Zeba strained her eyes to see, staying mostly hidden behind the edge of the cell. She arched her back, her muscles stiff from sitting most of the day. She never imagined longing for Chil Mahtab this badly.

She could hear her mother's voice. She had started her appeal to the mullah before she'd even reached him. She waved one arm back in Zeba's direction. They were too far for Zeba to make out the con-versation, but she could see her mother's gesticulations. The mullah's eyes were cast on the ground. Gulnaz was pointing to the heavens, summoning God into her plea.

This much was to be expected. It was the following moment that made Zeba's stomach lurch. The mullah looked up slowly. He was trying to speak, but Gulnaz would not allow it. She was not finished. He took a step toward her and put his hand on her arm. Gulnaz pulled back sharply then stood staring at him. Her hand rose to her mouth and her left foot slid behind her, then her right. The mullah moved in closer, his head tilted to the side. He put both hands on her arms as if to keep her from running. Gulnaz's head drooped like an untended puppet.

Why was he touching her? Zeba dragged herself outside the cell. The shackle scraped at the paper-thin skin of her ankle and she winced. The mullah was motioning to the quarters he kept next to the shrine. Impossibly, the mullah reached up and touched Gulnaz's cheek. Gulnaz pulled away, but her feet were rooted.

Zeba wanted to shout. She wanted to run across the dry yard, climb that shallow hill, and claw at the mullah. She wanted to pull him off her mother who looked so uncomfortable under his touch. She pulled at the chain, but it yielded no more slack.

"Ayee!" she roared in frustration. She cupped her hands around her mouth and shouted. "Madar! Madar!"

Gulnaz turned at the sound of her voice, her fingertips over her lips. She slowly raised a hand to Zeba as if to say all was well. But all was obviously not well. What was he doing? The mullah led Gulnaz to the two-room structure with floor cushions and curtained windows Zeba could recall from her first day at the shrine. Her mother was walking with slumped shoulders. The mullah put a hand on the small of her back to lead her, and Gulnaz twitched, pulling away again but only enough that the mullah's fingers slipped to her elbow. She stopped walking again and stared at him. She was shaking her head. He was pointing at the door.

"Come back, Madar!"

Zeba's heart was pounding with the distinct feeling that her mother was in grave danger. What was this man demanding of her? They were in the middle of nowhere, essentially. No devotees had come to the shrine today, the heat driving them away. The only people who could hear Zeba's cries were chained to their cells just as she was.

"Madar . . . Madar! Don't go, Madar!" she shouted. Her cries exploded across the yard with enough force to ruffle the leaves of the acacia tree. Gulnaz turned once more to her daughter and nodded before disappearing behind the mullah's wooden door.

CHAPTER 37

"MY SON! YOUR LIFE WILL BE LONG, MY DEAR. I WAS JUST THINK-ing of you when the phone rang."

Yusuf smiled. He doubted that old superstition had much truth to it, especially not in Afghanistan.

"If I know you," he teased, "you were probably just thinking about what a terrible son I am not to have called you in so long."

"Eh, you know your mother well." She sighed. "Can I help it? If I hear your voice every day, it's still not enough for me."

"Do you not care about your other children at all?" Yusuf fell back on his bed. It felt good to joke with his mother. Her sense of humor surprised most people.

"Sadaf is having a love affair with her cell phone, and your brother doesn't appreciate my cooking enough to come home even once a week. As for Sitara, she's as self-absorbed as ever. Have you spoken to her, by the way? Have you heard that you're going to be an uncle?"

"Am I?" Yusuf exclaimed. He couldn't imagine his sister as a mother. She and her husband still lived liked teenagers though they were both two years older than Yusuf. "Wow, that's exciting news!"

"It is a blessing. It'll be a bigger blessing if the child doesn't inherit his father's laziness. That man thinks a full day of work is moving from the bedroom to the living room."

"Oh, Madar. He's not that bad. He's got a good job at the bank."

"Yes, a bank. For a man who's surrounded by money all day long, it's amazing how little of it he has. He wants to buy a used crib for the baby. If your sister would have listened to us and waited, she could have been married to a doctor. Imagine how useful it would be to have a doctor in the family. My cousin in California couldn't be happier. Her daughter just married a heart doctor. Or was it a lung doctor?"

"Maybe a plastic surgeon?" Yusuf asked sarcastically.

"Don't even start with me. Whatever he is, he won't have to have a child on a credit card. Anyway, enough about them. Tell me how you're doing? Have you found a way to help that woman yet?"

Yusuf pulled himself to sitting, positioning the pillow behind him and crossing his outstretched legs at the ankle. Two other lawyers had invited him to a local restaurant for dinner, but he'd turned them down, hoping a quiet evening at home would help him come up with a brilliant way to get Zeba out of that shrine.

"I'm working on it. I can't believe the way this case has turned out. As if the prison wasn't bad enough, they've sent that woman to a shrine to treat her insanity. They've got her chained up and barely surviving on bread and water."

Yusuf's mother clucked her tongue in dismay.

"Oh, don't tell me that! That sounds like a myth. We used to go to the shrine in Kabul but only to pray. I'd never heard of one used for the insane. Is it real?"

"It's very real, Madar. I think it's the only one in the country, but it just happens to be here. And that's where she is. Afghanistan of today would surprise most Afghans who left years ago. It's a totally different place."

"Your father and I have been watching the satellite television more and more just because you're there, but when we listen, sometimes I feel like they're talking about a country I don't know. But you're safe? Are *you* eating more than water and bread?"

"I'm eating very well—maybe too well." And he had been. He'd been hazed in his first week in Kabul, his digestive tract less accustomed to the microbiology of the country than he'd anticipated. Since then he'd had no troubles. He was still cautious with raw fruits and vegetables, but everything else moved through him normally.

"Where are you now?"

"Home," he said, surprising himself with how reflexively the word had come out. "I mean, my apartment."

This did feel like home, though. Yusuf had fallen into a routine. Drivers knew where to drop him off, and he could walk into a handful of shops and expect to be greeted by name. He knew which streets reeked of waste and which streets were clean. He knew the best street cart for *bulanee* and the places where his cell phone would get no reception.

He smiled to think of the day he'd come off the airplane, that intoxicating blend of excitement and apprehension. It was good to be here. It would be even better if he could get this case to move in the direction he wanted it to.

"So what's going on with that poor woman? Did she tell you why she killed her husband?"

Yusuf, trained in the Western concept of attorney-client privilege, debated how much he should share with his mother. But he counted the miles between them and looked out his window at a street full of greased palms and decided there was no harm in sharing a few details with her.

"I haven't told you what I learned yet, have I? It turns out she walked in on her husband assaulting a young girl—in the worst possible way." Yusuf was careful with his language. There wasn't a Dari word for rape, Yusuf had realized when he'd begun his work here, as if not naming the act would deny its existence. Even in the judicial world, it was often called *zina*, or sex outside of marriage, equating the crime to a lusty and impatient couple having sex the day before their wedding. *Zina* was a blanket term that covered anything other than a husband claiming his wife.

"Oh no! God damn that bastard!"

"Yes. She won't tell me much, but from what I've put together, she killed him to defend the girl, one of her daughter's classmates. She doesn't want to say anything to the judge about what really happened."

"Good for her." Yusuf's mother sighed. "She's killed one person. No sense in her killing another."

"I know, but it's terrible that the truth can't help her."

"Truth is a hard sell. You know how we are. We prefer to be polite or to protect our honor. Did we ever tell anyone that we didn't want your sister to marry that louse? No, because having a disobedient daughter is worse than having a lazy son-in-law. We couldn't live without our lies."

Yusuf paused to reflect on this. Lies kept the whole earth spinning on its axis. This wasn't unique to Afghanistan.

"She's not a bad person, Madar. She is a bit of a *jadugar*, though. Did I tell you about that?"

"Really? Your murderess is also a witch? A woman of many talents!"

"She's inherited her talents from her mother, actually."

"Where else could children get their talents from?" Yusuf's mother said pointedly.

"Wait till I tell my father."

"He knows it's true. But you did get your hair from your father. You should thank him for that since he's the only man his age who can stand outside the *masjid* without his head reflecting sunlight. Now, I haven't asked in a long time because I didn't want to be one of those mothers with her nose in her children's business, but how are things with Meena?"

Yusuf winced. He debated telling his mother that Meena was in love with another man. He didn't fully trust his mother not to say something about it to Khala Zainab.

"We aren't a good match, so I would get that idea out of your head. You know, Khala Zainab hadn't even told Meena that she was giving her number to you."

"Is that what Meena said? She was probably just embarrassed about it and made that up. How could you not be a good match? You were so cute together as children, and you're both lovely adults. What more do you need?"

Yusuf shook his head.

"And, Yusuf, you can't make a decision on one conversation."

"It wasn't one conversation, Madar. We just reached a conclusion that it wasn't meant to be."

"What would I know anyway? I'm just a woman who's been married for thirty-something years." Yusuf's mother exhaled sharply. "Ay-ay, *bachem*. When are you going to have enough of that place? The stories you tell me and the chaos we hear about on the news are disturbing. How can you stand to be around these kinds of things?"

Were it not for the static on the line and the specifics of the case, Yusuf could almost have felt like he were only a train ride away from his mother, the way he had been when he lived in Washington. He could picture her, sitting on the living room couch, a basket of his father's white undershirts in front of her, still warm from the basement's coin-operated laundry machines. He knew when she hung up, there would be lines on her face from where she'd pressed the receiver against her ear. He pictured the furrows in her forehead and knew she was probably cupping her right hand over the speaker, a habit she'd developed from when conversations across continents traveled across tenuous fibers instead of satellites.

He could almost see out their apartment window, thick metal bars gridding the scene from the fourth floor. Though the view hadn't been much, Yusuf had spent hours at the window's edge staring at the building across from theirs and the others that flanked it. When he was twelve, Yusuf's father had given him a pair of binoculars, hoping he would use them to develop an interest in the airplanes that flew low over their heads. But Yusuf wouldn't become an engineer, despite his father's encouragements. Instead, he'd used the binoculars to spy into other windows.

He watched the woman who would undo her pink bathrobe to breast-feed her baby in the mornings. He saw the gray-haired man who flipped through channels with one absentminded hand down the crotch of his pants and another on the remote. He saw the thin, teenage girl who stuck as much of her arm and face as she could through the window grate to keep the cigarette smoke out of her apartment. Yusuf did not feel like a voyeur in watching these private lives. He felt more like a guardian of secrets.

But that wasn't why he was in Afghanistan. He hadn't come this far from home because he wanted to be privy to the sordid details of people's lives here. People had equally sordid lives in New York or Washington. His friends, his cousins, his parents, his colleagues—a hundred voices had echoed the very same question as soon as he'd booked his tickets to Afghanistan.

Why do you want to work there?

"Madar-*jan*, this is where I can do something real. The country needs a real justice system if it's going to survive as a society. I want to be part of that. It's rebuilding a nation and not just any nation—our nation. How shameful is it to leave it all for foreigners to do?"

"I'm proud of you, Yusuf. We're all proud of you. You should hear the way your father talks about you with his friends or with your uncles. Just last weekend we went to a wedding and he ran into an old classmate from high school. 'My boy is a hero.' That's what he said, honestly."

Yusuf's throat tightened. He rubbed his forehead and admitted to himself that he really missed home. He missed the smell of fabric softener on his undershirts and the feel of a gas pedal under his foot. He missed the paved roads and complicated parking signs detailing street cleaning schedules.

He missed Elena. He thought she might reach out to him even after they'd broken up. She never did, even when she knew he'd be leaving for Afghanistan. It was as if she'd agreed with him that they were too different to think they could be together. He'd not regretted his decision. He'd only regretted that he'd let things get as far as they had because it had caused them both unnecessary pain.

Sitting in the terminal at JFK airport waiting for his flight to Dubai, Yusuf had taken out his cell phone and deactivated his Facebook account. It was a sharp-edged moment, dulled only slightly by the number of people who passed him without noticing the bright young lawyer who had just disconnected himself from that world. Maybe it wasn't such a monumental decision after all. He deleted the app from his phone. He would immerse himself in his work, he'd resolved, and it would be best not to be distracted by pictures of his former classmates clinking glasses in dimly lit lounges in the East Village of New York City or biking through Rock Creek Park in D.C.

"I'm not going to stay here forever, Madar-*jan*. I'll be home once I feel like I've accomplished something here."

He could hear her tired exhalation, the acquiescence to her son's whims.

"I know that country better than you do," she said. "You'll accomplish a lot there, but the second you step away, it'll seem that you've accomplished nothing at all. You'll be the poor ant who drags grains of dirt three times his size to build a home only to have it trampled over with one person's careless footstep. It'll break your heart, and that's what I'm most worried about."

When he hung up, Yusuf felt the weight of quiet in the room. He rose from the bed and went to the radio on the dresser, flipping it on and turning the dial to scan through the stations. At the sound of a young man's voice, his fingers paused.

"You've called Radio Sabaa," the host announced. "Go ahead and speak whatever is in your heart."

"This is the first time I'm calling." The voice was nervous and Yusuf closed his eyes. He could picture the caller, a young man in dark denim and sneakers, a polo shirt with Coca-Cola embroidered on the pocket. He was on his cell phone, ducking into a side room of his home so his sisters and parents would not overhear his confession.

"I've been in love with a girl since I was a boy. I love everything about her. The shape of her eyebrows, the sound of her voice, the way she smiles. I used to follow her whenever she left her home, just so she'd know how much I cared about her. When she noticed, she looked back and smiled at me and it was as if . . . as if in that moment our hearts became stitched to each other."

"Ah, young love." The host sighed. "Please go on."

"In the last two years, we've talked nearly every day. We talk about our studies and our families and our hopes for the future. I want, God willing, to own a business one day, maybe a restaurant or a furniture store."

Yusuf smiled to himself, let go of the dial, and wandered back to the bed.

"I can only imagine doing all this if she's with me, by my side. I can't imagine life without her. I've never loved anyone else. I've never even looked at another girl the way I look at her."

"It sounds like she loves you as well. Is something standing in the way of your being together?" the host nudged, his voice thick with sympathy.

"There is a big problem. Her family has recently engaged her to another, a boy she does not love. He is in Germany and will be coming in two weeks for a wedding. After that, it's only a matter of time before she leaves to join him in Europe. She doesn't want to go. She told me that, but her family is insisting."

"How very heartbreaking!"

"It is. I cannot sleep. I have no appetite. I can barely do my job. If she leaves, I'm sure I'll be alone for the rest of my life. Nothing could fill the hole in my heart."

"Beautifully said, my young friend," said the host. He whispered something barely off air and cleared his throat. "I hope that if you and this young woman are destined for each other, nothing will stand in the way of your devotion. This is Night of the Hearts on Radio Sabaa. We're going to take another caller now . . ."

Yusuf chuckled softly to himself, thinking of a boy and girl who spent stolen moments talking on mobile phones, shooting each other lustful glances and thinking they knew true love. Then again, who was Yusuf to judge? He had chosen to walk away from Elena and had been more hurt that she had not put up a fight. She'd called him an idiot for wasting her time and moved on—just like that. He thought of the women in Chil Mahtab, the women who dared run off with men even though they were risking their freedom or their lives to do so. What love could possibly be that compelling?

CHAPTER 38

"WHAT DID YOU DO TO MY MOTHER?" ZEBA DEMANDED ANGRILY.
"Tell me!"

The mullah answered her through tight lips.

"I've done nothing to your mother. We spoke about your situation. Zeba-*jan*, I want you to be safe," he said in an oddly conspiratorial whisper. "Your lawyer says madness can be used to get you leniency in your case. I . . . I think it's important for you to spend some time here so that there is no question to your madness. I've promised your mother that I would watch over you. I'm going to keep that promise."

"God will never forgive you," she growled. "You can spend a million years praying and He will still condemn you for whatever it is that you've done to my mother."

She'd spat at his feet with whatever saliva she could muster, sick at the memory of the way he'd put his hands on Gulnaz.

The mullah rubbed at his temples.

"We're each haunted by our own sins, Zeba, but the ultimate judgment is left to Allah for a reason. With only five senses, we are limited in our ability to understand. Your mother will return today. You can ask her yourself."

Zeba turned her back to him and didn't move again until she was certain he'd left.

The other patients knew of her presence now and sometimes called out to her, "the woman." Zeba did not answer. There were too many ways for this situation to get worse for her. The best she could do was to maintain the solitude she sought. The nights should have been easy respites, but madness seemed to sparkle to its zenith under moonlight.

She was restless and unable to sleep. She needed to know that her mother was all right. She needed to know what the mullah had done to her and already reeled with guilt so poisonous that she almost wished Kamal back to life. That was how desperate she'd become. She did not question her mother's reasons for not lashing out at the mullah or turning on her heels. She understood now that everything Gulnaz had done, every bizarre behavior or act of madness, was a demonstration of love.

When the sun reached its highest point in the sky, Zeba felt her skin prickle. She sat perfectly still and understood, with the intuition of a woman who had endured much in the past few weeks, that she was moments away from another tectonic shift in her life. She focused on keeping her breathing even and pressed her back flat against the clay wall.

There had been a certain comfort to the shrine, Zeba admitted, before the mullah had shamelessly led her mother into his quarters. The small of her back ached. She pushed her shoulders back and felt the sharp pangs of protest in her muscles.

CHAPTER 39

"GENTLEMEN," SAID QAZI NAJEEB SLOWLY. "I'VE RECEIVED SOME interesting information related to the case of Khanum Zeba. I think we have to be very cautious with what I'm going to share with you. It could be a very ugly situation and would have been, no doubt, if her husband Kamal were not already dead and buried."

Yusuf listened carefully. The judge had called this meeting abruptly, and he half expected to hear that Zeba had starved to death at the shrine. Yusuf was already feeling guilt-ridden for not finding her a way out of there.

"I received a call from the police chief, Hakimi, if you remember his name from the arrest report. He's been approached by several people in the village who report that Kamal had been seen burning a page of the holy Qur'an a few months back. He wasn't sure exactly when or under what circumstances."

"Dear God, *toba, toba . . .*" the prosecutor groaned, shaking his head.

Yusuf bit his bottom lip and his brows lowered. Burning a page of the holy book was an unforgivable transgression. Yusuf couldn't put blasphemy past Kamal, after everything he'd learned about him. Still, his body tightened with unease.

"I don't want to have this weigh too heavily into the case, but I'm afraid we can't ignore it either. It's got to be considered."

At that statement, the prosecutor's ears perked.

"Murder is murder."

Qazi Najeeb leaned over his desk and peered over the rims of his scratched lenses.

"You know as well as I do that murder is not murder."

The prosecutor nodded in agreement. It was a truth the three men could agree upon.

"What else did Hakimi say?" Yusuf asked. He wished the police chief would have called him directly so he could ask these questions himself.

"Hakimi has been interviewing half the town, and it seems that lots of people have heard this story. He says it's hard to imagine how it could not be true with the sheer number of people who nod their heads when he asks if they've heard of this."

Yusuf could imagine it. A rumor started by one person, passed to two others, and then ten more when Hakimi began to ask his questions. Hakimi's questions, he knew, had likely added fuel to the rumor or truth, whichever it was. He'd seen the same happen in the past. Simply asking about Kamal burning a page of the Qur'an would have made it a possibility. A bit of attention from villagers and the possibility would take root. Soon its roots would spread through the ground, the seed breaking open and through the earth into the light of day.

"It's a surprising number of people who reported to Hakimi that they had heard the same story from others. One man said he saw Kamal smoking a cigarette in the evening a few months ago and that his hands had been blackened with ash, likely from Kamal wiping away the evidence of his sin. Another man said he heard Kamal saying he had no time or patience for prayers. And, worst of all, quite a few people said they had known Kamal to be a drinking man. He consumed alcohol regularly though no one would say where he might have gotten the drink from."

Yusuf put a hand over his mouth. He was afraid he would break into a grin, not because he felt good about Zeba's defense but because it was amazing how much things could change based on a rumor. He kept his eyes on his notebook so they wouldn't betray him.

"In other news, I heard from a guard that there's a reporter who is asking questions about this case. It seems this reporter has been to Chil Mahtab inquiring about the women in prison . . . you know how these young reporters are. That reporter got wind of Zeba's case, so I wouldn't be surprised if either of you receive phone calls about this. I want you to be warned, especially with what we're now hearing about Kamal and the story of that woman in Kabul who was murdered by the mob. This could get very ugly."

"People hear this kind of blasphemy and they want blood, but it's hard to get blood out of a dead man," the prosecutor mused.

"Precisely. Now let's summarize before we go too far with this new information," Qazi Najeeb said with more solemnity than he'd ever displayed. "This case has to be taken very seriously. In Zeba's defense, there were no witnesses, but the circumstances were so clear-cut that witnesses really weren't necessary. Yusuf has presented the argument that she may have been insane at the time the murder was committed. She has confessed to it in the arrest report and hasn't really refuted any of it in a convincing way. It's hard not to take that as an admission of guilt, then."

Yusuf shook his head.

"I disagree with that. Since she's been deemed insane by someone the judge feels is an expert opinion, then her arrest statement should be thrown out. How can an insane person write a true confession? You've seen her yourself, Your Honor. Do you think she would have been able to provide an accurate statement for the arresting officer to record? She was barely aware of what was happening even when they pressed her blue thumb to the page."

"Enough, Yusuf," Qazi Najbeen interrupted. "Let me speak. The prosecution has a strong case. I am trying to be very fair and open-minded about this case, but even if she's now been deemed insane, that's not enough to save her from being guilty of murder. Now, the only thing left to consider is this news about Kamal as a drunk who may have committed a horrible sacrilegious act."

Yusuf sat forward suddenly.

"You know, the case of the woman murdered by the mob in Kabul was an interesting one. The men who killed her were initially sentenced to death, but then the judge lessened their sentences, even dismissing some," the *qazi* added.

The prosecutor nodded.

"They were crazed. They heard someone had dared to burn Allah's words and they went wild. They were defenders of God in their minds."

"That's no excuse for murder," Yusuf shot back.

"Well, it seems people come up with all kinds of excuses for murder, don't they?" the prosecutor asked pointedly.

Yusuf resisted the urge to put in eyedrops as he sat in the judge's office. He rubbed at his sore eyes and knew he was only making matters worse. In a flash, he understood why it was that everyone in this country looked twenty years older than their actual age. He considered the street children who had swarmed him in Kabul—school-age boys and girls who would not have been allowed to cross the street in New York without an adult's hand clamped over theirs. Yusuf had been fooled by many of the women in the prison, their bodies and children and weariness making twenty-two-year-olds pass for forty. The men, thin and weathered by jobs that made three days pass between two sunrises. Their lives were in fast-forward but, in other respects, they didn't seem to be moving at all. Was this what his mother worried about—that Yusuf would spend the best years of his life toiling in a land that would give him nothing to show for it? It was possible, he had to admit, that she was right. But he still wasn't ready to give up.

"What do you want to do then? Would you feel better if Zeba were executed tomorrow? Do you feel that her children would be better off? Does that feel like justice to you?"

The prosecutor shook his head.

"We can't give a free pass to women who kill their husbands. I'm not heartless, my friend. I'm just doing my job—same as you."

"I'm doing my job and I'm also doing what's right." Yusuf's voice was thick and tense. He cleared his throat and began again. "I know that's what you want, too. Let's find a solution that will work for everyone. We've got someone's attention now, and I don't know if having a reporter following Zeba's case is such a great thing."

Actually, Yusuf was quite certain it was not in Zeba's interests to have the case scrutinized by a reporter. The trial of the lynched woman's murderers was still fresh on the minds of the people. College students were paying attention. Women's rights organizations were poised to march behind banners. What would start off as a battered woman retaliating against her blasphemous husband would quickly disintegrate into a witch hunt. Yusuf pictured, without much stretch of his imagination, a mob dragging Zeba's body down the street and taking turns beating her with sticks and bricks and car parts.

"What does the reporter want to cover exactly?" Yusuf asked. "Has he heard what people are saying about the husband?"

"I'm not sure," Qazi Najeeb admitted. "But if he's one of those pushy reporters from the city, he'll be asking lots of questions and it's possible that'll come up. Hakimi was pretty surprised by the number of people who came forward in this mess."

Yusuf's fingertips rubbed circles at his temples, his elbows on his knees. It was hot today, and the buzzing electric fan in the judge's office was fighting an uphill battle, swirling the same hot air in the small space between the three men. Yusuf could feel the dampness of his collar and underarms.

Something had happened in that village after his visit. It was as if people had been biting their tongues and waiting for a sign that it was okay to shout out Kamal's sins.

"I'll tell you how I feel," Qazi Najeeb said, wiping his brow with a handkerchief. "I'm tired of the way things have been. People think just because I'm a judge that anything I have has come to me by way of bribes. I don't blame them for thinking so. Everyone knows the economics of having a case dismissed or a person let out of prison. I'm not immune. I can say that much."

The two lawyers shot each other uncomfortable glances. Qazi Najeeb seemed not to be speaking directly to them anyway. It sounded as if he'd rehearsed these lines in his mind and was using the lawyers as a live audience.

"You boys are young. Do you know what happens when you get old like me? You sleep more, you eat less, you choose your fights carefully, and you think about what people will say at your funeral. I want my time to leave a mark. Remember the shrine? Hazrat Rahman—that man left his mark and people are still thinking of his wisdom and praying over his tomb. I'm not asking for a shrine," he said with a fleeting smile. "But I want to leave something people will remember."

"Qazi-*sahib*, what exactly are you proposing?" asked Yusuf cautiously.

"We can make sure this case is handled better than the one in Kabul was—even if they are the capital. You know what they did in that case? When they vacated the convictions for some and lessened the sentences on others, they did not consult with the prosecution, nor did they notify the victim's family. People noticed. People *talked*. I am not going to be that judge. If people notice or talk about me, I want it to be for good reason."

"Okay, but if that's the case," Yusuf reasoned slowly, "then it would be best to remove Khanum Zeba from the shrine. If we want this case to set a good precedent, we can't have our defendant starving in a thousand-year-old shrine. I've talked to the head of the local hospital, Qazi-*sahib*, and that's not the way mental illness is handled here."

The prosecutor nodded in rare agreement. Qazi Najeeb uncrossed his legs and leaned back in his chair. He thumbed through his prayer beads, getting halfway through the loop before addressing Yusuf's argument.

"I know. Gentlemen, neither of you have seen the things I've seen—especially in the last twenty years. My job is not an easy one. I'm supposed to balance tradition against progress in a place where people are suspicious of everything. We hate things staying the same as much as we hate things changing. You know what the real problem with corruption is? It's not the money that it costs to have your way. You can treat that as a living expense. The problem is that we're all puppets. We all have strings on our heads and arms and someone else pulls them: the Russians, the Americans, the warlords, the mullahs, the Taliban. Who isn't working for someone? You, Yusuf, you'll be called the American spy, sent here to corrupt us with the laws of the West. They've stayed too long. They pulled out too early. They killed innocent people. They got rid of the Taliban. The entire mission was in vain. We people are not of one heart."

"Your Honor, I respectfully disagree," said Yusuf. "I'm not anyone's puppet and I don't think my colleague here is either. I think there are plenty of people working for the good of the country and our countrymen. I think we do all want the same things."

"At the end of the day, Yusuf, no one will trust you. They barely trust me. If you don't see that now, you'll see it soon."

Yusuf sighed deeply. The judge was right and he knew it. He'd seen it in the way the prison guards had looked at him, the way the villagers had refused to open their doors more than a sliver, and the way the taxi driver kept looking up into his rearview mirror.

"Yusuf, go to the shrine, get Zeba, and bring her back to Chil Mahtab. Get an idea of how she's doing now." The fan had stopped oscillating. Trapped in one position, it clicked and buzzed in vain, barely ruffling the pages of Yusuf's notepad. The judge didn't seem to notice. "I'm going to spend some time thinking about this, and then I'll talk once more with Hakimi to see if anything new has come up in the village."

Yusuf left the judge's office and headed directly to the bathroom. He wet a paper towel and wiped down his face and neck. He dug into his bag and found the bottle of eyedrops, shook it, and leaned his head back to catch the drops in between his lids. He blinked rapidly, feeling the coolness move from his lashes to his cheeks like tears.

CHAPTER 40

GULNAZ WATCHED FROM A DISTANCE, WISHING SHE COULD SEE through the outer walls of the house. There was no way of knowing who was home. The apprehension she felt had sharpened considerably during the taxi ride coming over.

She closed her eyes and pictured her grandson, her granddaughters. Basir bore an uncanny resemblance to his uncle, Rafi. When he'd been a baby, Gulnaz had often slipped and called him by her son's name. It was, she knew, her heart's urge to return to the days when she could wrap her arms around a child and breathe in the scent of his sun-warmed hair or feel him fitting himself perfectly into the curves of her body. Rafi's children were blessings, but they pulled away from her quickly. Gulnaz knew it was their mother's doing. Shokria tolerated her presence and acted as the dutiful daughter-in-law but they'd never had the closeness Gulnaz had craved. Shokria knew she could never replace Zeba, and Gulnaz kept her daughter-in-law at arm's length, as if it would be a betrayal to her own daughter to do anything else.

There was no alchemy that could change the past. There were only the days ahead, be they few or many. There was only the chance that an ember could be recovered from the ashes and breathed back to life. That was why Gulnaz stood in front of Tamina's house and tried to will the door to open. She would have waited longer, but the sun was beating down on her and it was unbecoming for a woman her age to loiter in an unknown neighborhood.

Gulnaz moved toward the house, planning her words with each step. She knocked on the gate and moved back, adjusting her head scarf and straightening her back. She wiped the moisture from her upper lip with a handkerchief and put it back in the black handbag hooked on her elbow.

She heard a flurry of footsteps and shouts. Never, in all the times she'd knocked on her daughter's door, had she heard the excitement of childhood—a certain sign that Zeba, Basir, and the girls had been too ashamed to invite anyone in. When Zeba had opened the door, it had always been just a crack, wide enough only to see who had come calling. The children would peer out from windows or inner doorways. There was a reluctance in the way Zeba would step back and pull the groaning metal door wide. The door, too, had been complicit in the resistance.

Gulnaz had known something was wrong, but she'd only seen part of the picture. She shuddered to think of how much she'd missed.

"*Salaam*," said a young girl close to Kareema's age. The sun was on Gulnaz's back, making the child squint and curl half her mouth in a lopsided smile that she reserved for strangers.

"*Wa-alaikum*, little girl." Gulnaz tried to peer behind her without gawking. The small courtyard looked tidy. There were no immediate signs of disarray. "Is your mother home? I've come to visit my grandchildren. Basir and the girls—are they here?"

"Yes, Khala-*jan*," she exclaimed politely. She motioned with one grand sweep of the arm for Gulnaz to step inside. "Please do come in."

"I don't want to intrude," Gulnaz said. "If you don't mind calling them to come outside, I'll wait for them here."

The young girl looked uncomfortable. She was probably around ten years old and knew better than to leave an older woman standing on the street. She shifted her weight and tried once more.

"Please, Khala-*jan*, it's nothing. Come inside and I will call them. It's not right for you to stand in this sun."

The sound of laughter came from within the home. It propelled Gulnaz forward despite her reluctance to enter the home of Kamal's sister. She could be thrown out at any moment. Just as Gulnaz entered the courtyard, Tamina came out to see who had called. She was drying her hands on her skirt and didn't recognize Gulnaz immediately. The branches of a sparsely leafed pear tree brushed against her shoulder. The moment she realized who stood before her, her feet came to an abrupt stop.

"Tamina-*jan*," Gulnaz said softly. "Forgive me for coming to your home unannounced."

Tamina's eyes grew wide and her breathing slowed. She stood perfectly still.

It was up to Gulnaz to fill the silence with some kind of explanation for her presence.

"I'm here only to see my grandchildren. I do not wish to disturb you or your family in any way. I know you've been generous in caring for them after what happened to your brother, God forgive him."

When Tamina still failed to respond, Gulnaz debated leaving. Pleading was beneath her, but this situation was different. She had every reason to believe her daughter had killed Tamina's eldest and only brother. His family had the right to demand blood for her crime, even if the justice system hadn't yet reached a conclusion. She took a deep breath and continued.

"I never wanted such ugliness to affect this family, especially the children. They are innocent souls. If I could please see Basir and the girls, I will not bother you. I can walk with them outside and not disturb you or your children."

Gulnaz snuck a glance at the house. She could hear voices within, talking and laughing. She hoped Tamina's husband was not home. She had no interest in facing more people from the family.

"Madar-*jan*," said the young girl softly. "Should I go call Basir and the others?"

Tamina took a deep breath and shook her head.

"I cannot believe you've come here," she said in a voice husky with anger. "You've traveled a long way to see your grandchildren."

Gulnaz cleared her throat.

"I did."

People were always impressed with how far she'd gone, as if the physical distance between two places were the greatest obstacle she had to overcome.

"What made you think it was all right to appear at my door . . . in my home?" Tamina shot her daughter a look and motioned for her to go inside the house. Her daughter vanished without a word of protest, understanding that if she was to continue listening to this conversation she would have to do so from inside. Tamina was no longer still. She'd taken a step closer to Gulnaz, bringing the distance between them to the length of a man's body.

"I am not here for any purpose other than to see my grandchildren," Gulnaz repeated calmly. She raised her hands in a gesture of surrender. "I am not here to offer explanations or deliver messages of apology. I will not bother you with any empty words of condolence."

"Condolence?" Tamina scoffed. She rested her hands on her hips and shook her head. Her head scarf draped softly at the nape of her neck. "I don't need your condolences. I need you to leave my home. I need for my neighbors not to see me entertaining you in my home. What will people say? My brother is freshly in the ground and I am serving tea to his killer's mother in my home?"

"Tamina-*jan*, no one knows I'm here. Not a soul from my own family knows, not even my son. And your neighbors can't see through walls."

"Walls are as solid as tea bags," Tamina blurted. "Do you know what's happened in this town? Do you know what people are saying about my brother and what this has done to our family? They're saying that he had committed the ultimate act of blasphemy—burning the Qur'an, Allah forbid!"

Tamina tugged at both her earlobes and looked to the sky, begging God for forgiveness for having uttered such terrible words.

Gulnaz was stunned. She'd heard nothing of the sort, though it had been over a week since she'd spoken to either Zeba or Yusuf. Was this true?

"I . . . I hadn't heard a word about . . ."

"That's what this village is saying. People are looking at me now as if I'd handed him the matches to do it. And I've never heard such an accusation about my brother! Whatever my brother was in his life, I never let his sins touch my children. Now I'm afraid to take my children out of the house. My family's name is blackened! People will not speak to my husband, and my sister has been shamed in front of her in-laws. Our walls are covered in spit and curses. They hate us—as if I had anything to do with my brother's insanity. What else do you want to do to me? What else?"

She was furious now, her rage loose and her breathing heavy enough that Gulnaz could see the rise and fall of her chest below her collarbones. Her hands were clenched in tight balls.

"I didn't know," Gulnaz mumbled, covering her face with her hands. Her handbag had fallen to the ground with a defeated thud. Her fingers made a triangle at her mouth. It was time to reconsider her plan. She was doing her grandchildren no favors by poking a stick at their keeper. "I was wrong to come."

She lifted her bag from the ground, her back aching in protest.

"I'm feeding his children with whatever we have for our own family. Did you come here to thank me or check on what I'm doing? Leave and do not dare to come back! If you care about these children, you'll leave them in peace!"

Gulnaz half expected to feel Tamina's fists pummel her back as she fled the yard. She heard the door creak to a close behind her and walked to the end of the block without pausing to wipe the tears from her cheeks. When had she become so powerless? When had she lost control over everything in her life?

Gulnaz stood with her back flattened against a clay wall. The small street crossed a main road buzzing with shops and the rumble of car engines. A Toyota Corolla drove past, the driver slowing to get a better look at her as she lingered in the alley. Gulnaz pulled her head scarf over her nose and mouth and let out a long, soft moan that drowned in the town's bustle.

She'd been so close to her grandchildren. Had she done right to leave without putting up more of a fight? Perhaps Tamina needed more time. Maybe when the rumors circulating about Kamal died down, so would her anger.

She could predict Zeba's disappointment already. Gulnaz had wanted only to hug the children and bring them news that their mother thought of them every moment of the day. She knew what Zeba feared most was for her own daughters to look at her the way she'd looked at her mother—she desperately feared the day they would glare at her with icy eyes or refuse to open the door when she came calling on them—if she were ever able to call on them.

Zeba was still in the shrine. Gulnaz wondered what the mullah had told her after she'd left. She hadn't been able to bring herself to face Zeba after she'd left his quarters. At least, though, he'd vowed to take good care of Zeba.

Gulnaz, consumed in her thoughts, did not hear the soft footsteps that crept behind her. When the hand touched her arm, she jerked backward and shrieked.

"Bibi-*jan*."

A small gasp escaped Gulnaz's lips. She stared at the boy's face before reaching out to touch him. He stared back at her and waited for her to speak.

"Basir . . ."

She could say nothing more than his name before her throat swelled so thickly that her breaths slowed. Hesitantly, she touched his shoulder. He blinked, slowly, but did not pull away. She drew him close to her with this small permission and held his face between her hands. He closed his eyes, and two rogue tears slipped through the mesh of his lashes.

"My sweet grandson." Gulnaz pushed his hair back from his face. She brought her lips to the top of his head and kissed him, feeling his hairs bristle against her lips, the way Rafi's once had.

In her life, she'd never been apart from her children. They'd been at her side always, especially once their father had disappeared. Sometimes she'd even told herself that his absence was a blessing because it gave her an undiluted relationship with Rafi and Zeba. There was no one to second-guess her decisions. There was no indulgent partner to make her appear severe in comparison. How relatively easy it seemed, in hindsight, to pull the curtains and shut the world out of their small world.

"Bibi-*jan*, I didn't think you would come."

Gulnaz shook her head.

"Of course I would come. I am your grandmother," she said softly. "No matter what happens or where you are, I would not turn my back on you and your sisters. Your mother's been so worried, too."

"I know," he said. "I . . . I went to see her."

"She told me."

Basir looked up abruptly.

"You've gone to see her?"

"I have. And she was so happy to have at least seen you. It was a long way from here and a dangerous trip for a boy."

He winced at being called a boy.

"I had to go."

"I suppose you did," she agreed. "You had questions for her, didn't you? Were your questions answered?"

"I wish I hadn't asked any questions," Basir admitted reluctantly. He scratched at his head, not wanting to share what his mother had revealed to him. It felt like a personal shame, like his grandmother would slap him for his father's sins. It was that shame that made Basir realize he believed every word his mother had told him even if he'd stormed away in anger that night.

"You're right to ask questions and you're right to be scared to death of the answers. But God gave you the parents you have, and nothing they've done is your fault," Gulnaz said pointedly. She would not shame this boy by naming the sins of his father.

Basir nodded, not daring to look his grandmother in the eye.

"Your Ama Tamina is very angry with me for coming unannounced. She has a right to be angry after what's happened to her family."

"She cries a lot."

Gulnaz let out a sigh.

"She's lost her brother," she said simply.

Basir looked up. His brow furrowed in disagreement.

"I don't know if that's why she cries. She says things when she's upset . . . she says . . . she says my father never brought anything but problems to the family."

"She's a distraught woman. Hopefully, she has the heart not to take out her anger on you and the girls."

"She's mostly fine with us. I told my mother that, too."

"Mostly?" Gulnaz was caught on that small word, and it tore her apart like chiffon on a nail.

"Yeah, she's fine."

"You said mostly."

Basir shrugged his shoulders, and Gulnaz waited patiently. Something was coming to the surface, and she needed to hear it. The buzz of the main road filled the silence as Basir chose his words carefully.

"I . . . I feel like she's angry with me. She doesn't let me near her daughters and sometimes she . . . she doesn't even let me near Kareema or Shabnam. She keeps them all in one room with her at night. They're scared, Bibi-*jan*. I know I'm supposed to look after them and Rima, too, but she acts like . . . she screams at me sometimes to get away from them. It's easier for me to be out of the house. That's why she didn't even realize I'd gone to the shrine to visit my mother. I sleep in the courtyard most nights, but I don't mind it. I don't mean to complain."

He was carefully reeling in his words, as if nervous that he might be making his situation worse by saying them.

Gulnaz bit her lip. She thought back to what Tamina had said in those few angry moments.

"Oh dear Allah," she breathed with a hand over her mouth. She turned her back to Basir as the truth hit her. Tamina's anger hadn't come from a sense of mourning. She'd not said a single word about losing Kamal or about Kamal being killed senselessly. Tamina, who had lived with her brother every day of her life until she was married, was only angry at what had been done to her family, not to her brother.

She did not trust Basir because Tamina could never trust the son of Kamal. Tamina had no love for her brother. Every cell of her body had seethed with resentment that Gulnaz should have recognized, but she'd not wanted to believe that evil could run so deep. How could she have been so blind?

Basir watched her mutely. It was not his fault that he looked dark with guilt, Gulnaz wanted to tell him. It was the color of the sky reflecting on him. It was completely out of his hands.

"Bibi-*jan*."

Gulnaz nodded. This was the truth. This had always been the truth. What had Zeba's life been? What had her granddaughters suffered? Gulnaz felt ill, as if the contents of her stomach might empty into the street if she let herself think of it a moment longer.

She cleared her throat and choked back tears. She looked at Basir who was pressing the heels of his palms against his eyes with all the stoicism he could gather. How much did he really know? How much of what he felt was just that—feeling?

"We've got to get you back," Gulnaz said, curling a loving arm around her grandson's hunched shoulders. His head leaned into her as he would have leaned into his mother if she could have been here at this moment. At least Tamina's house was a safe place for her grandchildren. Tamina would let nothing happen to the children. She wouldn't let Kamal reach from the grave and violate her peace. Not again.

CHAPTER 41

ZEBA WAS AWAKENED BY THE FEELING THAT SOMEONE WAS standing over her.

"Zeba-*jan*, what can I do but pray over you?" a shadow whispered. "Gulnaz is right, even if it pains me to admit it. This is no place for you."

Zeba's tongue felt thick and heavy in her mouth.

"You . . . what do you want with my mother?"

"Drink this," the mullah said as he handed her a bowl of broth. Zeba heard the clink of bones against ceramic, greasy steam rising into her face. He nudged the dish toward her lips and barely flinched when she batted it away violently. Though her eyes had not yet adjusted, Zeba could tell that his clothes were wet with hot soup, the smell of salt and onions mixing with his sweat.

Zeba waited for the mullah to strike her, to yank her up by the hair the way a toddler lifts a doll—he did not.

"What did you do to my mother?" she asked; her question had gone unanswered the last time she'd seen him.

"I wish things could have gone differently. I'm an old man now and I'm looking back at my family and wondering if I made the right choices for my children. I'm still not sure."

"My children," Zeba whispered, speaking more to the night than the mullah. "My daughter Rima should be taking her first steps with my hand to hold her up."

"She might be running." Habibullah sighed. "Children have a way of moving on even after they lose a parent."

That, Zeba thought to herself, *was the kind of foolishness only a man would speak.*

"Your boy looks content. He follows you. He respects you and, more important, he does not fear you. That's why I thought you to be a decent man before you dared put your hands on my mother."

The mullah went quiet. The three-quarter moon cast pillars of light high into the sky. The mullah was crouched at the mouth of her cell, pressing his eyes with his thumb and pointer finger.

"I am old," he said finally. "I am too old and too tired to be anything but this. Your mother looks like she could be your sister. She's the only one time hasn't touched in this entire country. I am not surprised. She is so unyielding, she puts the mountains to shame."

"You dare to speak as if you know her."

"Once upon a time, I knew her very well. Once upon a time, I took her as my bride."

Zeba sat straight up. If this were a dream, she would have to shake herself from its grip before it went further.

"What are you saying?" she demanded, her voice uneven.

The mullah nodded solemnly. Zeba stared at him and traced time backward, undoing his beard and the grays of his hair. She looked into his eyes and followed the shape of his nose and shoulders.

"You . . . you are not dead?"

"Not yet, *janem,*" he answered flatly. Zeba's heart skipped. She fought the urge to let out a cry, to put her hands on his face. She focused on her breathing, closing her eyes as she whispered the question she'd asked so many, many times.

"Where were you?"

Zeba wondered if he would name a single place, as if a geographic location would do anything to explain a lifetime of absence.

"I went everywhere. I became a nomad."

"I prayed for you."

Zeba thought of the many times she'd gazed fearfully at the mountains to the east and thought of the four hundred twenty-three rickety wooden steps that linked their province to the next. Many had died there, she'd learned even as a child, losing their foothold or frozen with fright. She'd prayed to God that her father not be at the bottom of a ravine.

"I had to leave, Zeba. It was the best thing I could do—to free us both."

"The boy . . . you have a family now?"

The mullah shrugged.

"I did what any man would have done. I married and began again."

Zeba blinked rapidly. It sounded so easy, like putting one book down and opening another. But it made sense to her, too, because she was not completely unlike this man. She, too, had turned her back on Gulnaz.

There was a new, spectacular lightness in her chest. Zeba sighed. It seemed she was only as crazy as her parents had made her.

"Sing to me," she said to the man who'd left her so long ago. It seemed like a small request to make while she sorted out whether to love or hate him.

His voice, thick with nostalgia and with a rasp that showed his years, broke the silence of the heartbreaking night. They were two forlorn beings, the distance between them dissolving under the twinkling of the stars. They did not look at each other.

"*Tonight, you will listen to the sorrows of my soul*," he croaked. "*Though tomorrow, you will forget all that has been told.*"

Zeba's father touched the top of her head. His thumb rested on her widow's peak, the very center of her forehead, and she felt like he was reaching into her soul.

His song floated into the night. It was a confession. It was a prayer. Zeba raised her voice with his even as the tears slid down her cheeks.

CHAPTER 42

YUSUF HAD JUST GOTTEN OFF THE PHONE WITH RAFI, ZEBA'S brother. He was pleased to hear that his sister would be returned to Chil Mahtab after spending nearly three weeks at the mullah's. He'd wanted to visit her there, Rafi swore to Yusuf, but couldn't leave his wife when their fourth child was due to arrive at any moment. Yusuf could hear the guilt in his voice but wasn't sure if it was his place to reassure Rafi. Every man had his choices to make.

He was sitting in the interview room at Chil Mahtab waiting for Asma, the guard who would be accompanying him to the shrine to bring back Zeba. He was toying with his cell phone when he saw Latifa standing idly in the hallway. He recognized Zeba's cellmate and, seeing that she was staring directly at him, greeted her with a slight nod. At the acknowledgment, she opened the door and poked her head inside.

"You're Zeba's lawyer," she blurted.

"I am," he said cautiously. "Did you need something?"

"When is she coming back? We know they took her to some shrine for crazies, which is stupid. Do you know why that was stupid?" Latifa did not wait for Yusuf to answer. "Because she's not crazy. She's powerful and we need her back here. When is she coming back?"

"Soon," Yusuf said, hesitant to get into the details. "The judge has approved her return."

"The judge has!" Latifa grew angry, something red and hot rising in her, the kind of swelling that had created the dent in the door of their cell. "Well, I suppose you think that's good news, but that only means he's done playing around. Two other women were charged with murder and sentenced to decades. It's just a matter of time before he sentences one to death."

"Have faith. Things could change," Yusuf said carefully.

"As long as men are the judges, nothing will change."

Yusuf suddenly felt a bit defensive on behalf of all men.

"There was a woman nominated to serve on the Supreme Court last week. Things may change."

"Did you not hear the rest?" Latifa shot back. "She was rejected because she dares bleed once a month."

Yusuf had heard that news, actually. A Supreme Court justice would have to touch the Qur'an every day, one parliamentarian had argued. How could a woman be a judge when she could not touch the Qur'an one whole week out of the month? The reasoning had made Yusuf groan. Aneesa had hurled a book across the office when she'd read about it online. She was still ranting when Yusuf slipped away to get to Chil Mahtab.

"Actually," Yusuf said, putting his phone down on the table and turning his full attention to Latifa. "I'm going today to bring her back. But what makes you say that she's powerful? I'm curious."

Latifa's hair was pulled back in a messy ponytail. She reached both hands back, parted the swath in two, and tugged to tighten it. Yusuf, who had spent his life sharing a room with two sisters, felt a twinge of homesickness at the familiar gesture.

"You don't know what she's done for the women here," Latifa said, her eyebrows raised for emphasis. "The problems that keep women up at night—she's made them go away. I've never seen anything like it."

"What do you mean?"

"She's like her mother or maybe even better. I didn't believe it at first. I don't buy into that *jadu* stuff usually, but this is the first time I've seen it myself. Are you really going to bring her back today?"

"That's the plan." Yusuf was still considering Latifa's revelations. Had the prisoners ranked the black magic of the two women? "But what do you mean better than her mother?"

"Better than her mother the *jadugar*," Latifa said, drawing the words out. Believing that she knew something Zeba's lawyer did not know, she gained confidence and stepped into the interview room. "You know her mother's a *jadugar*, right? Don't tell me you didn't know that."

Yusuf chuckled lightly. Zeba and her mother had made quite an impression on the prisoners, it seemed. He feigned mild surprise.

"I'm here to deal with other issues," he said lightly.

"Oh, you're wrong to laugh this off, mister," Latifa chided, her hands resting on her wide hips. It was at this moment that Yusuf realized she was wearing a butter-yellow Pinocchio T-shirt. While Latifa wondered if he was gawking at her heavy chest, Yusuf noted the elongated wooden nose, faded to a splintered memory. This cartoon fibber, a gentle warning to children not to lie, struck him as particularly odd plastered across a prisoner's body. "The worst thing you can do is doubt a *jadugar*. You tell Zeba that the women of Chil Mahtab are waiting for Malika Zeba."

"Malika Zeba?" Yusuf repeated, scratching at his head. "You've named her a queen?"

"Just tell her," Latifa whispered, shaking her head with a sly smile. "The women will be on fire to hear she's coming back."

Asma walked in just as Latifa was turning to leave. Asma's red hair curled around her forehead, moist with beads of sweat. She straightened her jacket and shot Latifa an expectant look, but Latifa had already backed her way out of the interview room with a bowed head.

"Godspeed to you both! May your trip be quick and successful," she shouted as she made her way down the hall, her hands cupped around her mouth. Her words echoed against the alphabet-covered walls. "Ladies, good news! They're bringing back the queen of Chil Mahtab!"

Asma looked at Yusuf expectantly. She did not seem the least bit surprised by Latifa's booming announcement.

"Ready?" she asked with a quick nod toward the door.

THE SOUNDS OF THE PRISON CAR'S ENGINE DID NOT INSPIRE confidence, nor did the lack of air-conditioning. The fan purred but blew only hot air into the car. Yusuf sat with his head nearly out the passenger-side window to catch the dusty breeze. He kept his eyes shut. He was down to his last bottle of eyedrops and was unconvinced he would find anything decent in the local pharmacies. The midnight blue upholstery was heavy with the smell of old tobacco and scarred with tears and holes. The driver, a male prison guard, drove with two hands on the wheel, his fingers drumming as he hummed to himself. Asma and another guard sat in the backseat.

Yusuf was not sure what to expect. Qazi Najeeb had called his friend, the mullah, to let him know that they were going to be bringing Zeba back. The mullah hadn't made much of an argument, apparently, which surprised Yusuf. When the driver pulled up on the parking brake in front of the mullah's quarters, Yusuf saw a curtain pull back slightly. By the height, he could tell it was the mullah's son. He stepped out of the car and shook his legs, feeling the sweat on the backs of his thighs. It had been wise to wear black slacks today.

The mullah did not emerge until they were all out of the car. The wooden door opened slowly, and he stepped out calmly to meet them. The guards were the first to speak, the male guard putting a hand over his heart in respect. The mullah nodded and looked to Yusuf.

"Quite a caravan to accompany one woman. I did not expect so many of you," he said without smiling.

Yusuf shielded his eyes from the sun.

"The warden thought it necessary."

The mullah nodded.

"How has she been?" Yusuf asked. He looked over to the row

of cells in the distance. Two men sat cross-legged in the open space, under the dappled shade of a tree thirsty for rain. There was no sign of Zeba, which should not have made Yusuf uneasy but it did. He'd hoped to find her sitting in the plastic chair outside the mullah's door, just as he'd left her.

"She's been well," Mullah Habibullah replied. "She has a strong spirit, but you knew that already, I'm sure."

"Absolutely."

"I'd like to speak to you for a moment," the mullah said.

"Of course, Mullah-*sahib*," Yusuf replied respectfully. "And then we'll be glad to take Khanum Zeba off your hands and get her back to Chil Mahtab. The judge has given me specific instructions. I'm sure you understand."

"A moment, young man."

Asma and the other female guard exchanged a quick look before walking over to the metal fence of the shrine where devotees had tied pieces of multicolored ribbon and even some strips of tattered paper. The guard who had driven them took out his cell phone and began dialing. The mullah led Yusuf back into his quarters. Yusuf's stomach sank a bit, anxious to leave. He'd brought a bag of chips, a chicken kebab rolled in flatbread, and a bottle of water for Zeba, anticipating that she might be very seriously malnourished.

It had not been a full forty days. The mullah was likely not happy that his treatment was being cut short, and whatever protests he had not lodged with the judge were sure to come Yusuf's way now. He wondered if he could count on the guards to help him forcibly take Zeba back into custody if push came to shove.

Yusuf stepped into the room and prepared a rebuttal for the mullah's argument. He was so distracted by his thoughts that he almost didn't notice Zeba sitting on the floor cushion where he had sat on that first day at the shrine. In front of her was a steaming cup of black tea and two ceramic bowls, one of pine nuts and the other of green raisins.

"Zeba! You're . . . you're here." Yusuf's eyes darted from his client to the mullah who had already taken a seat on another floor cushion. He sat just a few feet away from her, close enough that if he stretched his arm out, his fingertips would touch her. She could have been mistaken for a houseguest.

Yusuf had imagined he would find Zeba starved and unkempt, weakened by exposure. He had counted every day that she had spent in this shrine as a personal failure. He'd thought of her Spartan cell with every forkful of rice he'd brought to his mouth. He'd braced himself, in these nineteen days, for word that she had succumbed to hunger or that she'd descended into a new depth of madness.

"Are you all right?"

Zeba nodded.

"I've come to take you back to Chil Mahtab."

"I know," she said, stealing a glance at the mullah. "I was told yesterday. I'm ready to leave."

The mullah cleared his throat and absently thumbed the onyx beads of a *tasbeh*. He sat with one leg bent and the other stretched straight. He wore a gray cotton tunic and pantaloons. Yusuf noticed, for the first time, his thick salt-and-pepper sideburns, curly patches that thickened along his jaw and gathered in a short beard at his chin. He wondered what this man would look like with a shave and change of clothes.

"Before you go, I want to know what will become of her."

Yusuf turned his gaze to the carpet. Was there a polite way of telling the mullah it wasn't any of his business?

"Her case is yet to be decided by the judge," he answered. "Now if you could tell me what you think of her condition today as compared to her first day here, I'll gladly take that information back to Qazi Najeeb."

"I'm a simple man," the mullah said, his voice melancholy. "The people who come to me are suffering and it is my job to sit with them, to pray over them, and to help them find a path to healing. Their illnesses are burdens to them and to their families. It's their collective suffering that I work to heal. This woman," he said, looking at Zeba thoughtfully, "was in bad shape when she first arrived. She had been overcome by evil djinns. They controlled her thoughts and her actions. They were her arms and legs. Since your last visit I've prayed with her. I've prayed over her. She's followed the diet that washes the toxins from her body. She's exorcised the poison from her mind. I think she is much recovered, and, it is worth saying, she was able to do so in fewer than the usual forty days."

"So you think she's now of sound mental condition at this point," Yusuf summarized.

"I think much has changed for her in these few days. I think she has a better understanding of many things." His eyes were still trained on Zeba, who did not flinch at his description of her progress. She looked up at the mullah, and her lips parted slightly, as if she were about to speak, but no words came out. She clasped her hands together on her lap.

"Zeba Khanum, if you're ready, then we should be going. Asma and the others are outside waiting on us."

Zeba nodded again and pressed her palm to the carpet to support herself as she stood. She looked underweight but not deathly so. There was color in her cheeks and light in her eyes, even if she did move like an ungreased joint.

"Do you need help?" Yusuf reached out a hand instinctively, but she shook her head. The mullah watched carefully before he rose from the ground to walk them out.

"Young man," he said, putting a hand on Yusuf's forearm. Yusuf turned abruptly. The physical touch had been unexpected. "Fight for her, please. Do your best to defend her, and Allah will reward you. She does not deserve to be punished. She's a good woman. I wish I could have helped her more."

Zeba turned around and looked at the mullah. There was a sadness in her posture, not the anger Yusuf had seen when he'd left her.

"You've done the best you could," Zeba said softly. She fixed the head scarf on her head, flipping the loose end over her shoulder gracefully. "I was . . . glad to meet you."

"I will be praying for you," he said to Zeba, standing just a foot from her. "Just as I prayed for you here, I will continue to pray for you when you leave. God is great. You know what He can do."

Yusuf felt more like an interloper than Zeba's counsel. Had Zeba become a believer in the mullah's methods? Had his prayers affected her so profoundly in these few days? She'd been desperate, and it was quite possible that she grabbed onto his incantations as a drowning soul would reach for a life preserver. Yusuf noted a change in Zeba, a tranquility that hadn't been there nineteen days ago. Could there be some unearthly potency in this shrine? He shook his head and wondered if he, too, were somehow falling under the mullah's spell.

He walked out of the door and looked at Zeba expectantly.

"Mullah-*sahib*, thank you for all you've done," Yusuf said because it was the right thing to say at that particular moment.

The mullah closed both eyes and nodded slightly, a tiny acknowledgment.

Zeba followed Yusuf with heavy steps.

They stood by the car until the guards, seeing them emerge from the house, began trudging back to the vehicle. The mullah leaned against the wooden door, his hands resting just above his belly, with fingers intertwined.

"Good-bye, Padar," Zeba said softly, her eyes glistening in the sun.

Yusuf stopped short and looked at them both. His jaw went slack, and he cocked his head to the side.

"What did you say?" he asked Zeba, who stood at his side next to the car.

The mullah did not budge but kept his eyes on Zeba's. With every second that the mullah and Zeba ignored him, Yusuf felt a burgeoning realization that these were not the same two people he'd seen three weeks prior.

"What did you call him, Khanum Zeba?" he asked again, his voice sharper.

"Father," Zeba whispered, brushing a tear from her left cheek stoically. Any further explanation was cut short by the return of the guards. In a flash, they had all climbed into the silver Toyota, and its four doors were shut in succession.

Her father? Yusuf sat in the front seat, turning the words over in his mind. Did she mean her true father or had he completely brainwashed her into some kind of bizarre devotional relationship? Yusuf resisted the urge to swivel in his seat and press Zeba for an explanation. It was not a discussion he wanted to have with the current audience.

The engine turned over and they went back down the dirt road, the shrine and the mullah shrinking behind them.

CHAPTER 43

"SHE'S BACK! LADIES, LADIES, MALIKA ZEBA HAS COME BACK TO US!"

A prisoner in a black-and-green floral print dress stopped at the sight of Zeba and turned abruptly to shout down the hallway. They were just down the hall from the beauty salon.

Zeba blinked with surprise.

Three heads poked out of the doorway. One woman held a hairbrush, and another's head was crowned with curlers. She yelped when she saw Yusuf and ducked back into the salon.

"Zeba-*jan*, you're back! Malika Zeba, how are you?"

They were standing before her. More figures were appearing at the end of the hallway as news of Zeba's return rushed like water flowing downstream. Two little girls were pointing from a distance.

"That's the queen," one whispered to the other. "That's Malika Zeba. My mother told me about her."

"I thought she'd look different. Where's her crown?" the second girl said, giggling.

"What's going on here?" Zeba's words were breathy and low. She wasn't exactly asking Yusuf. She was merely dumbfounded by the nickname she'd seemed to have been assigned and the energy around her return.

Yusuf leaned in and said sharply to Zeba, "I want to talk to you before you go back to your room."

"Of course," Zeba said, somewhat distracted by the commotion in the hallway. "I just . . ."

"We've missed you so much! I need to tell you what's happened while you were gone. So much has changed, and there's only you to thank for it," a young woman said.

Zeba smiled wanly, unsure what to make of this welcome. The girl took Zeba's hands and turned her palms upward, pressing her lips against them. Zeba pulled her hands back, made uncomfortable by a gesture that should have been reserved for the gray haired.

"You saved me!"

"I saved you?" Zeba repeated. Slowly, she remembered sitting with this woman and watching her two young boys fidget as she told the terrible story of how they'd been conceived.

"Yes! This *taweez* you gave me," she said, pointing to the small bundle safety-pinned to the sleeve of her dress. "I've worn it every moment since you put it in my hands."

"What's happened?" Zeba asked.

"The shelter the boys were supposed to go to is full. They have no room for anyone else, and my family does not want to take them. They would have had nowhere to go, Zeba-*jan*. They would have been on the street, so easy for anyone to snatch up and sell for body parts or turn into slaves. I've imagined a million horrible things. But just two days ago, the director of the prison said they would have permission to stay for another two years. Two more years!"

Zeba's eyes widened.

"That's . . . that's fantastic news!" she exclaimed softly.

"It is, and it is all thanks to you. So much has happened, Malika Zeba. We have been praying for your safe return so that we can thank you for everything you've done." She snuck a bashful glance at Yusuf, whose curiosity had been piqued. "And just to show you that I will never forget your help . . . this is what I've done."

She slid the sleeve up her right forearm, wincing slightly as it rolled over a fresh scar. Raised green-black letters spelled out Zeba's name. Zeba let out a gasp.

"What have you done?" she exclaimed. She touched the woman's arm with one finger, grazing the letters with the pad of her fingertip and drawing back sharply to feel how real they were. She looked up, expecting to see the woman grimace, but she did not.

"I've printed your name on my body to match the print on my heart. What you've done for me, I will never forget." She had her two hands pressed against her sternum, her head tilted to the side so that her bangs hung away from her kohl-lined eyes. "I will always be grateful for the time you've given me with my sons."

"Oh, you foolish girl!" Zeba laughed. "What will your sons say?"

"My sons? They're lucky I didn't tattoo your name on them, too!" She glowed with relief, and Zeba felt her shoulders relax at this woman's happiness. "They would cry every time I talked to them about going to the children's shelter. You cannot imagine how happy they are to be staying with me now! Marzia is teaching the children numbers now, or they would be here to hug you themselves."

"Malika Zeba!" called another woman's voice. Her couplet echoed through the hallway, followed by a ripple of laughter:

"There is hope even for the rice ever burned
Since our Queen Malika has been returned!"

Four more women charged toward them with giddy smiles and eager faces. "Finally! I never had a chance to talk to you before. I'm so thankful you're back. You've got to help me!"

Zeba was swept away by a wave of women, leaving Yusuf standing in the hallway of Chil Mahtab. Asma laughed at his slack-jawed expression and shrugged her shoulders.

"She's got the women under her thumb with that *jadu* of hers. Last week, they had a tattooing session in the beauty parlor. Her name's been written on a dozen body parts," Asma whispered, scandalized.

Yusuf's mobile phone chirped in his pocket. He took it out and looked at the number that had called him three times in the last week. Three times he'd ignored the calls because he'd been in the middle of a conversation with the judge or Aneesa or his mother. He pressed the green button to take the call, still thinking Zeba owed him an explanation. Was the mullah really her father? Did her mother know about this?

"Hello?"

"Yes, hello. Is this the phone of the lawyer for Khanum Zeba, the prisoner at Chil Mahtab?"

It was a woman's voice. Yusuf wondered if it were someone from the office, though Aneesa hadn't mentioned anyone would be calling.

"Yes. Who's asking?" The last of the women disappeared around the far corner of the hallway. Asma followed, more out of curiosity than a need to control the swell of women around Zeba.

"I'm a reporter with *Dawn News*. My name is Sultana. I wanted to ask you a few questions about her case. I'm happy to chat with you on the phone or in person."

She spoke quickly and concisely. She was polite, but there was an edge to her tone. When Qazi Najeeb had talked about the reporter, it had never crossed Yusuf's mind that it might be a woman.

"Oh, so you're the one looking for a story on Chil Mahtab?" Yusuf went to the interview room. He needed to write up a report of what had transpired at the shrine today and the mullah's latest assessment of Zeba. He pulled the door closed, and the echo of the hallway disappeared. He threw his bag on the table and pulled back the chair.

"I am. Initially, I wanted to do a story on the crimes of immorality, but it seems that your client is a very interesting one and the charges against her are pretty serious. Do you know the women of the prison are entranced by her? She's become something of a hero to them."

"Yes, that's pretty clear," Yusuf agreed, the calls for "Malika Zeba" still ringing in his ears.

"And it seems she's got an intriguing background. Her grandfather was a *murshid* and her mother is a bit of a character. How did Zeba come to be charged with such a gruesome crime? Has she truly confessed to killing her husband or do you assert that the signed statement recorded in her arrest registry is false?"

"How did you hear about that?"

"By asking questions. So is it her confession or was it fabricated?"

Yusuf was taken aback by her direct questions. They'd been on the phone for only a moment, and she was already pecking at the heart of the case.

"I've raised serious concern about the validity of the confession," he said carefully. He'd already decided that he would use the press coverage in any way he could. If it meant pointing fingers at the muddied justice system, he would do just that.

"I see. And I've also heard that she was taken to a shrine to be treated for insanity. This is not at all standard procedure in a murder case. Was it your recommendation to take her to that shrine? How much longer will she be there?"

Yusuf undid the top button of his collar and peeled it away from the back of his neck, where beads of moisture made it cling to his skin.

"She's not at a shrine," he said simply. If Sultana wanted more information about the shrine, she would have to look for it elsewhere. He wasn't about to paint his client as an insane person when it didn't seem an insanity defense would get her anywhere.

"But she *was* at a shrine, a local one where a mullah engages in some fairly controversial treatment for the insane. Why was she taken there when we have medical facilities with trained professionals who could evaluate and treat her scientifically?"

"She is not at a shrine," Yusuf repeated without elaborating.

"Where is she?" Sultana asked with great interest.

"She's here at Chil Mahtab. We're preparing our final statements for her case, and the judge should be issuing a ruling in the next two days." Yusuf had been struggling with his final arguments, going through pages and pages of handwritten scrawl without sat-isfaction.

"And how do you think Qazi Najeeb will rule?"

"That's a question for Qazi Najeeb," Yusuf replied. "But my hope is that he will weigh all the factors in this complicated case and reach a fair conclusion for this mother of four young children. The sooner she can be returned to them, the better."

"You maintain her innocence?"

"I do," Yusuf affirmed.

"You've made a case that she is insane, from what I understand. Do you know that no one has ever been defended with an insanity plea in Afghanistan? This is quite unusual."

"I'm aware, but the circumstances of this case are unusual and Qazi Najeeb has been careful about sticking closely to the procedural and penal codes of Afghanistan. We have followed the law precisely to be sure that Khanum Zeba is receiving a fair trial. Just because there's no precedence doesn't make it wrong. Lots of things are happening for the first time in our country."

"You're speaking to the only female journalist willing to cover this province. I don't think you have to tell me that."

Yusuf's lips curled in a smile as he pulled at a stray thread on the strap of his messenger bag.

"When are you planning on printing this story?" he asked.

"When I feel I have enough to go on. As of right now, there's a woman accused of murdering her husband and her American lawyer is making claims that she is not guilty because she's insane. Not a bad lead, is it? Still, I want to include everything I can. Sometimes, crime in Afghanistan is more about rumor and gossip than anything else."

"There's a lot of truth to that." Yusuf sighed.

"But I don't want to be part of the gossip. Rumors can get a woman lynched in the streets. I want facts, and facts might just help your case," she suggested. "Anything I print could potentially sway the courts to act on the right side of the law here. Our reports sometimes catch the attention of the foreign media. A few international eyes on your case, and the pressure is on."

"Ah, so you're really calling to do me a favor!" Yusuf chuckled.

"I don't do favors. I just report the news," Sultana corrected. "Can you tell me about this woman's husband? Do you have any idea why she or someone else may have wanted to kill him?"

"There are rumors, but nothing I can commit to. And again, I'm insisting on my client's innocence. It's unusual for a wife to kill her husband. It's much more common the other way around."

"Again," Sultana said pointedly, "something an Afghan woman doesn't need to be told."

Yusuf felt a rising indignation in his chest. He didn't appreciate being painted as the stereotypical Afghan man. He took a look at the blank forms on the table in front of him, picking up a notebook and using it to fan himself.

"Look, I've got to go. There's nothing more I can tell you for now. Good luck with your story," he said quickly.

"Yusuf, just one more thing to ask. Did Khanum Zeba ever—"

But Yusuf cut her off, pressing his thumb to the red button on the cell phone while her question dangled on the line.

CHAPTER 44

ZEBA'S CLOTHES, A SMALL STACK THAT BARELY USED UP ONE shelf of the metal locker in their cell, had been freshly washed and folded. The sheets of her bed were stiff with starch and neatly tucked under the corners of her mattress. There was a red silk carnation and a small prism keychain on her pillow. The prism had a red heart at its center and spread fractured light in every direction as Zeba turned it over in her palm.

She'd returned to Chil Mahtab two hours ago but was just getting to her room now. Swarmed by her fellow prisoners in the hallway, she sensed that this place had become a shrine unto itself. It unnerved her, the way the women smiled at her, the way they offered her trinkets, the way their fingertips touched her body as if she were some kind of mystic. And Asma was right. Several women had tattooed Zeba's name on their arms or backs either because she had saved them or because they hoped that she would. Some believed that the four letters of her name inked into their skin was a talisman in itself. The anticipation of what she could do thrived and spread like vines through the stifling hallways of Chil Mahtab.

Latifa had hugged her, an awkward pressing of her thick body against Zeba's gaunt frame.

"Oh God, you've wasted away to nothing! It must have been so awful. You should eat something. Nafisa, run down to the kitchen and get her some food!"

Nafisa had seen Zeba in the hallway but had patiently waited for the crowd to clear before she put her arms around her cellmate. She'd been spooked by the idea that Zeba had been deemed insane enough to be shackled to a shrine. In the cell, she'd kept her attention on the television. She was watching the news from Kabul: a young man and woman sitting behind a long desk reporting stories of suicide bombers and cricket game results. She was about to tell Latifa to get the food herself when she took a longer look at Zeba. Her jaw snapped shut before she could protest being bossed around.

"Oh, Zeba-*jan!*" Nafisa exclaimed. "I'll grab you something right away. You do look pretty terrible."

"It's all right, Nafisa." Zeba motioned for her to stay where she was. "I had some food on the way here. My stomach still feels bloated from it."

"Hmph." Latifa smirked, eyeing Zeba's thin frame skeptically. "You don't look the least bit bloated to me."

Zeba did not know what to do with herself. She wanted to stand and stretch, because for nearly three weeks she hadn't been able to. She wanted to walk through the yard and put her legs to use again. She wanted to lie down on her mattress and sleep without worrying about scorpions or hearing the rattling of chains.

Zeba was relieved to be back in prison, a feeling that made her insides sour. She realized she did not have much to hope for. Yusuf was struggling with his defense, and although she had not meant to, Zeba had begun to think it might actually be possible to find a way out of this predicament and be returned to her children. There were moments when she considered telling Yusuf and the judge and the prosecutor the unfiltered truth of what happened on that day. She could tell them that she had not killed her husband. The truth, in its entirety, could not possibly hold her responsible.

Then again, Zeba knew that no one would believe the truth. Furthermore, she had silently and without ceremony sworn to herself that she would not hurt that little girl any more than Kamal already had. Was she forsaking her own children for a child she did not know?

Possibly. But she'd made the choice weeks ago and would not reconsider it. If she were released from prison and something more were to happen to that child, every day of freedom would be torture. One day, she would tell the girls the truth too. She did not want to hurt them either, but she needed for them to look at her as they once had.

The sooner she accepted Chil Mahtab, the sooner she could begin to survive. She had to build a new life for herself. She had to be stronger than she'd ever been before. There was nothing crazy about her, she'd realized at the shrine. Her thoughts streamed in clear lines. The only voice in her head was her own.

Her father, Mullah Habibullah, had spent hours and hours at her cell in those nineteen days. His voice, the soft rasp of it like a familiar song, soothed her. She forgave him for his many years of absence. Disappearing, she now knew, was not the worst thing a man could do to his family. And she did not want to lose him a second time.

"You're not insane, Zeba. If there's anything wrong with you, it's that you have too much of your mother's blood in your veins. Her blood is hot and vengeful. She says she believes in God, but she believes only in Gulnaz. I know her well. I loved her, too. Since you're an adult and almost a stranger to me, I can tell you that much. I loved her once."

Zeba had not argued with him. She'd had the same string of bitter thoughts about Gulnaz for years.

"But I told the lawyers to leave you here because once I realized who you were . . . once I realized you were a part of me . . . I could not tear my eyes away from you. You looked troubled. Just as troubled as the other souls who are brought to the shrine. Sometimes it's hard to figure out if you're crazy or if it's the world around you that's insane. Sometimes if you don't lose your mind a little bit, there's no way to survive. You're not broken, my daughter. That's what you have to remember."

ZEBA'S THOUGHTS WERE INTERRUPTED BY A KNOCKING AT THE door. She saw faces she recognized. They pretended not to see her sitting on the bed and addressed Latifa. They bit their lower lips and cast sideways glances at one another.

"Malika Zeba is not sleeping, is she?"

Latifa looked to Zeba for direction.

"Come in," Zeba said. After so many nights alone, she craved the company. "Come in, sisters."

Their faces burst into broad smiles, and they clogged the doorway trying to get in. They sat, cross-legged, on the floor in front of Zeba with their head scarves hanging casually around their necks.

"I wanted to thank you for helping me," began Bibi Shireen. She had been sentenced to twenty-seven years for murder after her son was killed for running off with a girl. Zeba felt embarrassed to be sitting above someone as gray haired as Bibi Shireen and slid off the bed to sit among the women on the floor. Zeba half stood and gestured for Bibi Shireen to take her seat, but the woman waved her off with a frown. "You saved my daughter. They were going to take her as a bride in vengeance. No amount of begging had changed their minds but you . . . I don't know what you did, but it's worked. They decided they didn't want her after all."

"Really?" Zeba exclaimed. For a family to give up their claim on a girl was unusual, even if the government had outlawed the practice of *baad*, giving daughters to resolve disputes between families, in 2009. "That's wonderful news!"

"I'm not going to live another twenty-seven years, anyway. They'll never get that much time out of me. It's more important that my daughter's life not become a prison. She's the one with that many more years in her, God willing."

The other women nodded and chirped in agreement.

"And we wanted to thank you, too." It was the sister-wives, the two women imprisoned for the murder of their husband though he'd actually been killed by his cousins. The younger woman spoke first, her voice as sweet as cream. She looked at the first wife who sat beside her, grinning. "Do you want to tell her or should I?"

"Go on. You tell her."

"Well," she said, smiling surreptitiously. "While you were gone we found out that one of the men who murdered our husband was killed."

"Killed? By whom?" Latifa asked. She loomed over the circle of women sitting on the floor, more attentive than any prison guard.

"The cousins who came after our husband turned on each other. They started fighting about the land among themselves, and one shot his cousin in the chest. The family is in shambles. They're all about ready to kill each other now, and we're the only ones in prison. We are safe here. It's almost funny."

"It's not funny at all, actually," the older wife said with a chastising look. "But let them kill each other. Leaves us with fewer enemies out there. In the meantime, we're probably in the best place we could be."

The younger wife nodded.

"You bet," Latifa interjected. "I'm sure someone from the family would be ready to snatch both you widows up as wives since your husband is gone. That's what happened to my aunt."

"You're right," the older wife said, her face grim. "There was talk about that even during our trials. Better to stay here if that's the option."

"Will you tell us what you did, Zeba-*jan*?" the younger wife asked. She was kneeling, her hands on her thighs and her head tilted. "What kind of curse did you put on them?"

Zeba was stunned. She remembered the day these prisoners had laid their problems at her feet. She'd had no answers for them. She'd managed only to say that she would think on their situations and she had—at the shrine. She'd prayed for each of these women, though only in vague terms, distilling her request to Allah down to one simple word. Mercy.

"I . . . I cannot say what I did. I prayed and thought about you all." Zeba stumbled over an explanation.

"But what did you use for the spell? Fire? A chicken bone? I'm so curious!"

Latifa sensed Zeba's hesitation and filled the silence with her booming voice.

"She can't tell you, of course! This is dangerous stuff she deals with, don't you see? *Lethal* stuff." Latifa's voice was a hoarse whisper as she leaned in for the last words. From where they sat on the floor, she appeared larger than life. "What Malika Zeba does is not a game. It is not for everyone. It stays in her capable hands."

The women exchanged glances, Latifa's words sinking in. The young wife bit her cheek in regret, and Latifa returned to her bed to observe from a distance. Zeba struggled to maintain her composure.

"I don't need to know what you did," declared Wahida. "I'm just thankful you did it."

"Yes, this is a good one." Latifa chuckled. She was happier now that order had been restored in the cell. "Tell Zeba what happened in your case."

Zeba looked at Wahida, a young woman who looked much more polished than any of the others at Chil Mahtab. She had finished high school and she had one brother living in Iran who sent her gifts. She sidled up next to Zeba and put a hand on her knee.

"It is a good thing. Latifa-*jan* is right. The boy I'd run off with begged his family to allow us to marry, but it wasn't until Zeba came along that they finally agreed. At last, we're going to be together!"

"Lucky girl! Are they planning a wedding for you?" the older sister-wife asked, leaning backward to see past the younger sister-wife.

"No," Wahida answered wistfully. "But they've pooled some money together to get us both freed. Just a few more days, they tell me."

Latifa clapped her hands together.

"It's just incredible. I've been here for years," she said with a moan.

"I've never seen anything like this. I've never seen so many women getting a break. Malika Zeba is a miracle maker!"

"Don't say that," Zeba said sharply. "I'm not a miracle worker at all. I prayed for you all while I was at the shrine. I didn't do . . . I mean, you shouldn't think of me as . . . some kind of miracle maker. I'm a prisoner just like you."

"Not a chance. No other prisoner has been able to do what you've done. I've been here long enough to know that."

"She's right," the older sister-wife confirmed. "And if you ever need anything, we are here for you. The women have been gathering in the beauty salon, in the classroom, in the prison yard. Everywhere the chatter is about what you've done to help us. For the first time in a long time, we feel like something can be done. You've lit this place like a full moon!"

"And the children are happier, too, those poor things," clucked Bibi Shireen. "They sense their mother's nerves, you know."

Zeba felt her eyes mist. She wasn't responsible for any of this—was she?

"That's why you've earned the name Malika Zeba," Nafisa said, tweaking the volume up on the television. It was time for the singing competition again, and she did not want to miss the finals. "You're the most famous woman in this prison. There's even a reporter who's been here, asking around. She heard about your case and wants to interview you. I wouldn't be surprised to see your story make the news. Your face on the television—wouldn't that be something!"

Zeba did not answer. Notoriety within the confines of Chil Mahtab was one thing, but Zeba was certain that the rest of the country would not view her through the same rosy lenses as her fellow prisoners.

CHAPTER 45

THE RAIN CAME DOWN IN SHEETS, DESCENDING FROM THICK, nimbus clouds that looked like unspun lambswool. Yusuf had dashed into the office moments before it started. The rain fell upon the glass windows of the office in a soothing, staccato rhythm. He would appreciate none of this later, he knew, when he plodded his way home on a muddied road. The rain was much needed though, as the town hadn't seen a drop of precipitation in over a month. Brittle tree branches snapped as easily as peapods, and dust floated through the air without any moisture to weigh it down.

It was a welcome break from the heat, and Yusuf felt his eyes drawn to the window often, as if he'd never seen rain before.

When he heard the ringing, Yusuf reached into his jacket pocket. This time, he recognized the string of numbers on his cell phone. He took a deep breath before pressing his thumb against the talk button.

"Hello?" he said, purposefully icing his voice a bit to sound pre-occupied.

"Yes, it's Sultana again from *Dawn*," she said as if he'd not abruptly cut off their last conversation. "I wanted to follow up on the conversation we had the other day regarding the case of Khanum Zeba."

Yusuf looked at the stack of papers on his desk, thinking to himself that all his preparation for the case of Khanum Zeba was a great big pile of nothing in the end. The insanity defense had looked viable when outlined on his yellow notepad, but in reality, it had choked pretty badly. The rumors about her husband, Kamal, had won her more sympathy from the judge and prosecutor than any argument Yusuf had put forth. All he had left was the truth, the horrible truth about what Zeba had seen Kamal doing that day, but Yusuf had been instructed by his client not to mention the girl. She was afraid for the girl's well-being and rightfully so. *A child had been sexually violated,* he thought, *but the world would only see her as damaged goods.* There would not be pity or rage for her, and even if there were, it would scarcely be enough.

"Do you have a specific question?" Yusuf asked. He was sitting at his desk in their main office. Aneesa was at her desk on the opposite side of the room, a phone cradled between her tilted head and shoulder. She adjusted her glasses with her free hand and then rubbed at her forehead and temples. She was busy working on a brief for a new client, a young woman who had been sold into servitude after she'd lost both her parents. She'd been taken from a village to Kabul, and after the family she worked for discovered both of their adolescent boys had been sexually assaulting her, she was passed on as a bride to a man in his seventies. The old man had turned her out two weeks after their marriage because she'd not been a virgin. Now the client had been arrested for *zina* and was to arrive in Chil Mahtab in the morning. Aneesa might need his help on that case, and he didn't want to waste time on a reporter.

"I realize you don't want to give me specific details on this Zeba case," she explained. "So maybe we can talk about the imprisoned women more generally. I've been to Chil Mahtab a few times and the stories in that place range from tragic to absurd, but no one seems to be paying any attention to how easy it is to cry 'immorality' at the sight of a woman doing anything."

"How did you get interested in this topic?"

Sultana's voice relaxed noticeably when Yusuf asked the question, as if she were afraid he might have hung up on her.

"There was a report that circulated in the NGO world. It talked about the crimes women were accused of and the sentences they received. I read the report and, at first, I was so bothered that a foreign organization would come in to our country and judge us by their standards, but then I took a step back. I realized it wasn't useful to be annoyed if I didn't do anything about it, so I decided to investigate for myself. Afghans aren't going to read the NGO's report, but they will listen to our news service."

"I suppose there isn't much faith in the foreign NGOs."

"There's either too much faith in them or too little faith. Some people want them to do everything for our country, and others see them as spies or missionaries. Either way, we've got to pull our own weight too."

"Not many people see it that way."

"You're here with a legal aid organization. You might be hearing only one side of the story. Speaking of your organization, what do you think of the representation women are getting once they are arrested? Do you think it's fair or adequate?"

Yusuf's head dropped. He struggled for an answer. He knew Sultana was asking him about the general defense women received and the counselors appointed to them. But the words changed as they met his ear, turning into the same question that breathed uncomfortably down his neck each night as he tossed and turned his way to sleep each night.

Are you doing a good job defending Zeba?

"Are you still there?"

"Yes, I'm here," Yusuf muttered. He sat up and noticed Aneesa was off the phone. She shot him a look of concern, her arched eyebrows raised. He nodded back at her in reassurance then returned to Sultana's question. "Look, some of the women are getting a reasonable defense, but others aren't. A lot of the lawyers are putting together cases that make me wonder what kind of training they've received. Their defense arguments are actually pleas for mercy and almost sound like confession statements of their own. It's an injustice, especially for women who are arrested on trumped-up charges in the first place. That being said, I don't know if anyone in Afghanistan is getting a fair trial. Those murderers in Kabul who were tried and sentenced in a week . . . that wasn't really a fair trial either. That was an abomination in the opposite direction."

Was Sultana taking notes? There was a faint crackle on the line. He listened for the sound of her breathing.

"Did you do all your schooling in the United States?"

"I did," Yusuf answered.

"What made you want to be a lawyer?"

"I have an unquenchable need to be right at all times," Yusuf joked. He heard Sultana laugh lightly.

"And you? Did you study journalism abroad?"

"No, I graduated from Kabul University."

"Really?" Yusuf was surprised. He'd half expected Sultana to be like him, an expat who had returned to the homeland with a foreign education. He wondered why he'd made that assumption. Maybe it was her forwardness or the way she asked questions that didn't skirt the topic.

"Yes, really," she said sharply. She'd detected his surprise and was unimpressed by it. She switched into English to make her point. "We do have an educational system here, you know. You don't have to go to the United States to learn something."

"I didn't mean that. Tell me, then, why did you become a journalist?"

"Because I like to know the truth," she replied without hesitation. "I have always asked a lot of questions, even when I was a child. My family tolerated it so well that I decided to make it my work."

"Good thinking."

"Thank you," she said brightly. "I'm planning on going to the prison later this afternoon to do a few more interviews. I'm hoping to catch the warden as well. She's been pretending to be busy, but I'm going to corner her today. Any chance you'll be there?"

"I'm at the office this morning." And he was, but as the words left his mouth, Yusuf felt a tug to change his plans. "I'll probably be at the prison in the afternoon though."

"Great, I'll be there at two o'clock. Maybe I'll see you then."

Yusuf hung up the phone and tapped his pencil against his notepad. The afternoon was looking less dreary than the morning.

CHAPTER 46

ZEBA STOOD AT THE EDGE OF THE FENCE AND WATCHED HER mother approach, just as she had months ago. She'd last seen Gulnaz at the shrine when she'd turned to look back at Zeba before entering the mullah's quarters. Zeba thought back to her shouts, the warning cries she'd sent out to her mother from across the shrine's open yard. But Gulnaz had never been in any danger. Mullah Habibullah had never intended to hurt her—not when they lived together, not when he left, and not when they sat together to discuss the fate of their imprisoned daughter.

The rain had cooled the air but made a mess of the yard. Zeba's sandals were wet and the bottoms of her pantaloons had wicked the water from the earth. They could not sit for today's visit or the mud would cake their clothes. That suited Zeba fine. This was a conversation she wanted to stand for anyway.

Gulnaz met her daughter's eyes even from a distance, but she did not speak until she reached the thin fence that separated them. She looked at the slick beneath her feet and shook her head. Their feet sank into the ground, weighted by mud and the discoveries of the recent days.

"*Salaam*, Madar," Zeba said softly.

"*Wa-alaikum, janem.* Your color is better." Gulnaz's eyes flew over Zeba's shoulder, scanning the yard for any of her cellmates. She felt compelled to ask about them, as if she needed polite conversation to fill the space of time she was going to spend with her own daughter. "The others aren't outside today."

"They do what they can to stay out of this filth."

Zeba felt her throat knot. Ever since she'd been a small girl, she'd looked up to her mother. Even when she felt that her mother was vengeful with her *jadu*, she'd believed her to be someone larger than life and invincible. That's what made it acceptable to push her away. Her mother was not frail or needy. She was an island of autonomy even when the world around her was at war. Zeba did not push her mother down—she had merely walked away from her.

But this was a different Gulnaz. Before her stood a simple woman, made of flesh and scars and regrets. She was a story with an arc that fell suddenly and tragically when it should have lifted. Zeba did what she could to banish the pity from her eyes. That was not what she wished for her mother. It was cruelty to have a light shine so brightly on the one lie she had built her life upon, the one fallacy that allowed her to carry on each day and walk with her head held high. Zeba hated that she knew the truth about her father, that he had simply walked out on her because he couldn't stand to be around her mother. That her father was not a wretched man or an insane man or a dead soldier only made matters worse. He was alive and well, a decent person who'd made a drastic decision—choosing to walk away from everything he had and every person he'd ever loved simply to get as far away from Gulnaz as possible. He'd left her with as much dignity as he could until their paths were forced together once again.

Zeba could see the lines on her mother's face and wondered how she'd never noticed them before. The green of her eyes didn't sparkle. Was it because they sat beneath a sky of hammered metal or because they had lost their luster years ago and Zeba hadn't noticed? The bend of her spine, her shrunken lips, the slight tremble in her hands—all were tiny revelations for Zeba.

"Madar," she started. Why did it have to be like this? Why were she and her mother like two survivors floating on rafts, reaching out for each other only to be bounced apart by wave after tumultuous wave? Would they ever reach still waters?

"Now you know," Gulnaz said, her moist eyes half hidden by heavy eyelids. "Now you know everything. And I'm glad you do. It surprises me to say it but it's true. I hid it from you because you were a girl. You couldn't have known what a husband was." Gulnaz stared off into the distance. She spoke softly, a thin attempt at lightening the heaviness in the air. "But I don't have to tell you now, do I? You know better than most, *jan-e-madar*, that some husbands are quite burdensome creatures."

"They are, aren't they?" Zeba laughed, bringing a trace of a smile to her mother's face. Zeba went on, "I always dreamed of trekking across the country, climbing the mountains and finding some green flag somewhere or a pile of stones and being struck with this knowledge that somehow I'd stumbled upon my father's grave. I imagined him a martyr, a hero who had spilled his blood for freedom."

"It was a different kind of freedom he was after. He was no martyr, neither was I."

"I suppose not."

"I knew he would speak to you," Gulnaz said. "I begged him that day not to say anything, but I could tell from the look on his face that he wouldn't be able to hold his tongue for more than a few moments once I left."

"How could he? I would have hated him for it."

Gulnaz looked up sharply.

"You wouldn't have known to hate him for it. He could have simply left things alone."

Zeba shook her head.

"That's not the way it should be. I needed to know."

"Did you? Has it made anything better? Has it restored anything in you? I bet it hasn't."

Zeba wouldn't answer that question. Her mother looked pained enough.

"Have you told Rafi?"

Gulnaz nodded.

"I had to. No sense in waiting for him to hear it from you or, worse, from your father."

"Father" fell from her tongue like a drop of poison. Zeba saw just how much her mother despised her husband and knew resentment was at its root. Gulnaz had wanted him to be something better and he'd disappointed her.

"What did Rafi say?"

"Not much. I don't know if he'll try to see him or if he'll just pretend he never heard about this. He was almost a young man when your father left to—" Gulnaz caught herself before she completed the phrase with the lie she'd been telling for so long that it had grown roots in her mind. "When your father left. He's angry about that."

"He has a right to be. We all have a right to be angry at him for leaving."

Gulnaz looked up, grateful for the bit of anger that survived in her daughter after learning the truth.

"Those were difficult years."

"I'm sure they were, Madar. I don't doubt that for a moment."

"Shame is a terrible thing."

Zeba knew it well. It was terrible. Shame was more binding than the shackle around her ankle at the shrine. Shame, in its many shapes and colors, was what had broken Zeba, Gulnaz, and the girl Kamal had raped. It threatened to cast them out of their communities. It threatened the promise of a new day. It was an indelible stain on their spirits.

"I'm sorry you felt ashamed," Zeba said. It was the best she could offer. She could not tell her mother that she should not have felt shame or that she should not feel shame even now. She would not compound one fallacy with another, not when her mother could see right through it.

"It's done," Gulnaz said flatly. "I should have expected this to happen. Nothing stays buried, especially in a place like this where people are always sticking their hands into the dirt and trying to dig

things up. But he doesn't want to come back. Nothing will change
with the family. Your father turned his back on them, and for him to
return now would bring shame to him, too. He'll stay hidden behind
that beard and shrine until the day he dies and his wife can bury him
there as the great mullah who spent his years helping the troubled."

"He is not a bad person. He told me he meant you no harm."

"I didn't disagree with his choice," Gulnaz admitted. "We were
once happy, but that was before I knew him. When he was only my
fiancé and we were at arm's length, we were very happy with each
other. But by the time my wedding henna had faded from my hands,
I hated being his wife. I would have hated being anyone's wife, to tell
you the truth, and I told him that at the shrine."

"What did he say?" It was a bold question for Zeba to ask, such a
private matter between her parents. She asked anyway because boundaries had already been crossed.

"He knew it. He's always known it. That was why he did me the
favor of not divorcing me. He could have, just to free himself, but it
would have been a bigger shame than his walking out. He could have
stayed and taken a second wife, but even that didn't appeal to him. He
wanted to wander, and hating me gave him a good excuse to do it."

Zeba hooked her fingers on the metal fence and pressed her face
against the mesh, the rings making impressions on her skin. Her
mother touched her cheeks and nose with a fingertip, a caress as light
and warm as sunlight.

"I don't think any less of you, Madar-*jan*. I would have done the
same. I probably will do the same, actually, when it comes time to tell
Shabnam, Kareema, and Rima about their father. I'll come up with
the prettiest version of the truth I can and pray that they believe it
until we're all dead and buried."

"What did happen, Zeba?"

Zeba bit her lower lip and grimaced. She shifted her weight and
felt the softened earth give way beneath her, molding itself to the
shape of her feet.

"I found him attacking a girl I'd never seen before—a girl barely older than Shabnam. I'd never expected to see something so evil in my own home. It was the blackest thing a mother could see. He . . . he ruined her."

Gulnaz inhaled sharply. She'd recognized the darkness in Kamal long ago, but she'd not guessed it was this. She looked at her daughter and felt pride rush through her veins.

"You were strong. The judge doesn't know?"

Zeba looked at her mother.

"Why would he believe me? I'm only half a witness as a woman. And if it comes out what happened . . . she will be destroyed again. I have to think of my own children, too. People would say such horrible things to them."

Zeba's reasoning was sound. Girls without honor were better off dead, many thought. And then there was vengeance. If the girl's family was disgraced in town, they could seek retribution. Maybe they would demand Shabnam or Kareema be given to them as a wife or servant.

"One day, you'll talk to the children about all this," Gulnaz predicted, her heart torn between her own mistakes and those her daughter could still make. "When you do, don't spare them too much. It's much better to believe your children can be your friends. Look at Basir. He knows what you've done and why, and when I spoke with him, his eyes glow to hear your name. There is no shame you need to hide from him."

Zeba nodded. Her throat swelled at the mention of her son's name. To believe he could still love her was everything. She'd told him so much more than a boy should hear about his parents. She'd yearned to tell him everything, every cold detail, but he was only a child himself, and she could not trust him to keep the fact of her innocence to himself.

She'd told him what she'd seen and that the hatchet had been lying there. She'd told him even that she had been most afraid it was one of her daughters hidden beneath Kamal's figure. She'd told him she'd acted without thinking. He'd looked at her in fear, as if the most frightening thing in that night had not been the long way he'd traveled alone or the cries of the insane in the shadow of the shrine.

She resisted, though, telling him that she'd picked up the hatchet and swung it, sideways, at the back of his father's head, only managing to knock him over. She'd stepped on Kareema's plastic doll, lost her footing, and crumpled on the ground, the hatchet a few feet away. Kamal had howled at her in anger while on his hands and knees.

You whore! I'll kill you!

He'd leaped onto her, straddling her as she kicked. She'd covered her face with her hands. His heavy hand had clamped over her mouth so that she'd tasted the salt of his skin. She felt a tightness in her chest. Breathing was difficult. She'd not seen the girl crawl away. Like Kamal, she'd not seen what was coming next.

"I think Tamina is going to bring them here soon," Gulnaz added. "She hasn't said for sure, but I think she will."

"Tamina? Why . . . what makes you think she would do such a thing?" Zeba's voice was a whisper.

"She does not have the fondest memories of her brother. It seems he was a menace in her childhood as well, which is why she wanted to take in the children when he died. She doesn't trust Basir completely, but she's decent to him and I think she'll come around once the dust settles. I didn't understand completely, but now I do. The past months have been hard on her, especially with the rumors about the Qur'an. She'll come once it doesn't look like she's spitting on her brother's grave to do so. It's actually better for her that the village hates him so, even if he's dead. It gives Tamina more freedom not to hate you."

Tamina. Zeba could only imagine what Kamal had done to his younger sister in the privacy of their childhood home. No wonder she'd kept her distance from their family entirely. She, too, shuffled through life with shackles.

"Poor Tamina. I had never even thought . . ." Zeba groaned.

"But she's survived. Most do, in some way."

Zeba nodded and prayed that her mother was right.

Little girl, she thought, recalling the way pale-faced Laylee had dropped the hatchet after striking the fatal blow to the back of Kamal's head. Her hair clinging to her wet face, her hands shaking, and a bottled scream in her throat, she'd looked at Zeba wild-eyed.

Go, Zeba had screamed at her, half expecting Kamal to rise from the dead and strike them both down. She'd faltered, staring at her bloodied hands, before frantically wiping them on her dress.

No, no, no, no, no, the girl had cried in a voice so small Zeba could barely hear it over her own thunderous heartbeat.

Little girl, she thought as she stood inches away from her mother and thought of how many women kept secrets in the vault of their hearts. *Just a little girl and already so much to hide.*

CHAPTER 47

YUSUF TRUDGED ALONG THE ROAD, HIS SHOES MUDDIED AND his socks damp. He'd rolled up the hems of his trousers, hoping to spare at least part of his clothing from the mud. The taxi driver had dropped him off as close to the entrance of Chil Mahtab as he could.

He should not have come today. There was no true urgency to this visit, nothing he was going to do that could not have been done tomorrow when the sun had been given the opportunity to dry the streets. Yusuf told himself that engaging with this reporter was strategy, not an act of desperation. He stood in the interview room while two guards rambled past, greeting him with a nod. He'd gotten to know their faces, if not their names, and put a hand to his forehead in a friendly salute before unfurling his trouser legs.

He checked his phone and saw that it was just a few moments after two o'clock. He opened his messenger bag and removed his notepad. He spotted his bottle of eyedrops and appreciated the rain for what it did to the air quality. He'd woken that morning without feeling like the insides of his eyelids were made of sandpaper.

He'd missed a call. He looked at the long string of numbers and realized his mother must have called with a calling card. She purchased them from the Afghan market she went to for bread, lamb, and thermoses, items she refused to purchase from any other retailer. She took two buses and walked a quarter of a mile to get to the Afghan store but never complained about the inconvenience.

Everywhere else you go, she would say, *they give you beef and call it lamb. They think people won't know any better. And these thermoses know how to keep tea hot for hours!*

You think your fellow countrymen are above cheating you? his father would retort with eyes still trained on the television set. *They just speak your language while they're doing it. We haven't had real lamb in years.*

The longer Yusuf stayed away, the more he found himself imagining what his parents might be doing at any given moment. On his phone, he switched between local time and New York time. It wasn't that he wanted to be back in their apartment with the wafting smells of the neighbors' cooking and rattle of air-conditioning units perched precariously on windowsills. It was more that he thought of his parents with a certain fondness. Nostalgia, he thought, was far more elegant than homesickness.

He would call his mother tonight, when it would be noon in New York and she would be home, cooking lunch for his father. She was, doubtless, delivering daily packages of food to his sister as well to keep her well nourished as she thickened with her growing baby.

"Have you been waiting long?"

Her voice startled him. Yusuf looked up and found himself staring into the kohl-rimmed eyes of a woman who had to be Sultana. She wore a knee-length army green jacket, with sleeves rolled at the cuffs. She had on slim-fitting jeans tucked into brown boots, smart wear for the day's conditions. She stuck out her hand and tilted her head to the side.

"You are Yusuf, aren't you?"

"I am," he said and pushed his chair back to stand. He shook her hand, surprised both that she'd offered it and that her grip was as firm as it was.

"Sultana-*jan,* I'm assuming," he said, pointing to the chair across from his. He waited as she put her shoulder bag on the ground and flipped her brown cotton head scarf off her head, fluffed the top of her hair, and let it fall lightly back into place. She smiled politely, small dimples appearing at the corners of her mouth like apostrophes. She had no other makeup on her face and not a single piece of jewelry.

"Correct," she confirmed. "Thanks for meeting me."

"Of course," Yusuf replied. It was inherently uncomfortable for the two of them to be seated in a room—alone. It didn't help matters that Yusuf felt stirred by her face, the way her cheeks tapered to give her a heart-shaped countenance. "I'm glad you're looking into this place, actually. When you start looking into the cases of these prisoners, it tells you a lot about where the justice system's priorities are."

"Exactly," Sultana agreed. "When we need the police, they throw their hands up and cry 'what can we do without funding or training?' It's amazing how capable and resourceful they are in finding a woman who's escaped from a deadly home. No criminal is worse than a woman who wants to live for herself."

"It must be hard to report on this as a woman," Yusuf commented. "Frustrating to watch this happen."

"I suppose so. It's not shocking, of course. Just a reminder of how things really are. I could easily be them, I think. Other women might choose to believe differently, but any one of us could end up here."

Yusuf thought of the cases he'd reviewed with Aneesa: the woman who had strangled her husband after he'd prostituted her to strangers for money; the woman who had left the husband who had tried to stab her with a screwdriver; the woman who had refused to marry the man thirty years her senior. Yusuf thought of his own sister, who had dared to fall in love with a man his parents did not like. They'd shouted and protested, but in the end, it was her choice and they'd paid for her wedding and smiled when their friends congratulated them, never revealing how disappointed they'd been.

His sister could have been on the roll call of Chil Mahtab, Asma the guard watching over her and Qazi Najeeb deciding her fate over a cup of green tea. That was why Yusuf was here—because he could imagine his family or himself in every tragedy in this land. He could have been the ill-trained prosecutor, incapable of framing a true legal argument. His sister could have been locked up here. His brother could have been arrested for being caught with his girlfriend. Hell, Yusuf could have been arrested for the same. Even his parents could have been arrested for some conflagration of the truth.

"What kind of article are you trying to put together, exactly?" Yusuf asked.

"I want to talk about the specific crimes and the way women are locked up without a second thought. The problem is that none of the women want their names or faces in the news. They'd be happier talking to foreign press about it, but the thought of their stories anywhere in the Afghan news makes them want to run and hide. Of course, it's impossible to get the judges or the police to talk about any of this. They're all doing the right thing, in their own minds."

"I don't think Zeba's going to want to talk either, to tell you the truth," Yusuf admitted. "She's got children she's thinking about and doesn't want her name smeared any more than it already has been."

"I'm sure. That's why I'm not really talking about highlighting any particular case. I'd rather make it about the system as a whole."

"You know, I never asked you," Yusuf mused. "Why did you call me? I mean, there are a lot of lawyers with much more local experience here."

"Good question," Sultana said, laying her hands on the table as if to come clean. "I've been asking around and it's pretty hard to get anyone to talk. The attorneys who have trained here don't want to speak to a journalist, especially a female journalist. I thought you might be different. Plus, Zeba's case is fascinating. There aren't many murder cases, but in the few I've come across, the motivation is pretty clear. The women offer up exactly what it is that drove them to kill. She's not really given any kind of reason and"—Sultana's pointer fingers rapped on the table in synchrony—"I'm sure she must have had one. The fact that she won't reveal it only makes me more curious."

Yusuf took off his glasses and rubbed the bridge of his nose. There most certainly had been a reason, a very good one he wanted to say. Instead, he turned to her first reason for approaching him.

"How'd you know I came from abroad?"

"Ask enough questions, you eventually discover a few things. Simple as that. Speaking of which, where is home for you?"

"New York. Or Washington," Yusuf answered, knowing it was all probably one big America to her. "I've lived in both places."

She peered at him, divining something from the contours of his face.

"You were young when you left."

"I was," Yusuf admitted. "We went to Pakistan."

"We did too for a while. But you . . . you were one of the lucky ones." She smiled. "You went to America. We came back in 2003."

Yusuf shifted in his chair. He was among the fortunate and knew it. It was the reason he felt uncomfortable around anyone his age in Afghanistan. They should have been peers, equals. They should have felt like countrymen, but they didn't. It was as if they were all in the same car accident, but only Yusuf walked away without a scrape. Sultana must have sensed this.

"We were lucky, too. So many others were not."

Yusuf rubbed the back of his neck. He was thankful for the drop in temperature, a hint that fall was approaching and bringing with it cooler winds from the north. After fall, winter would settle in with its bone-chilling temperatures. He'd be watching the street children shiver in their threadbare sweaters and thin-soled shoes. If summer was brutal, winter was death itself. Yusuf's worst fear was that Zeba would be released from prison only to meet the justice of the outside world. Kamal's family might choose to avenge his death. If they did, they would do it quickly, Yusuf knew. She would be dead before the first villagers' toes turned white with chill. He thought of his grandmother's funeral, the browned *halwa* his mother had made and folded into halved pita bread rounds. The crispness of the caramelized sugar was forever melded in his mind with the sound of his mother's quiet sobbing and the feel of the *masjid*'s cold linoleum through his dress socks. It would be the same for Basir, Zeba's son, he knew. Maybe it would be the snow. Maybe every winter's snowfall would make him think of the day he lost his mother.

Yusuf kept his eyes on Sultana's hands, her tapered fingers and slightly rounded nails. He was a good lawyer. He'd been told so by law school professors, classmates, mentors, and supervising attorneys. He had an appreciation for statutes, precedent, formulating arguments. He liked the inherent rationality of the procedural codes and the penal codes. They were guidelines, blueprints for how to approach and build a case. They were anchors, preventing a society from becoming a ship unmoored in wild waters.

But he had traveled to the other side of the world. Sometimes, it felt as if he'd traveled back in time. The laws and codes were changing. The judge didn't have the full story; neither did the prosecutor. Sultana had an inkling that there was more beneath the surface, but she didn't have a clue. As things stood, Zeba's fate would not be based on facts—it would be based on the absence of information, which made it inherently unjust. Yusuf looked at Sultana and wondered if it just might be time to work within the set of unwritten codes that governed this land.

"What if I told you where you could find information about Zeba's case?"

Sultana cocked her head slightly and blinked.

"What do you mean?"

Yusuf tried to ignore the dampness settling into his feet. His mother would have stripped his wet socks off long ago. *You don't know it now because you're young,* she would say, *but you'll have arthritic legs the rest of your life if you don't get out of those things. I know you've got all those diplomas, but there's a lot you learn from living, too.*

Yusuf tapped the tip of his pen on his notepad, then looked up. Sultana watched him, her shoulders even and poised. She knew not to push him. She only needed to be patient.

"You're right. Zeba's case is an intriguing one and there's a lot more to it than can be found in her arrest register," Yusuf said. A confidence bloomed in him that this was the right thing to do. It was, in fact, the only thing to do. "There's been a lot of buzz in her village lately. Things people are saying about her dead husband that might shed a lot of light on what happened that day."

"Really?"

"Yes. There's a lot of talk about things he had done in the months before he was killed. It's worthwhile getting to know what kind of man he was, I think."

"You're suggesting I go out to her village and speak to people?"

There wasn't time for that. Yusuf knew just how long it would take to get there, knock on doors, and find the few willing to speak.

"Everyone's been interviewed by the chief of police—a man named Hakimi. It seems the deceased had a penchant for alcohol."

Sultana's eyebrows perked with interest.

"Did he?"

"Yes. Among other vices. But the worst that came out of the police chief's investigation was that he'd destroyed a page of the Qur'an. Seems he didn't have much respect for God's book. A man who does something like that with the holy book—well, you can just imagine how he might have treated his wife throughout their marriage."

"I see," Sultana said, her lips pulling together grimly.

"This information hasn't really made its way outside . . . it's not likely to weigh too heavily on the judge's decision because he's looking just at the physical evidence."

"Is there proof the husband did these things?"

"It's what a lot of people have been saying."

Sultana said nothing. She leaned back in her chair and narrowed her eyes on the pen Yusuf twirled between his fingers.

"Anything else?" she finally asked.

Yusuf shook his head.

"It . . . it explains a lot, doesn't it? I think it would make an inter-esting piece for the public to read about."

"Which would then get back to the judge and force him to be lenient with Zeba because her husband was such an awful man that he dared to burn a page of the Qur'an."

Sultana's tone had a distinct edge to it. Her eyes were narrowed so that the kohl and lashes and dark irises meshed together into smoky half-moons.

Yusuf wiggled his toes. His legs were starting to ache.

"You know, I didn't expect this." Sultana pushed away from the table. Her face was stony with resentment. "I expected better from you, honestly. I'd heard you were trying hard to build a real case for your client. Really trying to defend her instead of moving from her file to the next dismal imprisoned woman."

"What are you talking about?" Yusuf was thrown by her reaction. He leaned forward, stealing a glance toward the glass door to see if any of the guards might be eavesdropping.

"You want a reporter to do some dirty work for you? That's not me. Rumors have done enough damage in this country—they're a poison. Look at the women in this prison. You've seen their files, haven't you? How many of them are here just because someone pointed a finger? I'm not going to be part of spreading another lie just because you're about to lose your case. If Zeba doesn't want to talk about her husband that doesn't mean you can come up with something to justify another lynching like they tried to do in Kabul. I was there, you know. I covered the protests after that woman was murdered in the street because of a rumor. Thousands came out against street justice."

"Look, that's not what I was trying to do. Sultana, just let me explain."

She stood from her chair and shook her head indignantly. She picked up the strap of her bag, nearly knocking her chair over in the process. Yusuf stood as well, his hands remaining planted on the table. This had gone all wrong.

"Just give me five minutes."

"Good luck with your case, Yusuf. Sorry this has been a waste of time."

CHAPTER 48

YUSUF BIT THE END OF HIS PENCIL, A RESURRECTED HABIT FROM high school. Qazi Najeeb had summoned both lawyers to return to his office on Monday for the verdict and sentencing. Both sides had presented their entire cases, and he had had ample time to deliberate.

Today was Monday.

Yusuf sat in the floral armchair with Zeba on a wooden chair beside him. The prosecutor took the seat opposite Yusuf with a nod. Yusuf stuck his gnawed pencil in his bag, the taste of metal and rubber still in his mouth. The prosecutor settled into the chair and placed a folder of papers onto the table. The two men looked at each other and exchanged half smiles.

"Whatever it is, it'll be over today," the prosecutor said, shrugging.

Yusuf nodded. He'd been utterly unimpressed with the prosecutor's halfhearted approach, but he'd been judging the man by his own set of criteria.

"I . . . I have to tell you, the way you use the letter of the law . . . I've not seen anyone work so hard to defend a criminal."

"She's not a criminal yet," Yusuf quickly corrected. "That's the point."

The prosecutor nodded deferentially. He would humor Yusuf for today.

"You know what I mean."

Qazi Najeeb entered and moved past the two lawyers and Zeba to take his seat behind the desk. Both young men put their hands on their knees and started to rise when he entered. Zeba saw no point, given that the judge's back was turned to her already. She remained in her seat.

"*Salaam wa-alaikum.*" Their greetings were synchronized.

"*Wa-alaikum,*" replied Qazi Najeeb. "Take your seats."

The judge leaned back in his chair and grew quietly pensive. He slipped his hand into his vest pocket and pulled out his *tasbeh* and held it in the palm of his left hand. He stretched the moment as long as he could, wanting everyone to feel the importance of today's meeting.

"It's time to bring this matter to a close," the judge said, turning his attention to Zeba. "The two attorneys here have argued about the facts of this case a great deal. We've taken a lot of time to be sure the proceedings fell in line with the letter of the law. Even if we are not Kabul, we were no less diligent."

Zeba sat with her hands clasped on her lap. She watched the judge, but blinked and looked downward often so as not to appear too brazen. Qazi Najeeb sat back in his chair and considered her for a moment.

"You are not the same woman who was brought into this office months ago."

Yusuf's body tensed.

"You came in here months ago looking like you'd been overcome by djinns. You were like an animal, nothing human about you. I can see now that you feel differently. This has nothing to do with your guilt or innocence and everything to do with what kind of person you are."

Yusuf felt a sinking feeling in his stomach. Zeba did not flinch. In fact, her shoulders pulled back a bit and her chin lifted. She did not appreciate being compared to an animal even if the judge talked of a transformation since then. She knew he was right, though. She'd been dragged out of his office kicking and screaming, feeling a wildness in her bones because she no longer knew what or who she was. What mother would not go mad if she were pulled away from her children just when they needed her most? Complacency in that moment—that was the true madness.

"You're not saying much. You never have throughout this trial. All we know about you is your signed confession," the *qazi* said.

"That's not her confession," Yusuf interjected, raising an index finger.

The judge raised his hand in Yusuf's direction. Yusuf bit his lower lip.

"You think you control us, don't you?" asked the judge. "You think, like your mother, that you can move the world in whichever direction you'd like because you are who you are. You're the granddaughter of a *murshid* who has sometimes been described as holy and sometimes as a spy for the enemy states. You're the daughter of a *jadugar*—"

Zeba tried not to flinch, but the judge caught the way her muscles twitched at the mention of her mother's sorcery.

"Oh? Did you think I didn't know about her tricks? She's been a crafty woman all her life." Qazi Najeeb looked away and sucked his teeth. Why couldn't he see Gulnaz as just another plotting, graying woman? He scowled and thought of the ungodly way she commanded attention.

"Qazi-*sahib*, the reputations or habits of her grandfather or mother shouldn't have anything to do with this case," Yusuf said in a controlled voice. Defending his client without infuriating the judge was an art form that required continued practice.

The judge didn't bother to acknowledge Yusuf's comment but resumed speaking without further comment about Gulnaz, who seemed just as important to him as Zeba.

"You, Khanum, have been arrested for murdering your husband. Is there a worse crime? Is there something worse than depriving your children of their father . . . of . . . of depriving his family of their brother? Is there something worse than taking the life of a person?"

Zeba felt her body tighten with resignation. In a matter of moments, few or many, he could declare her fit to be executed for Kamal's murder. Her children's faces appeared behind her closed eyelids.

Yusuf saw her withdraw and instinctively said a prayer. He wanted to put a hand over hers but resisted. She was not who the judge thought she was. She was the bravest woman he'd met, willing to submit herself to the judge's mercy to save a young girl from having her life destroyed before it had even begun. He had profound respect for this woman whose behavior had maddened him at times.

"You've given me no explanation for why you killed your husband that day."

Yusuf closed his eyes. He could not look at Zeba. Not yet. A smile broke out on the prosecutor's face, his head bobbing ever so slightly in vindication. He was pleasantly surprised by the judge's apparent decision.

Qazi Najeeb brought his hands onto his desk, his thumb still moving one amber bead at a time though he could not possibly be reciting anything holy as he spoke. The soft click of the stones against each other grated on Yusuf's nerves. What kind of judgment was this? Had Qazi Najeeb not heard the stories about Kamal the drinker, the blasphemer? Had he chosen to ignore that Zeba's husband had been the worst kind of man?

Zeba's hands began to shake. She turned her head to the side as if moving away from an oncoming blow.

"I find you guilty of murder," Qazi Najeeb explained grimly. "Because that is what the evidence indicates. I have not seen anything in the defense's case to give another explanation for your husband's brutal death."

"Well done," whispered the prosecutor, who could now log another victory. The particulars of Zeba's case may have affected him as a person, but he also had to worry about his professional record. It was how he would be judged.

Yusuf's elbows rested on his knees. He knew the penal code. He'd studied it and then reviewed it again when he first picked up Zeba's case. She could be hanged. If he looked at her now—if he dared move his gaze from the tassel of the carpet on the ground—he would see her suspended in the air, neck snapped like a plastic doll and body limp with defeat.

"Let me be even clearer. You, Khanum Zeba, have been found guilty of murdering your husband. It is a deplorable crime against Islam and a crime against the laws of our country. There can be no excuse for it. We will meet again in three days and I'll announce your sentence."

CHAPTER 49

AFTER HEARING THE GUILTY VERDICT, YUSUF HAD SLOGGED home. He had planned to go directly to his apartment but decided, halfway down the road to his house, that he would stop at the gym first. He needed to do something physical.

He'd joined during his first week in the city. Inside were floor-to-ceiling mirrors, bright recessed lights, and the familiar hum of treadmills. Weight machines were scattered throughout the room as were dumbbells. There were men of all different sizes, some in Adidas tracksuits and others in faded T-shirts with sleeves cut off at the shoulder. One man in a short-sleeved T-shirt pulled outward the two ends of an elastic resistance band. A thick vein ran down the center of each bicep like the crease on a pair of pants. The place smelled of rubber, sweat, and metal.

The treadmill kept Yusuf sane. There was something soothing about the rhythm of his sneakers hitting the belt as it spun around the conveyor. It gave him a place to think when his apartment was too quiet and the office was too empty.

Inevitably, his thoughts returned to Zeba and the mullah. He had to know if Habibullah truly was her father, though he was still unsure whether or not it would make a difference. Shortly after Zeba had returned to Chil Mahtab, he'd called her to ask about it.

What kind of question is that? she had replied. It was neither confirmation nor denial.

Yusuf, with beads of sweat trickling down his back, decided to find out from Mullah Habibullah himself. If it were true, there might be more to chat about.

THUS, IN THE MORNING, YUSUF TRAVELED BACK TO THE SHRINE and knocked on the mullah's door. The mullah's son answered, looking back into the living room with raised eyebrows.

"Padar! It's the lawyer!"

Yusuf peered into the sitting area and saw the mullah sitting on a floor cushion, the same exact spot he'd been sitting in during their last conversation. He had his back against the wall and his legs crossed. He wore a white crocheted prayer cap on his head and a black vest over his brown tunic and pantaloons. He glanced at his watch as if he'd been expecting Yusuf at this particular moment.

"*Salaam*, Mullah-*sahib*," Yusuf said with a hand on his chest.

"*Wa-alaikum.* Welcome, young man."

"Could we speak for a few minutes? I have an important matter to discuss with you. It has to do with Khanum Zeba, of course."

The mullah motioned him to come in. Yusuf took two steps into the room. As he moved past the wooden door, he saw that the mullah was not alone. Across from him sat Gulnaz, her back straight as a hairpin. Her legs were tucked under her and hidden beneath a navy blue shawl with red embroidery. She looked from Yusuf back to the shawl spread across her lap, a deep sigh escaping her lips.

"*Salaam wa-alaikum*," Yusuf said to Gulnaz, bowing his head. She nodded. "I did not expect to see you here."

The mullah's son returned from the back room with another empty teacup.

"Have a seat," the mullah said. Yusuf sat on the same floor cushion as the mullah, leaving a generous gap between them. The mullah's son placed the teacup on the carpet before him. He brought over the teapot and filled it sloppily, his carelessness disappearing into the worn carpet. The boy then disappeared too, slipping into the next room and out an unseen back door.

Gulnaz had her eyes fixed on the mullah.

"I've interrupted your conversation," Yusuf declared, feeling quite certain that he was sitting with both of Zeba's parents. Though Yusuf had never been married, he'd felt the same tension when he'd visited an aunt and uncle who had stayed married only to avoid the embarrassment of divorce. He'd felt it on the phone in his last conversation with Elena. It was a special brand of anger, a brooding, an ire that existed only where there had once been love. Yusuf cleared his throat. "I came here to ask a question about something Zeba said the other day but . . . well, I think my question's been answered."

Neither the mullah nor Gulnaz said a word.

"I don't need to get into your family affairs or history. My concern is regarding the judge's verdict. I am sorry to report that the judge has found your daughter guilty. But I'm not ready to give up on her."

Gulnaz's hands flew to her forehead.

"Guilty." She sighed, her voice as thin and delicate as the red threads of her shawl. "Of course."

"As I said, I'm not going to give up on her case."

A small shift of the clouds brought a wash of sunlight into the room. Dust motes floated in the shaft of brightness that fell on Yusuf's feet.

"You," the mullah said, his voice spiny with resentment. "How is that you couldn't find anything to grind up or set on fire to save your daughter? I suppose you only have tricks for an evil sister-in-law or the woman who looks at you sideways."

Gulnaz's splayed fingers pressed into her lap. She lifted her head and turned her narrowed eyes to her husband.

"What a thing for you to say! You, the great holy man of the shrine, you pious wretch! You with all your prayers tied to the fences and unsaved mad men—how much have you done for your daughter?"

"What a fork-tongued witch you are," he muttered.

"I'm the woman who raised your children and put up with your family after you left! If that makes me a fork-tongued witch, so be it. But imagine what a dog you must be—the man who didn't care to watch his children grow. You left us with nothing when rockets and bombs fell around us like rain."

"I left you in the folds of a respected family."

"You took me from the folds of a *revered* family."

"Revered," the mullah scoffed. "You told me yourself the tricks you helped your father play to make believers out of your poor neighbors."

"You ungrateful bastard. If you think so little of my father, why are you so desperate to be like him? He was respected because he helped people. Unlike you, he did it in a civilized manner. He never shackled anyone or starved them."

"What I do works. Talk to the families of the people I've helped heal. They'll tell you. Or don't. I don't need to prove myself to you."

"No, you don't. You already have proven to me just what you are," Gulnaz spat. She turned her head to the door, refusing to look at the man who'd walked out of their home a lifetime ago.

Yusuf considered leaving. They would likely not notice his departure. He couldn't waste valuable time listening to them rehash the past. Zeba was going to be sentenced in two days, and Qazi Najeeb's desire to follow the letter of the penal code meant he would hang Yusuf's client without blinking an eye.

"It's not my place to intrude," Yusuf began cautiously. He was acutely aware of the difference in years between himself and Zeba's parents. They were old enough to be his grandparents, old enough to be treated with deference even if they were acting like fools. But social etiquette had been cast aside when Gulnaz and the mullah had aired their history before Yusuf. "But rehashing history will not help your daughter. Her outlook is bleak. I have a few ideas, but I'll need your help—both of you."

The mullah slurped his tea and Gulnaz scowled, giving Yusuf a snapshot of their past.

"I would do anything to help Zeba. I told her that before she left here," Habibullah declared, swirling the unfurled tea leaves at the bottom of his cup.

"Good. Then I'll ask you to speak to the judge. He's a friend of yours, isn't he?"

The mullah nodded.

"Does he not know who you are?" Gulnaz asked. "His family is from the same village."

"We were boys then," Habibullah said quietly. "He's not once recognized me, and I don't expect him to. I'm a different man now in many ways, including in my appearance."

"That much is true," Gulnaz muttered. "You've aged badly."

"Then speak to him," Yusuf said quickly. "He respects you and your efforts here. He considers you an expert and a pious man. Tell him Zeba is your daughter and beg him for leniency."

"Tell him who I am?"

"Yes. He's got to feel an obligation to do something for you. You can't just be speaking up for a person who's passed through your shrine. You've got to give him a real reason to listen to you."

"That's exactly what I was telling him," Gulnaz said quietly. "The *qazi* may have mercy on her if he learns that she's your daughter. It's Zeba's only hope."

The mullah scratched at his beard, his thick eyebrows drawn together and his bottom lip puffed out. He was pouting, Yusuf realized.

"What's wrong with you?" Gulnaz snapped. She was irked that there was silence where there should have been agreement. She turned her head just fractionally to address her husband. "Is that too much to ask of you?"

"Listen." The mullah's voice was a low roar. "I'll do anything I can for her. I told her I would. But that doesn't mean I have to jump headfirst into a well. I want to know if there's a better way."

"A better way that doesn't involve you, isn't that what you mean?"

"And for you, Khanum," Yusuf said, tracing the rim of his teacup with his index finger. Gulnaz lifted her head but did not look at him.

"I need you to do what you do best. Pay the *qazi* a visit and ask for mercy. She's the mother of four children. She was a good daughter. Her husband was a terrible man. Tell him all of that and, most important, remind him of your talents."

"My talents?" Gulnaz repeated softly.

"Yes, you know what I mean. It's not something I would normally ask, but these are unique circumstances."

"I understand," Gulnaz nodded. "I'll speak with him."

Yusuf did not doubt that she would.

"And what about you? What else are you going to do?" the mullah asked.

Yusuf looked at the door and remembered the sight of chained men in the yard by the cells. He thought of the many hours he'd spent under the green lamps of the law library and the way Zeba had steeled herself when he suggested approaching the judge with what she'd seen Kamal doing to that girl.

He was not proud of his tactics, but he'd been troubled ever since he'd learned why Zeba had done what she'd done. He thought of Sultana and the way she'd walked out on him, indignant and beautiful.

Yusuf put the teacup back on the floor and clapped both hands against his thighs before pushing himself to stand.

"As for me, I've got one other idea, but if it's going to do anything for Zeba, I need to get working on it. You both have my mobile number. The sentencing is on Thursday. Call me tomorrow and let me know what's happened."

They remained in their places long after he'd left, the irresistible need to retrace their steps preventing them from leaving. Age demanded that they not leave anything unsaid.

Once upon a time, Gulnaz recalled sullenly, there had been an afternoon when she had peered into a window and felt giddy at the thought of her life tied to this man's by an invisible silver thread. Such an idea seemed astonishing now as they sat seething in each other's presence.

CHAPTER 50

YUSUF OPENED THE PLASTIC CONTAINER OF SAUTÉED SPINACH and rice Aneesa had brought him, the contents resembling a green-and-white yin-yang symbol. Famished, he took in the aromatic steam of the white rice, a blend of cumin and salt. She'd even brought two squares of fresh bread. Yusuf tore off a piece of bread and shaped it around a lump of spinach, pink threads of rhubarb mixed in. His cheeks were round with food when Sultana walked into the office.

Yusuf could not conceal his surprise. He stood and grabbed a napkin. Holding it over his mouth with one hand to conceal his chewing, he motioned her over. She'd seen him and nodded, making her way to his desk.

"I'm interrupting your lunch," she said somewhat apologetically.

Yusuf hoped not to choke as he forced the food down quickly. He swiped the napkin over his lips and slid back into his chair. They were across from each other, just as they had been in the interview room of Chil Mahtab.

"Don't worry about it," he said, snapping the top back on the container. "Are you hungry? I could offer you some but—"

"Thank you, but I ate not long ago," Sultana said. She was wearing the same olive-colored jacket with the sleeves rolled up. A yellow-and-green head scarf hid her hair, knotted high on her head. "Don't stop on my account, please."

"It's fine. I wasn't that hungry anyway," Yusuf said, clearing his throat. There was one other lawyer in the office, but his desk was on the opposite side of the room and a half wall separated them. He'd looked up with interest to see Sultana enter and kept glancing over as he spoke on the phone. It was unusual, of course, to have a young woman visit.

"You got my message. I'm surprised to see you."

"I'm sure you are. I could have called, but I thought it might be better to stop by."

"I'm glad you did. Look, let me say that I'm sorry about the way our last conversation went. I didn't mean to try to use you or manipulate you into a story."

"But that's what you were doing, wasn't it?" She still had her handbag on her shoulder, and Yusuf wished she would set it down. She looked like she might walk out at any second.

"It . . . it was," he admitted. "Look, I've been struggling with Zeba's case. It's a tragedy from many angles, and as much as I've tried, well, the court just won't see why she shouldn't be hanged. The holes in the prosecutor's case are forgiven, when they really shouldn't be."

"I'm sure that's true. But do you honestly think that a man who burned a page of the Qur'an, if that's what he did, should be killed by his wife? I don't think you do, and that's why I wanted to speak to you again. Maybe there's a better angle to the story."

Yusuf rested his elbows on the desk. It was Wednesday, about twenty-four hours from the time of the sentencing. He had yet to hear from Zeba's parents. He'd called them both, but neither had answered the phone.

"I could tell you the whole story, but it's an ugly one and not anything that you can print. The details can't go public."

"What is it?" Sultana was, of course, curious. It was her job to ask questions, and that was precisely why she'd made the trip into this office.

"I need you to promise to respect what Zeba's kept private."

"I promise." Sultana slid the strap of her bag off her shoulder and let it rest on the floor. She sat back in the chair and listened as Yusuf told her about the little girl, his voice low and grim. She flinched, almost imperceptibly, but did not interrupt or move from the seat. Yusuf told her about Zeba's fears that the girl would be shamed publicly if word got out, that the village would seek out the victim and her life would be ruined once again. He didn't have to explain Zeba's concerns. Sultana understood them in the way any woman would because it all came down to honor.

The girl had been stripped of her honor, of her future. If the world knew, she would never live a life without shame.

It was the greatest injustice, and it made Sultana's blood boil.

"She has four children. Zeba is all they have. If they lose her, they lose everything."

"Are you certain about this story?" Sultana asked. She didn't doubt it though. There was no reason to.

"I'm certain," he said, nodding. "The way she talked about it . . . it's the truth. That's the reason why I said what I did to you. She's going to be sentenced tomorrow, and the judge has made it pretty clear that he wants to honor the law. I think he wants to see her hanged."

Sultana crossed her legs and tapped a finger on her chin.

"What can be done? Even if I go to the judge with rumors about her husband, what good will that do?"

"It's a long shot, but it's all I have. I've tried everything else." And he had, even using the mullah and Gulnaz to sway the judge toward mercy. It was a tragic shift, he realized, that he was now simply asking for mercy instead of justice or freedom.

"And you're thinking that if I tell the judge I'm going to run a story about the dead husband, that I'm going to write about the accusations made against him about Qur'an burning, that he'll feel pressured not to hang the woman who killed him?"

"I think it's a possibility . . . based on what I've seen of this judge."

"I just don't know." Sultana pursed her lips and considered Yusuf carefully.

The other attorney was off the phone now and looking in their direction. He raised his eyebrows as if to ask Yusuf who his visitor was. Yusuf raised a hand and looked back at his desk. He was in no mood to explain.

"Village rumors. I've never wanted to have anything to do with them. They'll be the death of all of us, I swear," Sultana whispered.

Yusuf ran his fingers through his hair. He had every reason to anticipate defeat in this case. The odds had been against him from the beginning. A dead husband, a reticent wife, no witnesses or possible suspects. She should have been hung long ago.

Sultana stood up abruptly, smoothing her jacket over the seat of her pants. She reached for her handbag.

"You're leaving?" Yusuf said. He didn't want her to go. If nothing else, he wanted her to stay and tell him that he'd done everything he could have done. She was the only other person who knew the truth.

"I've got to be getting back," she said. She met his gaze and saw the dismay in his eyes. He saw the determination in hers. "And I want to call the judge before it gets too late."

CHAPTER 51

QAZI NAJEEB HUNG UP THE PHONE AND RUBBED THE CURL OF HIS ear between two fingers.

"Who was that?" his wife called from the next room.

He didn't notice, his ear still buzzing from his conversation with Mullah Habibullah.

"Was it Shazia? Did she say if they're going to Kabul for the holidays?"

He felt the dull ache of acid rising in his chest and wasn't sure if he should blame his wife's *qorma* or the news he'd just received from his friend. He marveled at how little he'd known of this man, even after all these years, accepting blindly that the mullah had moved from another province to serve the people. That was only a sliver of the truth. The judge, who was on a daily basis presented with lies and false stories, felt he should have detected the holes in this one.

But he hadn't.

"Old man, have you gone deaf?" his wife shouted. She was standing in the doorway, an arched frame between the two rooms. She held a half-washed frying pan in one hand.

"Did you say something?"

"Did I say something?" she repeated in disbelief.

"Okay, it's clear you did. What was it?"

"I asked if your sister called."

Qazi Najeeb shook his head.

"Then call her and ask her if they're going to Kabul for the holidays. I want to ask her to pick up some fabric for me."

"I'll call her tomorrow," he mumbled. "Is there any tea left in the pot?"

"No. I'll put some water to boil," his wife said, turning to go back into the kitchen. She paused just before she disappeared completely. "Have you thought about closing your eyes for a few minutes? You look exhausted."

Qazi Najeeb nodded. She was a good wife, he admitted, even if she did strip him of all his airs the moment he walked through the door. She had the decency to do it only when they were alone and often reminded him that she saw it as her duty to do so. *The rest of the world bows their heads to you, dear judge. It's my job to remind you you're just a man.*

"I'm going to walk for a few minutes. My legs feel stiff."

"Those knees of yours are getting worse. I'm going to steep some herbs and ginger for them."

As the judge bent one knee and pushed himself to standing, he considered the way he'd thought of Gulnaz. Those eyes of hers, that pair of emeralds had entranced him, made him regret that he'd not courted her with more gusto in his youth. Would his body have ached the way it did if he'd spent a lifetime with her? Or would she have driven him away the way she had the mullah?

"When are you going to be declaring the verdict for that case?" she called from out of view.

"Tomorrow." He straightened his tunic, scowling to see two splotches of red grease on his shirt from lunch.

"Thursday? Just before the weekend? Really, are you so callous that you would announce a death sentence on the eve of our day of prayer?"

"Is there a better day of the week to be sentenced to death?" he asked facetiously. Najeeb heard the low whistle of the teakettle.

"You know what I mean."

"Look, I've already got two lawyers pestering me with this case. I don't need a third one at home."

"Can you imagine me working as a lawyer?" His wife laughed. She had reached only the fourth grade before being pulled out to tend to her younger siblings. And though she was literate, she'd never contemplated working outside the home, nor had any of the women in her family. It was not an idea the *qazi* would have ever entertained even if she had.

Qazi Najeeb's thoughts flitted back to Zeba. She might very well be the mullah's daughter, but as far as he could tell, there was no question that she'd killed her husband.

He stood and made his way through the front door and into the courtyard. He inhaled deeply, the sweet fragrance of his wife's dill plants restoring him. He paused to touch the yellow umbrella flowers and dragged his fingers through the feathery leaves.

Habibullah had sounded embarrassed on the phone, though more so because he'd lied about his background than because he'd left his wife and children. Najeeb wanted to do his friend a favor, but he felt genuinely torn. He'd wanted so badly to make this case a landmark one. He'd envisioned himself as a pioneer, a man who would be remembered for ushering in a new age of Afghan jurisprudence. It was not crazy to imagine that he might be sought out for a position on an appellate court or perhaps even the Supreme Court, forever tying his own legacy to that of Afghanistan.

Zeba's four children probably grieved their father. They deserved to see justice, he reasoned, even if Habibullah saw it differently.

He was a terrible man, his old friend had said at last, *a man who didn't deserve the wife and children he had. Zeba's a good woman. She's devout and pure in her heart. Her husband is responsible for this mess, not her.*

My friend, Najeeb had replied somberly, *I understand this is disappointing for you as a father. But how could she not be responsible? And I have to wonder how well you could know her anyway. I know she's your daughter, but you haven't seen her in decades. Think of how different every one of us is compared to how we were thirty years ago.*

In the end, he'd promised to take the mullah's entreaties into consideration and do anything he could to honor his friend's request. He swore not to breathe a word of their relationship to anyone else and he'd meant it. If this case did attract attention, Najeeb did not want too much scrutiny to land on the shrine. The mullah was truly helping people there, and the judge didn't see any reason to drag a man of God's good works through the mud.

Najeeb stepped into the street, pulling his *tasbeh* from his vest pocket. He lived on a lane of similar one-storied homes, each bordered by an outer wall that lent privacy to their inner lives. It made the road into something of a corridor, high walls on either side. Najeeb closed the metal door behind him, shuttering his sanctuary from the view of neighbors and passersby. He thought of the swarms of people who'd entered Zeba's home that day and surrounded her, as the police report had described. How many had there been? Dozens of gawkers trespassing a family's private life. That was what these women did not understand, Najeeb thought. All the women of Chil Mahtab had taken down their walls with their crimes, they'd pulled aside their *purdah*, their protective veil. Some had flaunted their relationships with men. Some had worked late hours with male colleagues. Some had left their fathers' homes. They should have anticipated the consequences.

Najeeb had not made it to the end of his block when he stopped abruptly. He narrowed his eyes and wondered if his vision was not in worse shape than his knees. There was no mistaking her, though.

"What are you doing here?" he asked incredulously.

"Qazi-*sahib*," Gulnaz said, her voice even and purposeful. "I need to speak to you."

"How did you find me?"

"I asked people. You're well known in this neighborhood."

He'd stopped thumbing the beads of his *tasbeh*.

"What do you want?" he asked, wondering if he should turn her away without waiting for an answer. He'd already begun to suspect that he'd been too lenient on Zeba in the first few weeks of the case. He felt manipulated now, knowing that Gulnaz was the type of woman to drive a decent husband away. It gave him all the more reason to believe Zeba had begun to follow in her mother's footsteps but then veered down an even deadlier path.

"I need to speak to you."

"Quickly. I have things to do and you're interrupting my evening." He folded his arms across his chest, the beads draped over his elbow. Gulnaz took a deep breath and began the speech she'd rehearsed on her way to the judge's home.

"Qazi-*sahib*, you and I are from the same village. We met as children. We lived in the shadow of the same *masjid* and waded through the same streams. You've known my family and have been welcomed into our home. I am coming to you now to ask for mercy. My daughter suffered with that man, and it is no secret what kind of man he was."

"Because we are from the same village does not mean I should ignore a crime. It's my duty as a judge to mete out justice."

"We all want justice."

"Then you'll understand that I must do the right thing here. I know she's your daughter, but I'm responsible for making sure the law is respected. We cannot afford to let our nation fall into anarchy again and this is where it starts."

"What about his crimes? His crimes went unpunished. He was a drinker, a man without a decent friend. He did not pray or fast or follow the words of God. A black carpet is not made white by washing. My daughter did her best to live with this man and be a good wife to him, but she could not absolve him of his sins."

"She didn't need to absolve him. She could have left judgment up to the law or to Allah."

"I'm asking you to consider her children. Her son is devastated, her three daughters have no one now. They've lost both their parents. Do we really need more orphans in this world? Let them have their mother back, please!"

"Criminals cannot hide behind their children." It was not that he was a callous man. Of course he'd taken into consideration that Zeba had left four children behind when she'd been arrested. He also knew the youngest was barely a year old. He'd memorized these details the first day he reviewed her case and could almost picture her little ones, their anonymous faces sometimes replaced by those of his grandchildren. He kept these things to himself.

"I do not have money to offer you, Qazi Najeeb. The days when my family lived comfortably are long gone. I've been alone for most of my adult life, and my son struggles to feed and clothe his family."

Najeeb grew angry at her implication.

"I've not asked you for a penny! Khanum, I have always been grateful to your father, the *murshid*. He gave my own father much hope when we had nearly none. My brother survived his illness and is alive and well even now. Do you really think I would ask for money after all that?"

Gulnaz said nothing. The sun had dipped behind wispy clouds, the sky a canvas streaked with paprika and saffron. The spiny profile of the mountains cut into the sunset. She wasn't really asking for mercy. She was asking for justice.

"There's something else you need to know."

Gulnaz scanned the street and saw children playing with a bicycle tire nearby. There was no one within earshot.

"It was someone else who actually killed him."

The judge nodded as if he'd expected Gulnaz to come up with something more unbelievable in retort.

"Like who? I'd be very interested to know who else might have been there. No one's said anything about someone else being there that day, including your daughter!"

"If you hang my daughter, you'll be making her a martyr."

"A martyr?" he scoffed. "A martyr for what?"

"She is at the court's mercy because she tried to save a life that day. What I'm about to tell you is the absolute truth though I cannot provide any evidence for it, and my daughter does not wish for anyone to find out about this. She's not breathed a word of it to you since her arrest because she fears for the safety of a young girl."

Najeeb felt the ache in his chest start up again. He would eat a spoonful of yogurt before going to bed and see if that settled the acid.

"Explain."

Gulnaz bit her lower lip. She had not bothered to tell Zeba she would be speaking to the judge and had certainly not discussed with her daughter what she would be telling him. But what would happen if Zeba were to find out about this conversation? She would either go right back to resenting her mother, which Gulnaz had become accustomed to, or she would be grateful. It was a chance she was willing to take.

"The day came when Zeba learned what kind of man he truly was. She found him attacking a young girl in their own home, defiling a school-age girl. That, dear judge, is the heart of the matter. All that came after, including her enduring nineteen days of the shrine, was a woman trying to protect the honor of an innocent child."

Najeeb huffed in exasperation. At every turn, there was some new disparaging revelation about the dead man. *Convenient,* he thought, *that the man was in no position to defend himself.* His family didn't do much to defend him either, probably because of the nasty rumors floating around about him and the desecration of the Qur'an.

"A child," Gulnaz repeated slowly for emphasis. "You're a father and a decent man. Imagine how Zeba felt to see such an atrocity in her own home."

"Yes, Khanum, I am a father," Najeeb said defiantly. She'd come here because she thought she could sway his thinking. She thought she could tease his decision in Zeba's favor, but it wasn't as simple as she'd anticipated. Qazi Najeeb felt a bit smug. He knew her better than she thought. "I have three sons and two daughters, all grown and raising families of their own. If there's one thing I know as a father, it's that a mother would do anything for her children."

Gulnaz pulled her shoulders back sharply. She shook her head.

"You've misunderstood me."

"No, I don't think I have," Qazi Najeeb said.

"I've come to you with the truth," Gulnaz insisted.

"You think you're so smart. You always have."

Had she done her daughter any good by coming here or had she simply made matters worse? She would call Yusuf tonight and tell him what she had done. The judge knew it all now, for better or worse.

The sun was nearly hidden behind the mountains now. Sunsets were odd in that sense—seeming to move in accelerated time. It was Wednesday, and this was the last sunset before the judge would announce Zeba's sentence. After that, how many sunsets would her daughter have left and how quickly would they pass? Time had never pressed on Gulnaz's heart as it did now that days and hours measured her daughter's life. Gulnaz lowered her gaze slightly so the judge wouldn't see that her bewitching eyes had misted.

"It doesn't matter what I think, Qazi-*sahib*. That's the problem. This world revolves around your opinion and your opinion alone."

"I don't think there's anything more to say on the subject," he said, not knowing what to make of her comment.

"No," Gulnaz said slowly. Her throat was thick with angst, and it was an effort to get the words out. "I suppose there isn't. But I'm sure you have plenty to think on tonight, so I'll let you get back to your walk."

She had attempted to reason with this man, to appeal to his decency on behalf of her daughter. But so often reason did not seem to work with people, which was precisely why she'd spent a lifetime getting her point across by other means.

She turned her back to the judge, and he resumed his walk. He was only a few meters from her when it happened, close enough that she could hear the light clinks and his soft gasp. *Tap, tap, tap.* It was not unlike the sound of hail on a roof. Gulnaz did not have to turn to see it. She closed her eyes for a second and imagined the scene behind her back, feeling a twinge of satisfaction. She pictured Najeeb, mouth half open, nothing but a tassel in his open palm. How many times had he worked his way through those thirty-three perfectly oval stones? Still it came as a surprise to Qazi Najeeb, who gave such little thought to the thin line of thread that held the stones together.

Hidden from view, the string of the *tasbeh* had frayed to nothing, sending the beads scattering to the hardened earth.

CHAPTER 52

"WHEN I WAS A GIRL, I BELIEVED THERE WOULD BE ONE JUDGment Day for us all," Bibi Shireen said. She sat cross-legged next to Zeba, her upper half swaying almost imperceptibly from side to side. Her eyes fluttered as she recalled the stories she'd been told time and again in her youth. "There are the signs of Judgment Day: the earthquakes coming one after another, people disregarding their prayers, heathens running through the streets. The mountains would flatten and the moon would splinter to warn us that Judgment Day was closing in. Those beastly creatures, Yajuj and Majuj, would be let loose and swarm the earth and wreak havoc among us. I believed that the dead would be resurrected, all of us glowing with youth and waiting to cross the thorny Bridge of Sirat together. Some would fall into the hellfires below, but the righteous would reach the other side where Heaven awaited."

Nearly half the prisoners of Chil Mahtab had gathered in the yard, where they sat in a semicircle around Malika Zeba. Word had spread that she would be sentenced to hang in the afternoon. The temperature had dropped quite suddenly so that the women could now sit outside without fanning themselves. A half dozen rolled-up sleeves revealed Zeba's name inscribed on forearms. The mood was somber.

"And what do you believe now?" Latifa asked.

Bibi Shireen's eyes closed tightly. She dabbed at the corners of her eyelids with the end of her head scarf. Her voice was thin and choked.

"Now I believe Judgment Day happens every day. Every day. Why, God, were so many of us created only to be sacrificed?" she lamented to the sky.

Zeba rested her hand on Bibi Shireen's.

"She's right." Heads swiveled to look at a woman who'd been sentenced to twenty years for running away. It had not mattered to the judge presiding over her case that she'd had three broken bones and a stab wound to her leg at the time she'd fled her husband's house. Her voice sang out:

"Our womanly blood men seem to revile
While the rest of our blood brings them a smile."

"I have one, too," called another, hesitantly. Zeba recognized her as a woman who'd been betrothed to a man who had never bothered to claim her. When her family arranged her marriage to another man, the family of her uninterested fiancé reported her for *zina* out of spite. She was young, her complexion still plagued with acne.

"If an accusing finger is aimed your way
You'll never see the light of day."

The couplets had become a way for the women of Chil Mahtab to pass time. Some were clever and some were stilted. They were all bits of freedom, though, in a world where most of the women did not know enough of letters to sign their names. This had been Zeba's unwitting gift to them.

Zeba was prepared for the judge to make his announcement today. She'd been prepared, she realized, since the very moment she'd been alone with Kamal's body. It was the reason that she'd slumped to the ground and sat motionless, waiting for her children to come home and the world to discover what had happened. Basir, her neighbors, Yusuf, her mother, and even her father had all made valiant attempts to change her fate, but it was not to be.

The women of Chil Mahtab had clung to her, wondering if they were witnessing the last days of Malika Zeba. If a woman could be imprisoned or lashed for being seen with a man, she would surely be hung for murder. It was as if the prison had already begun to mourn her.

Zeba had spent the past two days distilling her prayers down to what was truly important. She wanted only for her children to speak her name without shame or resentment. She wanted them to think of her and know that she'd nurtured them as best she could, that she'd watched over them while they slept and cried when they'd lived forty days, and that she'd winced when they'd stumbled and scraped a knee. Food had no taste if she did not see her children enjoy it. She'd not felt alive until the moment she felt Basir stir in her womb. That was when time began, when the eyelash began to move across the dial and measure seconds, days, and months.

She hoped they would know all this.

Latifa snapped her fingers.

"I've got one! I've got one!" she called out. "It goes like this:

"These hardheaded men from their pulpits won't budge.
How the world would be different if a woman could judge!"

There was a trickle of applause and a chorus of praise. Latifa beamed for a moment until the weight of her words fell upon her own ears. She looked at Zeba.

"I'm sorry," she said softly. "Maybe it wasn't the right time."

"Latifa, what better time could there be? It was wonderful," Zeba said. A box of chocolates was making its way through the crowd, generously shared by one of the prisoners. The women used a spoon to cut each sweet square into quarters, so that everyone could have at least a taste. "For a house with no windows, Chil Mahtab is not that bad. Sometimes I breathe easier here than I ever did at home."

"Exactly," called another woman. Zeba couldn't see her face. She was embedded among the others, only identifiable by the hand she raised into the air like a flagstaff. "Malika Zeba, they call this place Chil Mahtab, because that's the time we spend here. Forty moons at least. But you, you've lit these halls with the light of forty moons. No matter what happens, your name will be painted on the walls of this jail, in our blood if that's what it comes down to, for as long as each of us stays here."

Zeba felt her throat knot. She'd given them so little and received so much in return. They could return to their petty squabbles over who'd gotten more than her fair share of food or who had pilfered laundry detergent from her cellmate another day. Today, they gave the bickering a rest.

"God is merciful," called another voice, just as a northern breeze sent a quiet rustle through the leaves of the *arghawan* tree at the corner of the yard. Even the fence glinted in the sunlight, looking more like radiant silver than harsh metal. "*Inshallah*, He will hear our prayers. Have faith, sisters."

Latifa broke the melancholy mood with one final couplet.

> *"If I'd known Chil Mahtab could bring me such joy*
> *I would have happily let myself be used by a boy!"*

A roar of laughter erupted, and hands clapped in delight. Zeba's and Latifa's eyes lit upon each other and they agreed, without breathing a word, that there was much to be thankful for, even on Judgment Day.

QAZI NAJEEB'S OFFICE WAS A TIGHT FIT FOR YUSUF, THE PROSECU-tor, Zeba, Gulnaz, and a guard. Mother and daughter squeezed into the floral armchair, Gulnaz's hands wrapped around her daughter's. She'd spoken with Tamina in the morning, she'd whispered to Zeba. They would be paying her a visit in the next day or so as the villagers had begun to cool their attacks on Tamina's family.

The prosecutor twitched with nervous energy. He'd gone so far as to wear a tie for the occasion, even if it did remind him of a noose as he tightened the knot at his neck. He was eager to see this case come to a close. Yusuf sat opposite Zeba and Gulnaz, looking at his client from time to time to gauge her state of mind. She seemed more composed than he would have anticipated, but then again, she was a woman full of surprises. He tapped his foot and avoided looking at the prosecutor who sat to his right.

Qazi Najeeb had entered his office last, wanting to wait until everyone had taken their seats. Out of habit, he reached into his vest pocket as he moved behind his desk. His *tasbeh* was there, the beads rethreaded by his wife at his urgent request. He stole a glance at Gulnaz and decided to leave the string in his pocket. He coughed twice, the end of his turban bobbing with the movement of his head. He cleared his throat and looked at the papers on his desk as he began to speak.

"Today, I'll announce the sentence of Khanum Zeba," he said evenly and deliberately. "We've all spent our time working through this case, giving the victim the attention his death deserves. It is a tragic case. A husband is dead and a mother is in jail. Children are left without their parents. Sins have been committed and must be handled according to the law. There's been much talk about mercy, but mercy is best left for Allah to manage.

"I'm sure you all know the saying: 'Let justice find its rightful owner.' It's a common phrase though most people don't know the story behind it."

Yusuf squeezed his pencil between his thumb and index finger until the pads of his fingers went white. The way the judge said "justice" made his stomach drop.

"There was a thief who, just before dawn, was caught trying to steal food from the home of a decent family to feed his own children. Someone heard a noise and lit the wick of a lantern. When the man saw the burglar backing out of his window, he shouted so loudly that he woke his neighbors. The thief took off running, but half the neighborhood gave chase, swinging sticks and knives and whatever else they could find.

"The thief ran through the darkness and came upon the *masjid*. He thought he could hide out in the house of worship and ducked inside. As his luck would have it, the mullah had gone out to the stream behind the *masjid* to perform his ablutions. The thief slid into the mullah's bed and pulled the blanket over himself just as the angry mob approached. They entered the *masjid* and assumed the man sleeping was the mullah. Just then, the mullah returned from his ablutions and was surprised to find an irate crowd of people. Seeing him return, they assumed him to be the thief and dragged him outside, waving sticks and fists at him. He denied being a thief and begged them to consider carefully before they imposed punishment upon the wrong man. He cried and beseeched them, 'Let justice find its rightful owner!' whereupon they chopped off his hand. It was the penalty for stealing. Amid the chaos, the sorry thief returned to his hungry family.

"On the occasion of the mullah's death, he reached the gates of Heaven and met the angel of death. He asked the angel why God had allowed him to be punished for a crime he hadn't committed and why the true thief had been allowed to go free. Where was the justice in that?"

The judge paused for a moment, allowing his audience to ponder the question. He cleared his throat and continued.

"The angel told him that the thief had only intended to feed his hungry family. As for the mullah, while he hadn't been guilty of that particular theft, he'd once swatted a cricket and broken its fragile leg. It was a sin without witness but that made it no less of a sin. 'Just as you said, my friend. Let justice find its rightful owner,' the angel explained. What looked like injustice was actually justice overdue."

Gulnaz flipped the end of her head scarf across her shoulder. She looked at Yusuf, who dared lift his eyes from the floor.

The prosecutor nodded intently, his eyes narrowed as he awaited the actual sentence.

"In this case, there has been much to consider, and as I've said all along in this case, I want to follow the laws that now govern our country. It's the only way to move past the dark times when there was no order or when order was dictated by the individual. For that reason, I turned to the penal code."

Yusuf blinked rapidly. He looked at the judge whose eyebrows were raised as he read through the lower part of his lenses.

"Article 400 of the penal code tells us that an individual who 'kills another by mistake' shall be imprisoned for up to three years or fined up to 36,000 afghanis." Qazi Najeeb looked up, turning his gaze to Zeba. "From what I've seen, this woman did not have the intention of killing her husband. She had no plan nor had she made any statements to neighbors or loved ones that she was going to. Given her behavior and condition, we were even prompted to have her evaluated by an expert to assess her mental condition. She was determined to be in a very weak state and, after discussion with the mullah from the shrine, likely suffering from remorse. I do not believe she meant to kill her husband. I believe she meant to defend herself in light of his behavior—behavior that was both un-Islamic and illegal—and prevent her home from becoming a den of sin. It's become clear that she intended to turn him in, which is why she'd approached the chief of police before her husband's death. His deplorable behavior would have been punishable by law according to article 347, which makes blasphemy a crime."

Yusuf felt a pounding in his chest to hear the judge citing specific articles from the penal code. The prosecutor's face had contorted from a look of snide satisfaction to confoundment. How had things gone so wrong so quickly?

"And so, with Zeba having been found guilty, I have the responsibility to find an appropriate sentence for her crime, which I have decided will be the time she has already served in Chil Mahtab and a fine in the amount of one thousand afghanis."

The prosecutor was on his feet, mouth agape. Yusuf's nervous energy had taken him from his chair as well. If there had been more room in the judge's office, he would have leaped on the back of the armchair. As it was, he turned to Gulnaz and Zeba to see if the sentence had registered with them.

"But Qazi-*sahib*, this is not right. Don't make me go through the pain of an appeal. How could you find her guilty and then—"

The judge waved a dismissive hand in the prosecutor's direction. The electric fan buzzed in the background.

"The time for arguments has passed. I strongly suggest you focus on your next case," he said. He closed a manila folder on his desk and rested his two open hands on it protectively. "This decision is final."

The prosecutor blew through pursed lips. He wouldn't appeal, he knew. This case was rife with inconsistencies and he wanted nothing more than to move on.

It was just starting to sink in. Gulnaz's hands pressed harder against Zeba's. Zeba looked into her mother's eyes, her green irises like tiny prisms through the pooled tears. It was the greatest gift for them. It was the chance to start anew, their secrets no longer hidden in the folds of their skirts. Judgment Day had come, and Zeba would be free to embrace the four angels she'd been kept from all these months. Anything she ate would be sweeter than the fruits of Paradise. Anything she drank would be richer than the river of unspoilable milk. Zeba would enjoy the humble heaven that was this world.

Zeba would live.

CHAPTER 53

YUSUF SCANNED THROUGH HIS CALL LOG AND PRESSED THE green button when he saw her name. It was Thursday evening, and the events of the sentencing were still fresh on his mind. The prosecutor had walked out without saying a word, a sulk that did not go unnoticed by Qazi Najeeb. Gulnaz and Zeba had pressed their foreheads together and sobbed. Yusuf had looked at the judge, but he had already risen from his chair and mumbled something about seeing to another case. He had paused only to put a hand on Yusuf's shoulder and nod. He said nothing more.

When Sultana answered the phone, Yusuf pressed his back against the seat of the taxi in relief.

"She's free," he said, his words sparse so that he could get them out without his voice breaking. "Zeba's free."

"Honestly? You're serious?" Sultana exclaimed.

"Yes, very serious. It happened just this afternoon. If I hadn't been there, I wouldn't believe it myself!"

"But . . . but . . . why? What did he say?"

Yusuf recounted the judge's reasoning, a new jurisprudence incongruous with his age and the traditions of the city. Yusuf was left to wonder what constellation of influences had pushed the judge to set Zeba free.

"That's astounding."

"It most certainly is. Listen, I don't know what you told the judge and whether or not it had anything to do with this afternoon. What did you tell him?"

"Yusuf, I didn't say much. I only told him that I was thinking of interviewing the folks from Zeba's village and investigating the rumors circulating around her husband. He asked me why I would want to do that and I said because I thought the dead man deserved to have his name cleared if all the horrible things being said about him were lies. I asked Qazi Najeeb for his opinion on the matter, but he refused to say anything else. He was in a hurry to get off the phone."

"Something clicked, Sultana. I don't know what it was, but something worked."

The taxi had just rounded the corner of his road. His apartment was half a block ahead, and it was that time of day that men were milling about the streets. The electronic rhythm of a pop song spilled out of a kebab shop along with the aroma of charred meat. A young boy offered to shine the shoes of pedestrians.

"She's really going to go free? Completely?"

Sultana's disbelief echoed the thoughts in his own head. Had Qazi Najeeb been turned by the mullah's entreaties? By Gulnaz's pleas? Or had he feared the attention that Sultana might bring to the case, revealing what kind of man Kamal was and inviting criticism of the judge who dared punish the defender of the Qur'an? There was also the possibility that the judge had reached this conclusion based on the truth, having finally received all the facts, even if it had not come in the form of the defense's case.

"I wanted to thank you for what you did. That phone call you made, it just might have been the thing that got to him."

"I doubt it." Sultana sighed. "He didn't seem too affected by what I said. He sounded annoyed that I was interrupting his evening, honestly."

"It's not the way I imagined the case going, but it is the result I wanted. I'm happy about that part."

"That's the frustration of trying to do something good here. Even when there's a real judicial process, the result can make you think we've gone back to Taliban times. There was a woman lashed in Ghor Province just this week for *zina*. Her case went through a real court and in the end, an audience of men watched as they carried out one hundred strikes against her."

But Yusuf wasn't discouraged by that bit of news or by the way his attempts to bring the procedural code to life had failed in Qazi Najeeb's office. He understood that courtrooms could look like anything, briefs could be handwritten and scribbled on sheets torn from a composition notebook. He knew arrest registries could be works of fantasy and that *zina* could be deemed more criminal than murder. It only meant there was more work yet to be done.

"And what's next for you?" Sultana asked as if she'd read his mind. "Back to the United States?"

"No, not yet," Yusuf replied, smiling to hear Sultana ask about his plans. His mother would have the same question for him, though she would frame it more as a demand. He would go back to New York . . . eventually. He would be back on his parents' sofa soon enough—maybe even in time to hold his new niece or nephew—but it wouldn't be this minute. "I think I'm going to stick around for a while."

"You are, really?" Sultana asked, a hint of playfulness to her voice.

"Absolutely. So if you have any other questions you want to ask me, I'm still available."

The taxi stopped at the door of Yusuf's apartment building. He could see the awning of the gym down the block and made a mental note to get back there later today, feeling a boost of energy. He slipped the cabdriver a few bills and stepped into the street. The smell of diesel and freshly baked bread hung in the air.

"Good to know, Yusuf-*jan*," Sultana said. That she'd addressed him by his name and in such a familiar way was not lost upon him. It was the way things were done here—the land where rumors, hints, and insinuations were as solid as the mountains that contained them.

CHAPTER 54

THE CHILDREN HAD BEEN DELIVERED TO HER A WEEK AFTER HER release, brought to her by Tamina, who did not dare step foot in her brother's home. She'd come in the evening, once the sun had set, arriving in a taxi that parked at the end of the block. She'd paid the taxi driver to wait for her, knowing it was costing more than she and Mateen could afford, but she did not want to be seen by the neighbors whose ears prickled for news from the home of the freed murderess.

The girls had fallen into Zeba's arms. Basir had stood next to his mother, nestling his head against her side at first, then pressing his face into the sleeve of her dress to blot his tears.

Zeba had turned to thank Tamina, who stood straight as steel.

"I think it's best you stay away from me," she'd said, staring at the backs of the girls' heads. "We are nothing to each other anymore."

"Tamina-*jan,* I am so grateful that you—"

"Don't say anything, please. There's nothing to say. I did what needed to be done. That's what a mother does, I think. We do whatever it is God asks us to do."

Zeba had only nodded, knowing she would not see her husband's sister again. Kamal was buried beneath two meters of earth and with him was buried everything Tamina wanted to forget. This was her chance to do so, and she would not squander it.

Tamina had turned to slip back into the street when she paused and, without turning, said: "I'm glad for the children, Zeba. You didn't deserve to die."

Zeba, her arms still tightly wrapped around her daughters, her cheek pressed against the top of her son's head, had sobbed loudly and fallen to her knees.

ZEBA HAD SPENT THE FALL AND WINTER AT HOME WITH HER children. Her grandfather, Safatullah, had given her ownership of a plot of land the family had leased to farmers. The rent payments she received were not much, but they were enough to sustain a small family. They'd seldom left the house during the three-month school winter break. Zeba used the time to recover. She'd opened the windows of her home to air out the stench of rotted food and vacancy. She'd raked over the dirt in the courtyard, though Kamal's blood has been washed away by the heavy rains that had fallen while she was in Chil Mahtab. She cut away the dead branches of the rosebush and let her fingers linger in the softened earth beneath it.

Inside, Zeba swept the floors and washed every pot, pan, and glass in boiled well water. She did so in peace, noticing as she wiped down the walls of their living room that she did not sense the blackness. It had disappeared just as furtively as it had entered. In the room she had shared with Kamal for seventeen years, Zeba separated her husband's clothing from her own, holding his shirts and pants at arm's length. She folded each piece and stacked them in the center of an old bedsheet, tying the ends of the sheet into a tight knot. On the coldest days of winter, she'd opened the bundle and used his tunics and hats as fuel for the cooking fires, stoking the flames with a twinge of satisfaction.

The children did not speak of their father. They did not need an explanation, having known what their father was in life. That he was no longer part of their world did not trouble them. They would not miss his violent outbursts, the way he would leap at their mother's cowering form. Their ears still burned under his twisting fingers, their cheeks still stung from his slaps. They did not miss the sound of breaking glass or the anxiety that sent a stream of urine running down their legs in the middle of the night. It was better and fair that he was gone and their mother was returned.

Let justice find its rightful owner, the judge had said. It was a truth her children had understood without hearing the fable. The jurisprudence of a child astounded Zeba.

It was spring now. Frigid temperatures were giving way to milder days. The palette of the world outside shifted, a spin of the color wheel. Yellow turned to green and gray turned to blue. The snowcaps of the mountain receded. The river waters ran cold and fresh, a new generation of fish filling its beds. It was time for her family to reenter the world, Zeba decided. Should the villagers gawk and stare, so be it. Should they point fingers and whisper or shout, it would not matter. She had not left Chil Mahtab only to make her children prisoners of their own home.

Rima's small fingers, the soft pad of her palm, fit snugly into Zeba's right hand. Basir carried a black plastic bag they would use to bring back fish from the river. Zeba followed her children, her chest bursting to see them in the warm sunlight. Basir, Shabnam, and Kareema were a few meters ahead of her, close enough that she could see their profiles when one turned to laugh at something another had said.

Kareema stopped abruptly, turned, and called back to her mother.

"Do you promise we will see Bibi-*jan* tomorrow?"

"Yes," Zeba nodded. "We'll leave in the morning to go to your uncle's home. We'll have to bathe well, though, so we don't stink of fish when they hug us."

Kareema burst into laughter and hopped a few steps to catch up with her siblings.

These are my children, Zeba thought to herself. *Look at those brilliant faces, the way their arms swing as they walk, the way they nudge one another with a playful shoulder. There's no part of the devil in them. They are mine.*

Gulnaz would be waiting for them, as would Rafi and his wife.

Without Kamal to spoil things between them, Zeba felt like she'd been returned to her childhood. Knowing the truth about their father had freed Rafi and Zeba to love their mother more completely, for they could finally understand her as a whole person. They didn't need their father's explanations nor did they have much desire to be part of his life. It was enough to know he was there, not a martyr, but not the devil, either.

Many of the villagers had come to the river, enough that the sight of them made Zeba hesitate for a second. She considered calling the children back and turning around, promising them to come another day. But then she thought of the women she'd left behind at Chil Mahtab. She thought of Latifa and Nafisa, Bibi Shireen and the young woman with the twin boys. She remembered that they'd called her Malika Zeba and burned her name onto their bodies.

We are so happy for you, they'd cried the day she was freed. *Pray for us, Malika Zeba. You know no one else will.*

They'd rejoiced in her release because that, too, gave them strength. If a murderess could be set free, there was some hope for the rest of them.

Bolstered by their voices that echoed still in her head, Zeba lifted her chin and pushed forward, nearing the villagers she'd avoided for two seasons. Boys laughed, carrying sticks strung with trout, their silvery-green skins dotted with red. A family was flash-frying the fish by the side of the river, just feet away from the stones where small children sat perched, dipping their fingers into the icy waters and shivering.

Zeba settled on a flat area, not far from where the river took a gentle bend. They were close enough to others that she could make out their faces but far enough away that she could not make out their words. She spread out the bedsheet she'd brought and they sat, cross-legged, while Basir went off to try the fishing net he'd borrowed from a neighbor. Shabnam and Kareema brought jacks and began their quiet game, bouncing the ball and deftly grabbing the silver spiders from the ground. Rima giggled each time they softly batted her meddling hands away.

The river water shimmered in the afternoon sun, and Zeba put a hand to her forehead to shield her eyes from the glare. She looked for Basir's silhouette and found him amid a group of boys his age. While some stood on a cluster of rocks, Basir and a few others had sloshed into the waters with knees high, dragging their nets.

Zeba heard a rustling behind her, and her head swiveled instinctively. Seeing a mother and father making their way back home with a young girl walking between them, she turned her attention back to her daughters.

She had leaned over to brush Shabnam's hair from her eyes when she suddenly felt her breath catch in her chest. She turned once more, slowly, half hoping the family would not notice her and half hoping they would. There were people around them, but no one paid them much mind, as if Zeba and her children were the most ordinary people.

The wife was speaking to her husband who nodded. The little girl's hand was clasped in her mother's. They were coming closer and would soon pass Zeba and her three daughters. Zeba lowered her gaze and felt her eyes mist. She blinked but could not look away. What a beautiful girl she was—just as lovely as the three who sat before her.

The girl's slender frame came in and out of view, half hidden by her father's form. He looked to be a good man, Zeba thought, a wave of peace washing over her. He looked to be the kind of man who knew right from wrong, the way he walked with his wife and daughter and not ahead of them.

Something the mother said made the little girl look up and laugh, a bashful expression of cheer on her precious face. Zeba let out a soft cry, quiet enough that her own girls were not distracted from their play. But as if her breath crossed the open ground between them and tapped on the little girl's shoulder, her head turned.

She looked in Zeba's direction, and her mouth opened slightly. Zeba still could not bear to turn away, meeting the girl's eyes and feeling her heart pound in her chest. Would she say something to her parents?

But she did not. She only blinked her eyes and smiled, a soft curve of her lips that felt to Zeba like tiny arms thrown around her neck. The many words left unsaid between them, the many questions each had about the other dissipated into the spring air, replaced by the sound of the babbling river, renewed with mountain water.

From this distance, Laylee looked distinctly unbroken. Her father's hand absently touched the top of her head, as if to confirm her presence even as she walked beside him. She had lived over four thousand days but spent the recent months reliving the one day that had been infinitely worse than all the rest. While Fareed's angry hands tried to wring the life from Zeba's neck, Laylee's mother had been bent over her daughter, her tears mixing with the ghastly crimson she was dabbing away from between Laylee's tensed and bruised thighs. At the moment when Zeba had thrown her head back and screamed in the judge's office, Laylee had begged her mother to end her misery. *Kill me,* she'd pleaded. In the next room, her father, Timur, had fallen to his knees to hear his daughter make such a quietly catastrophic plea. They had no other children. Laylee was everything.

You are a good, good girl, he'd whispered to her over and over again. Laylee's mother had to turn away, broken a second time to see the way her husband cradled his daughter. His spirit was shattered but his honor intact.

Only because her father's hand touched her head with pride and only because her mother had nursed her day and night back to health had Laylee survived to live these spring days. She would never be the little girl she'd once been, but her wounds would continue to heal.

Zeba lifted a hand and pressed it to her chest. Her eyes could have followed the girl forever, until she became nothing more than a purple dot against the sparse trees, but Zeba closed her eyes, burning the image of that timid smile into her memory.

"Madar, are you all right?" Shabnam asked, looking at her mother nervously. She and Kareema had paused their game, giving Rima a chance to scatter the jacks with one mischievous sweep of her hand.

Basir was on his way back to them, a glittering trout tied to the end of a stick, raised in the air like a triumphant scepter.

"I am more than fine," she told her daughters, and for the first time in a long time, she believed those small, precious words to be true.

ACKNOWLEDGMENTS

The time, motivation, and inspiration to write are gifts that my family so graciously gives me. Thank you to: my husband for keeping my stories (and our story) exciting; my parents for, as ineloquent as it sounds, everything; my children for making these stories important to tell and for their nascent love of books; my friends and family for sharing my stories with their own circles; and my colleagues for believing art and medicine are closer than they seem. I am indebted to and in awe of Heather Barr, whose Human Rights Watch report *"I Had to Run Away": The Imprisonment of Women and Girls for "Moral Crimes" in Afghanistan* was a window into the inner workings of the women's prison system there. Heather, you were generous with your time and wisdom of the penal and procedural codes of Afghanistan, and this book is more authentic for it. Any errors related to said topics are my own. I am grateful that the very dedicated Manizha Naderi put me in touch with Heather. Thanks to Dr. Esmael Darman, editor in chief of Rawan Online, for his insights into the stigma, prevalence, and treatment of mental illness in Afghanistan.

I am one lucky writer to have my work represented (and titled) by the sagacious Helen Heller. I am just as fortunate to be edited by Rachel Kahan. Your passion for purposeful books behooves us all. There are so many to thank at HarperCollins: Jeanie Lee and the sharp-eyed copy editors and proofreaders, Mumtaz Mustafa for a third wonderful cover, Virginia Stanley and the energetic library marketing team, Amanda Mulvihill and the international force (we've got lots of fun ahead of us), Camille Collins, Kate Schafer, Ashley Marudas and the marketing department, and the many, many others who help bring my stories to readers.

And of course, my gratitude to book clubs, coordinators of book festivals, librarians, booksellers, and all those who persist in celebrating stories and the transformative power of reading.

ABOUT THE AUTHOR

Nadia Hashimi is an Afghan American pediatrician living in suburban Washington, D.C. She is the author of the international bestsellers *The Pearl That Broke Its Shell* and *When the Moon Is Low*.